REALMS OF SECRETS

A SOVEREIGN SISTERS NOVEL

Teanna Lynne

Cover design by: Delilah Cay

Interior artwork by: Delilah Cay

Map design by: Cody James King

Printed in the United States of America

Authors Note: This edition of Realms of Secrets was updated February 2025 and page numbers vary in previous editions.

For Sharity, because you taught me to always fight for myself, and when I couldn't you were there.

Author's Note

Content Warning: This book contains topics that may be difficult for some readers. Such as: grief, parental loss, mental illness, panic attacks, torture, kidnapping, explicit sex, breath play/choking, and other topics that one might find triggering.

Read with caution.

Pronunciation Guide

Estarynn - (es-tare-rin)

Vulca - (vulh-ka)
Queen Elani - (queen el-on-e)
King Basc - (king bask)
Eve- (eve)
Mar - (marr)
Rian - (ree-in)
Nat- (nat)
Cyrus - (sigh-ruhs)

Sena - (sen-uh)
High Lady Ayana - (high lady a-on-ah)
Terran - (tare-in)
Oliver - (ol-iv-er)
Rose- (rose)
Oak - (oak)
Reed - (reeed)
Aine - (eye-nn)
Farai- (fah-rahyi)
Lina- (lean-ah)
Symone- (see-moan)
Hala- (hall-ah)
Mateo- (muh-tay-oh)

Gael- (guy-el)

Rayan - (ray-in)
Queen Mira - (queen meer-ah)
King Callan - (king cal-in)
Cay- (kay)
Finn - (fin)
Nalei- (nah-lei)
Regan Auger - (ray-gan awh-ger)

Eteri- (eh-tare-ee)
Chief Zion- (chief zi-on)
Imani- (ee-mah-nee)
Asha- (ah-sha)
Azariah- (az-uh-rye-uh)

Cansu - (con-su)
Yuta- (you-tuh)
Teru- (te-<r>u)
Taka- (tah-ka)
Chien- (ch-i-en)
Eri- (ee-<r>i)

Prologue

800 Years Ago

Dead leaves crunch under my bare feet as I follow along the edge of the forest. The air is hot and dry, typical for Vulca this time of year. I pull my pack tighter across my back, securing it in case I need to run again. It's been weeks since I've had a safe place to rest, that small village in the north is still the closest thing to sanctuary I've come across.

Not that it lasted.

They found me too soon. I had barely begun the next phase in my plans when I heard the sound of screams. I didn't have time to waste so I grabbed the bag I always keep packed, jumped out the window, and made a break for the treeline. It may have saved my life, but there is no saving the bottoms of my feet. They're calloused and cracked, aching with every step. I wince as a thorn lodges itself in my heel.

I'll need to stop soon. I ran out of water two days ago and the only thing I've had to eat are the half rotten berries I've found in bushes. As if to emphasize my dire situation, my stomach rumbles loudly. I place a dirt covered hand over my belly and use a small bit of healing magic to stave off the ache. It won't replace the need for food, but it will take away some of the pain.

Hours pass and eventually the sunlight disappears, I stumble almost blindly through the darkness. If I had heightened senses like other species this would be much easier, but no, fauns are not blessed with such eyesight. My species is known to bring happiness and fertility which I have yet to find much use for on my mission.

A loose root seemingly jumps out of the earth and I fall forward, barely managing to catch myself before my face lands in a pile of mud. Rolling over, I free my foot and draw my knees to my chest. I reach down, unable to see my ankle, but feel the dull throbbing that fills me with dread. I can't run on a twisted ankle. Taking a deep breath, I use more healing magic, feeling the drain on my limited well of power.

Vana save me, this just keeps getting worse. I close my eyes, clasping my hands together and sending a prayer to the goddess for guidance. In the centuries of my existence, I have found both allies and enemies. I have trusted and been betrayed. I have seen my faith in the realms waver as villages were burned to the ground, crushed by earthquakes, and wiped out to sea by floods. All while the leaders preach about peace. Yet my faith in *Her* has remained sure.

I use the tree closest to me to stand, testing out my ankle with a small bit of pressure and thankfully finding the pain gone. My time in the mortal lands taught me much, but never about magic.

No.

I was forced to learn what little I know while on the run.

The extent of my abilities remains confined to basic healing and a handful of charms. My control over the earth element is practically nonexistent.

As I take a step, ready to continue on, I get another vision. It's nothing more than a flash of a cave entrance, but I already know that this is where I must go. I allow myself to be guided through the woods until the cave appears in front of me, real and inviting. This isn't the first time that Vana has blessed me, each vision a gift that I am most grateful for.

I rush inside the cave, finding the ground warm and dry, the heat rising from beneath the stone. The cave is narrow, but I suspect deep, not that I can tell in the darkness. I set my pack down then quickly get to work gathering up some twigs and dried grass. I make a small pile and then strike two rocks together until the sparks light and a small fire burns.

Sitting close enough to the fire to use the light, but far enough that the heat won't make me sweat, I begin pulling out items from my pack. I start with my map, spreading it out so I can see the entirety of Estarynn. I pull out my pencil and add new markings, circling the villages that seem to hold potential and crossing out those that appear to already be corrupted.

Three are lost causes, but there are five that could prove useful. The leaders of the villages took the time to hear my pleas at the very least. It's risky to speak so openly, but I must do it. My mission demands it of me. I look over the map again, planning out my next stop and hoping that this might be the one. Praying that it will be.

I stare at those markings until I am sure I have memorized them. I close my eyes and summon the image, ensuring that I can see it in perfect clarity lest something happens and I am forced to destroy the physical copy. It wouldn't be the first time. It took them a while to catch on, to realize just what was happening within the realms.

Then, they began hunting.

I had been expecting it. Vana made sure of that. They have hunted me for more than half my life, yet they've never gotten close enough to catch me. If the reactions of the villages I visit are any indication, I am led to believe that they see me as more of a myth than anything. A phantom that spreads nothing but lies, and poisons the minds of the people.

With a sigh, I tuck my things back into my bag and move it further away from the fire, setting it against the cave wall. I do my best to heal my feet, but there is little point. They will be damaged again by this time tomorrow.

It's better to save my magic. I'll leave them for now and then wrap them in a poultice come morning, hoping to stave off infection.

Despite reconnecting with my near immortality, I am still aware of the danger of mortal illnesses. After all, I was raised to welcome death, to know the signs and accept my time when it comes. Even if I have been forced to prolong my existence for the sake of my mission. I must care for this body long enough to accomplish my goals and then I am free to join my mother in eternal slumber.

I lay down, resting my head on my pack and letting my mind roam. There is never truly any quiet within the confines of my own mind, not when there is still so much to do. Spreading the word is only part of the plan. I still must find what has been stolen and what has been lost. Without it, there is no hope for the future and my mother's vision will come to pass.

My lids grow heavy and I let them fall shut as sleep claims me, bringing me an endless loop of visions that I will decipher tomorrow. For now, I will rest.

~~~

A vision startles me awake. I barely have time to sit up before the male walks through the cave's entrance, shocked to find me there. His eyes widen and his mouth drops open. His skin is pale, stained pink by time spent out in the sun. His hair is a light shade of brown and hangs loosely at his shoulders.

He holds out his hands as he approaches, his deep voice kept low so as not to startle me, "I'm not here to hurt you."

"I know." And I do, Vana showed me why he is here.

He stops a few feet away from me, standing up straighter with a look of awe. "So it's true? You're really her?"

"Yes," I confirm.

"What is your name?" he asks, looking around the cave with a frown, as if he finds it lacking.

"I have none. I am merely the messenger."

His head cocks, "surely you must have a name."

4

I shrug. That part of me is gone. I left my name behind in order to fully embrace my duty. I'm not sure that I truly remember it, even now. It has been so long since I have heard it spoken.

"Well, my name is-"

"I already know," I say, cutting him off.

He nods, "Of course. I had heard rumors of your sight. I should have known that you would see me coming."

I watch him as a kind smile spreads across his lips. I feel heat rise in my cheeks, but I ignore it, standing up and wincing as my feet scrape against the stone. He notices and rushes over, grabbing my calf and staring up at me with light brown eyes.

"May I?"

I nod, bracing my hand against the cave wall. He grimaces as he looks at my destroyed feet and then lightly wraps his hand around the arch of my foot, spreading healing magic through my body. I fight back a groan as I feel my small cuts and bruises slowly disappear. As he sets my foot back down, I realize that both feet feel new again.

He pulls a small bag out from behind him and reaches inside, pulling out a pair of thick soled boots. He passes them to me with a grin. "They might be a bit big, but it's better than nothing. Go on, give them a try."

Slipping my feet into the boots I find just a bit of extra space, but he's right, I already feel better. I give him a reassuring nod as I reach into my own pack, grabbing the map and holding it out to him without any hesitation. This is it, this is the next step. He takes it with his brows raised, but I merely hold up a hand. "Let us begin."

PRESENT

Chapter 1

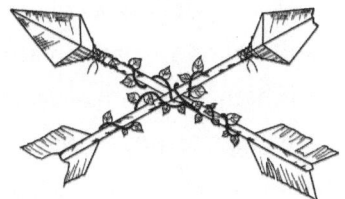

Oak

In this world of secrets and lies there is one thing I know with absolute certainty. My aunt is a bitch.

The moment I am dragged out of her study, a bag is thrown over my head and my arms are cuffed behind my back. I kick and thrash, trying to do everything I can to escape Aine's harsh grip, but it's no use. The hand wrapped around my arm is firm, unrelenting. I try to call on my magic, but find it dormant, there but unresponsive. Panic grips me and I start to struggle harder.

A shift in the ground beneath my feet has me stumbling forward. I expect to be yanked backward, instead, the hand releases me and I go careening down. My face smacks against the hard ground sending vibrations skittering across my body. Groaning, I roll over onto my back and squirm into a half sitting position, leaning back against my elbows.

"Really? Now you let go?" I mumble.

"Let's go," Aine bites, grabbing me by my shoulders and hauling me to my feet.

Something sharp pokes me in the middle of my back and forces me to move. My feet are unsure as we make our way forward, the bag over my head letting only the faintest bit of light in. I reach for my magic again, hoping to use it to guide me at the very least.

It won't respond to my call.

Still.

No matter how hard I pull, it is just outside of reach, taunting me. Anger bubbles up inside of me and clouds any rational thoughts left in my mind.

Taking a deep breath in, I channel my inner Eve and say *fuck it*. Whipping my head back and forth, I manage to loosen the bag enough that I can see a sliver of ground. The moment I see the moss beneath me I take off in a sprint, moving with nothing more than instinct driving me on.

Somehow, I manage to stay upright even as my feet get caught on fallen branches and exposed roots. My heart pounds as adrenaline floods my system, but I can't stop. Each step forward means keeping my promise, and this time I won't fail. I can't afford to.

Just as I begin to feel more comfortable in my escape, vines shoot up from the ground and wrap around my legs. They force my legs together, tightening at my ankles and thighs. A large hole opens up beneath me and I go tumbling through an abyss, the bag ripping off my head, but the world around me is still black. A sharp tug at my feet sends me tumbling backwards until I'm left dangling upside down, held up by the vines circling my ankles.

Blood rushes to my head as I fight to steady my breathing.

"Well this is-"

My words are cut short as I am yanked upwards and flung through the air as the world around me comes back into view. Aine stands proudly over the hole she formed beneath me, all the while twisting her arms and controlling the vines as I am whipped back and forth like a ragdoll. The wrap around her head doesn't budge as she uses the powerful magic that traps me.

Bile rises in my throat and seconds before I am about to puke she slams me into the ground. The impact makes my ears ring and my breath stutter. Small rocks dig into nearly every inch of my body and my cheek feels like someone took a cheese grater to it. I groan, writhing on the ground as my entire body aches and burns.

"Up," Aine's voice is cool and demanding. Her tone leaves no room for argument as her eyes, peeking through the gap in her head wrap, bore into me with disgust.

I stare up at her with a grimace. With a great deal of effort, I force myself to my knees, half hunched over as my breaths come out in pants.

"What," I inhale deeply, "did you do that for?" I watch her for any sign of reaction, but aside from her slow blink, she gives nothing away.

"Up," she says again, this time raising her hands and allowing the vines to drag me to my feet. My toes barely brush the ground as she steps forward, leveling our eyes together. "Try that again and you'll regret it."

Biting the inside of my cheek I hold back the words that burn the tip of my tongue. I have two choices here. Continue to fight without my magic and having no idea where we are. Or... I could go willingly and escape as soon as I have a better handle on the situation. I weigh the options in my mind quickly and decide that maybe Eve's approach *isn't* the best in this situation.

Lifting my chin, I meet Aine's fierce, dark brown eyes. "Fine. You win."

Her eyes narrow, regarding me carefully as she looks me over from head to toe, searching for any sign of a trap. When she seems content with my concession, she releases the vines around my legs, leaving one loosely around my waist like some kind of lead. Wrapping her hand around the end of that vine she pulls me forward.

"Move." She turns on her heels and marches on, half dragging me behind her as we make our way through the dense woods.

I let my eyes roam over our surroundings, searching for anything familiar. The deeper we press into the forest, the more difficult it becomes to discern one big tree from the next. Frustration rises inside me as my magic continues to remain inaccessible. After another hour of walking I finally break the silence. "Why doesn't my magic work?"

Aine ignores me, staring straight ahead and keeping a firm grip on my vine.

My teeth grind together. I'm not one to shy away from silence, but everyone has a breaking point. We've been walking for hours and my entire body aches. The least she could do is answer a few questions. Maybe even heal some of the injuries that *she* caused. Light fades from the sky and darkness envelopes us. The only sign that Aine even notices is the slight slow in our march.

"We're going to need to stop soon. It's getting dark and we *both* need rest," I mumble.

The sound of rumbling earth echoes through the woods until a solid wall is built around us. Stone, ten feet high forms an impenetrable barrier that no one would get through, at least not without magic. Aine whips around, releasing the vine as it falls to the ground around me. Without another word she creates a stone bench and shoves me towards it. "Rest."

Dropping onto the bench I let out a satisfied sigh. My feet throb and my thighs shake from exertion, sweat pools down my back and across my forehead. I hadn't realized just how badly I needed a break until I got one. Though I still don't trust it one bit. Aine might have released me from the vine, but the walls around us paint a perfectly clear message. I'm not going anywhere.

I watch as Aine moves around the walls, casting charms that will no doubt hide our presence and alert us to anyone who gets too close. Her hands move in quick, precise motions, drawing runes into the air beautifully. I've never seen anything quite like it.

Spells and incantations are different from our elemental magic or the power we get from our creatures. It's not something we're born with, but something that has to be learned and practiced. Most people spend years studying and might never have a full grasp on more complex spells.

Similar to potion making, there is a delicate balance that requires perfect concentration and control. The way Aine casts, it's like watching an artist paint or a dancer dance. There is a fluidity and grace to the movements so unlike what I was taught. Private tutors were brought in for my cousins, Reed, and myself, but in all the years I practiced under them, I have never seen them move like *that*.

"Where did you learn to cast like that?"

Aine finishes what she is doing and turns to face me. "With the Ghosts," her words cut through the air.

I can't hide the surprise on my face. I hadn't expected her to actually answer. A million more questions bombard my head, but I have to be deliberate. If I want to have any chance of escaping, then I need to ask the right questions, things that will help me. But I also have to be careful not to jump into the deep end too quickly. "What's it like? Being... a Ghost?" my question comes out hesitant, not quite sure how to phrase it.

Aine considers me a moment before creating her own bench and sitting down gracefully. Every time she moves, it's fluid, like every part of her body is in perfect sync. "Why do you want to know?"

"I figure if I'm being sent to train with the Ghosts, to become one, I should probably know what to expect," I answer with a short laugh, the words half truth, half lie. Sure, a part of me is deeply curious about this super top secret group of spies, but the other part of me knows it won't matter because I won't be sticking around long enough to find out.

"Becoming a Ghost is no laughing matter. We are elite spies who have trained for years to master skills you can barely imagine," she bites, the annoyance clear in her tone.

"Apologies, I didn't mean any insult. I just mean that I didn't exactly sign up for this. I want to understand better and to know more about you. How long ago did you... become a Ghost?" I really need to figure out the correct way to broach this subject before Aine decides to wrap a vine around my neck and strangle me.

Aine stands suddenly, walking forward until she is right in front of me and I am forced to stare up into her deep brown eyes. "Enough questions."

Before I can even process the blow, my eyes are falling shut and I am dragged into unconsciousness.

Chapter 2

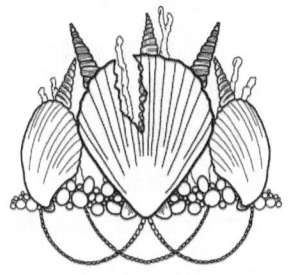

Cay

*W*ild, terrifying magic encircles me. Power radiates through the air with a low hum, buzzing deep within my bones. Gritting my teeth, I push against it, putting everything I can into protecting them.

Around me, my friends and family lie unconscious, blood dripping from their nose and eyes. I feel a trickle of it roll over my lips, the metallic taste invades my mouth. The only sound in the room is the roaring water pouring from the palms of my hands and a silvery song. Sparing a glance back, I look into each of their faces.

Rose.

Oak.

Mar.

Eve.

Then, my mother and brother, laying side by side, their hands outstretched towards each other. Their breathing is shallow, barely enough to move their chests. A stutter in the motion distracts me, that one little *movement drawing just enough of my attention away that dark magic crashes into me.*

I am thrown backwards, landing in a crumpled heap beside the people that I hold closest to my heart. I gasp for air as I begin to raise my head, trying to look at my attacker's face, but something snaps before their shadowy form is revealed to me and I am torn away.

I bolt upright, nausea churning in my gut as my heart races. Stumbling out of bed, I race to the bathing chamber and barely make it to the toilet before the contents of my stomach burn my throat and force their way out. It takes several minutes before I calm down enough to process the dream. It felt so real, like I was standing there, fighting the man cloaked in shadows. My palms burn from the power of the water I was pouring against him.

The metallic taste of blood still lingers on my tongue and I race to the mirror, searching for any sign of it. My face is clean, ghostly pale and covered in a sheen of sweat, but not even a hint of blood on my skin. I force back the hair that is plastered against my cheeks and grab a ribbon off the counter to tie it away from my face. Once it is secure, I turn on the water and splash it against my face. In the past, I would just use magic for something like this, but the thought of using my power now sends an unexpected stab of fear through my chest.

Slowly, I make my way back to my room, walking over to the bed and trailing my hand over the delicate fabric. I can't help that my eyes wander to the pillows. A deep indent remains in the pillow that rested beside me, beneath a head of chestnut curls. I hadn't expected him to be here when I woke, but something about his absence aches. Like the illusion has shattered and reality has set back in.

But there is no time to waste standing around staring at a bed, there is someone that I need to see.

~~~

The moment I enter the room and see her still frame, I crack. I sit by my mother's bedside and feed healing magic into her, holding her frail hand in my own. The tears come out in streams and I quickly begin to hyperventilate.

Thankfully, Flora is here. She grabs me by the shoulders and whispers reassurances that my mother is stable, that she has been responding well to the magic and seems to be breathing better. Flora's soothing words calm me down enough that I can really look at my mother.

Dark brown hair, barely a shade darker than my own, frames her face. I examine every detail, committing them to memory. Oval face, long pointed nose turning up ever so slightly at the end. Wide lips, usually a dark shade of pink, now dull and chapped. Her cheekbones are more defined now, carved out even though it has been less than a week since-

No, I can't go there. I can't think about it anymore. I force the thoughts from my mind, and focus on my mother instead. She's here. She's the one I can protect. The one *alive*. Taking a long, deep breath, I push everything I have left into her. Praying to Vana, our goddess and protector, that she will save my mother.

After hours of sitting by her side, I make my way back to my rooms. Luckily, I don't encounter a single person on the way. As soon as I step inside I close the door behind me and lean against it, sliding down to the ground and pulling my knees to my chest. But this time no tears fall. No sobs steal my breath. Instead, a cold and empty feeling spreads inside of me until all I can do is lay down on the ground and close my eyes.

~~~

Days go by with the same routine. I wake up. I get dressed. I visit my mother. Food is brought to my room, though who is doing so is a mystery to me. I spend my evenings staring up at the ceiling, the longing for home consuming my thoughts.

It's bright here, the sun peeks through my drawn curtains, but there is no rainbow. No myriad of colors that dance across the walls. When I look out the window there is no stained glass, just a clear pane that feels *empty*.

Eventually, Rose comes to the door, trying to coax me out. She begs me not to shut her out again, to let her help me through this. But the only answer I have is to ask her for time. To allow me to live in this despair for a little while longer.

Because if I don't, I'll crack again. But this time I don't think Flora or anyone will be able to put the pieces back together. No amount of fake smiles or empty laughs will fill the void left inside me.

I spend another three days wallowing. Barely leaving my room and never talking to another soul. Rose still comes knocking every day, but I stopped responding in the hopes that eventually she might understand I don't *want* to feel better.

I don't want her help to heal because if I do, then it makes it real. The moment I acknowledge what happened it means there is no going back. No changing the outcome. It means losing him all over again.

When the familiar pounding on the door sounds again, I stifle a groan. Marching to the door I summon the courage to turn Rose away face to face.

"Rose, please just-" my words dry up in my mouth as I take in the figure standing just on the other side of the door.

Oliver.

I haven't seen him since the night we slept beside each other. Though in fairness, I've made a great deal of effort *not* to see anyone. Still, seeing him standing in front of me has our conversation playing on repeat in my mind.

"Can I ask you something?"

"Anything," he breathes.

I take a deep breath. "Was my father's death my fault?"

"No," he says without a moment of hesitation.

My heart pounds inside my chest. Words of gratitude stuck in my throat choke me as I stand here, staring at him with my mouth agape.

"Like the view, princess?" Oliver says with a smirk.

My jaw snaps shut. Of course. How could I be naïve enough to think that *nice Oliver* was anything more than a hallucination. After all, he is incapable of anything other than arrogance, condescension, and general assholeness.

"Oliver, to what do I owe this displeasure?" I groan.

His smirk only widens. "Nice to see you too."

"What do you want, I'm busy."

Oliver peeks over my shoulder where my bed remains unmade and a collection of food trays sit untouched, "I can see that." He leans against the door frame, his forearm resting over my head as he leans in close, invading my personal space. "Come on, you're coming with me."

I pull away, taking a step backwards and into the comfort of what has been my sanctuary for over a week now. "What? Absolutely not. I'm not going anywhere with you."

"Oh, I wasn't asking, princess," he says with a dry chuckle.

"Too bad, because I am not leaving this room. So you can go and find someone else to torment." My heart is pounding, fear flooding my senses at the idea of being forced from the room. To face the others and have to meet their pitying stares. Yet, as I look into Oliver's eyes, I find determination there rather than pity. "Just leave me alone, Oliver."

"Nah, I don't think I will. You've been holed up in this room throwing yourself this little pity party instead of actually doing something about what happened."

I stalk forward, shoving him in his chest hard enough to push him out of the doorway. "Fuck. You."

"You'd like that wouldn't you?" he smirks.

"I swear to Vana, Oliver, if you don't leave in the next 10 seconds I'll blast you just like I did on our way to Sena the first time."

His jaw ticks, a muscle popping as his eyes grow heated. Oliver steps forward, getting up in my face and staring down at me as I refuse to back down. "Have it your way, princess, but know that while you're in here, hiding, the world is still moving just outside these walls. Don't regret not being a part of it." With those parting words he turns on his heels and stalks away.

17

Slamming the door shut, I release a scream of frustration. At him. At myself. At the world and everyone else in it. Yet even as rage boils inside me, I can't help but acknowledge the fact that Oliver was right.

Disgusting. Even thinking it leaves a bad taste in my mouth.

Oliver might be the biggest ass I have ever met, but he makes a good point and I hate that.

I can stay in here and let this pain consume me, or I can go out there and do something about it. And though the thought is terrifying, I know what the right decision is.

Chapter 3

Rose

I am no stranger to being alone. Loneliness is something that can be felt even in the most crowded of rooms. Physical presence and mental presence are not always as synonymous as they may seem. I used to walk through the halls believing that the attention I received meant that I would never be alone. But now I know that is not true.

I know people love me. My friends. My family. Yet there is this piece of me that can't help but doubt.

If they loved me, why would they lie?

If they loved me, why would they shut me out?

If they loved me, why can't they see that I need help?

Constant questions infest my thoughts, and corrupt the parts of me that once were whole.

Still, I walk the halls smiling at my people. It's a skill that I have perfected since we returned from Rayan. Something changed the moment I set foot in my mother's chamber. The image of the loving, caring, mother was stained with this cruel, monstrous beast. Watching Oak be dragged away clouded every memory of my life with this haze.

If she could do that to Oak, who's next? Does she truly care about any of us at all? About me? Knowing that I was lied to my entire life has changed my perspective. Made me more cautious.

I can't afford to take things at face value anymore. No, I need to analyze everything to make sure I never fall victim to my own naivete again. I won't be made a fool of, I won't let her feed me pretty lies disguised as love. *Never again.*

The mantra that has guided me through my days for the last week. When I eat, *never again.* When I bathe, *never again.* When I train, *never again.* Every moment, a reminder that I need to be more, to do better.

Familiar halls guide me to the library, the sanctuary that has provided me the smallest reprieve. As I turn the corner to enter the grand room, I run face first into a pile of books. Or more accurately, someone *carrying* a pile of books.

I fall backwards, hitting the ground and sending shooting pain up through my tailbone. Vana that hurt.

"Are you okay? I am so sorry! I couldn't see where I was going," the voice calls from behind the books. A head peeks out and I am unsurprised to find my cousin, Reed, on the other side. "Rose, I am so sorry!"

For once, a real smile splits my lips. Reed is the kind of person who just radiates warmth, who makes everyone around him feel safe. Like they can trust him. Laughing to myself, I slowly stand, brushing my hands off on my thin, cotton pants.

"It's fine. Nothing to worry about."

"Are you sure? I can escort you to the infirmary if you need-"

"Really, I'm okay. Nothing but a bruised backside," I say cutting him off. The books start to topple to the side and I reach out instinctually, pulling half of them out of his arms. "Here, let me help."

Reed and I walk into the library and quickly set the abundance of books on the closest table.

"In hindsight, I guess I couldn't carry all of them in one trip. Though I absolutely despise having to walk back and forth between the apothecary and here. This castle is too big, honestly." Reed releases a long sigh, but the deep dimples in his cheeks tell me he is only partly serious.

"You're not wrong. I wouldn't blame you if you used an enchantment to carry the books for you."

Reed's mouth drops open. "I didn't even think of that. Rose, you are a genius, do you know that?"

Laughter bursts from me as I shake my head. "I am in no way a genius. I've just got a few years on you is all. Besides, with how much I read I had to find some way to make things easier on myself."

"You're only four years older than me, you know." Reed gives me a pointed look. He's only a few inches taller than me, but his personality makes him seem so much bigger. He looks so much like Oak that for a moment I just take him in, allowing myself to think of her for the first time since she was taken.

Forest green eyes, light brown curls, deep olive skin, and the familiar splatter of freckles that runs in our family. They even have the same wide nose. The only noticeable difference is Reed's sharp jawline, towering height, and... muscles?

"Reed, have you been working out? When did you get all these muscles?" I examine him.

Gone is the boyish male who I grew up beside; his thin frame has been replaced by broad shoulders and full biceps. I guess carrying all those books has been more of a workout than I would expect.

Reed's cheeks are dusted peach, and his eyes look anywhere but at me. "Kind of. I've been training with the guards sometimes. Nothing crazy, just some basic maneuvers and practicing using my elemental magic. I love my apprenticeship with the apothecary, but I realized that I want to be more than that. I want to be strong, a fighter, like Terran and Oliver."

My heart squeezes. "I'm proud of you," I say and his cheeks darken. "You know Oak is going to want to see what you can do as soon as she is home." I fight against the dark thoughts that threaten to cloud my mind.

"Hey, can you help me with something?" Reed asks, distracting me.

"Of course, what do you need?" I'm not sure if it was intentional, but Reed pulled me back from that edge, dragged me back into this moment instead of reliving all of the mistakes I have made in the past.

"I was supposed to gather some supplies for a potion we're working on and I would love some company. That is, if you aren't busy."

Something sparks inside me. "You know, I would love some company myself. Besides, it's been too long since we've spent time together, just you and me."

~~~

Reed leads me through the forest, following a trail I didn't even know existed. I listen as he tells me all about this potion, how it can be used to amplify magic. The way he talks about his apprenticeship makes me almost as excited as he is. Then, he grows quiet.

"You know, I don't really remember my parents. The closest thing I have to a mother is Oak," his voice wavers, "it might not make sense since she is only a few years older than me, but it's true. Oak was the one who has always taken care of me. She made me feel better when I was sick. Helped me when I struggled with my studies. Taught me my first spells and fixed things when an incantation went wrong. She is who I think of when I think of a mother." He stops walking, staring at his feet. With a long sigh he looks up to the treetops, searching for something.

My mind empties, searching for the right words, but coming up with nothing. But then I remember what it was like after losing my father and I realize, there is no such thing as the right words. The only thing you can do is speak from your heart.

"I remember my dad. I have all these memories of things we used to do together and how it felt to be loved by him. But now, when I think of my father, I think of Terran. Being a parent is about more than having a child.

22

It's about raising them, teaching them, and showing them that they are loved *unconditionally*. For you, that person was Oak. And there is nothing wrong with that, you never have to feel bad about that because it is *your* truth."

Reed smiles, casting me a sideways glance. "You know, you're going to make a great mother one day."

"I don't know about that," I laugh, "besides, I don't even know if I want to have a child."

"Well lucky for you, you have plenty of time to think about it. And lucky for me I will never have to worry about it." We both laugh, Reed taking my hand, "come on, we're not too far from the meadow."

A few more minutes of walking and the forest opens up revealing the meadow. Lush grass is covered with morning dew and a large wisteria tree stands proudly in the center. Beautiful bright purple flowers hang down in a canopy, reminding me of our secret garden.

"I'm surprised the flowers are still in bloom! Most of those surrounding the castle have already begun to change with the autumn weather." I step forward, a gentle breeze sneaks through my thin cotton pants and makes me shiver. I won't be able to dress so lightly for much longer.

Reed walks straight for the tree, ducking under the hanging flowers. I follow after him, sitting down amongst the white flowers that cover the ground. My cousin sits beside me, carefully examining every petal and only picking those that seem to match his criteria. He uses his magic to create a basket of vines and places the flowers into it gently. I listen as he explains what we're looking for before falling into a peaceful routine. We pick flowers side by side in silence, the rich, sweet, fruity scent surrounding us.

"Rose," he breaks the silence, "do you… do you know anything about where they took Oak?"

My throat clenches as my heart begins to race. At this moment, I have a choice to make. *Do I trust Reed and risk everything? Or do I keep this to myself and protect myself from whatever horrible thing could happen?* It feels like hours tick by as I consider my options.

I'm not afraid to admit to myself that I need help. Yet a part of me also thinks that I would just be better off alone from now on. That mantra starting up in my head. *Never again. Never again. Never ag-*

"Please. She's my sister," he pleads, his voice barely above a whisper.

I know my answer. "Do you know anything about a group of people called the Ghosts?"

Reed turns to me, confusion written across his face. "What? I don't understand. Like dead people?"

"Not quite. *The* Ghosts. I didn't know about them until we returned from Rayan. When- when my mother sent Oak away. My mother said that they are some kind of group of elite spies, ones that are kept secret. After she told us about them, one came in and dragged Oak away. That was the last time I saw her."

The memory of that moment is seared into my mind. A reminder that I allowed my mother to control me one last time. To force me to stand by and do nothing even as everything inside of me was screaming.

"So, these Ghosts are like Oak? Spies for the high lady?" Reed asks.

I shake my head. "I'm not really sure. I think they're more than that. I have never heard about them before and," I hesitate, "I've been researching them, but I have found nothing. Not even a hint that they exist. It's like they have been wiped from every record. Everything I've tried has come up as nothing more than a waste of time."

"Let me help. I've read hundreds of books in the library and maybe I can think of something that you haven't already thought of. Aren't two heads always better than one?"

"I'm sure a hydra would agree with you on that one." This gets a chuckle out of him. Reed is right though, if I'm ever going to make any progress I'm going to need some help. Normally I would ask Cay or the others, but- I let the thought drift away

"Okay, you can help. The most important thing is figuring out where they are."

Reed's brow creases, "Why? Shouldn't we be focused on *who* they are, not where?"

"No. Because we're going to rescue her." As soon as the words pass my lips something large and black drops from the tree and lands behind us with a heavy thud. My magic comes to life inside me as I whip around, ready to defend us.

The figure rises from their crouch and shakes their head, a mane of loose black curls flying everywhere. Amber eyes are set against bronze skin. Wide, downturned lips tilt into a charming smile. "What's this I hear about a rescue mission?"

Reed takes an audible gulp from beside me. "Mateo?"

Chapter 4

Terran

The moment the door closes to my mother's chambers, I breathe a sigh of relief. Ever since the attack on Rayan, I have been inundated with meeting after meeting. For the court, the military, and everything in between. I walk through the halls begging internally that I don't run into anybody else. But of course, that is too much to ask for. Voices approach from just around the corner and I contemplate a concealment spell before deciding against it.

I can't run from my responsibilities as much as I may want to. So instead of turning and walking the other way or literally hiding from whoever is about to emerge from around that corner, I continue walking straight ahead, ready for whatever fire I need to put out now.

Two of my advisors lock eyes on me the moment they turn and their faces light up as they have me trapped.

"Your highness, how good it is to run into you. We have some urgent matters that must be discussed," Dagen says. He is a small male, a faun who barely stands to my waist. His bald head is such a contrast to the wiry white beard that sticks out from his chin. He's served on this court for hundreds of years now, going as far back as my great-great-grandfather. While many might consider his *experience* a benefit, I have found that it is difficult to promote change when so many of those who hold power cling to the ancient ways.

"Your Highness, might we discuss the unrest with the centaurs? Their hoards have become an increasing problem following the... incident," Norok pushes. He's far younger than Dagen, close to my mother's age if I had to guess. He is one of the more reasonable council members, perhaps due to his parentage.

He comes from a long line of merchants who travel the roads all across the realms, delivering goods and making the trek that few others are willing to make. If what I've heard is true, he grew up on those roads and understands the plight of the people far better than anyone else in his position.

Plastering a smile on my face, I allow them to lead the way into yet another meeting. For the next two hours the pair drones on about some sort of issue with the centaurs.

It is not as though I do not care about my people, but truthfully this *issue* seems blown out of proportion. A few centaurs pushed into wolven territory and challenged them for land. The guards I have already sent to monitor the situation have reported that the two groups have settled it themselves and the centaurs backed off, conceding to the claiming of the land in the name of the wolves.

"Thank you for following up on such an important matter. I would love to share that this matter has been resolved already," I explain. Their faces share a look of surprise and confusion at my proclamation.

"Sir? What exactly do you mean resolved?" Dagen asks with a hint of irritation. He likely is upset I allowed them to talk on and on about the matter while also claiming to have already taken care of things.

But my motives are clear-to understand both perspectives you need to hear both perspectives. If my men claim things are settled, then I believe them. Still, it is reasonable to assume that the council is privy to new information that my guards may not be. Unfortunately for me, that wasn't the case.

"Exactly as I said, the issue has been resolved. There is no need for further action. Now, if you'll excuse me, I would like to retire for the evening." I stand, not giving them time to argue before exiting the room with haste. I practically run back to my room and as I take a sharp corner I bump into someone.

"Apologies, I should have watched where I-" I freeze at the sight of the person who stands in front of me, "Cay?"

Cay looks up at me with a hesitant smile. Her sea-green eyes wide and sparkling with surprise and a hint of trepidation. "Terran," my name comes out in a whisper, the sound has my heart racing.

"I am glad to see you up and about. How are you?" I immediately want to slap myself. *How are you?* Could I ask a more stupid question? Her cheeks blush a beautiful shade of pink and I have to fight the urge to reach out, to feel the heat radiating just beneath her porcelain skin.

She doesn't answer my question. "What are you doing wandering around the castle so late?" she raises her brows and shifts on her feet, an arm coming up to wrap around herself protectively.

Her dark hair is tied up for once, the sight so different that I am caught off guard. My eyes roam over her, catching on the dip in her collar, exposing the smallest hint of skin. I continue down as her dress cinches at her waist before billowing out over her full hips.

She looks stunning. The dress gives just a small hint of skin while emphasizing her curves. I could stare at her all night in this dress. Which is the exact thought that makes me realize I *have* been staring... this entire time... and *completely* ignoring her question. "I-I'm just leaving a meeting. Heading back to my chambers, yourself?"

Cay smiles, her face lighting up. "I'm just returning from visiting my mother."

"How is she doing? Any improvement?" Her smile dips, but she pushes through, forcing a smile that I know all too well. It's the same smile that I see in the mirror every day. "You know you can always come to me, right?"

Her cheeks turn crimson, the color spreading to the curved tip of her ears. "I-yes, of course," she says quietly.

"You don't have to do this alone. I can help with handling the refugees and you can focus on your mother. The entire court is here to support you however you need," I reassure her. I will use every resource and guard that I have, whatever it takes.

Cay's face contorts into one of shame, another expression I am well acquainted with. "Can I be honest with you?" she asks hesitantly.

"Always." There is no hesitation. I would do anything for her. Perhaps more than I should.

Ever since the attack, I can't help but feel as if I failed her. Out of all the people to rush to her aid, *Oliver* was the one to do it. And seeing her stuck to his side made me realize something, something that I have tried to ignore for the last year.

"I haven't even really thought about my people since we escaped. I've been so focused on my mother that I…" she words fade off.

"Of course you haven't. You lost your father, it makes complete sense for you to want to stay by your mother's side. And I am sure that your people will understand that," I grab her hand, "but I do think that seeing your face would be good for them. Knowing that you're alright, that they still have a leader here."

She scoffs. "I am not their leader."

I squeeze her hand, and use my free one to tilt her head up so she is forced to look into my eyes. "Listen to me, being a leader is so much more than a title. It's about bravery and trust and standing up for what is right. Defending those you love. You did that. You came to the defense of your people, and stood your ground against an enemy that most would shudder at. Do you understand? You *are* their leader."

A single tear rolls down her cheek and I brush it away with the pad of my thumb. We're standing so close that her saltwater and citrus scent swirls between us. Memories of another time being this close to her surface and I have to force myself to take a step back, to put distance between us as I release her hand.

Clearing my throat I try to gather my thoughts and one thing stands out that I know will interest her. "I've been researching Cansu. Looking into everything I can find about them and why they disappeared. About their magic."

Cay's eyes widen and she seems the most alive I have seen her since we first bumped into each other. "Really? What have you found? Is there anything that could help my mother?"

"I-" a noise behind me cuts me off as more voices approach and I know we're on borrowed time. "Meet me in my father's private library tomorrow night at dusk. I'll tell you everything."

I don't wait for her response. I am rushing down the hallway and slipping into my chamber before anyone else can find me. How very high lord-like of me to hide in my room as if I were still a kid. Somehow, Cay brings this out in me, a side of myself that I thought would be locked away forever.

I smile to myself before getting ready for bed.

Chapter 5

Mar

When I was sixteen years old, I watched as my mother gave birth to my youngest brothers, Flint and Hagan. Twins are more than rare, they're practically unheard of, which is why my mother was careful throughout her pregnancy. She took tonics, made sure to eat well, got plenty of sleep, and never did anything too strenuous. She was healthy.

Despite all of that, I was by her side as she bled out in her bed, helpless to stop it from happening and unable to look away. The twins' father screamed and begged the goddess to save his wife. I begged too, but no matter how much I prayed to Vana, my mother still died.

The days after her death I was numb. I simply went through the motions each day. My brothers' father was distraught over my mother's death, so I had to help.

I made sure Keegan ate breakfast and attended his lessons. I watched over the twins as they slept and cried for a mother that they would never know. All the while, there was no one there to care for me. Eventually I learned to live with the numbness, and then one day someone taught me how to feel again.

Eve.

Eve sparked a fire in me that I thought had sizzled out. She reminded me who I was and brought so much warmth back into my life that it was impossible to feel numb.

Until now.

It's been nearly two weeks since she was taken. Two weeks since her mother collapsed. Two weeks since everything changed again. The familiar numbness crept in again and I didn't fight it.

What is the point when Eve is gone?

I spend my days helping my father solve problems and attempt to keep the kingdom running smoothly. But at night, I train. There in that familiar room, I let it all out. Each punch reminds me that I am still alive, and that I have someone worth fighting for. When my body is exhausted, but sleep remains out of my grasp, I research. I spend hours trying to find some way to save my sister without collapsing our entire realm and causing mass panic.

I need help. There is too much for me to do alone, not while being the face of our family and constantly stepping in where my father cannot. But I have heard nothing from our friends. Oak never made it to our meeting, she has sent no letters and no explanation for her absence. Rose has also failed to respond to my many letters and I fear writing to Cay will be too much of a burden.

So I wait. I wait and hope that they will be here soon, regardless of whatever is keeping them from helping me immediately.

Someone clears their throat and I am reminded that we're in the middle of a council meeting. Few people know about the queen and Eve, only the most trusted advisors, and this meeting is to determine the next steps.

"I understand your sense of urgency, princess," the head advisor, Soren, pauses, "but we must consider the consequences of our actions. Fear is already brewing throughout the realm and we're trying to maintain the delicate balance." His jaw is set, this is an argument that we have had before and his opinion remains unfaltering.

"We cannot ignore the people's fears, but we must also consider how much of the truth they can take. Learning that their queen is ill and their heir stolen…" Ebba, second to Soren, continues. She seems more open to conversation, though if I have made any progress swaying her to my side, she has yet to show it.

"I understand the risks, and of course they are certainly things to consider. However, I still believe that at the very least we should gather the guards and form a rescue crew to search for my sister. We can never hope to find her if no one is looking." I stare them down, refusing to look away so that they are sure to see just how serious I am.

Nothing is going to stop me from finding Eve.

Ebba looks between Soren and I before letting out a deep sigh. "Very well, we will take this to the other advisors and see what the best course of action is." In other words, it's not going to happen. The two of them rise and exit the room without saying anything else.

The moment the door clicks shut behind them I slump forward, folding my arms atop the table and resting my head against them.

"Taking a nap?"

A deep sigh escapes me and I don't bother lifting my head. "What do you want, Rian?" It's the first time that I have seen him since we arrived back in Vulca. His departing words gave me more than enough reason to stay away.

I am a male who takes responsibility for his own failures. I know what hand I had in your sister's capture. If you would rather place all the blame on me then I will bear it, as is my duty. But beyond that, I have nothing more to say to you. Goodnight, princess.

"Nothing from you. I came to track down Ebba, I was told she was here." His voice reveals no hint of emotion, only cold indifference.

I turn my head so that my cheek is resting against my forearm. "She already left," I say, staring into his ice blue eyes. I take him in, his hair is cropped shorter now, his face freshly shaven. He looks put together, like he has not a care in the world.

If only.

"You look like shit," he says blandly.

Rolling my eyes I stand, walking straight past him to the door.

"When was the last time you fed?" he asks from behind me.

I pause. "I ate breakfast this-"

"No, you know exactly what I meant. When was the last time you *fed*, Mar. Don't avoid the question."

I turn around, giving him a tempered smile. "I don't believe that is any of your business. So, if you'll excuse me," I say with a slight dip of my head.

"You're my princess, it is my job to care. Ensuring that you have eaten is just another part of my duty to protect the crown." His voice is right behind me, too close. His familiar cedarwood scent wraps around me, caressing me and filling the air until I can't help but breathe it into my lungs, allowing it to consume me entirely. "That sounds awfully inconvenient. I am sure there are far more important tasks for you to complete. Allow me to assure you that I have things well in hand." I pull open the door but a hand shoots out beside my head and slams it closed. I turn around slowly, my brows raised. "Was there something else that you needed?"

"What's going on with you?" he asks, searching my face.

"I don't know what you mean." I steel my face, revealing none of the emotions that swirl inside me. I know what he is trying to do and I won't let him. Not this time. He's made it perfectly clear where we stand.

"You know exactly what I mean," he growls, "this isn't you. Where is that fiery girl who likes to go toe to toe with me? Why don't you let her come out and play."

I glower at him. "She disappeared the moment her sister did. Now, if you'll excuse me, I *do* have more important matters to take care of."

"That's a load of shit. This isn't you, it's some imitation, some messed up piece of who you really are. I don't recognize this person."

He finally achieves his goal, he hits the target right on its mark and I crack. I am messed up, but he doesn't get to say that.

"You don't know me. You've never known me. While you sit here and preach to me about whatever image you have created in your mind about who I am, I am busy trying to hold myself and this entire realm together. So screw you, Rian, go find somewhere else to ride that high horse of yours."

My gaze shifts to his hand and he removes it from the door, actually pulling it open for me so that I can walk away. As I pass through the doorway I hear him mutter under his breath, "you're right, I don't know you at all."

The door slams shut behind me and I flinch. My heart pounds in my chest and my head swims. From the moment I heard his voice, I feared what he might do to me. The small spark in the pit of my stomach is exactly the reason why I go straight to the training room and work out every bit of frustration and anger I have left inside me.

After three hours, I make my way back to my rooms. I stand in the doorway, staring across the hall at Eve's door. I haven't opened it since I've come back. Part of me is scared to find it cold and empty. That her scent will be gone and it will be like she never existed.

It's only been two weeks, but it might as well have been a lifetime. I can't go on like this for much longer. It's time I take action, even if it means doing so alone.

Chapter 6

Eve

I know that I'll be dead soon. The past two weeks have gone by slowly, my fate sealed with every passing hour. *And to think, this will be my downfall?*

Boredom.

I mean seriously, if you're going to kidnap a girl and lock her up, the least you can do is entertain her. Maybe a little torture, mocking, playful banter. I would give anything for just one tiny sliver of entertainment.

Of all the things I worried about when Teru stole me, boredom wasn't one of them. When they delivered me into the hands of their king, I prepared myself for the worst. I fortified my mind and readied my body to endure whatever they planned to put me through. But oh no, the only thing the mysterious so-called king has done is ignore me.

Part of me is a bit offended, truly.

Am I not worth his time? Am I of so little importance that he feels he can just lock me away and forget all about me?

You would think that after going through all the trouble of stealing me back in Rayan that they might actually *want* some answers.

My best guess is that he is busy. I mean, running a kingdom is a lot of work after all. I've watched my father run around handling problem after problem for my entire life. On top of that the entire kingdom has been gone for the last millennia.

Or so we thought.

I have to admit that even as Teru brought me through the mist and showed me the outskirts of the kingdom, I was still convinced that it was all a ruse. Now looking back on it I realize that it was naïve of me to think such a thing.

I know very little about Cansu, the land of the mist, but I know *nothing* about its ruler. The memory of the first and only time I saw him is seared into my mind. Golden skin, dark waves, beautiful golden brown eyes beneath long, full lashes. As if that wasn't bad enough, his jaw is carved into a straight line that squares out just below his chin. He's absolutely devastating. That is the only word that seems accurate enough to describe him.

The first few days of my captivity, I yelled and pounded on the door of my room. Yep, room, not cell. Complete with a small cot, basic bathing chamber, a single table and chair, and a lamp. Slightly less than what I would consider the bare necessities.

Three meals are left on the table and I am mysteriously asleep every time they are delivered. No matter what I try, I am never able to remain awake to figure out the source of the food. At first I was hesitant to eat anything, but on day three I gave up, giving in to my stomach while the empty pit of my magic gnawed at me from the inside.

Now, I am too weak to do much aside from staring up at the cracked ceiling. I've counted the tiles on the floor a dozen times. I've noted every irregularity in the stone walls, every single bump and divot. Yesterday it became difficult to stand, and I had to crawl to the bathing chamber.

The pain keeps me awake at night. The place where my magic should be is a void that pulses with need. A constant ache that I have no hope of replenishing. With not a flicker of a flame around and no way to steal pleasant emotions, my succubus powers are completely cut off. I am entirely defenseless.

Maybe that's their plan. Ignore me until I am too weak to fight back, save themselves some time when it comes to the whole torturing part. I wonder who will do it. Teru is a likely guess, though the king seems like he wouldn't mind getting his hands dirty.

I'm curled up in a ball on my bed, my face scrunched up tight as I fight my way through the throbbing pain. My chest aches and my entire body is covered in sweat from the strain. Every few minutes my entire body will begin to shake, my muscles tightening and cramping up until I can hardly breathe. This time is the worst. A small, pained moan slips past my lips and I have to think that maybe boredom won't be what kills me after all.

A creaking noise fills the room, but I can hardly open my eyes to look at where it came from. Hands grab me harshly and I am pulled off the bed, landing in a heap on the floor. A whimper escapes me and I double over, clutching my stomach.

"Get. Up." The command comes from a deep, harsh voice.

Forcing my eyes open I peek through my damp hair. He's dressed in all black, a simple tunic with cut off sleeves and matching pants. It's the one who looks like Teru. He has the same nose and lips, the eyes only slightly different. Where Teru's appear more angular, his are straight and narrow, though they share the same steel-gray irises. The shape of their faces are just barely off as well. This one has a more angular jawline and rounded chin. The most noticeable difference, however, is the way he looks at me.

If Teru's face can be described as exasperated at best, this one looks at me with complete and utter disdain. Like I am not worth the dirt beneath his shoes. This observation is confirmed as his mouth contorts into a vicious sneer.

"I said. Get. Up." He punctuates his words clearly, his grip on my arm tightening and drawing a new pain different from what I have grown familiar with.

"Maybe," I gasp, "you should ask nicely." Each breath comes out in pants. My heart races as adrenaline begins to surge through my veins.

He grabs my other arm, his fingers biting into my skin sharply, and yanks me to my feet. My legs start to give out, but he holds me upright. "I don't do *nice*. Now move or I'll make you move." His eyes narrow further, the gray swirling and becoming darker. The sight sends a shiver down my back.

"Yeah, well, I guess you're going to have to because I can't exactly stand on my own." I give him my best smile and shrug my shoulders. Before I can blink he is dragging me out of the room. The moment we cross the threshold, everything goes black and I recall the feeling of their unique magic, evanesce. The power to dissipate like smoke and appear somewhere else entirely.

The moment the blackness clears, he releases me. I fall to my hands and knees coughing. I force myself upright so that I am sitting on my heels, and examine the room. It's a small chamber. Maybe double the size of my *room*-which should say something about my current living situation. The walls and floor are the same ancient stone, cracks are filled in all over with something smooth and black. The contrast catches my eye and I nearly miss the people standing in the corner.

The same people from when Teru first brought me here are standing side by side against the wall. The tall one with the shaved head and scarred face. Then the small one, only recognizable by her height. Whereas before she had painted black lips and a white sheen covering her skin, this time you can see her rich, tawny skin. Teru, of course, is standing by their look-alike where they flash me a smug grin and a condescending wave.

I roll my eyes at them and continue to search the room, trying not to get my hopes up that there will actually be a way out. Then my eyes land on *him* and my muscles lock, frozen. My breath catches in my throat.

He sits in the center of the room on a simple throne, not needing anything extravagant as his commanding presence is enough to draw attention. This time he is wearing a black, sheer shirt that exposes every hard line of his stomach and the deep v below his hips. His pants are hung low, the color a rich emerald green. Devastating.

"Hello there," he says, voice smooth as silk. It glides across the room and whispers against my cheek making goosebumps rise across my skin. His lips tilt up in the corners with a smile that says he knows exactly the effect he has on me. "We have a few questions for you."

"Sorry, gonna have to pass." I force myself to sit up straighter. A small chuckle comes from the side of the room, drawing my attention away momentarily. The tall one is clenching his jaw shut as he makes a sort of coughing noise. I narrow my eyes at him before turning my attention back to the king.

As our eyes meet, his smile widens. He stands, his height towering as I sit here on the floor, and walks towards me slowly. Once he is in front of me he crouches down so that we are at eye level with each other, dark gray meets honey brown. "Cute. Let's try that again, shall we?"

I lean forward until our faces are only an inch apart. "Screw. You." Before the words have even fully left my mouth my head is being ripped backward. My hair is wrapped around a tight fist as it pulls so that my neck is tilted up, exposed.

"Learn some respect, whore," it's the one who dragged me from my room. He pulls harder on my hair and I am forced to lift off the ground to relieve some of the pressure from my burning scalp.

"Taka, enough," the king says.

Taka releases me and I fall forward again, my hands reach up and rub at my head trying to ease the pain. I look up furiously at the king and sneer.

He laughs to himself. "You'll have to excuse Taka, his manners could use some work."

"Consider him unexcused," I spit, shooting a glare in Taka's direction back over by the wall. He moved so quickly that I wonder if he just evanesced around the room.

"Fair enough, still, let's start with something easy. How about a name? Unless of course you're more comfortable being addressed as whore?"

This male may be beautiful, but every time he opens his mouth the only thing I want to do is knock his teeth out. "You go first."

A low grumble starts up from the wall, but he raises a hand, silencing them without a single look. He tilts his head at me before running his gaze over my entire body. "Yuta."

"Yuta?" I test the sound of it on my tongue, drawing out the *u* sound and the clipped *ta*.

"Exactly. Your turn."

I consider my options here. If I refuse to give him my name I have no doubt he'll just continue to call me whore, though I've certainly been called worse. As far as insults go for a succubus, whore is pretty tame. But what if I do give him my name? There is a chance he'll recognize me as the heir to Vulca and it will put me and my entire kingdom in even more danger. As I'm about to accept his offer for my temporary nickname, he cuts in.

"Don't," he commands, "you owe me a name. Tell me, *now*."

Asshole. "Fine. My name is Eve."

"Eve?" he echoes my earlier response.

"Yup," I say, popping the p.

"Good. Now, let's try a new question. Where are you from, Eve?" He says my name like it's our own little secret. His eyes glow with flecks of gold. His tongue traces the seam of his lips as he waits for my response.

"I have no home," I answer with a shrug.

He nods his head. "I see. Well what about your family? Tell me more about them?"

I sigh dramatically. "I'm an orphan, never met my parents. No siblings. Just me. All alone."

Yuta tilts his head to the side, his eyes becoming more cold. "And your magic? I know you use the fire element, Teru already told me. Anything else you'd like to share?"

"Like my creature?" I ask, genuinely confused.

"Sure, you could say that."

"How about you guess," I smirk.

"I think I'd rather hear you tell me yourself."

I pretend to think about it. Pursing my lips and shaking my head back and forth. "You know, I think I've had enough questions. How about we play another game?"

Yuta shakes his head with a deep sigh. "Eve, if only you would cooperate," he says standing, "we could have done this the easy way."

Teru appears between us, "I would say it's nice to see you again, but it's not."

As they raise their hands I prepare myself for the strike. I take a deep breath and harden every muscle that I can to take the hit with minimal damage. Only a physical blow never lands.

Teru's magic shoots out like a whip and forces its way inside my mind, cutting off all my senses and sending me plunging back into darkness. But this time, something is different, the tiniest sliver of light remains, and I latch onto it as hard as I can.

Chapter 7

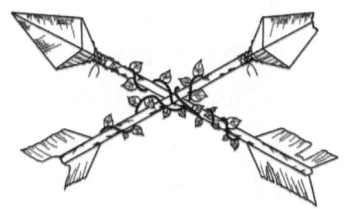

Oak

My head is pounding as I blink my eyes open, temporarily blinded by a bright light. It takes a few seconds for my eyes to adjust and when they do, I take in a harsh breath.

The first thing I notice are the towering walls that wrap around us, smooth and white, solid and without a single crack. The second thing I notice is the crowded courtyard that I lay in. The ground is covered in a thick layer of straw and leaves, small paths winding around the space with packed dirt. There are females everywhere, carrying baskets, beating against large quilts, some are chatting, sitting beside a fire and laughing as they sip from their mugs.

"Come on, it's time to go," a voice says behind me.

I stare up at Aine with a mixture of confusion and awe. She has pulled down the cloth covering her lower face, revealing an angular jaw, full lips, the tip of her nose ever so slightly slants down. She's quite beautiful, her features so gentle, completely at odds with the harsh look in her eyes.

"Do not waste any more time, up," she commands.

Pushing up from the ground I wipe my hands against my pants, trying to rid myself of the feeling of the straw pressed into my palms. Without waiting for me, Aine begins to walk through the center of the courtyard, her steps sure and graceful while I continue to kick up dust in my wake.

"Where are we?" I ask, already expecting the answer.

"The Crypt," she answers blandly.

"The Crypt?" I echo. Talk about being on the nose. Ghosts, Crypts, next thing you know they're going to start talking about the reapers of souls. For as much of a mystery the Ghosts are, they're not exactly furtive.

"Yes, now hurry up, we're late." Her tone is laced with irritation as she parts a thick curtain and walks through. As I follow behind, she lets the curtain fall closed, hitting me in the face.

"Was that really necessary?" I mumble. I've been here for all of ten minutes-that I know of- and already Aine has found a way to unsettle me. I pride myself on staying under the radar, of not drawing any unnecessary attention upon myself. But at this moment, I would really love to tell her exactly what I think of *The Crypt*. As I pass through the curtain any protests die on my lips. A large dais sits in the middle of the room, raised up a few feet off the ground and enclosed with vines strung up between bamboo shoots. Two women circle each other wearing the same thick, black pants as the first time I saw Aine. Only instead of a tunic wrapped around their chests, they have fitted tank tops, revealing the defined muscles of their arms and shoulders.

One has pale blonde hair tied back, and porcelain skin, a light flush staining her cheeks pink. Otherwise, it's like all color has been leached from her. The other has deep umber skin, her black hair falling in loose curls around her face.

The two are warriors, their movements precise and controlled. Sweat drips off of them as they hold their hands out in a defensive position, their feet gliding across the floor, crossing one over the other so that they never turn even an inch away from their opponent. Their breaths are even, steadily coming in and out as they contemplate their next move.

"Who are they?" I ask, unable to take my eyes off them.

"The blonde on the left, that's Lina," a girl answers from beside me, "the one on the right is Farai."

The smallest twitch of Lina's hand and Farai attacks. She spins around, balanced on the balls of her feet, her back leg comes off the ground and kicks out, hitting her target in her stomach.

Lina is thrown backwards, curving her body inwards and landing on her upper back, rolling upright into a crouch. She doesn't wait to retaliate, jumping up and doing a full turn before her leg arcs forward and slams into Farai's shoulder.

A harsh grunt leaves Farai as she blocks, shifting her hand to grab hold of Lina's ankle. As soon as her hand is wrapped around it she drops to the ground, twisting in a move that ends with Lina pinned on her stomach, as Farai sits atop her back.

I examine the hold, searching for any way Lina could escape. Farai is pressing her body weight into her hips so that she can't roll. Her hands force Lina's face into the ground from between her shoulder blades, all while Lina's hands are caught underneath her, immobilized. The most impressive thing is how Farai has managed to trap Lina's legs between her crossed ankles. Everything about the hold is perfect.

"How did she do that?" I ask, mesmerized.

"Training," Aine's cold voice answers. Aine stalks forward as the two girls untangle themselves, Farai helping Lina stand.

"I don't know how you do that every time, one of these days you're going to teach me," Lina says excitedly.

The pair turn and greet Aine with easy smiles and a dip of their heads. She returns the gesture before calling me forward. As soon as I step up beside her the other two lock up. "Lina, Farai, this is Oakley."

"Oak," I cut in.

"Oak," Aine emphasizes in annoyance, "will be training with us from now on. The order has come from the high lady herself."

Words hang unspoken in the air, the temperature chills as wind whips around us. An unsettling feeling creeps up inside me.

"Oak, this is Lina and Farai," Aine says by way of introduction. "Farai is my second in command and Lina is my third." Lina gives me a broad smile, her nearly translucent eyes bright and shining. Farai barely acknowledges my existence beyond a sweeping gaze from head to toe.

My brain catches up with Aine's words and my mouth drops open. I fear that my brows may merge with my hairline from the shock. If Lina and Farai are second and third in command then that must mean that Aine is number one.

The number one Ghost is in charge of watching me which means my escape plans are going to be a lot more difficult than I thought. Not to mention if Lina and Farai are watching me too.

I force a smile onto my face, trying to play it cool. "So, how did you become the top three in the entire compound?" If I can get them to confirm my suspicions then maybe I can get them to reveal something else. And if they won't tell me themselves, then I'll just have to persuade them to.

Farai finally meets my eyes and I notice the three discolored lines near the corner of her eye. *Scars.* "Here, secrets are earned, and you have not earned *anything* yet," her voice is smooth like the edge of a blade, and her attention cuts into me.

Before anything else can happen Aine steps in. "Lina, I want you to take Oak around the compound, show her where everything is and have her get changed. You can meet us back in the courtyard, I need to debrief with Farai."

Lina nods her head and gestures for me to follow her as she descends the steps of the dais and walks back through the curtain from before. "Over there is where we clean and sharpen our weapons," Lina explains, pointing to the spot where a few people examine their blades.

She continues guiding me around the perimeter. "Laundry is over there, everyone is responsible for their own things, and you must always have clean clothing, so don't wait around to do it, the crowds get pretty big towards the end of the week."

I look down at my ragged clothes, still dirty from the days of travel from Rayan. "I don't have any clothes but these," I explain to Lina.

She looks me over from head to toe before shaking her head. "That doesn't matter. We all are given specific pants and tunics to wear for missions. You'll also be given training attire and two pairs of sleep clothes. Those are the only ones you'll get, so I recommend showering every night. Though, after training, I can't imagine you wouldn't want to shower anyways."

We continue through the courtyard and I truly realize how many people are here. There are easily two dozen women milling about working on things or walking out of corridors. A pair exits from one and Lina points them out. "Over there is the kitchen, we all rotate cooking duties and meals are prepared three times a day. No eating outside of those times so don't be caught with food in your room."

So much information. I have no idea how I'm supposed to remember all of this. *Maybe I should be taking notes?* That's what Reed would have done. My heart throbs at the thought of my brother. What he must think of me, being sent away like I was. He must be so ashamed. He has always idolized our aunt and he's probably glad to be rid of me. I wish I could have explained before I... left.

"This way to our rooms," Lina says, drawing me from my thoughts. We head down a narrow hallway until we emerge into another wide courtyard, this one has many stone benches and tables all throughout the soft grass. This space is surrounded by wooden doors two stories high, a set of stairs in each corner. A quick count reveals 24 doors, 12 on the top and 12 on the bottom.

"This section has four squads in it, those 6 rooms are our squad's. That one is Aine's, then Farai's, then mine, then Hala, Symone, and yours is on the end," she explains, moving left to right.

"So, I'm in your squad, just like that?" I ask, hoping to get at least something small out of her.

Lina turns to me with an unexpected sneer. "Apparently." She shakes her head and her smile returns to normal. "Now, there is a small bathing chamber in each of our rooms. Go get cleaned up and changed and meet me back here in 15 minutes." She gives me a little shove before making her way up to her own room.

~~~

I only take ten minutes and make it down to the courtyard before Lina returns. A kind of nervous energy is running through me as I bounce from toe to toe. Whatever happens is going to help me determine what my next move is going to be. I've already wasted too much time here when I need to be looking for Eve. I can't afford to sit around and wait for someone to save *me*.

"That was fast," Lina says, appearing behind me, "good. Aine has this whole thing about being on time. Better remember that unless you want to endure one of her *punishments*." She cringes.

"Right." I follow after Lina as she walks back to the first courtyard. As the familiar space comes into view Lina grabs me by my arm and pulls me to a stop.

"A piece of advice? No one is happy you're here. Let alone that you're in our squad. You haven't earned that right and the girls know that. You being here stole that away from one of them, that's not something they'll easily forget. So keep your head down, don't cause problems, and do what you're told when you're told to do it."

"I've been doing that my whole life."

"Good, then we won't have any problems." Lina walks over to a group of tables where Aine and Farai are sitting down, heads bent towards each other as they talk in whispers. "We're back," Lina announces when we're close.

"I take it that everything is in order?" Aine directs at Lina who gives her a thumbs up as she quickly starts up a conversation with Farai. Aine turns back to me and hands me a piece of paper. "This is your training schedule, stick to it. And this," she says handing me another paper, "is your chore schedule. Everyone has to pull their own weight around here so don't go thinking that just because you're related to the high lady that you'll be getting any special treatment."

I snort. "Yeah, well clearly we're not that close so no worries there."

Aine gets up in my face, "It is an honor to be chosen as a Ghost. Disrespect us again and you'll find your time here to be exceedingly unpleasant."

"Understood," I say, quickly skimming the papers as I notice something odd, "why isn't there any training with magic?" How can they expect us to get any better when we can't practice our magic?

"Magic is an extension of us which means that if our bodies and mind are weak, so too will the magic be. We do not allow beginners to train their magic until they have completed the tests and have earned the right, and trust, to unlock it."

I gape at her. "Are you telling me that there is no magic here? None at all?"

Aine shakes her head. "There is magic. Just not for you. There are very few people who have earned their right to magic and you are not one of them, and I doubt you will be any time soon." She points to the papers clutched in my hand, "your first training session is at dawn. Your partner will be Lina. Now, it is dinner time so get yourself food if you would like or return to your room. Those are your two choices." With those parting words Aine, Farai, and Lina all walk away side by side.

Chapter 8

Rose

I've spent the better part of the morning and afternoon in the library, bent over a table covered in ancient tomes on the entire history of Sena. None of which have revealed anything about the Ghosts. No matter how much I search, it is like every trace of them has been wiped clean, almost like they never existed at all.

The book sitting in front of me is closer to the time of my great-great-grandfather. It talks about the source of the power that flows into the land, how each species- fauns, centaurs, gargoyles, wolves, and the fae- all contribute to the land. This particular fact has held my attention for the last half hour. I always believed our power came from the rulers directly. It's why Terran is away so often, bleeding power back into the land. Yet according to this, that's not the case.

Each species has their own magic outside of the basic spells and enchantments, which can be taught, and their elemental power of course. For the most part, those powers are closely guarded by the species themselves, only those most trusted know the true depth of the power they hold. Some of the more notable powers, like Eve's ability to feed off of pleasure, are not as hidden, especially in comparison to more elusive creatures like gargoyles.

Growing up I spent a lot of time studying the different species that made up my kingdom, but even still, I have very limited information on the unique magic outside of the fae. Similar to mermaids' preternatural healing abilities, the fae are strategists by nature. Something about my species gives us the ability to calculate and analyze a situation far beyond that of any other. It's also what drives us to seek our knowledge. Especially in regards to our enemies.

I flip through the pages, searching for anything that even hints at the secret spies that have taken Oak. After another half hour I give up, flipping the book closed and coughing as a plume of dust fills the air. As soon as I am able to breathe again, I search the table for something else to review, but the piles of books have all been gone through. Twice. A groan escapes me as my head thumps against the table, my eyes squeezed shut.

"I'm not sure I've ever seen you quite so vexed, cousin." Reed's voice breaks the silence.

"If you're not here to help, then please leave," I say, not bothering to lift my head.

"Well I was going to bring you these books I found that might have information on the Ghosts, but you're right, I'll just go."

Smacking a hand against the table I look up at him, my chin resting against the wood. "Did you really find something that might *actually* be helpful?" Skepticism is thick with every word. We've been down this road before, and every time only leads to more disappointment and fury directed entirely at my mother.

"Maybe you should take a look for yourself and find out," Reed offers with a shrug, the corners of his lips tugging up into a teasing grin. Since our time in the woods Reed has become more open with me, his personality truly shining through. He is so much more than everyone else sees.

Reed is clever, he uses critical thinking to solve whatever problem captures his attention and does so with a level head. Beyond that he is observant, intelligent, and far too kind for this new world. Not to mention, he is incredibly strong and powerful, fast on his way to rivaling my brothers. He is also a bit of a smartass, also like my brothers, albeit far more loveable.

"Just bring it here please."

He crosses the room in three long strides until he is standing across the table, setting the books down in a stack before me. The spines are worn, the fabric bindings torn and faded, luckily I can still make out the titles. Most are unfamiliar and seem to relate to plants, which begs the question as to why exactly Reed thinks this will be helpful. I ask him as much.

"Because, in all of these books there is mention of a root that can be used to act as an antidote to most poisons. It's actually very interesting the-"

"Reed, what does this root have to do with the Ghosts?" I ask, cutting him off.

"Right. Well, the thing about this root is that it is extremely difficult to find. So difficult that no scholar has ever been able to locate it." He raises his brows expectantly.

"I'm still not getting what this has to do with Oak."

He sighs, clearly becoming exasperated. "If no scholar has ever been able to locate it, then how do we know of its existence? Someone must have found it."

"Okay so…"

Reed leans forward, resting both his hands on either side of the books. He looks left and right like he is checking for someone who might overhear. "If you ask me, who better to find a mysterious root than a group of mysterious spies."

I shake my head, "That is a reach and you know it. Just because this plant-"

"Root."

"*Root*," I correct, "is so difficult to find doesn't mean the Ghosts are the ones who found it." I stare down at the books, wondering if this is really the best we can come up with. A hidden root? There is barely a slight chance that this has any connection to the Ghosts.

"Listen, I know it sounds absurd, but I think it's worth looking into. Maybe one of these books explains how the root came into our realm's possession." He rests a hand atop the stack, looking at me expectantly.

There are at least half a dozen books here, some extremely thick. It will take hours to go through all of them. But if Reed is right, and there is even the slightest bit of information, then it will be worth it. At this point, I would be happy to find any piece of information.

Anger stirs deep inside me, resting there like hot coals ready to be set ablaze. If my mother would just answer my questions and tell us what we want to know, then there would be no need for this. But of course that would be too much to ask for and my mother continues to guard her secrets even from her flesh and blood.

"Okay," I sigh, "let's look through these and see what we can find. Make a note of anything that even remotely hints at the Ghosts."

Reed sits down across from me and quickly divides the stack and half, cracking open the one on top and immediately diving in. I follow his lead and immediately regret my decision. My eyes cross from just looking at the words on the page. My head swims as my stomach constricts. I can't remember my last meal, but who has time to eat when there is work to be done?

When we're both on our second books a low whistle sounds from behind us and my entire body locks up.

"Wow, that is a *lot* of books."

I meet Reed's panicked gaze across from mine as our uninvited guest saunters over. "What do you want, Mateo?"

The wolf shifter walks straight over to our table, stopping at the end and letting his amber eyes rake over the sea of books spread out around us. "I don't want anything. Other than to help you."

I allow my eyes to flick to his for a moment and find him giving Reed a sexy smirk, power rolling off of him in waves.

He looks my cousin over and then winks.

I watch as Reed's face turns bright red and he tries to hide behind a book. His eyes peek over the top of the pages and I stick him with a look that screams *pull it together*. At the moment, Mateo is no more than a thorn in our side. But if we don't handle this right, then he could go to my mother and we would have a far worse situation on our hands.

"I appreciate the offer, Mateo, but I am going to have to decline… *again*," I say pointedly.

Mateo pulls a chair over and flips it around so that he is leaning over the back, his arms crossed over each other and acting as a sort of ledge for his squared chin. Black curls surround his head, the coils loose and fluffy. His bronze skin is a touch darker today, like he has been spending extra time outside. Unsurprising for a wolf shifter. Even when they aren't running with their packs, they tend to lounge around in the clearings. Usually nude.

Reed sets his book down, looking between the two of us and silently begging me to send him away. There is an odd sort of tension between the two of them, and I get the feeling that there is a story there. One I will absolutely be coaxing out of my cousin later.

Heeding his silent plea, I turn back to Mateo and focus on him. "Thank you for your concern, but you are truly not needed, please leave." The words come out a touch harsher than I mean them to, but that only makes the wolf smile more, his eyes brightening.

"I think you do need me. I can be really helpful if you'd let me."

Everything about him screams overconfidence, yet I don't hate him for it. The quality is almost… endearing. We've already turned him away twice now, yet he keeps coming back. I find it difficult to believe it has anything to do with the rescue mission. Not with the way his eyes keep straying to Reed.

I lean forward, lowering my voice to barely a whisper, "Listen, I normally wouldn't turn down help, but this whole thing is extremely dangerous. Especially for someone like you. I can't risk putting you in danger." I hope he hears the sincerity of my words and understands that the repercussions could be catastrophic for him. Maybe even for Reed and I, given my mother's apparent disregard for family. Or at least those of us who are of no use to her.

Mateo leans back, his gaze locked on Reed who is deliberately avoiding making eye contact and staring at the same spot over my shoulder as he has since Mateo first approached us. "Listen, if that's what you're worried about, then don't. I can handle whatever is thrown my way. I've never backed down from a fight before and I'm not about to start now."

There's that confidence again.

"This isn't like anything else you've ever faced. It goes beyond just fighting, it," I hesitate to speak the words aloud, "it could be seen as treason." The words hang thick in the air. The energy around us seems to buzz like it knows what I said. Like it inhaled the confession and is ready to release the breath directly into my mother's face.

Mateo focuses on me now, his amber eyes swirl beneath his thick brows. His features are so unique that for a moment I am trapped in his stare. Perhaps it is his power as an alpha, but something about him commands attention. "I understand the dangers. But I also know that I am exactly the person that you need to help you. *Let me.*" His voice was unwavering, his conviction inspiring something that terrifies me, trust.

We sit in silence, him waiting for my answer, Reed pretending he is invisible, all while I search for any ulterior motive that might be guiding his declaration.

What does he get out of it? Why would he *want* to help? There are too many things we don't know about him. Before he appeared in the woods, I barely knew he existed beyond being the alpha of a pack. Still, something deep within me tells me I can trust him. To put my faith in him. Fear holds my tongue captive all while a wild need to accept him throbs inside me.

I narrow my eyes. "Are you using magic right now?"

Mateo smiles. "Maybe." His tone is teasing, everything about him light and easy, disarming. He laughs, the sound releasing something in my chest. "Sorry about that, I didn't mean to, really. It just happens," he says with a shrug.

"What magic is that?" Curiosity outweighs my anger at having magic used against me.

"Nothing special really. Just a wolf thing, or at least an alpha thing." He stares Reed down waiting for his reaction and getting completely ignored.

"Interesting. We'll get back to that later, right now I care about why you think we *need* you to help us." I need a lot of things right now, but I can't think of any reason why his help would be included in that list.

Mateo's posture shifts, his entire body tensing. "Because," he leans in, "I have information on the Ghosts."

Every part of me focuses on that single bit of information. "What information do you have? Be specific." It takes every ounce of willpower inside me to not get my hopes up. If what he says is true, then that means we have wasted all this time on pointless books, all while Oak is still hidden away and Eve remains captured by the enemy. A fact that I refuse to forget, even while my focus remains on Oak.

"I know where you can find a Ghost."

This gets Reed's attention. "How? Where?" Reed demands. This is one step closer to finding his sister and bringing her back home. Then, we can focus on saving Eve.

Mateo tsks. "See, if you want that kind of information, then you'll have to let me in on it."

"Do you even know what *it* is?" Reed bites. Okay so I definitely need to know what happened between them if it's got *Reed* all worked up. My cousin is the master of control, he never lets his emotions get the best of him, yet somehow Mateo seems to have gotten under his skin.

"Fine." Both of their heads whip towards me, Reed's eyes going wide. He opens his mouth to argue, but I hold up a hand. "If what he claims is true, then we do need him. Besides, we've looked through all of these books and found nothing, it can't hurt to try something new."

"That's not true we found the root and-"

"Reed, stop. I'm sorry, but we are going to accept Mateo's help." Even as the words pass my lips my heart begins to race, fear creeping up inside of me and making my blood run cold. I can't help but question whether or not this is another moment of me being naïve, of allowing someone to manipulate me into doing whatever they want. Of being a puppet.

"Rose, do you honestly trust him?" Reed asks, meeting my eyes.

I know the real answer, but for the sake of Oak, I can't let it get in the way of finding answers. "For now, yes. Only so long as he makes himself useful," my gaze shifts to Mateo. "You can start by telling us how exactly you can find a Ghost."

"See, I can be helpful," he says to Reed before turning to me. He takes another moment to steel himself, "we have to go to Eteri."

Chapter 9

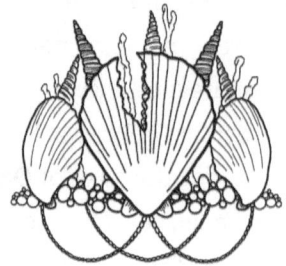

Cay

Days pass by in a blur. My mornings are spent by my mother's side, healing and talking to her. Hoping and praying to the goddess for something to change, for some small sign that she is getting better, that I won't lose her too.

My afternoons are dedicated to my people. No matter how much time I spend with them, I can't help but feel like an imposter. The legacy my father left behind lingers like a shadow over my shoulder. I always imagined that when I took up the crown that he and my mother would be by my side, guiding me, teaching me what it means to be a queen and lead a kingdom. Instead, I'm left here stumbling through the dark and failing at every turn.

Regan assures me every day that I am doing a great job, but I know that without her, my people would crumble much like our home has. I listen to their stories, I try to make things better in whatever ways I can. Sena's generosity is what keeps us going, yet I can't help the bitter taste left on my tongue knowing that they didn't truly come to our aid when we most needed it. They sat by and allowed my home to be destroyed.

The best part of my days are the evenings spent with Terran. Every night he arrives at my room as the warm glow of the fading sun guides our way to the library. Though we rarely see each other outside of these stolen moments, I love the routine we created.

We've claimed a spot in a corner on the second floor as we search for answers. So far, we've found nothing. Throughout all of the history books there is no mention of that ominous mist that destroyed my life in a singular moment. We've combed through books on elemental magic. Spells. Incantations. Potions. Even curses.

Nothing.

In my worst moments, when it all feels pointless, Terran is there to bring me back. He grounds me to a place in reality that doesn't feel so hopeless. It's a feeling I can't truly describe. Everything is easy with him. He is the singular point of normalcy left in my life. All of the other people in my life have changed or disappeared.

The day after *it* happened, I finally got to see my brother, Finn, again. After being separated through everything, I expected to feel a sense of relief and comfort from him, and at first I did. As he ran into my arms, throwing his arms around my neck and crying into my shoulder, it felt like a weight had been lifted. I still felt weighed down, but at least one small part of me was able to breathe again.

Then, the dread creeped in. I was told before seeing him that he didn't know what happened. Only that he needed to leave and now they were staying in Sena for a while. I was given the task of telling him that his father was dead and his mother lay sick and possibly dying in a room just down the hall.

As soon as the words left my mouth I watched the change happen. I saw the moment things clicked into place and this small, innocent boy became hard and unreachable. The love he had for me faded from his eyes, leaving behind a burning stare of anger and resentment. He blamed me. He stared up into my eyes and whispered *I hate you* before turning on his heels and walking away.

I let him go.

I hate me too.

He has refused to see or speak to me since that day. So I chose to give him space, the same thing I asked for myself. Only I fear that in giving him that space I may have created a rift so extensive that we might never be able to cross it again. Another bridge burned, another piece of my family lost forever.

Now, I walk through the halls no more than an empty shell. Avoiding the one person who might be able to bring me back to myself. Rose. We have been each others' rock through everything for our entire lives. The five of us each a piece of one soul that without each other is left broken. Oak and Eve are gone, taken by people that we have no hope to find. Mar is struggling to fill the hole that her sister's absence has left. I am barely holding my fractured kingdom together. And Rose, she is the one who can make it all better. But what if I don't want to feel better?

I turn down a hall leading back to my room, my thoughts running through the constant loop I can't escape. Voices interrupt them and I am momentarily pulled out of my mind. The training room is just up ahead and the sounds of metal clashing draws me in. As I approach, the voices grow louder, recognizable. Poking my head in, I can't believe what I see in front of me.

Oliver has his back to me, his body poised to strike as a large sword arcs over his head. Heading straight for my brother. My *barely* 10 year old brother. Oliver towers over him, twice his size and easily 200 pounds heavier. Still, his sword clashes against Finn's, the impact making him stagger backwards and ultimately falling to his butt. Finn's sword lays discarded by his side as he works to steady his breathing.

I march in, heading straight for Oliver and wasting no time in using my magic. A torrent of water shoots into his back and sends him careening across the room. He's standing within a few seconds, stalking straight towards me. I raise my right hand and he moves to block the magic, not paying attention to my left hand as my open palm cracks against his cheek.

His face shifts from anger to shock and then back to anger. "What the fuck do you think you're doing, princess?" he growls. He wraps his large hand around my wrist and tugs me forward until we are chest to chest, his completely *bare* chest. I pull against his grip and he releases me, refusing to put even an inch of distance between us.

"I could ask you the same question. What in Vana's name do you think you're doing with my *brother*," I say, my magic stirring inside me and my throat beginning to burn. I force myself to take a step back, swallowing hard. The burn only intensifies.

Oliver's eyes narrow on me, his eyes flicking to my throat before leering at me. As he opens his mouth to retort, he is cut off by my brother who steps between us.

"Get out of here. I don't want to see you." He stands straight backed, his chin lifted up in defiance. Sweat beads along his brow and bruises cover his own bare chest. His ribs are a mottled kind of black and blue, his arms a mix of purples and yellowish greens. A few of his knuckles are split.

Power pulses inside of me. My hands begin to tingle as magic flows through my veins and threatens to overspill. Oliver did this. He bruised and bloodied my little brother in a fight that he knows Finn never had a chance at winning. I curl my hands into tight fists, droplets of ice cold water dripping between my fingers as my control begins to slip.

"Finn, leave," Oliver bites, not even bothering to spare my brother a glance as his eyes stay locked on me. "No! She's the one who should leave. You told me you would train me," Finn cries indignantly.

"Now, Finn. I won't say it again," he says, leaving no room for argument.

Finn storms out of the room, muttering under his breath as he goes. We wait in silence until he has left the room.

Oliver steps forward as I take a large step back. This was the first time I have used my magic in weeks, and I can feel how unsteady it is. He holds his hands up placatingly as he continues to walk forward hesitantly. "You need to calm down."

"Are you fucking kidding me right now? You did not seriously just tell me to calm down." Water begins to pour in a steady stream from my fists against my will. Energy hums beneath my skin as the burning in my throat intensifies.

"Yes, I did. You need to get control of that magic, princess." He continues to walk forward, forcing me back until I am up against a wall. He reaches out and grabs my fists playing with my limited restraint.

"Oliver..."

"It's okay. Just take a few deep breaths and focus on me."

"Looking at you right now is only making it worse. I really want to hurt you right now, possibly even maim."

He chuckles, "Fair enough. Try not to focus on *that*, don't let that anger control you. Think about something else, something calming."

My magic grows stronger and my options become limited so despite my better judgment I decide to listen. Taking a deep breath, my thoughts shift, playing my memories out for me one by one. I picture walking through the halls with Terran. Sitting in the garden with the girls. I picture my last birthday, surrounded by my family as they handed me their gifts.

Then, unbidden, I think of Oliver when he found me in the throne room. I feel his arms wrapped around me like a protective shield. I think of the way he laid beside me in my bed.

The pressure begins to ease. I take a few more deep breaths and then my power recedes deep inside me. My well is filling up as my veins cool and the burning in my throat finally dissipates.

"You back with me?" Oliver whispers.

I open my eyes, meeting his hazel stare. "Yeah, I feel a lot better now."

"No longer picturing murdering me?" he teases.

"Don't test your luck, the feeling is always there, jussst beneath the surface."

"Let me guess what you were thinking about," he smirks, "me. Naked. Probably in your bed on to-" He catches my hand barely an inch away from his cheek. "Hitting isn't nice."

"Remember that murderous feeling? It's reached the surface." I have to fight the urge to hit him again.

"Noted." He examines my face before taking a few deliberate steps back. "So, let's talk about your little tantrum."

"Tantrum?" I say with a scoff.

"Yes. That little display just now? What else would you call it?"

"I call it defending my brother after you attacked and seriously injured him."

"Please, it was a few bruises. He knew what he was getting into when he asked me to train him. It's part of the process, get over it." He rolls his eyes.

"Part of the process?" I throw my hands up in the air as I begin to pace. "He is only 10 years old, Oliver. He's just a kid. The training room is no place for someone that young."

"I was younger when I first started training," he shrugs. "If anything, he is behind. You can't just ignore the fact that your kingdom was attacked, Cay," he says my name with abhorrence, "ignoring the problem isn't going to make it go away."

"I am not ignoring the problem!" I scream, "And what does that even have to do with Finn?" I continue to pace, throwing my hands up in the air again and looking over my shoulder at him where he leans casually against the wall.

"He needs to be prepared for what comes next. What happened in Rayan, that's just the beginning. He needs to train so that when the time comes, he can defend himself," Oliver says pointedly.

I whirl on him. "No, he does not. Because I will be there to protect him."

"Like you protected your mother? Like you protected your father?"

Something inside my chest cracks. "I'm done." Without another word I march from the room. The moment I cross the threshold, I run straight into a large form. My face smacking against a hard chest.

"Oh, there you are," Terran says with a smile, "I went to your room, but you weren't there, I thought you might already be in the library."

My chest is heaving with lingering fury. I school my face as I look up at him. "Sorry, I got caught up in something."

His eyebrows pull together as his lips turn down. "Are you alright? You seem kind of flustered."

I plaster on a smile. "Absolutely, let's get going."

"Good, because I think I found something," he says with excitement.

"After you," I gesture. He turns to lead the way and I follow after him, looking over my shoulder and finding Oliver standing in the same spot, staring after us with a blank stare. No smirk.

Chapter 10

Mar

I roam the kitchen, opening cabinets and the same ice box that hasn't changed since the last time I opened it three minutes ago. Sighing, I close the door and make my way to the small table in the corner of the room. I'm taken aback as I realize my father is sitting at the same table, slumped in his chair with his head drooping as he struggles to keep it up.

"Hey, I didn't realize you were here. Are you alright?" I ask, already knowing the answer. Neither one of us has been alright for the last three weeks.

He looks up at me, his eyes are ringed with darkness and his face paler than usual. His hair is disheveled, like he rolled out of bed. It's been the image that only I see, usually in the dead of night as he takes up residence in his office, sorting through paperwork and trying to keep things organized. He rubs at his eyes, clearing the sleep though I already know neither of us has found it today. "Hey, sweetheart. What are you doing up?"

I tilt my head back staring up at the ceiling in an attempt to hide what I know is so plainly written across my face. "Just looking for something to eat."

He nods his head. "I think there is some flavored ice left. Mint if I remember correctly."

My heart squeezes with the reminder of sitting on my bed talking to Eve well into the night. I still haven't been able to go into her room. This is the longest we have spent apart in years. She has been a constant presence by my side, our routine so familiar that it feels wrong to go through the motions. The disruption too much to handle on top of everything else.

I ignore my fathers suggestion and redirect the conversation. "When was the last time you fed?"

He shakes his head. "You don't need to worry about me. I want to know about you, what have you been doing?"

"I've been keeping busy."

"Don't overwork yourself. You should rest, take care of yourself."

I roll my eyes. "You're one to talk. Have *you* been taking care of yourself?"

"I'm managing." He chuckles before his eyes grow distant, lost in thought. After a few moments of silence his face grows despondent. "Though I have to admit, your sister's absence is something that haunts me every moment. Between that and Elani..."

I've never had a problem opening up to my father. He has been nothing but supportive my entire life. He has guided me and shaped me into the person I am today. Yet somehow he feels more distant now and I can't bring myself to burden him with my own troubles when he is already going through so much. Still, I can't hide what I am feeling now. "I know. I feel it too."

The air feels thick as we sit together, neither one of us talking as we each process what has become our lives. Only a month ago we were sitting at the dining table joking about Rose's birthday. It feels like years. I hear the echo of her laugh in the halls and chase the sound. I can only imagine how much worse it is for our father.

"How are you doing, really?"

His shoulders begin to shake as he crumbles before me, gut wrenching sobs tear out of him and he folds in on himself. "My heart has been ripped in two, Mar. I fear for your sister while praying to the goddess to save Elani," he chokes, "my kingdom continues to look to me for guidance and I can barely hold on. I have failed them and they don't even know it yet."

I watch as a king breaks before me, becoming a male, a mate, a father. This moment is where things change, I can feel the shift. When a ruler cracks, the kingdom fractures with him. Someone has to hold the pieces together. "You're doing everything you can," I assure him, pushing aside the desire to fall apart with him.

"It's not good enough. I should be ashamed."

"Absolutely not. You are a wonderful, caring king. You always put our people first. *That* is what they need. They will support you through anything because they know you will support them. You need help, let me be that person."

He shakes his head, slowly pulling himself back together. Hesitation flickers in his steel blue eyes.

"Let me help you," I repeat as my heart begins to race.

Finally, with a deep sigh, his shoulders seem to relax and he nods. "Okay. But are you sure? I don't want to give you too much."

"I'm sure. I want to help. These are my people too and I want to do whatever I can. If taking some of that work off your plate is what it takes, then consider it done. Where should I start?" I choke back my own tears, shoving aside this overwhelming need to cry so I can take care of my father.

He seems to consider it for a minute. "There are too many meetings, I can't be everywhere at once. The council needs to meet, but we haven't been able to because of my schedule. You've been present enough that I

67

feel comfortable with you guiding these discussions," his cheeks flush, "I would like to spend as much time with Elani as possible."

"Of course. Whatever you need. Give me more." I can already feel the nausea rising in me at the thought of all that needs to be taken care of.

"I've neglected the guards. With everything that happened in Rayan, we should be reinforcing our defense, but I haven't had time to create a plan. Until we do, we remain even more vulnerable than we already are."

Fear seizes me as the realization dawns on me. Still, I can't back out now, this is too important for my own anger to get in the way. Besides, I can avoid a certain asshole well enough. "Consider it done. I will have it taken care of within the next few days."

"You should partner with Rian. He was present during the attack and he'll have a better understanding of what we should do and how best to prepare. Let him take the lead, but remember that you're still in charge, you have final say." He winks at me.

Fuck. So much for avoiding him. I hesitate for barely a breath, but it's enough to give my father pause.

"I knew it. It's too much. I shouldn't have-"

"No, it's not too much. I was just thinking about where to start first. I swear. I can handle it."

"Are you sure?"

I smile. "Yes, it's no problem. Get some rest. Spend time with your mate. Let me carry some of your burden."

He leans across the table and places a kiss on my forehead. "You've always been the one I could depend on." With those parting words, he rises and leaves the room, most likely heading to the royal infirmary.

I replay those words over and over again for the next hour. I mindlessly walk up the stairs to my room. I change into shorts and a loose fitted shirt. In less than half an hour, I am standing in the training room, staff in hand and a dummy set up in front of me. I attack. And attack. I don't stop attacking until the pain shifts from an ache in my chest to a full body ache.

Covered in sweat and breathing heavily, I walk back upstairs and hop into the shower. I lean my head against the cool tile walls and squeeze my eyes shut. As much as I have forced the thoughts away, my mind conjures images of Eve, filling my head with so many gruesome images that I can hardly remain standing.

Chapter 11

Eve

My head pounds as my senses return to me and the blackness recedes from my eyes. I'm curled into a ball on the cold ground, shivers wrack my body as I try to piece myself back together. My skin is covered in a thick sheen of sweat, my clothes clinging to me in odd places. I unfurl myself, forcing my body upright as my muscles scream at me, weak and sore. As the room spins around me, my stomach churns and I have to breathe deeply to quell the urge to vomit. Something that I have been doing a lot lately.

I raise my head, blinking away dark spots and staring up at Teru as they stand above me, staring down with a mask of rage painting their face. I meet every ounce of loathing with my own, pouring the pain and anger into my scowl until they take a step towards me. My muscles tighten in anticipation of another attack.

Bring it asshole.

"Enough," Yuta's baritone voice cuts through the silence, "leave us." His imposing form remains at the center of the room, commanding attention from his simple throne. It is then that I notice the detailing carved into the arms and back, exquisite.

I watch as they all leave the room without a hint of protest. Their eyes looking straight ahead as they file from the room one by one. A faint whisper drifts towards me followed by a grunt. The moment they are gone I fix my furious eyes on the one male remaining, the orchestrator of my capture and every moment since.

"What are you doing to me?" the words come out grating.

A phantom wind disturbs his black hair as he stalks forward. He stops right in front of me, crouching down-the warm, sensuous scent of jasmine envelops me. He reaches out, grabbing my chin with long, smooth fingers and tilting my chin up so I am forced to stare into his honey brown eyes, more of a warm golden now. "What is it about you?" he purrs. The juxtaposition of his personality and breathtaking appearance sends me off kilter in my weakened state.

I gather every ounce of strength I have left to slap his hand away, falling forward as soon as he releases me. My arms flail out, barely catching myself before my face meets granite. My heart begins to race, my head swimming as my vision begins to blur. I stay like that for longer than I would like, fighting my body to remain conscious.

Fuck, this sucks.

"Get the fuck away from me before I gut you, rip out your insides, and feed them to a dragon." A flicker of red hair flashes in my mind, but I can't afford to lose focus.

I barely have enough strength to force myself into a kneel, sitting back against my heels with my palms pressed firmly against my thighs, supporting my upper half. In another circumstance this might be the beginning to a fun evening, but the only thing in our future is someone's head rolling across this polished floor. Preferably his.

"You're making a big mistake, keeping me here. I have people, people who will come for me. When they do," I laugh, "you'll wish you had never left your hideout." A newfound strength fills me as I imagine my girls, Rose,

Oak, Cay, and Mar, all rushing into this room and fighting alongside me as we always have. The moment we're all together again, we will rain hell down on all of these fuckers.

Yuta laughs at me, his rich voice filling the room and reverberating off of the walls as he gives me his back and glides towards his throne. His fingers dance over the ornate arms, tracing the intricate swirls and symbols carved there. He eases himself into it, watching me with amusement and interest. The corners of his lips tip up ever so slightly as his eyes swirl with whatever is going on inside his mind. A buzzing sort of anticipation builds between us.

Pulling one knee up, I use the leverage to force myself to my feet. I search inside myself for ever a flicker of power, some kernel of magic that can change the tide. The deep well of power inside me is hollow, aching from the emptiness. If I had access to my succubus charm I should be able to control him long enough for me to get to fire. I don't need much, just enough to get me out of here and closer to my sisters. All I need is to get to them.

Yuta's lips curl into a full smirk. "You can search all you want, but you'll find no magic inside you." Mist curls from his fingertips, pooling around his feet and spilling down the steps, creeping towards me with a taunting whisper.

A tight tug on my center has me taking the smallest step towards it, like a string pulled taut. Something buzzes inside me, but it's not my magic. That remains entirely cut off. Anger rises in me until a raw scream tears from my throat as I throw my hands up in frustration.

"What did you do to me," I demand. My chest heaves, my skin becoming oversensitized as the phantom winds begin to grow making the mist swirl. A wisp reaches me, curling up to caress my leg and my legs lock up.

"Nothing really," he says with a shrug, "we simply looked into your mind to find the truth about who you are."

My blood runs cold, the color draining from my face as I lose all sensation in my fingers. I'm so screwed. He can't know who I am. If he knows who I am, then he will attack Vulca. He can get to my father, my mother, *Mar*. My memories will betray me and everyone I love if I allow him access to my mind. No matter what, I can't let that happen. I won't.

"Oh?" I say with false bravado, "and what is it you think you found? I'm nobody, completely irrelevant, nothing."

Yuta smiles knowingly, his eyes roaming over me from head to toe. There is nothing heated in his gaze, just this unique curiosity that lights his eyes. "Oh, little minx, you're far more than nothing. You just might be everything," he says, his already deep voice dropping an octave.

"What's that supposed to mean?" The frantic pounding of my heart throbs in my neck as my pulse beats erratically. I need to get control, to appear completely unbothered. *Pull it together, Eve, now is not the time to lose your shit.*

"You really have no idea, do you?" he cocks his head. His magic begins to recede as he pulls it back to him, the vapors evaporating the moment they touch his skin.

I shrug. "How about you enlighten me?"

It's a risk, playing into his game. But if there is one thing I need just as much as magic, it's information. Something to help me not only escape, but understand why they are doing this. What they hope to gain. Still, in this moment it is easy to play dumb because I am absolutely fucking lost.

"No, I don't think I will." Before I can even process his words, Yuta claps his hands and that empty vortex consumes me, sending me tumbling through the darkness yet again.

As I am deposited on my bed, my stomach churns and this time I can't fight it. I barely make it to my bathing chamber before collapsing into a ball on the ground, shivering and switching between burning hot and freezing cold for what feels like hours. My magic is too low. My power is unreachable as the effects begin to set in and the clock starts ticking.

No one can survive long without their magic. It's why deprivation makes for a great form of torture. The body slowly starts to deteriorate until nothing but a husk of a person is left. First, we grow weak, our bodies using every ounce of energy to keep us going, to give us a chance to survive. When that is not enough, our hair will fall out in clumps, our nails turn brittle. Then, our bodies will begin to attack itself until we are no more than a pile of bones wrapped up in shriveled, leathery skin. Finally, our eyes and brain will swell until they burst from their sockets, the contents of our skulls seeping out through our ears, nose, and mouth.

Yummy.

I've never seen it happen before. It is considered to be the cruelest form of torture known, so horrific that it was banned hundreds of years ago. But I guess laws don't apply to hidden kingdoms. Not surprising, though I am not exactly looking forward to it. Within weeks I will begin to see the more serious effects, at least if I don't feed. The smallest of fires would provide me with enough magic to sustain myself a little longer. But what I really need is the magic that will feed my creature.

Pleasure.

I scoff to myself as I crawl to my bed, dragging my body against the floor. Being a succubus is something I have always loved. I am comfortable with myself, in knowing my wants and needs. It's not that I have anything against other creatures or the way they replenish their magic, it just never felt right to me. My creature is who I am. Yet here, in this small, dark room, completely cut off from everyone that I love, I can't help but resent it.

If I were a mermaid like Cay, I could use the water in my bathing chamber. If I were fae like Rose and Oak, all I would need is access to the earth, flowers, anything connected to nature. If I were a vampire like Mar and our father, then I could do some real damage all while replenishing the magic they have denied me. But I'm not any of those things. Which means I have to find some way to steal pleasure from the people who only seek to bring me pain.

Easy enough. Curling in on myself I push aside everything other than keeping my strength. I only have a short amount of time to do this and only the vaguest idea of how. If it's going to work I'm going to need every ounce of power I have left in me. I'm not usually one for planning, but in this instance, I can't afford to be rash. I need to think, calculate, make a plan, and stick to it.

Chapter 12

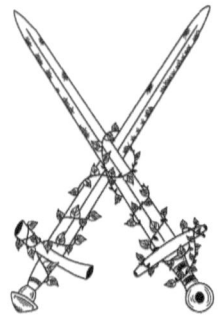

Oliver

Magic hums beneath my skin incessantly as I walk the halls of the castle. Each passageway is cast in shadows, only the faintest light painting the walls from the sconces placed every few feet. I rub my fingers together, feeling the familiar build of power as I suppress my magic, forcing it to remain buried deep inside me.

Clearly I didn't spend enough time training today if it is still overflowing like this. I'll have to do more tomorrow, make sure that I have control of things. With tensions running high, now is not the time to slip up. Especially with our *guests*.

A lyrical whisper reaches me from around the corner, halting me mid step. My heart begins to beat faster, my magic pushing to the surface like a battering ram demanding to break free. The voice drifts away and I feel the vice grip on my throat loosen, the tension releasing from my shoulders.

Standing in the hall, I wait until I am sure she is gone, unwilling to risk running into her so soon after our little disagreement. I mean honestly, what an overreaction. We both know that Finn needs to be trained, she's just too stubborn to admit it. She puts all this pressure on herself, and I try to do this one thing for her and somehow I am, *once again*, the bad guy. Typical.

I turn down the hall her voice had come from, wondering where exactly she was leaving so late in the evening. Midway down, the familiar archway leading to the library opens up. I let my eyes roam over the wide space, taking a moment to note my sister, our cousin Reed, and some dark haired guy half asleep on a table.

I don't even want to know what's going on there. Not my problem. Though my sister's presence eases something inside me. The rest of the space is empty, and I dismiss the scene in front of me as completely ordinary.

Turning on my heels I head back to my rooms, focusing on the faint chirps of crickets hiding outside the windows. I let it ground me, taking away some of the strain of holding back my magic. Each step feels a little more strained until the uneasiness is too much and I pick up the pace, changing course and heading back to the training room.

The next few hours are spent expelling every bit of magic I can until I feel the perfect level of emptiness inside me, all while knowing that by the time I wake it will be near full again. Though for what I plan to do in the morning, I might need it.

~~~

Guards stand at attention outside my mother's door, their gazes fixed straight ahead with not even the slightest acknowledgement of my approach. I roll my eyes as I reach forward and open the door for myself. The room is perfectly put together, not a book out of place, not a pillow unfluffed, every small detail accounted for. Behind the desk, my mother sits with her chin raised in the air, dignified. I have to fight the urge to laugh.

"Mother," I say flippantly. I take the seat across from her, kicking my feet up on her desk.

"Oliver," she says with a resigned sigh, "must we have this conversation *every* time? Remove your feet. Now." Her voice is clipped, eyes flashing in a warning.

I give her a mirthless smile. "Of course, high lady, my most sincere apologies."

Her jaw ticks, a wave of power whipping out at me and bouncing off of my imperceptible shield. She sets her palms down against the mahogany desk, letting her fingers trail over the smooth surface. "I see you are in one of your moods again. Tell me, *son*, what is it this time?"

"I'm sure I don't know what you mean, *mother*," I say in mock bewilderment, "it was you who requested my presence, was it not?"

This dance has become a routine for us. Her, filling the room with the poignant stench of complete and utter bullshit. Me, throwing it right back in her face. So far, I have never lost a challenge. I simply allow her to think she has won. What she doesn't realize is that each concession I give is chosen. I won't let her control me like she tries to control the others.

The creak of the door opening behind me announces just the puppet I was thinking about. Heavy footsteps grow louder as he makes his way across the room, lowering himself into the chair at my side. I turn to him, flashing a smirk with a raise of my brows. "Brother."

He heaves a deep sigh, his eyes flicking to my feet where they are still propped upon our mother's desk. Ignoring me, he turns to greet her. "Mother, how are you today? You look lovely as ever."

What's that sound? Oh wait, that's just the sound of my brother's lips puckering as he prepares to kiss our mother's ass.

Everything about him irks me. His clothes, perfectly pressed with not a wrinkle in sight. His hair, styled so that the curls remain perfectly in place. His back straight and chin pointed out proudly. The sad thing is that he didn't used to be this way. In fact, there was a time where I even looked up to him, wanted to *be* him. Now? I will do anything to ensure I am nothing like him.

"Terran," our mother says affectionately, "thank you, dear. This gown is new." Her hands glide over the plum gown, caressing the high neck and beaded collar. It's extravagant, something that should be worn to a ball. Yet here we are, sitting in her office.

This time I can't hold back my laugh and it comes out as a choked snort.

"Is something funny?" she bites.

"I just find it humorous that while an entire kingdom is crowded inside spare rooms, their entire lives uprooted, you are here getting new gowns." My blood begins to boil and the pulse of my magic thrums inside my veins.

"That is uncalled for. I have opened my home to those people. I have graciously offered them sanctuary, food, water, and anything else that they should need."

"Sure, after you left them on their own while they were being attacked. While their king was slaughtered and their entire kingdom was destroyed. Did you forget about that, mother?" I cock my head.

An ear-splitting screech echoes through the room as my mother pushes her chair back, standing above me with her hands clenched into fists. "How dare you-"

"Please, let's all take a moment to calm ourselves. I'm sure Oliver didn't mean anything by it," Terran raises his hands placatingly.

"Oh I meant something," I scoff, "from the moment that we learned Rayan was under attack we have done nothing but sit on our assess and pretend to be saviors. But look around, the thousands of refugees that crowd our halls are a constant reminder of our failure. I don't know how you can look at yourselves in the mirror. How you can go about your day as if everything is fine."

"Enough. I will hear none of this. If you are not here to help with truly pressing matters then you can leave," my mother bites.

My feet hit the ground with a heavy thud. I push my chair back and it topples over, cracking against the stone floors. "Gladly." Before I can take a step away, Terran grabs my arm firmly, his hand wrapping around my bicep.

"Wait," he growls close to my ear, "it's not worth it. Just stay and we can talk things through." He stares into my eyes, the same shade of hazel as mine, our faces are mirrors of each other, yet I don't recognize the person standing before me.

"There's nothing left to say. It's too late for words." With that I rip my arm out of his grip and march from the room, the door slamming shut behind me. My nostrils flare with harsh puffs as rage pushes me forward. Magic is pulsing off of me in violent waves and I consider heading back to the training room. Again. Barely 12 hours since my last visit.

My feet move unconsciously, carrying me to the one place that seems to truly relieve the throbbing inside me. I walk through the long room, beds laid out on either side of me. I slip through the door at the back of the room and weave my way through the narrow corridor.

"Olli? I wasn't expecting you today?" Flora says, surprise written across her wrinkled face.

"I thought I would check in on her, see how she's doing." I grab a stool and take my place beside the unconscious queen, watching the shallow rise and fall of her chest. "Any change?"

Flora comes to my side, placing her brittle hand atop my shoulder. "Nothing yet. We've had healers coming in for hours at a time, only leaving small gaps between sessions. Still, their magic doesn't seem strong enough to make a difference."

Without thinking I reach out, laying my hand over Queen Mira's, and push healing magic into her. I let out a deep sigh of relief, chills skating down my back as my magic finally has an outlet. Intoxicating warmth flows over me with each passing second.

"Oliver," Flora hisses, "don't."

"Flora, I know what I'm doing," I laugh.

"You know nothing. This magic is dangerous, so much is unknown-"

"I'm fine," I smirk at her, "trust me."

Her frail hand tightens on my shoulder. "It's not you I don't trust. It's the magic. You don't understand what you're playing with. Magic like this is volatile, if you lose even an ounce of control there is no telling what kind of destruction will follow. What will happen to *you*," she says pointedly.

My power finally begins to wane until it feels much more comfortable. As I watch the queen, her breathing seems more even. Her skin has more color and she is not as cold to the touch. Rising, I turn to look down at Flora, placing a soft kiss against the top of her head. "You don't have to worry about me."

Without waiting for whatever lecture is sure to come next, I make a hasty exit and begin my search for something to entertain me. Maybe *someone*.

Chapter 13

Mar

I sit in my bed, thinking of how best to approach things. I stare into my closet and consider my options before deciding to embody the exact person that he *thinks* I am.

I choose a deep burgundy gown, the fabric is thick and heavy. Long sleeves cover my arms and end at a point above my wrist, the neckline dipping into a slight v that emphasizes my collarbones without revealing too much cleavage. My golden hair is braided back, short wisps perfectly curled so that they frame my face. The perfect mix of reserved and powerful and every bit the princess that he imagines me to be.

Finishing off the look I grab a pair of golden heels, a swirling design curling up the side and meeting the thin strap wrapped around my ankle. I admire my reflection in the mirror, my eyes lined with kohl making them appear bigger. My lashes are curled in a way that gives them a full and sultry look. I turn back and forth, admiring the finished product as my dangling gold earrings sway, brushing against my neck.

He wants a princess, he'll get one.

Without a second glance, I let my door fall shut behind me, making my way to the lift and allowing it to take me up to the second to highest floor. The doors open to a long corridor that I am more than familiar with. Memories of walking by my father's side as he tells me stories of his own father, all while the windows let in the bright glow from our kingdom.

The rhythmic clack of my heels against the black tiled floor echoes as I make my way to this dreaded meeting. I walk the hall like it's a death march, my shoulders drawn back and chin held high. My body is tense despite how hard I fight it, each step is stiff and jarring. Forcing myself to keep going, my heart begins to race as I approach the room, guarded by one of my father's men.

They open the door silently as I tip my head in acknowledgement. The moment I have crossed the threshold they close the door gently behind me. I don't have to look for him in the room. He stands in front of the window, staring out at the glowing city below. The bioluminescent lights reflect off his white blonde hair, giving it a bluish sheen. He doesn't turn as I enter, doesn't even acknowledge my presence.

Fine, he wants to play it that way then so be it. I walk to the far end of the room, pick up the glass decanter and pour myself a glass of wine. The dry taste coats my tongue as I sip on it, crossing the room again so I can make myself comfortable. Without a word I take a seat beside Rian, the cushioned chair soft and so comfortable I could sink into it. I swirl my glass, allowing the heady aroma to waft through the air.

With a quiet sigh he turns to look at me, his jaw locked and eyes darkening. He leans against the window sill, watching me with intense purpose. Neither one of us speaks, both waiting for the other to set the tone for what's to come. I win the standoff as he rolls his eyes.

"You look…" he trails off.

"Beautiful? Elegant? Regal?" I taunt.

"Tired," he chuffs, "actually if I'm being honest you look like shit."

I shrug. "I've been busy."

"Clearly," he says with blatant irritation. When I don't respond he moves until he stands directly in front of me, staring down at me in my comfortable chair. I'm going to get one of these for my room, it will make the perfect spot for reading once I have some time again. *If* I ever have time again.

"Tell me what I'm doing here," he demands.

"Awfully pushy today, Rian. Do you have somewhere better to be?" I ask with a quirk of my brow. My blood rushes with the thrill of the fight, the deep inherent need to push him, to test his limits and see what will make him snap.

"Enough games, just tell me what it is you want so we can both leave."

I tilt my glass back, finishing off the wine in a loud gulp. I set the glass on a small table beside me and cross my legs, leaning back casually. "My father has asked me to take care of some things for him."

"And? What does that have to do with me?"

"Well, he would like me to focus on security, of ensuring that our kingdom is prepared should we find ourselves under attack."

Rian's eyes narrow as the puzzle pieces begin to fall into place. "He wants me to help." It's not a question. He sees the truth on my face and knows that this is serious, otherwise he wouldn't be here.

"Yes. Unfortunately for the both of us, it seems to be non-negotiable. My father wants the best, he wants someone trustworthy, and for some reason he thinks that person is you."

"What else is happening?"

"I don't know what you mean."

"There's something else, I can tell. It's written all over your face."

I take a moment to consider my options. I never asked my father about his opinion on sharing the real secrets with him so it is safe to assume it is a no go. Still, telling Rian would make things so much easier. Not to mention… it would ease some of the tension that has built up inside me at not being able to tell anyone. The weight of the secret would lessen by a fraction.

Mind made up I walk him through everything that has happened since we got back. He already had an idea of the Eve situation since none of his guards have been mobilized to form a search party. Still, he lets me get it all out, never interrupting and listening intently, focusing on each word and finding meaning in everything.

"No one else can know," I emphasize, "this secret is something that could destroy the foundation of the kingdom, we cannot let anyone outside of those we trust with our lives know."

He nods with understanding and resolve. "I'll help."

A laugh burst from me, chaotic and broken, becoming choked as I try to force myself to stop.

"What exactly was so funny?" he growls.

"Oh, just you thinking you had a choice. You're under my control now, like it or not. My father put me directly in charge of this whole thing so you'll be reporting to me, following every single order I give and listening to every word that I say." What I don't say is that neither do I.

My father needs help, the kingdom needs protecting, and if this will give me an opportunity to find and save Eve, then even better. I push to my feet, feeling a rush of blood to my head from the wine. I barely waver, but Rian steadies me all the same. His hand wrapped around my forearm is hot, his skin burning against mine.

"Careful, little one, you better reign that in before someone gets the wrong idea. Wouldn't want their princess to go all dictator on us now, wouldn't be good for the public image."

I pull my arm from his grip, push past him and head for the door, ready to walk away without engaging. Who am I kidding? I barely make it three steps before I am whirling on him, never one to back down from a fight. Especially when it comes to this arrogant asshole.

"Don't act like you know me. We've been through this too many times before and I don't have the time or energy to fight with you anymore. This is getting old, Rian."

A blur of motion has me pinned up against the door, his hand wrapped around my throat and squeezing slightly, not enough to cut off my air, but enough to prove he is in control. His chest heaves with his ragged breaths. The pointed ends of his fangs peek out between his full lips. Our bodies are pressed close together, every point of contact burns. He leans forward, his lips barely brush over my throat as his fangs graze the skin, a shadow of rough stubble scrapes behind his trailing mouth.

He stops just below my ear and breathes me in as he squeezes my throat a little tighter, drawing a gasp from my lips. My chest presses more firmly against him, completely outside my will. Everything is sharper, my senses heightened and my magic stirring as he draws my creature out of me. The conflicting need to push him away and pull him closer raging inside me.

"What, Rian? What do you want," the words come out breathless and weak. *Damn body, betraying me at this pivotal moment.* I can't let him think he has any more control over me than he already expects.

I am the powerful one, I am the decision maker. If he wants to resent me for it, then fine, but I'm not about to allow him to try and change me.

"Stop pretending. This isn't you." His gaze rakes over me, taking in my *princess* attire. His eyes linger on my collarbones before fixating on my neck.

"Isn't this exactly what you claim I am? A perfect princess. What's the matter, you having second thoughts?" I goad.

"Don't. I won't have this conversation with you."

"Oh, of course, because this is all on your terms. You decide when we talk. You decide who I am and how I should dress or act. I'm done," I scoff, "let's get one thing clear, I am the same person I have always been and I will not change for anyone. Especially not a male. If you have an issue with who I am then that is your problem, not mine. So mind your business and stop pretending you know what's best for me."

I reach behind me, my hand circling the door handle and pushing it open. I half stumble through the door, but I manage to catch myself, quickly slamming the door behind me, leaving him on the other side.

The guards stationed outside do a good job of hiding their expressions at whatever it is they just heard as I make my way straight back to my room so I can rip this dress off.

Chapter 14

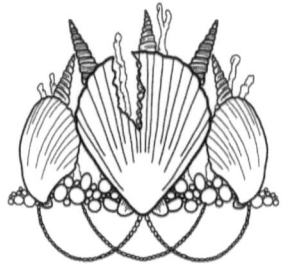

Cay

Warm, golden light filters through the nearly sheer blinds as I roll over in my bed. The fresh, sweet smell of roses fills the room from where they sit on the windowsill. I push the blankets away, tugging on my night slip as I pad over to the window, inspecting the flowers.

There's no note, same as the last few days. I pick one up, wrapping my fingers around the stem. I notice that the thorns have been removed again as I bring the flower to my nose, inhaling deeply.

The flowers first appeared four days ago, each morning a new bouquet is left by the windowsill waiting for me by the time the sun rises. It has become the thing I look forward to the most every morning. I carry the flower with me as I walk to my bathing chamber. I turn the faucet on the tub, allowing the water to warm without using my magic, reserving it for my visit with my mother.

I set the flower down gently on the counter, the red standing out against the black granite countertop. The water fills quickly, and it's only a few minutes before it reaches the top and I have to turn the faucet from where

I am perched on the edge. Rising, I grab the hem of my night slip where it has bunched over my rounded thighs. The silk glides easily over me and pools on the ground as I discard it.

Dipping a toe into the warm water, I feel the rush of magic wash over me. I lower myself in as water splashes over the sides onto the stone floor. Fully seated, I close my eyes and allow myself to transform. The moment my legs turn into my tail my creature hums in approval.

Many of the residents of Tepis have felt the disconnect from their creatures and a constant source of water. Back home, we have pools to relax in throughout the day and we can exit the barrier and swim directly in the sea if we choose to do so.

It's been an adjustment to say the least.

For the most part, we have managed, allowing ourselves moments like this to replenish ourselves and allow our creatures to be free. Thankfully, Terran managed to assist in getting a sizable lake built not far from the castle grounds so that our larger creatures have a safe space to transform. Believe me, no one wants a giant hydra to transform in their bathtub. The mermaids, gorgons, nymphs and... sirens, don't have to worry about their size.

I don't spend too long in the water, just long enough to ease that inner ache and fill my magic up to the brim. Emerging from the tub, I use my magic to dry myself quickly as well as the small puddle on the floor. It's small tasks like these that I am getting back in the habit of using, things that don't require too much power and are relatively safe.

I gather up my slip and the rose, and walk back into my chambers, quickly throwing on a simple dress and before beginning the familiar walk to the infirmary. As I enter, I am greeted by the few soldiers who are still kept in these quarters. Odd burn-like wounds that won't leave their skin keeping them here. I walk straight to the back and slip through the narrow passageway to Flora's small chamber.

The moment I enter the stone path, I know something is wrong. Charged energy buzzes through the air with the massive use of magic. I force my way through, the stone grazing my shoulders and leaving a stinging mark. My entire body locks up as I lay eyes on my mother.

Her entire body is jerking wildly, thrashing on the bed as some kind of black liquid leaks from her mouth. The sight of it spurs me into motion. Rushing forward I immediately try and hold her down all while forcing healing magic into her chest. The force of her thrashing throws me off of her over and over again as I start to scream for help.

"Somebody! Somebody please help!" tears are flowing down my cheeks, "please! Anybody, we need help here!"

I flick between staring down at my mother and checking the passageway. Just as I look up again, a shadow emerges from the darkness.

"Cay, oh Vana, what happened?" Rose's voice is shaky and far too quiet.

"Rose, please help me," I beg.

Flora emerges just behind her and immediately starts to move around, gathering up supplies. I peek over my shoulder as she begins to grind herbs in her mortar and pestle. She moves remarkably fast as Rose and I continue to hold my mother's body down, I never stop pushing magic into her. Flora pushes us out of the way suddenly and forces the potion down my mothers throat.

Standing off to the side, I can only watch as my mother slowly stops jerking, becoming so still I fear the worst. Sharp, shallow breaths speed up until I am overwhelmed by them, my entire body shaking as it struggles to take in enough air. I stumble back until I am pressed against the wall, sliding down as my head begins to swim.

"Shh, Cay, I've got you," Rose says assuredly, wrapping her arms around my shoulders as she kneels beside me. Her body is tense, but her focus is on me. "Try and focus on breathing. Take a deep breath in for four seconds. That's it, hold it in. Now let it out and hold. Again."

I follow along with her instructions until it feels like my lungs are actually taking in air. My head falls back against the wall as exhaustion takes over.

"Rose, get her out of here," Flora's sharp voice commands.

Rose pulls me to my feet and tries to drag me away, but I struggle against her. "No, please, I want to stay with my mother," I beg.

Flora shakes her head. "She is stable, you'll be of no use to her here. Go, find somewhere else to be and take care of yourself, take some time to calm down."

This time I let Rose guide me from the room, following her blindly as she leads me through the castle. The ground shifts as we emerge into our garden. The two of us walk straight to the stone bench, sitting down side by side. Rose doesn't say anything, just holds me by my shoulders and lets me process everything that just happened. It was so fast, maybe a few minutes at most, yet the weight of it sits heavily on my chest.

"I could have lost her," I whisper.

Rose's sharp intake has me leaning into her more, her grip on me growing tighter. "I know. But you didn't. That is what you have to try and focus on now."

I push to my feet, pacing the small space as I ponder those words. She's not wrong, everything she said is factual. So why can't I do it? Why is it that the only thing I can think about right now is the image of my mother thrashing and the sound of my father's body falling to the floor? I thought I had control over this, that the grief had passed and I could manage the fear. *How stupid am I?*

"Cay, you can't blame yourself for this. It was nobody's fault. And listen, your mother is fine now," she hesitates, "or at least no worse than before."

I focus on that, on Rose and what is true. Allowing myself to believe for a second that everything is alright, I lay on the ground, staring up at the sun, now high and bright in the sky above us. Rose lays down beside me, reaching out and taking my shaking hand. We lay there, side by side in silence, listening to the birds and the wind moving through the trees.

"Ever since we got back, I have felt so alone," Rose says quietly.

I wait for her to continue.

"Oak was sent away, Eve was taken, Mar is struggling back home, and I have no idea how to help any of them. And now? I am right here beside you, but there is nothing I can do."

I squeeze her hand, taking a moment before I respond. "I know. I feel so helpless, like everything is wrong and I don't know how to make it right." I turn my head to look at her as she does the same. I stare into her hazel eyes, glassy with unshed tears. "I'm terrified. What will happen if she doesn't wake up?" The words linger between us.

Rose sits up, staring down at me without letting go of my hand. "Nothing will happen to your mom. I promise. Flora is one of the best healers in the whole realm and your mom is being watched over constantly."

Sitting up, I turn to her fully. My heart begins to pound, the new plan that Terran and I came up with burning on the tip of my tongue.

She cuts me off before I get the chance, "I've been researching. With Reed and this wolf, Mateo. We've been trying to find the Ghosts so that we can get Oak back and then she'll be able to find Eve, and Mar can finally breathe again, and then we can all help you find a cure for your mom. Mateo thinks that the answers to finding Oak, and maybe more than that… are that we have to go to Eteri," her words come out in one singular stream, all jumbled together. The look she gives me is hesitant.

I open my mouth to respond, but she cuts me off again, "I don't want you to think that your mom isn't as important, but we have always been better together. The five of us are it, we make each other better in every way and with all of us together there is nothing we can't do. We *can* find a cure, Cay, I know it. We just need time and resources. We need knowledge." Something about her expression looks ashamed and makes my heart crack open even more.

Before she can say anything else I hold my hand up. "I know you think my mom is important, nothing you could say or do would change the fact that I know with absolute certainty you want what's best for her. And for me. I completely understand everything that you said and you're right, we are better together." I smile at her, taking a deep breath before continuing.

"I won't lie, I am a bit surprised that all along you've been doing this, but… I have something to confess myself."

Her eyes narrow, "Go on."

"I've been doing some research of my own," I hesitate, "with Terran."

"Terran like my brother Terran?"

"Yes."

Rose takes a moment to process. Her face goes through a wide array of expressions before landing on a teasing grin. "So, you and my brother? When exactly did this research start?"

Heat races over my entire body as my face turns a deep shade of crimson. "Oh no, don't even think about it. He's just helping me out of obligation." I laugh nervously.

She laughs. "Cay, my brother doesn't have a spare moment to piss, let alone spend hours helping you research something like this. If he is helping you, it's because he wants to, not because he feels some warped sense of obligation."

"Can we just focus on what we found?" I groan.

"Sure," Rose says with a smile, "but we'll be revisiting this later."

"Fine," I concede.

"So, what have you found," she asks, her tone more serious.

"We think we might have already found a way to help my mother. Maybe not a cure but at least a way for her to wake up."

"Cay, that is incredible! Tell me everything."

I bite my lip. "You're not going to like this."

Rose places a hand on my shoulder, "You can tell me anything, always. I will support you no matter what."

I wrap my arms around her, pulling her into a fierce hug and letting all of the built up tension between us and everything else happening fade away. I spent too much time hiding from Rose in fear of facing the truth, when the whole time she was exactly the person who I needed to help me through this. "We need to go back to Rayan."

Her entire body goes tense in my arms before she slowly disentangles from me. "Are you sure that is a good idea?"

A jittery laugh bubbles out of me. "Truthfully? No. It's probably the worst idea since…"

"Hey, I know," Rose gives me a reassuring smile, "but listen. Even if it's not the best idea, it's something right? If you two believe you can help your mom, then you have to do it."

My entire body relaxes, and so much fear releases from me, just like that. The support of one of the people closest to me is enough to make everything feel like it might actually work out, like there is hope again. That's the power that they have. They can pull you back from the brink and remind you that there is something worth fighting for. Even when that something is yourself.

"Okay," I breathe, "we think that the water in a special cavern can help give my mother enough magic to wake up until we figure out a more permanent way to fight off whatever it is."

Rose nods her head. "That makes sense. Where is this cavern? You said you have to go back to Rayan but…"

"It's in Tepis, in the castle."

She blanches. "What? Cay, that is insane, how are you going to get inside the castle?"

"I'll create another portal."

"I don't want to upset you, but…the last time you used a portal it didn't really work out the way you expected."

I nod. "I know. But this time I know what to expect. I can control my emotions. The spell *will* work."

She stares into my eyes, searching. "Okay, I trust you," she says with a resigned sigh. Rose bites her lip, clearly nervous about something else.

"What is it?" I prompt.

"It's just," she hesitates, "I can't go with you. I need to go to Eteri and they're on opposite sides of the world, you can't get much further away from each other."

I smile at her reassuringly. "I know, which is why I'm not asking you to come."

"But who will you go with? This could be really dangerous."

"I've already talked to Terran about it. We're going to partner with Regan and allow her to choose a group of guards to escort us."

"Us?"

My face heats. "Yes, Terran is insisting on going with me."

"Oh, wow. That-that is surprising, but there is no one I trust more to keep you safe."

"Enough about my plan, tell me about this trip to Eteri?"

Rose sighs. "Honestly, it is more of an idea than a plan at this point. Mateo claims that he knows what he is doing, but I'm not so sure. We still have a lot to figure out."

"Fair enough. I do have one question, though. Who's Mateo?"

Chapter 15

Rose

"How many times do I have to go over this, Mateo, we are not kidnapping anyone," Reed groans.

"I'm just saying-"

"No. Just no, Mateo."

I watch as the two males bicker back and forth, a deep crease set between Reed's full brows as Mateo's amber eyes shine with mirth at their ongoing argument. It's been like this for the last two hours, and in that entire time we have made absolutely no progress. A steadily building headache throbs beneath my fingertips as I drive my fingers into my roots, massaging my scalp. "Enough, we don't have time for this. Each day that we waste is another day of Oak being gone."

Silence fills the room, hanging heavy in the stale air. "You're right," Reed agrees, "we need to start taking this seriously." Reed glares at Mateo openly, his green eyes narrowing.

"What did I do?" Mateo asks defensively.

"Mateo, I understand that you have a lot of… ideas, but we don't have time to go through every single possible scenario. We need to look at the facts and make a plan from there. No more messing around." My eyes soften on the male as he genuinely seems confused.

"I thought that was what we were already doing?" His warm eyes flick back and forth between my cousin and I, a cluster of black curls bouncing over his lashes.

"Barely," I sigh, "we still have so much left to figure out and at this rate we'll never get it done."

"You're right, we need to focus," Reed echoes, guilt etched into his features.

The three of us adjust our positions at the library table. The small, round wood is covered with sheets of handwritten notes in poorly constructed code, as Mateo called it.

"We can all agree that the most challenging part of all of this is going to be getting out of the castle, correct?" Reed asks, looking between us.

I nod. "My mother has guards watching me constantly. She thinks I won't notice them since there are more guards around now, but it's kind of hard to miss an extra set of footsteps following behind you everywhere."

"Let me worry about the guards and getting out of here. All I need from you two is to get the supplies we need and we're good to go," Mateo offers confidently.

Reed and I share a look and Mateo chuckles deeply.

"I know that you think I'm just fucking around, but I'm not. I won't mess this up." His eyes linger on Reed for a moment before flicking to me.

I search his face for any sign that he is lying, but instead I only find determination. Biting the inside of my cheek I steel myself. "Okay."

He leans forward, reaching out a bronzed hand and laying it over mine. "You can trust me." We stay like that for a moment before Mateo seems happy with my expression. He squeezes my hand and leans back, rolling a tight coil of his hair between two fingers. "Good, now once you both have the supplies that I asked for earlier, take them to the wisteria tree and wait for me there."

Reed and Mateo begin to go over the supplies again, double and triple checking that nothing is forgotten. All the while, that lingering kernel of guilt writhes inside me. Right now, Cay is preparing for a very similar journey, one that will hopefully save her mother, and the only thing I can focus on is how I won't be there for her. We both know that neither of us can be in two places at once, that we each have an important part to play in what is about to begin, yet I can't help but feel like I am letting her down.

Cay is content to suffer alone, to bear her burdens entirely on her own shoulders rather than share them and lighten her load. And now I am abandoning her to deal with all of this by herself. Again. I will never forgive myself for letting the distance grow between us this last year. I hate feeling like it is happening again.

We need each other, all five of us, and just when it felt like I got them back I lost them again. In a way I have never known before. Even still, I know that we are each on a path that is going to ultimately bring us back together, we just have to hold on a little longer. As much as it is killing me to do so.

"What do you think, Rose?" Reed asks, pulling me back to the conversation.

I glance down, quickly skimming over the list they have created and looking out for anything that would raise my mother's suspicions. It's all common enough, nothing exceptionally rare or valuable.

"Is this it?" I ask Mateo.

"That's it. Think you can manage it?"

"I think so," I look up at him excitedly, "so what does this mean?"

Mateo's lips curl into a broad smile. "We're ready."

My lips part, my eyes going wide as the words begin to sink in. "Are you sure?"

Mateo nods.

"When?" Reed gasps.

"As soon as you're ready. Tomorrow evening would be ideal," Mateo says with a yawn.

I look at Reed and find him staring back at me and suddenly things seem to be moving much faster than I thought possible. When we sat down at this table we had a loose idea at best. Now, Mateo seems to believe we are ready.

"Mateo," I start, "we're only going to get one shot at this, if we mess it up, my mother will have me on complete lockdown and I won't be able to wipe my nose without her knowing."

"Do you trust me?" he asks with thick, black brows raised.

Looking deep within myself I consider his words. *Do I? Can I?* Trust is not something I can freely give anymore. But since meeting Mateo he has given me no reason to doubt him, only help in doing the one thing that has been occupying my mind since the moment Oak was taken.

Taking a deep breath I shove aside any lingering doubt. "Yes. We'll leave tomorrow."

Mateo turns to Reed, waiting for his answer.

"You're sure that this is the way to get my sister back?" Reed pushes. His broad shoulders are pulled back stiffly, full lips set into a firm line. His entire body is one giant ball of tension locked beneath newly developed muscles.

"I swear on Vana's name. Eteri has the answers you're looking for. That is where we need to be." Mateo stands, looking down at us with sincerity.

"Then let's do this. We can leave tomorrow," Reed confirms.

The three of us share another look before we begin packing things up. Reed takes the list of supplies as Mateo and I start to destroy notes, ripping them up and using a spell that will turn them into sand so no one else can read them. Once everything is taken care of, Mateo excuses himself and heads back to his pack saying something about readying the troops.

Reed and I have very little information on what he is planning or how we are actually going to accomplish any of this, but Mateo seems confident.

The only thing we need to worry about is getting the things on the list and being in the right place at the right time.

"Rose?" Reed calls from behind me.

"Yeah?" I answer, pushing the chairs back into the table.

"Do you think this is going to work?"

I look up at my cousin. He's standing to the side, his hands gripped tightly around his list, his eyes brimming with hesitation. I smile at him. "This is it, Reed. We're going to do this and we'll get the answers that we need. We'll have Oak back before you know it." Even as the words leave my mouth I feel my own chest constrict with mild panic.

He nods before turning on his heels and heading away.

"Oh wait!" I call out to him, stopping him in his tracks, "what about your apprenticeship? Is this going to mess up all your hard work?" Reed has been working with the apothecary for a while now and the last thing I want is to cause more issues.

"The apothecary is pretty understanding, I'm sure I'll be fine. Especially since we're not planning on getting caught, right?" Reed asks with a small smile.

"Right. Just making sure." We exchange another set of smiles before making our way back to our rooms. As soon as I am back in my chambers I begin packing a small bag, nothing too big or obvious, but enough to get me through. It could take at least a week to make it to the Eteri border, and I want to be prepared. Once that is done I crawl into bed and stare up at the walls with a pounding heart.

This is it. By this time tomorrow we'll be traveling to Eteri. This is the next step in making things right again, of bringing Oak home. If we can figure out where Oak is then we can get her out, then we can help Cay save her mom and help Mar find Eve. One more day and then I will finally be taking the next step to bringing my sisters back to me.

Hours pass staring at the ceiling until sleep finally claims me, my mind conjuring the image of a garden and the sound of laughter.

Chapter 16

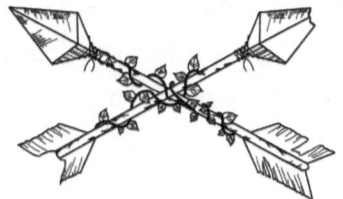

Oak

Ice cold water washes over me from head to toe, jolting me awake. Fabric clings to my skin as I flail my limbs, tangled beneath a pile of blankets. My eyes bolt open, staring up at Aine as she glares down at me.

"Get up." Without waiting for me to move, she turns on her heels and marches from the room.

I shove my blankets off with a racing heart, jump to my feet, and quickly change into the training gear I was provided with. Dark brown leather pants with a lightweight tunic. I tug on my thin soled shoes and race from the room, taking the steps two at a time and concentrating on not faceplanting. I carve a path through the courtyard and to the large stretch of tables where the others are already eating their breakfast.

I quickly scoop up some potatoes and eggs onto a plate and search for somewhere to sit. I catch a glimpse of pale blonde hair and make my way there. I'm assuming we're meant to sit with our squad, but if we aren't then this is about to be extremely awkward, especially since I only know three people.

Standing at the end of the table, I look between the four girls sitting in front of me. Lina, Farai, and Aine are all deep in conversation with someone unfamiliar and I hesitate to interrupt. Thankfully, I am spared as Lina looks up from her nearly empty plate.

A small laugh bubbles past her lips as she tilts her head at me. "Didn't I warn you not to be late?" Her eyes flick to my soaking wet hair as it drips onto my forehead and rolls down to my cheeks. "Sit down. We only have a few minutes before training starts and you and I are up first."

Taking a seat at the end of the bench I am across from the stranger. "Hi, I'm Oak, ni-"

"I know. We all know exactly who you are," she says, cutting me off. Short black curls frame her long face. Her lips are full on the bottom, the color a deep, dusty rose that stands out against her fawn skin. Thick lashes fan marbled gray, almond shaped eyes. Something about her is familiar, but I can't quite place what it is. Without another word she rises from her seat, gathers up all of the empty plates left on the table, and walks away.

"Don't mind Symone, she's just mad because she was on breakfast duty this morning and she didn't get much sleep," Lina offers with an amused smile.

Nodding, I quickly finish off my food and stand to take my plate wherever it is meant to go. I head in the direction Symone went and find her behind a table collecting others' plates as they drop them off before heading towards the training circle where I first saw Lina and Farai fight. I reach out to hand her my plate, but instead of grabbing it she lets it fall at the last second, the ceramic shattering against the hard ground.

"Symone!" Aine's voice shouts across the courtyard.

I watch as she drops to her knees and immediately begins cleaning up the broken shards, plucking them gently from the ground and placing them in the palm of her hand one by one. I drop down to a crouch beside her and start to help. As I reach to grab a piece, she smacks my hand away.

"Leave it. I don't need nor want your help."

Before I get the chance to respond I feel an arm tugging me to my feet. Lina guides me towards the training arena and whispers into my ear, "Making friends already I see." She releases my arm as I glare after her.

The moment we pass through the curtain I am surprised to find females everywhere. Paired off sparring or moving in small groups as someone guides them through movements. On the far side of the room someone is giving a demonstration of a takedown, moving step by step and showing exactly where to add pressure to make your opponent drop.

A flurry of excitement builds in me and I have to clamp it down. This is not something I should be excited about. Clearly the people I am up against know what they're doing, which only means that my job has become that much more difficult. Every single person here is a well trained spy and without my magic, the chances of me escaping are becoming smaller and smaller with every passing second.

"This way," Lina leads me forward. Aine and Farai are already on the ground, stretching out their muscles and preparing for training.

I follow their lead and sit down opposite Lina. "So, what are we going to be training on today?" The room is filled with various obstacles ranging from training dummies to towering balance beams and the same sparring ring from before. There are people everywhere, all working in small groups and moving efficiently through their chosen practice areas.

"Today is just to see where you're at, get a solid idea of what you know and what you don't. Once we have that, we'll go from there," Lina answers, bending in half and reaching for her pointed toes. Her nose touches her knees with ease and I inwardly cringe at the display of flexibility.

"I have a pretty good foundation," I offer, following her lead and bending at my waist. My nose hovers inches above my shaking legs.

Lina laughs, unfolding herself and pulling her feet in, pushing her knees out into a butterfly position. "We'll see." She bends forward again, this time touching her nose to the heel of her foot and I am pretty sure I can feel my own muscles screaming just looking at her.

"How are you so flexible? That looks extremely painful."

Lina expands again, crossing one arm over her chest and then switching. "I wasn't when I first got here, it just takes time and patience. You can't rush it. Your body has to slowly acclimate to the conditions you are putting it in, stretching the muscles day by day, pushing just past the point of pain until you can relax into it and let everything go."

"How long have you been here?" I ask, my heart racing. Maybe Lina will give me something I can work with, maybe she'll let something slip and I can use it to escape.

"I've been here most of my life. I first arrived when I was eight years old." She rolls her head, stretching her neck out before rolling over onto her stomach. She pushes the palms of her hands into the ground and arches her back as her head tips back, staring up at the clear sky.

"How old are you now?" I ask, continuing to follow her through each new position. It's not a rude question. Since aging slows at 25 it is possible that Lina could be anywhere between the 22 years that she looks or even well into her 6th decade. My cousin Terran is 50 and looks nearly identical to his brother Oliver who is only 35, both only look a few years older than Rose and I.

"I just turned 27 last week." Lina pushes her hips into the air, tilting her head towards the ground and tucking her chin into her chest. She holds the position for a few minutes before walking her feet towards her hands and slowly uncurling her back from the waist up. "Now, are we going to train, or are you going to keep up this inquisition?"

I jump up and down a few times shaking out my hands. "I'm ready. Whatever you've got for me, let's do this."

Lina flashes a deadly smile and a twinge of fear rises in me. "Good, let's start on the balance beam."

I follow after her as she walks up to a long tree turned over on its side and held up by two large concrete pillars towering at least twenty feet in the air. As soon as I move towards it Lina steps into my path. Confused, I move to go around her, but she is there again. Each time I try to take a step forward, Lina appears and blocks my path.

Quicker than my eyes can track, Lina spins and delivers a sidekick directly into my gut and sends me soaring backwards. My ass hits the ground and I feel a jolt vibrate up my spine from the impact. I quickly stand, marching back to where Lina is still blocking the way. "What was that about?" I shout.

Lina shrugs, "If you want to train then you need to get past me, simple as that."

My hands ball into fists as my frustration builds. I move forward again only to find myself staring up at the sky with my body aching. This happens over and over and over again until I fully realize, escaping is going to be much, *much*, harder than I thought.

~~~

Nearly twelve hours later and training is *finally* complete. For twelve hours straight I got kicked onto my ass repeatedly. In that entire time I only managed to touch the beam with the tip of a finger once. One. Time. In *twelve hours.*

I am so screwed.

Lina and I work side by side as we put away training dummies. Farai and Aine are on dinner duty so they both left early to prepare the meal. Symone arrived late to training alongside the final member of our squad, Hala. Both of them were assigned to breakfast so they had to stay late to clean things up. The brightside to that being they missed the worst of Lina kicking my ass though that didn't spare me from the other 11 hours of taunting and teasing I received.

As soon as everything is cleaned up we make our way to the dining area and sit down for our third meal of the day. Lunch was easy. Lina and I got pulled to help with making sandwiches around midday. I've already figured out that it is the best shift to receive. No waking up early and you get an added break to your midday training. Besides, it's not hard work, so I don't mind helping out.

Taking my seat beside Lina, I dig into the mountain of rice I have heaped on my plate.

"So, you're the high lady's niece," Hala says matter-of-factly.

Swallowing down my mouth full of food I nod my head. "Yes, my mother was her younger sister."

"What's she like?" Hala asks reverently.

"My aunt?"

Hala nods.

"Um, well, I mean she is beautiful." I shift uncomfortably, not ready to get into this at all.

"Obviously, we've all seen her before. What I mean is what is it like to be by her side? To watch her work and have her ear?" Hala practically crawls on top of the table, that's how far forward she leans in.

"I-""Enough, Hala, Oakley has no respect for our high lady, you will find nothing of interest coming from her mouth," Aine says, finally arriving after serving all of the others. Farai is just a step behind her. The two of them sit down side by side on the opposite side of the table, next to Hala who looks repulsed by my presence all of a sudden.

"Well what about the heir? Our future high lord?" Hala pushes. Her dark brown eyes sparkle with interest.

"Terran is great. He's going to be a great leader and I look forward to having him as my high lord," I say confidently with a true smile tilting my lips. I watch Hala's face fall, her eyes growing harsh and her lips thinning. "What? What did I say?"

"To wish harm against our high lady is the greatest of evil."

My mouth drops open. "Wait what? I didn't mean-""She didn't mean it like that Hala. She just means that he's a good person, right, Oak?" Lina jumps in.

I nod my head vehemently and Hala seems to slowly relax again. Once I feel sure that no one is going to chop my head off, I relax myself. Our table is quiet compared to the others around us, full of laughter and jokes. Clearing my throat, I try to brighten things up again. Maybe if I can gain their trust it will help me get out of here. "So, Lina told me that she came here when she was eight. What about you all?"

"My sister and I arrived when she was six and I was four," Hala answers with a small voice. As she does my brain finally connects a few dots and I see the resemblance between them. Symone's skin is slightly lighter, her nose a bit wider and of course her eyes are a different color, but other than that she looks so much like Hala.

"I also arrived when I was eight," Farai answers, surprising me.

"Wow, you were all so young. Why did you all end up here? Is this some sort of program your parents signed you up for?" I ask, looking between them all and locking eyes with Aine.

There is a moment of intense silence before Aine pushes out of her seat, picks up her plate, and marches off. Farai leaps to her feet and follows after her.

"We all came here because we are orphans," Hala whispers.

"We had nowhere else to go," Symone snaps.

My heart stutters in my chest as I look around the courtyard. So many happy and smiling people, warriors, spies, but beyond that… orphans. All of these females had one thing in common, their parents were gone. Mine too.

A well of emotion bubbles up inside me and I can't fight the single tear that slips past my tightly closed lids. "I'm sorry. I know how you feel, I'm an orphan too." I blink my eyes, clearing the blurriness and meet Hala's across the table.

"You don't. Not really," Symone answers, her voice clipped. The sisters rise without so much as a word to each other and they walk off towards the plate collection.

I turn to face Lina as she pushes the food around on her plate. "What did I say?"

She sighs, turning to look at me with nothing but pity and disgust. "The kinds of questions you're asking are things that you have to earn. Some things we just don't talk about and the sooner you learn that the better." She stares into my eyes, searching for something. With a deep sigh she rises from her seat and gathers up both of our plates. "Come on, follow me."

I traipse after her as she leads us down a corridor I haven't been down before. The first two weeks of being here I was locked in my room, this is my first time really exploring since my initial arrival. A few more turns and we enter into a small stone cavern, a waft of hot air blows over me as we cross the threshold.

A glistening pond rests in the center of the room, steam and the intoxicating scent of jasmine rising from the surface of the water and filling the small cave around us, thickening the air. As I get closer, I bend to test the water and it is deliciously warm. "What is this place?" I ask, looking over my shoulder I find Lina stripping herself of her training attire.

"It's a hot spring. I like to come here on days when I trained particularly hard, took one too many falls, or generally want to relax." The last of her clothing hits the floor and she steps into the water, walking down a small set of steps before sinking in until she is fully submerged. Her head quickly breaks the surface, sending water flying everywhere. "Are you coming in?"

I give only a second of hesitation while I take a quick inventory of my many aches and pains. Nodding, I quickly remove my own clothes and follow in after her. We each sit on a natural bench carved beneath the water, the surface is just below my chin, but I don't mind since the heat is doing wonders at soothing my aching muscles. As soon as training finished it felt like my entire body might fall off, now, I feel like I am being remade into something entirely new.

"This is incredible, I feel so much better already," I groan.

"We're not sure where it came from exactly, but there is a small stream that feeds into the pond. The waters have healing qualities," Lina explains.

"Amazing. Why aren't there more people down here then?"

Lina sinks lower, resting her head back against the edge of the pool and closing her eyes. "Most of them think this place should only be used for emergencies, that we shouldn't rely on the springs to heal us."

"Why?" I ask with a groan, "this place is here, why not use it?"

Lina doesn't respond, but she does float closer to me. "What was it like growing up in the castle?"

My entire body stiffens. Shit. I need to stay focused. "It was alright I guess. Nothing that different really."

She raises her brows at me. "Really? Growing up in a castle was completely *normal*?"

I shrug. "Pretty much, yeah. For the most part we were just normal kids." I leave out the part that I have been acting as my aunt's spy, no need to offer up any additional information if I can help it.

"We?"

"My brother, Reed. And I guess my cousin Rose too. I can't really speak for my older cousins, but the rest of us had a pretty normal childhood by my standards." I can taste the bitterness of the lie on my tongue, but I can't stop the words from coming.

Without a word, Lina rises from the water and begins putting her clothes back on.

"Leaving already?" I ask.

"Trust goes both ways, Oak," she says with her back to me. As soon as she is fully dressed she leaves the caves and I am left alone in the silence.

I only stay for another ten minutes or so before I head back to my room, grateful that I didn't get lost. The moment I am dressed in pajamas and sitting in bed, my mind races.

Breathing in, I search deep inside myself for the tiniest flicker of my magic. I push and push and push, forcing my body to its limits until I am once again drenched in sweat and panting from exertion. Hours go by like this, but whatever enchantment is keeping my magic from me, I can't fight past it.

Today I saw proof that others did have access to their magic, but were *choosing* not to use it inside the compound. Focusing instead on honing their physical skills and their mind. Well great for them, but I don't have time for all that so now that I know we *can* access our magic, it's just a matter of figuring out how.

My entire body is shaking from the force of my will until finally I can't take it anymore. Shifting my position, I sit with my legs crossed, resting the backs of my hands against my knees and against all instinct, I try to meditate. Sometimes, you just can't force it. For a while my mind is nothing more than fleeting thoughts, each one coming to the surface long enough for me to acknowledge it and then let it pass along. Eventually, I might have a thought that will reconnect me to my magic so I keep doing this until the sun is about to rise.

Just as I start to believe I have wasted an entire night's sleep, I see a light, one so bright and burning that I can't see through it. The only thing I can make out is a shadow of an image, a wisp of something dark and too fuzzy to distinguish. Before I can even process what I think I have seen, the image is gone and my body drags me under against my will.

Chapter 17

Eve

C reaking hinges drag me from a deep sleep. I roll over in time to see the door click shut. "Fuck," I say, stumbling out of the bed. My legs hit the floor with a heavy thud as I force myself across the small room, quickly grabbing the door handle and pulling with every ounce of strength I can muster. The door doesn't budge.

Exhausted already, I turn, placing my back against the door and sliding down it until my ass hits the cold ground. I look to the small table beside the bed, searching for the familiar tray of food. Instead, I find it bare.

Isn't that just fantastic? First they starve my magic, now they'll starve my stomach. Forcing myself back to my feet, I stumble towards the bathing chamber only to find a long gown hanging in the doorway.

"What the fuck?" I pick it up and turn it, alternating between looking at its front and back.

The gown is absolutely stunning. Sheer black mesh lays overtop deep burgundy fabric hung up by thin, barely there straps. A note is pinned to the collar. *Put me on.* I hesitate for only a moment before deciding there's nothing worse they can do to me in a dress that they can't already do without. Might as well look hot while getting tortured.

I slip the fabric over my head, tugging it down as far as I can. The gown cinches at the waist, the neckline straight across without exposing even a hint of cleavage. The left side of the gown has a long slit that reaches well past my upper thigh, stopping only a few inches below where the fabric cinches. Scandalous. Dainty ties hang off my hip and brush the bit of exposed skin at the peak of the slit.

It fits like it was made for me. Every drape of the fabric, every line that was stitched, all accentuate my body perfectly. Even the length is perfect. The gown just barely pools on the ground while I stand there with bare feet. With the right pair of heels it would just barely brush the floor.

Pushing up to my toes, I do a little twirl, loving the way the fabric moves against my skin. The satin lining is smooth and luxurious compared to the scratchy blankets I have been sleeping with. My hair is a mess, my eyes are ringed with dark circles and I'm pretty sure that disgusting smell is coming from me. My wrists are a bit too small, my collarbones too defined, all signs of my time already spent here. Sighing, I begin to remove the gown, reaching down to the hem and yanking it up.

The sound of someone clearing their throat has me dropping the fabric and jumping backwards.

"You've been summoned," the petite girl says.

"Vana, you scared me. When did you get in here?" I ask with a hand clutched over my chest. I swear my heart is about ready to burst right out.

"Let's go," she says, pulling the door open and gesturing me out.

"Look, I'm not sure what-"

"Move." Her arm shoots out and grabs me, yanking me forward until I trip over myself.

"That was rude," I mutter over my shoulder as I make my way out into the hall. She follows close behind me as I blindly walk forward, pretending to know where I'm going. Usually I just appear wherever they want me, I rarely am expected to walk which in hindsight is kind of convenient.

"Turn left."

I follow her directions without complaint, using this unusual opportunity to look at my prison. The walls are stone and lined with carved light fixtures lit up with magic. My bare feet slap against the stone floor. They're a dark marbled black with flecks of purple and red embedded in. A warm glow lights the halls as we make our way through. All in all, it's beautiful.

"Stop here," the girl commands.

"You know, you could ask politely," I offer with a raise of my brows.

"Put these on," she demands, offering me a pair of sleek black heels.

"Why didn't you give me these before we walked all the way over here?"

She shrugs, "You didn't ask." She reaches around me to pull open a door three times her size, gesturing me into the room before her.

My first few steps are a bit shaky. But come on, it's been a while since I've had heels on. Am I really to blame? Once I feel more confident in my strides I step farther into the room, admiring the tall ceilings and large chandelier hanging at the center of the room.

"Ah, thank you, Eri," Yuta's familiar voice says, drawing my attention from where he sits across the room. A shroud of mist blankets his dark hair, draping him in shadows. Between us is a large, formal dining table at which no one else sits.

Eri, as I now know, leaves the room, the loud sound of the door closing behind her sends a chill down my spine. Great, just me and the psychopath.

"Please, join me," he extends a hand towards the seat to his right.

Ignoring his request I choose a seat at the opposite end of the table. I open my mouth to ask what this is all about, but he silences me with a hand as a collection of servers appear out of nowhere, setting plates upon plates of food down the length of the table. Every time I think they're done, another will pop into existence beside me and place yet another plate of food in front of my chair. All the while, I glare at Yuta, waiting for him to say or do something.

Finally, there is a long enough gap that I feel safe to try speaking again, only for him to beat me to it.

"So, *Eve*, how have you been enjoying your time here in my kingdom?" he asks, drawing out my name.

"Oh you know, it's been a real blast," I say sardonically.

Yuta smiles to himself, watching as he carves into a plate of meat and brings the fork up to his lips. He chews slowly, until eventually swallowing and patting a crisp napkin against his lips. "Really? I would have thought the heir to the Vulca throne would be missing the comfort and luxury of her home by now."

Everything inside of me freezes, my blood turning to ice. *Fuck.* It only takes half a second before words of denial are spilling from my lips, "Me? The heir? You've got the wrong girl, buddy." I laugh, really trying to lay it on thick.

"No?" he asks, not bothering to look at me as he begins to slice into another section of meat.

Alright, think, Eve, think. How am I going to play this? What's my next move? A story begins to unfold inside my head and I quickly pull myself together. "Nope," I say, popping the p. I shrug my arms casually, taking great care to place my elbows on the table as another laugh bubbles up. "You've got me in the fact that I work in the Tower, but beyond that, it is absurd to even suggest I am anything but a servant." My heart is racing with each passing word.

He finally looks up at me, his eyebrows raised in amusement. "A servant? Really? With such immense power as yours?" he cocks his head again, seeming to consider his own words, "you must be extremely valuable to the crown then, since of course, as you said, you're not the heir."

Something about the way he says it has me floundering. Shit. Shit. Shit. If only Mar or Rose were here to take over. I'm not built for this kind of thing. They're the strategic ones, they're the ones who do the talking, not me. This kind of delicate dance is way outside my usual skill set. Still, it's not like I have much of a choice at this point.

"I wouldn't say I am any more valuable than any other servant. I do my chores as commanded and get on with my day. Why? Is this how the royals live?" I ask, gesturing to the mountains of food.

He watches me carefully. Examining every small movement as I take small bites from various plates. His eyes catch on the way I am bending over the table, trying to expose a bit of cleavage even though the dress isn't designed for that sort of thing. He freezes as I raise a piece of what looks like fruit to my lips and bite into it slowly.

"What is this?" I say, moaning like the taste is the most delicious thing in the world.

"It's a delicacy of my kingdom," he answers, his lips tight.

I slowly trail my tongue along the seam of my lips, lapping up the sour juices lingering there. "I could suck on this all night," I moan, fluttering my lashes.

"Enough," he bites. His voice is harsh and commanding.

"What's the matter? Do you not enjoy this fruit?" I ask, picking up another piece and rubbing it slowly against my bottom lip,

Suddenly he is in front of me and my fork is in his grip. "Stop."

I look up at him through my lashes, licking my lips as they spread into a sparkling smile. "What?" I ask innocently.

He drops into the seat to my left, lifting the fork to my lips and I get the tiniest hint of excitement on my tongue. The feeling is so unexpected that I have to bite my lip to keep from moaning out. Finally, finally I might get a taste of the pleasure they have been denying me. I open my mouth, pushing my tongue out every so slightly and wait for him to take the bait.

Only instead of the sweet and sour taste I am expecting, my mouth is filled with something tar-like and absolutely repulsive. I start to spit whatever it is out, but Yuta clamps a hand over my mouth and forces me to swallow down the vile taste. The moment I do his hand leaves my lips and I am left sputtering and coughing, bent over the table.

"What the fuck!" I scream.

"There, that's better," he says, wiping his hand on a napkin.

"You have some nerve to-" before I can finish that sentence I feel the familiar black vortex surround me. When it spits me out, I am not in the same room I have grown accustomed to.

No, this one is slightly bigger. The bed is wider and as I trail my hand over the top of it I can feel the difference in the quality of the bedding. Instead of one thin pillow I have two, slightly fluffier versions. The bed isn't the only thing improved. This room has a similar bathing chamber only much cleaner and again, slightly larger. As I turn the faucet on, the water actually runs hot, instead of lukewarm. The mirror isn't cracked and the sink isn't leaking.

Huh.

Small miracles.

Maybe now the sound of it dripping won't keep me up half the night. The biggest change in this room is that I have a small window, barely wider than the palm of my hand and only the length of my forearm in height.

Still, it's enough to see out and look down onto a narrow path distinguished by stones and lined with canopying trees. Most of the branches block my view, but there is just enough to watch as Yuta goes strolling by. His head tilts up towards the window like he knew I would be looking out and I have to fight the urge to scream.

Whatever it is he forced me to drink, I can't trust it. Especially as I can already feel something stirring inside me. The temptation to force the contents of my stomach back up is high, but doing so means getting rid of what little food I was able to eat. Something tells me that my days of food delivery trays are gone and I should take what I can when I can so I guess that's not happening.

I pull over a chair and sit beside the window, watching as Yuta walks away and silently cursing his name the entire time.

Chapter 18

Rian

"**I**s that everything you need, sir?"

I double check the luggage again, making sure all of the weapons and potions are prepared for our departure. "Looks like it. Thank you, Dordi. Make sure everyone is prepared to head out at dawn," I say to the guard.

When I was first given the task of securing the defenses of the kingdom, I thought it would be simple, yet as the days went by, I quickly realized that I did not have the people I needed to get this job done properly. Now, I am going to fix that issue.

Securing my own bags I set them off to the side with the rest of the things we will be taking with us. I don't expect to be gone long, maybe a week at most assuming everything goes according to plan, so they're fairly light. Only the bare essentials. Though after my last trip, I am not sure I even know what that means.

I march through the halls, heading for the chamber where I know the *princess* is finishing up a meeting with the councilmen. Each step feels like the slice of a blade carving into my skin as dread rises inside me. Why did it have to be me? Why did it have to be *her*? I would leave right now without a word if I didn't already know she would just come rushing after me.

No. Of course this particular princess will listen to no one but herself.

Lucky me.

The halls are mostly empty since I restructured the guard, focusing on reinforcing the first line of defense and keeping only our most trusted and talented guards here in the Tower. The council was hesitant at first, but with a little extra encouragement they seemed to come around. Not that I gave them much of a choice.

One new benefit of this role is that people don't get to question what I say or do. The king wanted me to make decisions, so I'll make them. Though, he technically also wants his daughter to be the one approving said decisions, but seeing as she is already handling so much, I'm sure it's better this way.

As I approach the room where she is meant to be, the doors open and a flood of people come rushing out talking in tense whispers. I stand at attention as they pass me by, not sparing me even an ounce of attention. Once the hall is entirely empty I make my way into the room, falling short just past the entryway.

Her face is buried in the crook of her elbows as she half lays on the table. Her blonde hair is spilling over her arms and down her back, the golden strands so bright in an otherwise dark room. I can practically feel the tension in her limbs from across the room, her entire body seems broken and neglected. A burst of heat flares in my palms as I fight to dampen my sudden rage and the immediate instinct to go to her.

I gently knock my knuckles against the wooden door and she raises her head, her tired eyes meeting mine instantly. My breath sticks in my throat for a moment. Even exhausted and stressed, she is one of the most beautiful females I have ever seen. Everything about her is sharp, her features carved in such a way that one look could make you bleed. Yet all I see is the delicate creature beyond it.

Crossing the room slowly, I watch with rapt attention as she stretches her arms above her head, the movement exposing the smallest sliver of skin as the hem of her shirt rides up. Her lips are pouty and begging to be kissed, licked, bitten. Fuck. Just the thought of biting her lips sends a bolt of electricity straight to my dick and makes my brain fuzzy.

This. This is why it is a bad idea for us to be around each other. Whatever it is about this girl, I need to focus, and when she is here that isn't possible. I force myself to stay a good distance away, always keeping that space between us just in case. Wouldn't want something to spontaneously catch fire and with us, you never know.

"Why are you so far away?" she asks, annoyance written across her face.

My fingers twitch with the urge to wrap my hand around her throat. Always such a damn brat. I give her a tense smile that barely lasts a second.

"Apologies," I say, moving closer until I am standing at her side, "better?" I stand there, stiff as a board as I wait for her response. Silently hoping she will bite back, while simultaneously praying she doesn't.

She looks up at me and swallows hard, making her throat bob with the movement. That one little second and my fangs are practically begging to sink into her neck. For fucks sake this is getting ridiculous. She's just a female. A princess for fuck's sake. I need to get this locked down before one of us does something stupid. Likely me.

"What do you want?" She massages the back of her neck.

I bet I could make her feel ten times better if I could just- no. Shutting that thought down right here. Right now. Clearing my throat, I focus on what I came here to do. "I have a plan."

"Okkaaay," she draws the word out, "and what is this plan of yours?"

"There is only so much I can accomplish here in the city with the resources I have been provided."

"Go on," she groans. Her shoulders seem to sink with the weight of the ask she assumes I am about to make.

"It will cost you nothing, only my time. I request permission to retrieve you additional soldiers." My heart thumps wildly in my chest, waiting to see how she might react.

"Oh? And who are these soldiers? Why are they so special?"

"Well," I say with a smug smile, "you already know one of them. Nat. She is one of the best guards we have and we need her here. Frankly, she should have never been able to return home in the first place."

"Nat? You want to bring Nat back?" Her eyes widen.

"Yes, and her brother, Cyrus," I explain.

She sits up, energy flushing her cheeks and sparking in the air. "Really? When?" she asks eagerly.

"I would like to leave tomorrow morning, at dawn."

Her brows pinch together, "you? Just you?"

"That is the idea, yes." Well, me and about half a dozen other guards.

"No. I'm going too, this isn't up for conversation." She pushes to her feet and immediately tilts to one side like she might topple right over.

Without thinking my arms shoot out to catch her, tugging her against my chest. The moment our chests touch I can feel the heat burning from her skin, mirroring my own. "Are you okay?" I ask, my voice breathless.

"Yes," she answers, leaning back against the table, "just have a lot on my plate at the moment."

I nod my head, slowly drawing circles on the outside of her arm where I hold her upright. "That's understandable. It is also why you should let me retrieve both Cyrus and Nat alone. I don't need anyone else to bring them back."

Once I have reinforcements, we can start on the *real* work. But I can't just bring in anybody, it needs to be people we trust. I know I can trust Nat, and Cyrus… I trusted him once before, maybe it's time I do so again.

"Of course you would say that. You never let a girl fight her own battles, do you?" she snorts, rolling her eyes.

I expected rage, or at the very least some strong words and maybe a slap to the cheek. This version of Mar? It irks me more than anything else.

I can't help myself, my fingers graze her cheek as I tuck her hair behind her ear. Her head pushes into the palm of my hand and I caress her cheek, the rough pad of my thumb gliding over her defined cheekbones. This is wrong. So wrong. We shouldn't be doing this. With a sigh, I force myself to take a step back, dropping my hands at my side.

"Are you going to try and force me to stay here?" she asks with a sigh of her own.

"No point in trying, is there?"

"No, I'm going. No matter what," she says, determined.

"Right," I push a hand through my hair, "well then… before we leave there is something I need to make sure you understand." My pulse pounds in my ears.

"Oh?"

"What happened in Rayan… I cannot allow it to happen again," I say, unable to hide the twinge of regret from seeping into my voice.

"*Allow* it?" Mar growls.

And here we go, the inevitable fight.

"Yes. If I hadn't allowed myself to get so distracted then I could have saved the heir," I answer, stating the obvious. I don't understand how she can't see this. Everything that happened can all be traced back to my being distracted. If I had just focused, I could have prevented all of this from happening in the first place.

"You don't know that. There is no guarantee that you could have gotten to her in time, that you could have fought them off, none of this is your fault so stop blaming yourself!" she screams.

The outburst is so unexpected that for a moment I don't know how to respond. Still, this argument is familiar, it's the same one we've danced since our feet first touched Vulcan ground again.

"Of course it is. I was sent with you both to protect you. And I failed. Do you understand that? I didn't do my *job*," I spit, irritation clouding my better judgment and feeding into the argument.

"Yeah, well we didn't make it easy on you. And I'm not making it any easier right now, am I," she says to herself, refusing to meet my eyes and opting to stare up at the ceiling instead. "Be prepared to leave at dawn."

I can only nod as she leaves the room. This is going to be fun.

Chapter 19

Rose

As the last rays of light fade from the sky, I slip from my room. The halls are mostly empty as I make my way to the garden. Every small sound makes my heart skip a beat, the fear of getting caught looms over me. Turning the final corner that leads to the entrance, I nearly run face first into my brother.

"Well, well, well. Look who's sneaking around the castle," Oliver mocks. Sweat drips off of him as his eyes sparkle with a manic gleam. Wherever he is coming from, he was certainly enjoying himself.

"I don't know what you're talking about, Oliver. I'm just taking a walk," I bite. The pounding of my heart is like a war drum, the beat growing louder and louder as we stand here in the open. I don't have time for this. I'm supposed to be meeting Cay before I leave and this is going to make me late. "If you'll excuse me," I try to slide past him.

He steps in front of me. "Why the rush?"

My palms grow damp as my hands begin to shake, my entire body alight with nervous energy. "No rush. Just really tired," I say, faking a yawn.

Oliver's lips crack into a smirk, "Tired? Yeah? Is that why you're going the opposite direction of your room?"

Heat builds in my cheeks. "I never said I was going to my room." I know I've said the wrong thing the moment my brother's eyebrows become one with his hairline.

"Oh? So then tell me, whose room *are* you going to? Which court boy is mother going to kill?"

"Again, I never said I was going to see a boy," I answer, rolling my eyes.

"Huh, interesting. I'm not entirely surprised, but still, good for you," he says, clapping a hand on my shoulder as he walks past me.

"Wait, what? Oliver-"

"No need to explain, have a good time."

"Oliver!" I call after him, desperate to understand what just happened. I can feel it deep in my bones, I'm going to have to answer for this conversation later.

The moment I enter the garden I am being pulled into a tight hug. I squeeze Cay back and let the slightest bit of tension ease from my shoulders.

"I was so worried. I thought for sure someone had figured out what you're planning and you were locked up somewhere," Cay whispers against me.

"Sorry, I ran into Oliver and got held up."

Cay heaves a breath as she pulls away. "Why doesn't that surprise me?"

"I'm sorry, but I don't have a lot of time now. I'm already supposed to be at the apothecary," I say regretfully.

"It's okay. I'm just glad I got to see you before you leave."

The words hang heavy in the air, neither one of us willing to acknowledge the weight of them. This is it. I'm leaving tonight, soon Cay will be heading back to Rayan, and neither one of us knows when we'll see each other again. My heart constricts with a wild kind of panic and then my arms are back around Cay's shoulders.

"Please be careful," I beg her.

"You too. I can't lose anyone else," her hands ball into fists at my back. "First my father and mother, then Eve was taken and Oak is missing. I just... promise me you'll come home." She squeezes me tighter.

My throat burns and my eyes sting. "I will. I'll find answers and we'll get them both back. You focus on helping your mom."

We finally pull apart, both wiping at our eyes and trying to hold it together. The sky is growing darker with each passing second and I know I've already stayed too long. Staying here could put the entire plan in jeopardy and I refuse to be the reason why this doesn't work. It has to work.

"I have to go. I love you. Be safe."

"Love you too," Cay says with worried eyes.

I run from the garden, heading straight for the apothecary. I'm halfway there when a large boom explodes from somewhere in the castle. My vision swims and I'm standing back in Rayan, watching the barrier fall all over again, my heart pounding in my chest. I force the image away and continue to race through the halls, running as fast as I possibly can.

Mateo warned me about this. Whatever his role in this plan is, it's loud and crazy and absolutely terrifying. Thankfully, I make it to the apothecary without another incident. The door to the workshop clicks shut behind me and Reed appears from the shadows.

"Where were you? I was scared something happened!"

"I know, I know, I'm sorry. Let's just get moving, we're already running behind."

Reed shoulders a large pack filled with the supplies Mateo asked for and hands me a small pack of my own which I quickly combine with my own bag.

"Is this everything?"

"Yes I made sure it was all in there. You could have checked yourself if you were on time," Reed taunts.

"Okay I get it, I'm sorry, let's go before someone catches us." We slip out the back door and take the hidden path back to the wisteria tree. The familiar dangling flowers provide a sort of blanket of coverage to keep us hidden while we wait. Mateo should be right behind us, but it feels like time is moving at half speed.

"Where is he? He should be here by now, right?" Reed asks, wringing his hands together. He's pacing back and forth, small bursts of magic sparking in the palms of his hands as his emotions grow more uncontrolled.

"Reed, you need to calm down. I'm sure everything is fine," I reassure him. My stomach churns as we wait, the nausea growing worse as my own anxiety elevates.

"You don't know that. Anything could have happened. What if he got hurt? Or caught? He's barely a member of court, Rose. Who knows what your mother will do to him after what she did to my sister."

"I know that and I'm worried too, but Mateo asked us to trust him."

"And do you? Do you trust him?" Reed asks, turning towards me.

"Yes." I still can't wrap my head around why, around what makes Mateo so easy to trust. But at this point I'm running low on allies and I'll take all the help I can get to bring Oak home. Together we'll find Eve.

"Right. Okay. Yeah, we just have to trust him. This is fine. Everything is fine. We are all fine." Reed continues pacing.

My brows knit together, a million questions forming in my head. "Reed, is something going on between you two?"

Reed spins around so fast he nearly trips over his own feet. His mouth is gaping open and his eyes are positively panicked. "What? Why would you say that?"

I shrug. "I don't know, you just seem extra worried. I thought that maybe som-"

"No! Nothing. I'm just worried about the plan, okay? Am I not allowed to be worried about the plan?" he bites. He crosses his arms over his broad chest, raising his brows at me.

"Hey, it's fine. Just a question. I won't bring it up again," I say, raising my hands up between us placatingly.

Reed is supposed to be the mellow one, this does not bode well for us if he's already this on edge.

Bushes rustle on the edge of the clearing and my heart stops beating for a second until a large curly mane appears. Mateo jogs over to us with a wild look about him. "Time to go," he says cheerfully albeit out of breath.

"Okay and how exactly are we going to do that? Remember, this is the part of the plan that you insisted on keeping to yourself," Reed asks, irritated.

"Someone's feeling grouchy," Mateo teases with a smile, his eyes roam up and down, looking over Reed. "I've got it all figured out, just follow me. It's time for phase two."

We walk through the woods for a half hour before Mateo directs us onto a small trail that leads into another clearing. The moment the woods open up we find nearly a dozen people scattered throughout.

I grab Mateo's arm, yanking him to a stop. "What is this? Mateo, who are these people?" I demand. Shit. This is absolutely the worst decision of my life and I once let Oliver give me a haircut.

"Relax, little Ro, this is my pack. Well, part of it at least," Mateo says, bumping his shoulder into mine before running off to join the strangers. He steps to the side, talking with a tanned male with a dark head of short hair.

"Did he just call you 'little Ro'?" Reed asks, flabbergasted.

"Yes."

"And you let him?"

"Apparently," I sigh.

Mateo introduces us to all of the wolves briefly and then he leads us down another, less defined, trail, explaining that this is the path we will be taking to get to Eteri. Mateo's so-called *genius plan* is that his pack is going to escort us to Eteri. That's it. That's the *entire* plan.

We're totally screwed.

As soon as introductions are over we head out. It's the middle of the night so we should be able to make it pretty far before we need to hide out.

Doing this all on foot isn't ideal, but considering Reed and I aren't wolves, just shifting and running isn't much of an option.

The first hour of the journey passes remarkably fast. Reed is grilling Mateo on every single detail of the plan including the exact use of each supply we have packed. From the look of anguish on Reed's face, I am guessing it's not going all that well.

Meanwhile, my mind is caught on something entirely different. How in Vana's name we are getting into Eteri. It's one thing to make it to the border, it's entirely another to be granted access to their cities, let alone an audience with the person we are looking for. So far, my only plan is to be as honest as possible and hope that they are willing to help us out. If they won't, well then we have a bit of a problem on our hands.

By the time the earliest rays of sunlight are breaking on the horizon, we are all completely exhausted. A couple of the wolves quickly get to work setting up a kind of camp using their magic- one building small, stone tents for us to sleep in while the other uses her magic to keep us hidden.

"Hey, Mateo, I have a question," I ask, walking over to where he and Reed seem engrossed in conversation.

"What's up, little Ro?"

"Please don't call me that."

"Nah, you love it," he says with a charming smile and damn him maybe I do.

Still, I ignore him. "How haven't the guards caught up with us yet? We aren't exactly moving super fast and I've gotta say, that boom from inside the castle was pretty loud. And slightly concerning," I tack on under my breath.

"Easy. I can use illusion magic. Very realistic. No one will even notice we're gone," he says nonchalantly.

Reed and I share a skeptical look.

"How can you do that?" Reed asks somewhat in awe.

Mateo smiles like Reed's interest is the best thing in the world and I again ask myself what is going on between the two of them. "I'm just good at enchantments, no big deal, I could work with you on it if you want," Mateo says with a shrug and a sexy smile.

Reed's face turns a deep crimson and I excuse myself from the conversation. As I walk over to the tent designated for me, I feel a presence lurking in the shadows. When I turn to find it, searching the treeline for any sign of someone there, there's nothing. Just the faint glow of the rising sun.

Chapter 20

Oak

"**S**tay focused, you almost had her on that last one," Farai calls to me from outside the sparring circle.

A bead of sweat drips down the side of my face as I watch Lina for any sign of movement. We've been at it for at least two hours now, but Aine says we can't leave until I pin her. Lina, of course, is determined to not let that happen. It would *ruin her reputation* or so she claims.

Most of the other units have already started packing up for the day, cleaning the equipment and heading out towards the dining area. Hala and Symone are both on dinner duty tonight so they were already allowed to leave, lucky them.

"What's the matter, Oak? Ready to admit defeat?" Lina taunts, flicking her pale hair over her shoulder. She flashes me a demonic grin before pouncing, launching herself forward and curling into a ball. She flips feet over head through the air and lands in a crouch directly in front of me. Without missing a beat her leg swings out, swiping the back of my ankles and making me fall on my ass once again.

"Fuck, that hurt," I groan, rubbing at the base of my spine where the pins and needles feeling is concentrated. Lina offers me a hand up and I take it, jumping to my feet and shaking out my arms and legs.

"Enough, that was sloppy. Lina, you can do better than that. Oak, at least try and react next time," Aine chastises from beside Farai.

Lina rolls her head out, stretching her arm across her chest in an attempt to keep things loose. She quickly gets back into position and gives me a nod to let me know she is ready to go.

Following suit, I take up my fighting stance. Aine forced me to spend hours holding the same position until I *got it right*. And as frustrating as that experience was, I can't deny that I feel stronger. My body is perfectly positioned to both attack and defend. Now, if only I could do either of those things and finally be allowed to leave this Vana's damned circle.

"Again," Aine commands.

We both move at once. I shoot forward, my fist arching out with perfect form, delivering a hard blow to Lina's shoulder. She takes the hit with nothing more than a grunt, quickly shifting to kick out at me. There's no time to dodge so I block the worst of the kick with my forearm, the impact vibrates through me.

"Good block, Oak. Faster, Lina, you should have gotten past that," Aine continues to yell out from the sidelines.

I hone in on the fight, forcing Aine's voice from my mind and directing all of my attention to the person in front of me. Lina's breaths are ragged, her movements slowing ever so slightly as she begins to show signs of fatigue. This is it. This is my opportunity. Sure, she's not at the top of her game, but that doesn't matter. A win is a win. All I need to do now is make it happen.

Lina spins around, ready to deliver a back kick, but the slightest hint of her hesitation is enough for me to dodge. I move to the side only to be punched directly in the face and knocked completely on my ass.

"I'm sorry! Sorry! I didn't mean to h-" Lina's words are cut off by Aine's grating voice.

"Never apologize for winning a fight. Back in position. Oak, Lina's strategy was blatantly clear, use your eyes and maybe next time you won't fall into one of her traps."

I roll my eyes and feel the anger begin to stir inside me. The entire day, all it has been is everything I do wrong. How I'm weak, stupid, not good enough to be here.

Hello? It's not like I asked to be.

My entire body starts to shake with rage as each command that passes from Aine's lips makes my blood boil hotter and hotter.

The next five rounds end in rapid succession, all with me sprawled across the floor in varying degrees of pain. My eyes widen moments before Lina's boot connects with my chin. Hot blood spills down my neck and a cry of frustration bursts from me before I can stop it. I sit up, touching a hand to my chin gingerly, wincing at the near blinding pain.

"Let go of your anger, let your instincts guide you," Lina whispers to me as she helps me to my feet.

My vision swims and I have to fight off the bout of nausea that greets me on my feet. I'm so fucking over this. Weeks have passed and I feel like I've made zero progress. I shake out my head, focusing instead on what Lina said to me while ignoring the way my body sways on my feet. Something has to give, has to change. I take a deep breath, calling all of my attention back to the fight and letting go of everything inside me.

No anger, fear, frustration, betrayal. I choose to be here, in this moment, whatever that means. When I open my eyes things seem sharper, and I blink to be sure I'm not hallucinating. Lina smiles at me knowingly before shoving me back. I don't budge and that's when the excitement builds. This fight is different, more even. I block each attack sent my way, returning with my own. Blow for blow we fight all while I am internally screaming about how well this is going.

One of my kicks breaks through Lina's defense and she stumbles back a step. I'm on her in a second, rapid firing kicks and punches until the only thing she can do is block. I have the upper hand and it feels fucking amazing. I take a half-step back, giving myself enough room for the kick that will end it all. I jump up, spinning and kicking out midair. Only my boot never connects. I land on unsteady feet and whirl around.

Lina's fist makes an impact with the center of my face and a harsh cracking sound deafens me. I fall to the floor in a crumpled heap, my hands both clutching my now broken nose as blood pours from it in a steady stream.

"That's enough for today. Lina, start cleaning things up and then go get some food. Oak, come here," Aine commands from beside Farai.

"Not too bad," Lina whispers to me as she helps me to my feet.

I stumble to the edge of the ring and hop down off of the platform, making my way to them. Aine reaches out a hand and pulls mine away from my face. She looks over my nose before quickly healing it. The small rush of magic sends a thrill through my bones. My entire body is sore and I have never been so exhausted in my life. That one tiny kernel of magic makes it all fade away almost instantly, leaving only a faint ache behind.

"I want you and Farai to spend some time working on your balance. It's still not good enough, and had you been practicing more, you might have been able to block that last punch," Aine says, clearly irritated.

"But what about dinner?" I ask, ignoring her subtle digs.

"I'll have Symone set two plates aside. Now go," Aine says, shoving me towards Farai who looks less than pleased at this change of plan.

Farai leads the way over to the edge of the training area and jumps right in.

"Aine is right, your balance is horrible, you need to fix that if you want to make any real progress."

"No, I swear I have really good balance. I don't know what happened back there." I groan.

Farai shakes her head. "You rely too much on your magic. You use it to sense the earth, right?"

I nod my head.

"*That's* why you are good at balancing. You're using magic. Maybe unintentionally, but it doesn't change that you're using it."

"What does magic have to do with balance?" I follow her as she begins some kind of fluid movements, slowly transitioning from one pose to the next without missing a beat.

"Your magic allows you to know more, to see a bigger picture, but that's not always going to be possible. It's important that you learn to trust and rely on your other senses and powers aside from magic alone."

Her words take a while to fully set in, but when they do I realize how right she is. I do rely on my magic too much. "Okay, you're right," I say, biting my lip and nodding my head in agreement, "I want to learn how to be better. Teach me how to be better." My words come out as more of a beg than I was hoping for, but the sentiment remains the same.

For the time being, I'm stuck here. Might as well learn a thing or two.

Farai stares at me down, monitoring my expression for something. Whatever it is, she lets it go. "Alright then, let's start with the basics. Get into a horse riding stance," she instructs.

I follow her directions without complaint and listen intently as she goes through every single baby step from the very beginning. Sometimes it's best to go back to the beginning, to learn something all over again, but this time pay attention to what it really means. It's time I start listening.

Chapter 21

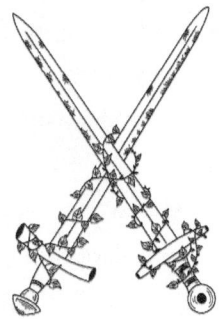

Oliver

My head swims with the buzzing of magic filling the air. My body hums in approval as I slowly release more and more, letting it strengthen me. I wait for the training dummy to stop its swaying from my last attack, the moment the base is secure I go back at it, kicking and punching. Energy builds inside me along with the power thrumming in my veins, intoxicating and utterly dangerous.

Opening my palms I let my magic swell, muttering an incantation as I narrow my eyes on my target. I lift my hands out in front of me, holding them palm out and forming a triangle with my thumbs and fingers. A white orb of pure energy appears at the center, pulsating wildly. My entire body tingles pleasantly, a feeling once foreign and terrifying, now something that I chase.

The orb grows larger than my fist, white wisps of power thrashing out and snapping in the air like a bolt of lighting. "Fuck," I mutter excitedly, unable to contain my smile. I pull my hands close to my chest slowly while taking a deep, controlled breath.

Thrusting my hands forward with a grunt, magic shoots forward in a brilliant beam of light and smacks into the door seconds before it is pulled open. My brother's face appears in the doorway, shocked and confused.

"Well I hope whatever that was wasn't meant for me," he says with a nervous grin.

I drag my arm across my forehead, wiping away sweat. "No, brother, if that was meant for you, you'd be dead."

"Noted. What was that anyway?" he asks, walking into the room and leaving the door partially open.

Shrugging, I walk over to the weapons wall, picking up a broadsword and testing the weight in my hand. "Nothing, just an incantation I've been working on. You up for a fight?" I ask, nodding towards the other swords.

Terran crosses the room and picks up a longsword, placing two hands on the hilt and cracking his neck. "Against you? Always."

We stand facing each other, my brother's eyes laser focused on me where he stands with perfect form. I wave the sword around a few times, testing the length and balance. It's not bad for a training sword, not that I'm aiming to do any real damage. Well, nothing *bad* at least.

"Are we going to fight or are you going to keep waving that thing around like a toy?" Terran mocks.

Tossing the sword into the air, I do a full circle before catching it with my non-dominant hand and flashing him a smirk.

"Always a show off," he says, rolling his eyes.

My body tenses just before I strike out, carving the sword through the air and straight for my brother's chest. He brings his arms up, blocking the strike with his long blade.

"I prefer to think of it as a demonstration. Care to learn a thing or two?" I say, my eyes flicking to the spots where our swords clash together.

"Need I remind you who taught you to fight?" Terran says, dropping his arms and bringing his sword arching upwards in the other direction.

"I seem to recall, dad teaching me to fight, not you," I say, countering his blow and meeting it with one of my own.

We move back and forth, exchanging one hit for another, the power shifting between us equally. Our footwork is nearly identical, our form mirrors each other as we move through the movements our father ingrained into us.

I take a step forward, dropping low and stabbing out with the tip of my blade. Terran spins out of the path of my blade and brings a knee up, catching me in the gut while kicking my hand and sending my blade clattering to the ground. I stare up at him in fury, thoroughly soaked with sweat and pissed the fuck off.

"Father might have taught you the basics, but it was me who taught you finesse. Maybe you need a refresher," he smiles down at me, extending a hand.

I scoff, ignoring his hand and rising to my feet so we are standing eye to eye. Looking at my brother is like looking in a mirror. The image I carved myself into was his and yet now, I feel like I hardly know the male standing before me. There was once a time I would have considered him my best friend, my idol, now he is nothing more than a husk of the male I thought he was.

"Don't you have some papers to sign?" I say bending down to pick up my sword. I cross the room to put it in its place and Terran does the same.

"Oliver, whatever I did to make you so mad at me, will you please just tell me? I hate being like this, let me fix things," he says wistfully.

I turn my back on him, my jaw locking as I fight to force down my rising magic. That one little orb barely did anything to quell the demand of the magic. "You can't fix everything, brother."

He sighs. "I know that. But I believe I can fix *us*. Just talk to me. You used to tell me everything, but now you just shut me out. Oliver, I know something is going on with you, I'm your big brother."

"Any chance I could join in?" a hesitant voice calls from the doorway, saving me from answering.

Terran and I both watch as Cay enters wearing a thin, lilac camisole and black skin tight training pants that show off her every curve. My eyes catch on the perfect divot just beneath her hips and the swell of her thighs. I bet if she turned around her a-

"We were just finishing up, apologies," Terran says regretfully. His gaze is fixed on her seagreen eyes accentuated by the way she has her hair pulled back today.

"Oh. Okay. Well maybe I could train with you another time?" she asks hesitantly.

I snort. "Sure, princess, if you're okay with losing a finger or two. Do you honestly think you could keep up?" I might not sever any of my brother's limbs, but that's not exactly from lack of trying. His skill has saved his ass more times than I've held back. I'm not sure I could control my power if we were to fight and frankly I'm not interested in testing that theory out.

"You're an ass, Oliver, you know that?" Cay's hands come up to rest on her hips in defiance.

I pick up my towel and a water bottle, pouring it over me. "Never said I wasn't," I shake the water out of my curls and run the towel over my face. The moment the towel lowers, a jetstream of water smacks into my face.

"You missed a spot," Cay says with a triumphant grin, turning around and sashaying from the room.

I watch her with a scowl as my brother laughs beside me. "Fuck off," I say jabbing him with my elbow. He raises his hands up in surrender and I roll my eyes. For a moment things feel like they used to. Terran opens his mouth to say something else, but I march from the room, not ready for that conversation.

Chapter 22

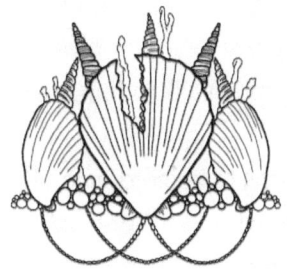

Cay

In the days since Rose left things have been eerily quiet. No one else seems to notice that she isn't around, whatever magic they used continues to work perfectly. And now that I've watched her plan succeed, I'm ready to take the next step in mine.

"Are you sure?" I ask, my nails biting into the palms of my hands. I've asked Regan to watch over the refugees and my family, a task that I know she won't take lightly. Yet even knowing that, I can't help but wait anxiously for her answer.

Regan places her hand on my shoulder, squeezing reassuringly. "Of course, Your Highness, it is my honor to look after our people." She gives me a smile before heading back towards the hall where the refugees have been relocated.

The burning in my lungs reminds me to breathe and I suck down air, finally feeling like I can breathe again. As much as I know this is the right thing to do, that going home means helping my mother, I can't help the fear that I feel just imagining seeing my home again.

Nightmares have plagued me for over a week now and I can do nothing to escape them. Even visiting my mother only seems to make things worse. Still, I refuse to let this hold me back from seeing her. Not when I am about to leave and who knows if-

I cut that thought off. I won't go there. Not yet.

I enter the familiar cave-like hall that leads to my mother's bed and find Flora there, standing over her and pressing a frail hand against her forehead. "How is she today?" I ask, pulling over a stool so I can sit by my mother's bedside.

"Steady. Her magic seems to be holding on for now. Though there were a few moments last night when..." Flora sighs. She hobbles to her small countertop, fiddling with a mortar of crushed berries. Her movements are slower than usual, her shoulders slumped forward more and the wrinkles around her eyes seem deeper.

"You've been doing so much for us both. You must be exhausted," I say, watching her as she grinds the berries with the pestle.

"Nonsense, I can keep up just fine, don't you worry about me," she tsks.

I smile at her, knowing it's not worth it to push the argument. Flora is going to do what Flora wants to do. No exceptions. "Do you think it's safe for me to leave? What if she..." I say as the thoughts creep in again.

"Whatever it is you need to do, wherever you need to go, you just do that and let me worry about keeping the queen here. I owe her that much," Flora says, walking over and handing me the mortar while she begins to rub the thick paste over my mother's lips.

My brows pull together as I let her words sink in. "Wait, what do you mean 'owe her'?"

Flora seems to pause, considering, her lips form a thin line as she nods her head. Grabbing another stool, she sits down beside me, taking the mortar from my hands and setting it to the side. "I have been the court healer for nearly my entire life. I have helped raise generations of this realm's lords and ladies. I helped raise Rose and her brothers."

I remain silent, watching her expression change, like she is lost in a memory.

"When Oliver was a young boy, he was often sick and very weak," she says wistfully.

"Wait, I don't understand. Oliver? But he is one of the most powerful people I know," I say bewildered.

"Now, but there were times where we weren't sure he would make it. His father and mother were desperate and one day the high lord left with the boy. When he returned, it was like Oliver had never been sick before. He was running around happy as ever," she says with a sigh, rising from her chair and taking the berries back to the counter.

"So where did they go? How did they heal him?" I ask, following after her.

"I don't know anything for certain, but I do remember overhearing the high lord talk about your kingdom and your parents. Your mother's name in particular was mentioned multiple times. Now, I might not know what exactly she did for that boy, but I am grateful to her all the same." Flora walks back down the hall, disappearing from view.

I look down at my mother's red lips, wondering how she is connected to Oliver and what she has to do with his sickness.

~~~

The sun set hours ago and there are only so many hours remaining until first light, the time when I am meant to meet Terran so we can leave, yet sleep is the farthest thing from my mind as I continue to pace the length of my room. It still feels surreal, how did we go from spending time together in the library to something like this?

Are we ready? What if we get caught? So much could go wrong and too many people could get hurt.

No. I can't do this. I can't leave. Can't go back there... to that place where my father died. It's too much. I'm not ready. I need to stop this before it is too late. I race from the room in nothing more than a silk sleep dress. But it doesn't matter, there's no time to worry about that now, not when I have to put an end to this before we do something stupid.

Terran's door is straight ahead and I rush forward, throwing it open without knocking. My eyes lock with his as he lays in bed, the blankets slung low over his hips leaving his entire smooth, bare, chest on display. I freeze on the spot, my mind going blank and my body becoming burning hot.

Papers are spread out around him, a stack is gripped tightly in his hand, but the moment he sees me he pushes it all away. "Cay? What's wrong? What happened?" he starts to get out of bed and I immediately turn around, walking straight towards the door while my cheeks continue to burn.

"Wait, Cay, what happened? Tell me what's going on," he calls after me, the sound of sheets ruffling stop and the soft sound of footsteps against stone chase after me.

I stop in the doorway, my back towards him. "I'm sorry, I was just anxious about tomorrow. I didn't mean to disturb you. Please, forget this happened," I whisper, squeezing my eyes shut against the embarrassment.

"Just, hold on a second," he says with a laugh. His hands wrap around my shoulder and he turns me so I am facing him. "Look at me?" he asks, his voice low.

My eyes crack open and I am grateful to find he has thrown on a tunic, albeit the buttons are still undone, leaving plenty of tanned muscles on display. I mean honestly, it's not the first time I have seen a male's chest. Why am I getting so worked up over this?

"Cay? You with me?" he asks and I nod my head slowly. "Good, I thought I lost you there for a second. You alright?"

I take a deep breath and try to concentrate on why I came here in the first place. "I think this is a bad idea. What if something goes wrong? What if someone figures out what we're trying to do or... what if someone gets hurt?"

He smiles down at me, bringing a hand up to caress my face and making my heart jump. The rough pad of his thumb skates across my cheek bone and a shiver makes its way down my spine. "Why don't we go over the plan again, would that make you feel better?" he asks, surprising me.

"Really?" I ask, my voice barely above a whisper.

He pulls me to his chest and gives me a tight hug that only lasts a second yet sends my heart racing. The sound of its beating is so fast I am sure he can hear it, yet he just takes a step back and begins buttoning up his tunic. "Of course, come in and we can talk things through. I know we can make this work."

I nod my head, letting him lead the way to the desk. We go through the plan together, twice, and when I finally feel good about things a huge yawn forces its way out. I slap a hand over my gaping mouth in horror. "Sorry," I mumble behind my palm.

Terran laughs. "No need to apologize. It's late. Why don't we both go to bed and get some rest."

My eyes widen and my hand falls away. *Is he suggesting we…*

His eyes mirror my own as he begins frantically waving his hands between us. "I didn't mean- I just- I-" he takes a raking breath, "I only meant to suggest that we each *individually* get some sleep. I am sorry if it seems as though I was-"

The tips of my ears nearly catch on fire from how hot they are. Of course he didn't mean *together*! *I am such an idiot!*

"No! No, no, no, of course. I knew exactly what you meant," I say with a nervous laugh. I play with the hem of my nightgown, unable to move from where I stand frozen.

Terran towers over me, his eyes roaming from head to toe. "You look…"I swallow hard. "Sorry, I ran straight here and I wasn't thinking properly. I should have gotten dressed."

"I didn't mean anything by it. I just… you look very pretty," he says, his eyes flicking to the thin straps holding the dress up. One has fallen to the side and he reaches his hand up, sliding it back into place and pinching the fabric between his thumb and forefinger. "It's so soft," his voice is more gravelly than before.

"It's silk," I breathe. Energy buzzes between us and I take a step forward, my head tilting back so I can look at his hazel eyes.

He trails a finger across my collarbone and over my shoulder leaving a trail of tiny bumps in its wake. He bends down, bringing our faces within a few inches of each other and I swear I forget how to breathe. His free hand reaches up, tangling in the hair at the base of my neck. "Your skin and hair are so soft, Cay," he says, tilting my head up further, "I remember how soft your lips are too."

The air around us evaporates and I am left panting, my mouth hanging open and waiting. He leans forward and my eyes flutter shut. There is the faintest brush of his lips against mine and then they're gone. Disappearing like a phantom that was never there. His hands drop away and when I open my eyes I find him halfway across the room already.

I don't wait to hear what he has to say, I just turn and head back to my room. I walk straight to the bathroom, shed my nightgown, and slip into a bath.

Chapter 23

Mar

I pull on a pair of training pants, the dark fabric clinging to my long legs like a second skin, and pair them with a dark purple tunic. My hair is braided back into two strands that meet halfway down and merge to form one thicker braid. Finally, I lace up riding boots that hit just below my knee, the soft leather perfect for long journeys.

Picking up my bag, I sling it over my shoulder and try to fight the urge to run to the landing platform where I am supposed to meet the others. Rian has arranged for a small squad of dragons to take us to Nat's village so that we can save time and not worry about horses.

The large cavern is the same as the last time I was here. When we first arrived home after what happened in Rayan. My heart races as I stand at the entrance, staring at the place where I truly realized that I was home and Eve wasn't.

Rian is standing with a small group on the dias, scanning the cave until his eyes meet mine. Neither of us moves as we stare at each other, silently acknowledging the last time that we both stood in this place together.

I smack my hands against my outer thighs and shake my head. There's no time to sit around living in the past. It's over, it happened, we're fixing it. That is all that matters. Sure I'm doing it alone. Yeah, I still have no idea why the others stopped answering my letters. Maybe I *don't* have any idea what to do after we get Nat. None of that matters. Because at least I'm doing *something*. I'm making progress.

Making my way to the top of the landing platform, I greet the other guards with a nod and walk straight up to Rian. "Are we ready? How soon can we leave?" Magic thrums in my veins excitedly, the urge to cast makes my palms itch.

"As soon as you want. We've got everything taken care of here," he says seriously.

"Really?" I whisper.

"Really."

I can't help the little sparks that shoot from my fingertips, and I am forced to ball my hands into fists. I haven't had the chance to dispel any magic since the last time I fed, now it feels like it's ready to burst from beneath my skin.

There is a delicate balance to wielding power, too much and it sets you on edge, the feeling of it just beneath your skin. But when you go too long without or you use too much power, it's like all of the energy and life force has been drained from inside you. It's better to keep it at an even middle.

"Are you ready? Seems like you've got a bit of a problem there," Rian says, his eyes flicking down to my closed fists.

I slowly unfurl my fingers, revealing a small fire burning at the center of my palm. It pulses, the flames shift from a warm orangish glow to a vibrant yellow and then cool blue. We both stare at it, watching as the flame grows larger. Power hums inside me, a pleasant buzz as warmth spreads through me.

"Mar," Rian warns.

"What?" I breathe, letting a little more power into the flame.

Rian grabs my other hand, wrapping his long fingers around mine and directing my magic towards him. The flames slowly fade from one fist and appear between our joined palms. Heat licks against my wrist as Rian continues to draw my power, not taking it in, but redirecting it. We lock eyes as I feel his own magic reaching out for me.

"What're you doing?" I ask, my chest rising and falling slowly.

"You need to get control of that magic, little one," he says, his thumb rubbing circles against the palm of my hand.

"What?"

"Control, baby," he says with a teasing grin.

My cheeks flush. *What is going on right now?*

"Rein it in, you're a little overexcited," he says with a chuckle, nodding his head to the side.

I look around us and find a ring of fire, rising from the floor and extending well above our heads. I'm momentarily mesmerized by the colors as they pulse throughout the entire ring, Rian's hair reflects their distinct glow as it shifts.

"It's beautiful," I say in awe.

"It's you," he answers. Magic pushes against me harder now and I follow Rian's lead as he guides me through the process of reining it in. Slowly the fire falls from around us, the heat fading from my palm until Rian releases my hand.

"What was that?" I ask, staring down at the ground, now singed with a black ring from the flames.

"Not sure, but whatever it is, you got it under control and that's all that matters," he says with a shrug, shattering the moment.

"What?" I ask, staring at him with my mouth agape. That was incredible and I wasn't even *trying* to do it. How can he be so nonchalant about this?

"What?" he echoes my question back to me, his brows raised.

"Did you not see how amazing that was?"

"Sure. It was very pretty. But we're running behind now."

"You're a dick, Rian," I groan, pushing past him to where the others stand waiting for us, pretending they hadn't been staring. "Let's go," I say, nodding to the dragon who will be taking us.

The guard quickly shifts, his large dragon form appearing before us with deep emerald scales. He's bigger than Nat, not by much, but enough that it is noticeable. The guard lowers a wing to the ground so that I can climb on easier. I settle down in the space between his shoulders and close my eyes.

"Feeling better?" Rian asks.

I can feel him standing above me as I choose to ignore him. Somehow Rian always finds a way to become an even bigger asshole and I'm not in the mood to deal with that kind of energy right now. Not when we're *finally* going to do something to help Eve.

"Hello?"

I lean back against my elbows, relaxing as I start to plan out our next move after we get Nat. I know that she'll be just as eager as I am to start searching, but I suppose we'll at least need to return to Izal to mobilize a bigger unit. Of course, my father will also want to know what is happening.

"Mar."

Even if my father doesn't agree, it's time. We've spent weeks now just pretending that everything is normal. Queen Elani is still unresponsive to all forms of healing and we need to start considering telling the people. It's wrong to keep them in the dark like this. I understand not wanting to cause panic, but if we just focus on finding Eve then we can figure out what to do to help the queen.

"MAR!" Rian bellows.

"What?" I snap, not bothering to open my eyes.

"Are you seriously going to ignore me? Like a child?" he growls.

I don't respond.

Rian huffs. "Fine. Have it your way. We can ride to the village in silence if that's what you want."

I listen as he walks away, mumbling under his breath. I feel him return after a few minutes and I crack an eye to look at him. His back is to me as I shoot daggers and internally hope he falls off this dragon when we take off.

"I can feel you staring at me. You better sit up, we're about to leave," he says without turning around.

Rolling my eyes, I follow his direction and within a minute we are in the air. The guard's flying isn't as smooth as Nat's was, but-much to my disappointment- no one falls off. Soon we are making our way through the cave entrance and emerging into the morning light.

It takes a while for my eyes to adjust after being in the perpetual darkness that is my home. Eventually, as we soar through the air and carve a path towards Nat's village, I can take in the beauty of the rest of Vulca.

Most of our people are concentrated inside of Izal, deep within the volcano, but there are a handful of villages and outposts that remain on the outskirts, closer to the borders. As we fly southwest the land becomes a lush green, the trees growing denser. Out of all the lands, Sena is the most diverse in regards to landscape, but Vulca is second.

I spend the first hour just watching the terrain change, the beautiful colors and distinct landscapes. Eventually, I sit back and close my eyes again, picturing everything that is yet to come, focusing on the desired outcomes and forcing myself to remain positive. Everything is going to work. It has to.

There is a bright flash of light and a silhouette of a figure at the center. My eyes fly open, fully expecting to see something, but nothing is there, just the endless blue skies and fluffy white clouds, the rising sun lighting the way as we soar through the air.

"And how long exactly do you plan on remaining silent?"

I look up at Rian trying to decipher if he was the figure that I saw, but he's too tall, his shoulders too wide, whoever or whatever I saw behind my eyes is gone.

He stares down at me expectantly so I return the gesture with a raise of my brows. We stare each other down, neither of us yielding, neither of us looking away, just locked into this moment waiting for the other to break. Eventually one of the other guards calls out that we're getting close and Rian is forced to prepare for our arrival.

I consider it a win for myself. Rising, I watch as the village comes into view. It's bigger than I expected, rows of houses repeat one after another, intersecting in a grid pattern. A large field seems to be our destination as we bank to the right, flying low over top the roofs. We touch down quickly and somewhat jarringly, I am thrown off my feet and start to fall backwards when an arm wraps around my waist and drags me upright.

Rian tightens his grip on me, leaning forward to speak directly into my ear, "This is the part where you say *'thank you'*."

I turn to him, softening my eyes, licking my lips, and smiling. I part my mouth as if I am about to speak, drawing a triumphant smile from his lips. I tilt my head back. He leans in. I sneeze directly in his face.

"What the fuck!" he screams, tightening his grip on me instead of letting go like I was expecting.

I smirk at him, as I grab the sleeve of his tunic and wipe it across my nose. I quickly move back as his magic begins to build along with his rage. That's enough taunting for now. Jumping down, I land on the lush grass with ease, quickly stretching out my muscles and getting my first real look at the village.

A few of the guards have already started gathering our stuff together and setting it to the side, the dragon who flew the entire way here takes the opportunity to shift. The moment he is back in mortal form he slumps onto his hands and knees, almost immediately rolling over to his back. It can be incredibly taxing to fly for such a distance, especially with so many people, something that makes what Nat did that much more impressive. *All the more reason we need her.*

Nat carried *all of us* out of Rayan and to land after a hard battle, *then* she managed to bring Rian and I all the way back to Vulca, without ever making a single complaint. She is a warrior. She is someone who we need to fight for my sister. Besides, it doesn't hurt that she and Eve had a little thing.

Walking through the village, a few people seem to recognize me and give me a slight bow, others run right past without paying me any mind. I see a sign for a healer and follow it, weaving through the crowds and walking straight through the door, a little chime rings as it falls shut behind me.

"Just a second!" a husky voice calls from somewhere deeper in the shop.

It's fairly small, but laid out well, the walls lined with various potions and tonics. Baskets of herbal soaps and oils sit in the center of the room filling the air with their fragrant scent. There is a small counter stacked with unopened boxes, behind it, a curtain hangs partially open.

"Sorry about that wait, how can I help you?" a male says, pushing through the curtain and flashing a brilliant smile.

Oh. My. Vana.

Fuck, he is gorgeous.

He's got a head of dark copper waves, full brows set over hooded eyes, the iris a pale, sage green. His nose is long and straight, but the end becomes rounded, giving it a softer appearance. His cheekbones are high and well defined beneath the cluster of freckles spreading from one side of his face to the other. His lips are a wide heart shape, the color a dark dusty rose, which matches his slightly sunkissed skin perfectly. Finally, his angular jaw comes to another rounded point at his chin, making everything appear so much gentler, even with his sharp features. Add in the bit of stubble he's got right now and this male is stunning.

"Miss? Can I help you?" he repeats, giving me a lopsided smile and revealing the most perfect dimple.

I mean come on. How can this male be real?

"Mar?"

The sound of my name pulls me from the fantasy slideshow I was about to enter.

Nat emerges from behind the male, her own wild curls are piled atop her head into a messy bun. She's wearing a simple tunic and cloth pants covered in grass stains. I look between the two of them and realize the male is wearing the same thing which must mean they both work here.

"Hi," I say breathily.

This is it. It's happening. Here she is, standing in front of me. Vana my heart is beating fast. One step closer. We are one step closer. *We're coming, Eve.*

"Um... hi?" Nat says questioningly.

"Oh, you two know each other?" the male asks, looking between us while raising those perfectly sculpted brows.

"Um, yeah. Cyrus, this is Mar, second in line to the throne," Nat explains, gesturing to me while the male seems shocked. "Mar, this is my brother, Cyrus."

"*Brother?*" I ask, taken off guard.

"That would be correct, Nat here is my little sister," Cyrus says, bumping a shoulder into his *sister*.

Wow. Talk about genetics. "It's lovely to meet you, Cyrus," I say with a smile, heat rising in my cheeks.

"The pleasure is all mine, my lady," Cyrus dips his head to me, his eyes flicking up and locking on mine with interest.

Someone clears their throat and our spell is broken.

"Mar, what are you doing here?" Nat shifts on her feet.

"Nat, I think you know why," I say, taking a deep breath and sending a prayer that things go easily, "we need your help."

Chapter 24

Eve

I flop down onto my back in my new bed, staring up at the less cracked ceiling and going over every detail of that dinner with Yuta three nights ago. I expected something new from him, but in the days since I was sent to this upgraded prison, everything has been quiet. There have been no torture sessions, no dinners, just me and the silence.

My thoughts are consumed by the girls. *Is everyone okay? Did something happen to them? Why haven't they come for me yet?* When I'm not worrying over their fate I focus on the happy memories. More often than not, living through the images that play inside my mind when I close my eyes.

Only my mind seems to be playing tricks on me ever since that dinner. My dreams at night are shadowed and difficult to decipher, muffled voices and a faint glow have kept me from reliving my favorite moments with my best friends. The one thing that has made all of this bearable. Then, there are the waking daydreams.

I'll close my eyes for a moment and get an onslaught of overwhelming feelings. Anger, sadness, longing, frustration, exhaustion, everything so intense yet seemingly without cause. Sometimes, I swear I can see them there, in the corner of the room, sitting at the table, even sitting beside me in bed. It's like they're here only when I reach out to where I can sense them, then I feel nothing and I'm alone again. The pain of knowing that it is all a hallucination is worse than not having them with me at all.

I have taken to torturing myself by talking to their phantoms, telling them stories about what I have been through since I was stolen away. In my weakest moments I beg them to save me, to give me even the tiniest flicker of magic so that this withdrawal might not kill me.

Not before I can say goodbye. I have to say goodbye. But then there are times where I consider it, just saying goodbye to these *images* and hoping that they understand, that they know I tried to hold on. It's just too much.

Sure, I haven't felt as sick the last few days, and maybe I haven't been deteriorating as fast as expected, but that ache inside me where my magic is supposed to be is still unbearable. And this momentary reprieve *is* going to end and I'll be back in that place, consumed by hunger and pain and wishing for a way out. I can still feel that something is missing, this hole left where that spark used to be and now it is hollow and cold, lifeless. It hurts and I don't want to feel it anymore.

The girls are what keeps me here. I have only the faintest hope that my plan might work, that it would give them enough time to find me, but I will hold onto it... for them. But something feels different now. When I woke this morning it felt like there were... threads, strings pulling me in all different directions from within.

Sitting up, I close my eyes and focus on one thread, following it as far as I can and letting it give me a sense of *something*. This thread feels very thin, like it is barely holding on from being stretched so far. I can feel the fibers beginning to pull away so I wrap my hand around it and smooth my hand down its length, pushing my energy in and asking for anything it will give me in return.

Waiting, I don't dare open my eyes or lose concentration, I give everything I can to whatever connection this is. Then, I see it, a barely there shadow of a mountain, the tall peaks no more than an outline on the horizon formed inside my mind.

I pull myself forward using the thread, a buzzing builds inside my mind growing louder and louder until it feels like my eardrums are going to burst. I release the thread and slam my hands over my ears to stop the noise, not realizing that in doing so I have broken the connection.

My eyes fly open, my heart racing.

"Fuck. What was that?" I ask myself aloud. Taking a few deep breaths I close my eyes again, searching for another thread and reaching out.

The next one is more relaxed, the thread hanging a bit like it has some slack to it. The fibers are stronger on this one, but still showing early signs of fraying. I follow the thread just like before, pulling myself further and further. The end is nothing more than a dark opening, nothing but a vast emptiness that seems to want to suck me in. Panic grips me and I quickly drop the thread, a bright flash of light chasing me.

I race to the bathing chamber, bending down over the toilet as the near empty contents of my stomach threaten to come up. Whatever that was, I did not like it. Not at all. It takes me a while before I feel calm enough to search again, to go back inside myself and see what the remaining threads have for me.

The third thread is barely a thread at all, more like a wisp, hard to grab onto and easy to lose. It takes a considerable amount of energy to follow this one. And at the end there is a dark, ominous room, the shrill sounds of screams echoing throughout. The worst part? I know those screams. It takes less than a millisecond before I release that thread, my heart racing as the screams slowly fade into the background.

I hesitate to reach for the next, but the moment I make that connection I feel an instant rush of relief. This thread is strong, thick like a rope, and very, very, short. It takes almost no energy to reach the end and when I do I gasp, tears springing to my eyes. Because there she is, riding atop the back of a dragon with the sun beating down on her. *Mar.*

The image is clear and vibrant, nothing like the others. She's coming, I know it, Mar is coming. My eyes remain closed, clinging to this perfect picture as hot tears splash against my cheeks. The sky is bright and blue around her, fluffy white clouds fill the air.

"Mar!" I cry out to her.

Her eyes remain closed.

"Mar!" I yell, screaming as loud as I can.

She doesn't react. Panic threatens to consume me again so I search deep inside myself, clawing at that well, desperate to find even a kernel of power. The image starts to fade and a sob bursts from my lips as I dig deeper and deeper. I wrap the thread around my forearm three times, anchoring myself. Something stirs inside me, a burning feeling rising in my gut along with hope.

I latch onto that feeling, watching my sister with ferocious determination, a feral scream rises in my throat as something cracks inside me. An explosion of power forces its way out of me and rips me away from Mar.

"No!" I bellow into nothingness as I am thrown backwards in reality. I slam into the wall, my head cracking against the concrete. I bring my hand up to the back of my head, feeling hot liquid beneath my fingertips. "Fuck."

My hand comes away wet, covered in sticky blood, the deep crimson color makes my stomach roll and then I begin throwing up. I collapse against the floor, writhing in pain and groaning at every small movement. It feels like a million tiny blades are being sliced into my skin while something tries to claw its way out from inside my stomach. I *really* hope nothing claws out of my stomach.

"What the-" someone says above me.

I force my eyes open, not even realizing they were shut, and find the tall muscular guy with the mustache. He runs a troubled hand over his bald head and curses, bending down beside me. He lays a heavy hand against my head and warm healing magic washes over me, soothing the pain in my skull. Yet somehow it does nothing for the rest of me.

Clutching my stomach I try to crawl away from him, tears falling freely over my cheeks as the worst pain I have felt in my entire life takes over.

Fuck.

What in Vana's name is happening to me?

"What hurts?" the male asks, thin eyebrows raised.

I clutch my stomach tighter, unable to formulate words.

"Stomach? Okay. Let me see," he says, reaching forward.

Shaking my head back and forth I continue to crawl backwards. "Stay away," I gasp.

"You clearly need help. Don't be stubborn," he says with a pointed look. His hand comes up between us and wisps of magic seep from his fingertips.

My vision goes black and I feel his arms come up around me. My mouth drops open on a scream that never seems to make it past my chest. I am jostled around as he starts to move, my protests dying on my lips and becoming nothing more than pathetic whimpers.

What the fuck is happening right now?

Time moves slowly as I remain in this black void, half in reality, half in my mind. I reach out for the threads again, but they're gone, filling me with disappointment. There is something about them, something important. If that last thread led to Mar then does that mean the other girls each have their own thread? I have to believe it does, even if the fear that they *don't* is crippling.

Sleep tugs at me as my body feels absolutely drained, more than it has felt in any of the days prior, but I welcome it. These threads mean something, it gives me the hope that I need again. I know now that I'm not alone, my sisters are with me even if not physically. And something about it, the way those threads feel, it's like something is changing. Somehow I know they're coming for me. However that might look, they're going to bring me back to them.

For now, that means I need to hold on. I need to keep my strength. I need to fight back and keep trying to make my shitty plan work. Right now, this is about trust. Trust in myself and trust in the people I love most in the world. I know that they will never let me down, that they will *always* come through in the end. I just have to give them time.

So for now, I let go of everything, relishing in the feeling of warmth and comfort that washes over me. A small part of me realizes just before I sleep, I don't feel so cold anymore.

Chapter 25

Terran

S hit.

Shit. Shit. Shit. Shit. Shit.

What. Am. I. Doing.

The door clicks shut behind Cay and I immediately regret the last 10 minutes of my life. Cay came to me, scared and desperate for a bit of comfort and what did I do? I took advantage of her. Again!

If somebody treated Rose like this I would never let them live and here I am, treating her *best friend* like-

"Shit."

Rose is going to kill me. What is it about Cay that has me constantly throwing aside thought and reason? This isn't normal. Something is definitely wrong with me. I can't be trusted around her, absolutely not. Tonight proved that well and true.

This mission is dangerous in too many ways already, let alone allowing myself to become distracted and jeopardizing Cay's safety. No. I need to fix

this. I quickly get dressed in presentable clothes and go to the one person I know who might be able to fix the mess that I got us into.

~~~

"Are you insane?" my brother screams in my face, his hands balled into fists at his side. A powerful wave of magic pulses from him and has my own writhing beneath my skin.

"Please, Oliver, I wouldn't ask you for help if it wasn't important," I beg. Telling Oliver about our plan is a huge risk, but given what he did when Rayan was first under attack, I have to believe that he will be on our side. Especially given his history with Cay's mother, Queen Mira. Though his initial reaction is not quite what I was expecting.

"Absolutely not. Call it off," he demands, "now." He stares me down from across the room, his rage palpable in the air. Finding him in the training rooms was hardly difficult but perhaps it would have been smarter to let him get his rage out *before* telling him about our impending mission.

"Why? You and I both know that this is likely the only way to save Cay's mother." If this was a mistake, if Oliver tells someone and I just ruined Cay's chance of getting her only living parent back, I'll never forgive myself.

"That doesn't matter. It's too dangerous, send someone else," he says, shaking his head vehemently.

I cross the room, coming within just a few feet of him before his power seems to stop me. "Oliver, I can take care of myself. I'll be fine," I say placatingly.

He scoffs, looking me over from head to toe with considerable disdain. "It's not your safety I'm worried about, brother. Or did you forget that this little plan of yours included a completely untrained princess, whose emotional state alone should be reason enough to keep her as far away from this as possible."

"Cay isn't completely untrained and you know that. She held her own back in Rayan and I will be with her the entire time to protect her. Besides that, you don't know what her emotional state is like. She is ready for this. She can handle it," I say adamantly.

"You weren't there. You don't get to tell me about what happened in Rayan. I saw it. I saw her fracture and break and become a shell of who she used to be. You might not notice the difference, but I do. I can see it written all over her," he says, walking closer to me with long, deliberate steps. He stops just before me, standing chest to chest and staring deep into my eyes, a mirror of his own. "And another thing."

"What?" I ask cautiously.

"I don't trust you with her."

There it is. My biggest fear. That someone else would see me for the failure that I am. Not as the future high lord, but as a male of honor. I can't even fight him on it because I don't trust *myself*. Which is why, despite my better judgment, the next words leave me without hesitation.

"So come with us then."

Oliver takes a step back, his face contorting into one of bewilderment. "I'm sorry, what?"

"Come with us. If you truly do not trust me to keep her safe then join us and *help me* do it."

He shakes his head. "You can't be serious."

"Oliver, why do you think I told you about this in the first place?"

He throws his hands up, starting to pace around the room, "I don't know! Fuck, I thought you were just having second thoughts and wanted someone to talk you out of it."

"And you thought I would come to you for that?"

"I never said you were smart," he glares at me.

I sigh, trying to figure out the best way forward. I need Oliver to make this work. "Listen, you're a skilled fighter, you know Rayan, and you're the only person I can trust to help me with this. Please."

Oliver tilts his head back, staring up at the ceiling silently. "Fuck," he says, seeming to have made up his mind.

"You'll help?" Hope sparks inside me. With Oliver's help we can absolutely do this, there is no doubt in my mind.

"Yes," he groans, "but to be clear I'm not doing it for you."

I pause. "Then who are you doing it for, brother?"

"Cay's already been through a lot. She doesn't need you fucking this up and making things worse for her," he bites, refusing to meet my eyes.

"I had no idea that you cared so much about her," I say genuinely surprised. I know that he went to Rayan during the attack-and of course there was whatever was going on when they got back-but, generally speaking, I've never seen the two of them have a single pleasant interaction.

"Don't think too much into it." He walks to the far end of the training room. There is a strange sort of energy in the room that has me feeling on edge, it seems to follow him as he moves about the room. "Are we done?" he asks, picking up a small bag and quickly pulling it closed before walking back towards the door.

I step in front of him as he moves to walk past me. "That depends, are you actually going to do this? Help us?"

He smirks at me, brows raised. "Did you forget, brother, who it was who helped the last time Cay needed it?" He pushes past me, shoving his shoulder into mine.

I curl my hands into fists, the truth of his words filling me with rage. Oliver and I agree on very little lately, but it appears that when it comes to two things, we are on the same page. The first, my many failures as a brother and leader. The second, matters that concern Cay and her safety.

~~~

The next morning I go straight to Cay's room, nodding to the guards as I walk through the halls. They smile at me and wish me luck on my travels. I told my mother that I was going to travel through the kingdom, replenishing the magic as a precaution. Usually I would wait longer between doing so, but given everything happening and how paranoid she has been, she didn't question it at all.

I chose a handful of trusted guards who will travel north, drawing attention away from us as we head to our real destination. The plan was simple enough and with Lieutenant Auger's help, no one will notice Cay's absence. I've ensured that a team is guarding Finn at all times to guarantee his safety, and Flora will watch over the queen.

Standing in front of Cay's door, I take deep breaths and clear my mind. There is only one thing left to do before we leave and I fear this might be the most challenging part of the plan. Knocking twice in quick succession, the door is pulled open almost immediately.

"Terran," Cay gasps, surprised to see me.

"I'm sorry. I know the original plan was to meet in the library, but there is something I need to discuss with you before we leave," I say quickly.

"Okay," she says, pulling the door open wider and gesturing for me to step inside.

"Thank you." I follow her direction, but stay close to the doorway, refusing to allow my eyes to wander and see what Cay's room here looks like. *Is it at all similar to the one in Rayan that is seared into my brain?*

"So, is everything alright?" she shifts from one foot to the other and bites her lip.

I swallow hard, suddenly only able to think about the feeling of her lips brushing mine just a few hours ago. When I don't answer immediately she steps forward, concern written across her face. I clear my throat. "Yes, I'm sorry, I didn't mean to scare you."

"Good," she says with a sigh of relief, "so what brings you here then? We still have another hour before we plan on meeting." Her eyes drop to my lips and her cheeks flush.

"Yes… you see-I-there-," I stumble, "there has been a slight change in the original plan." Only she has the power over me to make speech nearly impossible.

"Oh?"

"I thought about your concerns and realized that perhaps we needed some additional assistance."

Her brows pull together. "Assistance? What kind of assistance?"

"I have asked my brother to join us," I explain, forcing the words from my mouth.

We stand in silence, Cay's mouth hanging slightly ajar as she processes what I said. "Did you-did you just say that you asked *Oliver* to help us?"

"Yes."

"Oliver? Like, your brother, Oliver?"

"Yes."

"Why would you do that?"

"I believe that it is the best option. We could use the extra help and he is trustworthy. We can depend on him."

"I thought you said that this plan was good? That everything will be fine?" I can hear the worry rising in her voice.

"I did, and I still believe that," I say, taking a step towards her. "But I won't take any chances when it comes to your safety."

She considers me for a moment, her hair tied back from her face, accentuating her eyes. I get lost in them, their sea-green depths calling to me and ensnaring me in their grip. She is so beautiful. Effortlessly. Her eyes, her lips, her cheeks, even her forehead. It's times like these, when I get completely lost in her, that I think maybe I don't want to be honorable, maybe I want to ruin her.

"Terran?"

The sound of my name on her lips breaks the trance and I force myself to take a step away from her, slowly backing up to the door. "Cay?"

"Are you sure that this is the best plan?"

"Of course, I would never do anything that would put you in harm's way if I can avoid it," I answer.

"Okay. I believe you. So, what's next?"

"Next, we follow the plan as discussed. I have to make a few more rounds, show my face, be seen talking to my guards. And when the time comes, we'll meet in the library, same place as always."

"Okay," she breathes, her shoulders seeming to droop as some of the tension dissipates.

"I'll see you in an hour," I confirm, heading out to do exactly as I told her.

Chapter 26

Rose

After hours of walking through the forest, jumping at every snapping branch and rustle of leaves, I am officially on edge. Not to mention Mateo's constant talking. That went from cute to infuriating in a mere half hour, making things even worse. Now, all I can think about is how this must be a sign I should have gone with Cay.

We're already halfway to Eteri, which according to Mateo is great and means we're making excellent time. Reed and I on the other hand can only see the harsh truth of the matter... we have a whole lot more walking-and Mateo- to go.

"Maybe we can use an incantation that will seal his mouth shut?" Reed mumbles beside me.

I choke on my laugh, earning myself a suspicious glance from Mateo. "I'm not sure even that would stop him," I whisper back.

Reed smiles at me, looping his arm through mine and tugging me close to his side. "Rose, is it just me or do you feel..."

"Like someone is watching us?" I finish for him. He nods and I feel a heavy weight drop into the pit of my stomach.

There has been, and still is, this sort of lurking presence all around us, like the trees have eyes or something. I can't help but fear that my mother knows we are gone and has sent someone after us. If she drags us back to the castle, we'll never get answers about the Ghosts, and who knows how long it will be before we see Oak again.

"What should we do? Should we say something?" Reed asks, looking ahead to Mateo and his second in command, Gael.

Mateo fully believes that everything is going exactly as planned, that nothing could go wrong, and something about that just feels too good to be true. Yet somehow we haven't had even the slightest bit of trouble since we left the castle.

"Not yet. We're probably just stressed and overthinking things. We should just distract ourselves, focus on something else."

Reed runs a hand over his unruly curls, flattening them to his head. He stares after Mateo, watching as he walks with his packmate and laughs over something he says. Mateo's hand lands on Gael's shoulder and I feel Reed stiffen beside me.

"Did something happen between you two?" I ask, flicking my eyes towards Mateo.

Reed trips over his own feet, almost falling face first into the dirt, saved only by our interlocked arms. "What?" he asks shakily.

I squeeze him tighter to my side, whispering in his ear, "Is something going on with Mateo?"

"Why would you ask that?"

"There's tension," I shrug.

"There is *not* tension," Reed counters.

"Reed," I pull him to a stop and grab him by the shoulders so he is forced to look into my eyes, "it's me, come on."

He glares at me until finally cracking. He heaves a sigh and we start walking together again. "It happened on your birthday."

"My birthday?"

"Yeah… honestly it was all Evie's idea, so I'm sure you know how that went."

"Yeah, I understand," I smile to myself while my heart squeezes, "but what *exactly* happened?"

"I promise nothing as interesting as you're thinking. We talked for a while, danced a few songs, then people started to run around like crazy and panic because…"

Rayan.

Sometimes it's easy to forget that what happened was only a few months ago and not years. So much has changed in such a short time that I'm not sure I can even see myself as the same girl who entered that party.

Some moments in life change us for the better, some for the worse, and others change us in ways that make our lives difficult to recognize. I wish I could go back and tell myself to hug them all a little tighter. To stay in the garden and listen to more stories of the chaos Eve and Mar had been up to. Now, it feels like I lost that part of me.

"I know. The attack."

Reed nods. "He- he kissed me."

I turn to him with a knowing smile and he rolls his eyes. Laughing to myself I lean into him, resting my cheek against his shoulder. *Since when is Reed so tall?*

"It wasn't anything crazy. Just a peck honestly. Still, he told me he would find me and then he ran off. That time he found us at the wisteria tree was the first time I had seen him since that night," Reed sighs.

"Did you ever look for him?" I ask out of curiosity.

"No. But what was I supposed to do? We shared a few dances and a peck on the lips. I didn't want to seem too…"

"Clingy?" I offer him.

"Yes," he groans.

"Well maybe he has been looking for you all this time. Maybe him finding *us* in the woods was really him finding *you*."

Reed glares at me. "Not likely. Mateo is an alpha, he has a pack and plenty of friends. He doesn't need me."

I return his glare. "Reed. Honestly. I really don't think friendship is what he has in mind," I nod towards Mateo where he keeps looking back over his shoulder, his eyes locked onto Reed's. He's been doing that for the last five minutes without Reed even noticing. I wouldn't be surprised if he has been listening in on our conversation, not that I'll ever tell my cousin that.

"Why did we ever agree to let him help us," Reed groans, slapping both of his hands over his face and making me laugh.

"Do you want to know something that is sure to make you feel better," my heart begins to pound.

"What?" he asks from behind his hands.

"I've never..."

"Never?" Reed pushes.

"Never been with anyone," I rush out.

"Seriously?"

"Yes."

"At all or just..."This was a horrible decision. "At all."

Reed is struck silent for so long that I worry something is truly wrong with him. I slap his arm and he holds his hands up placatingly. "Sorry, I'm just surprised that's all."

"Why are you so surprised?"

He shrugs, "I just assumed. I mean, Rose, you are four years older than me."

"I guess..."

"I'm not saying there is anything wrong with it but-"

"Get down!"

Reed and I are thrown to the ground beneath two large bodies. I push my hair out of my face and look up to find Mateo pressing my cousin into the ground while Gael is doing the same to me. A burst of energy lingers in the air above us.

"What the-"

"Move!" Mateo yells, shoving Reed to his feet and pushing him forward.

Making it to my own feet I watch as the world around us descends into chaos. Mateo's pack has formed a ring around us in their wolf forms. They're huge-even on all fours, they still tower above us. With their wide shoulders and bared teeth, they look positively terrifying. Mateo and Gael are the only ones who haven't shifted.

The sound of a twig snapping in the woods draws our attention. Emerging from behind a cluster of trees is another large wolf, his coat is the color of ash, the hair long and matted. The wolf prowls forward, his paws nearly the size of my face.

"What is going on?" I ask under my breath to no one in particular.

"It seems that we may have wandered into another wolf's territory, and he doesn't seem too happy with my being here," Mateo answers, still clutching onto Reed's arm.

Something whizzes by my ear and I follow the sound in time to see Mateo yank Reed out of the direct path of an arrow. The deadly point gets stuck in a tree a few feet behind them. If that had hit Reed...

"Time to go," Mateo says, turning Reed around by his shoulders and shoving him forward.

Without a moment of thought I reach out and take Reed's hand, racing alongside him as we zigzag through trees. Mateo and Gael are hot on our heels, watching our back and barking out orders as arrows continue to whiz past us. The sounds of snarls and gnashing teeth grow distant as we run farther away from the rest of Mateo's pack.

Reed tugs me to the side as an arrow passes just beside my head, nicking the pointed tip of my ear and drawing blood. I curse at the slice of pain and send a burst of magic shooting behind us, being careful not to hit Mateo and Gael.

Two large wolves jump out between trees just in front of us and I am forced to stop, yanking Reed to my side. More wolves appear and we find ourselves surrounded, their deep growls vibrate through their chests and into the ground. Magic stirs inside me, called to the surface by the imminent attack and ready to defend me.

Mateo and Gael crowd into Reed and I, forcing us between them and forming a sort of barrier. One look between my cousin and I and we are pushing forward, standing with them side by side.

Mateo looks at us out of the corner of his eye. "Guess we're doing this then."

Magic erupts from the earth.

Chapter 27

Mar

"No," Nat says, backing away from the counter. She turns on her heels and walks straight through the curtain without another word.

Chasing after her, I round the counter finding myself staring at a broad, male chest.

"Sorry. Little sisters, you know?" Cyrus says with a shrug, as if that explains everything.

I shove past him, half expecting him to hold me back, but he doesn't. "Nat, just hear me out," I say, pushing the curtain aside. Behind it is a narrow hallway lit by burning torches on the wall. I walk through the hall with newfound purpose, my steps determined.

The hallway opens up into a small seating area, a two seater couch and one large chair fill the space, a small table sat at the center.

Nat is curled up in the chair, head buried in her knees where they are pulled to her chest with her hair curtaining her face. "I can't help you."

I cross the room in three short strides, squatting down in front of her. "Yes, you can. Eve is counting on us."

She whips her head back sending her hair flying everywhere. "Well then she is going to die."

My heart stops beating.

"If Eve is counting on me then she is going to be disappointed," Nat continues, "I can't be her savior. Not when I'm her ruin." Her words are firm and catch me off guard.

Rising to my feet I throw my hands out wide. "Why not? Explain it to me."

"Haven't I done enough already? I already failed her once. I won't do it again." She looks away from me.

"Exactly!" I cry out, "This is your chance to make things right. Help me find her. Help me bring her home."

Nat shakes her head. "The answer is no. You wasted your time coming here." She continues looking anywhere other than at me.

I stare at her, unable to process what is happening right now. I was so sure that she would help, that we would be leaving here and racing off after Eve. *How stupid was I to think I could rely on anyone but myself?*

"I'm sorry, Mar. Please leave." Nat stands, walking past me and back down the hall.

I take her place in the chair, leaning back and closing my eyes.

"You okay?" a deep voice asks.

Cracking my eyes, I find Cyrus standing in the archway, leaning against the wall with his brows raised. "Yup," I say, popping the 'p'. It's a habit I picked up from Eve.

"You sure?" he asks, walking forward and perching upon the arm of the couch.

"Yeah, I'll survive." *Eve might not though.*

"There's a guard looking for you, looks like a real asshole. Actually, I know he is. I would love to beat his ass if you give me a reason."

I can't help the smile that lifts my lips. "No, that's okay. I can take care of him."

"I really wouldn't mind. Besides, he probably deserves it," he says with a sideways smile.

"You're not wrong," I say with a laugh, pushing to my feet.

"So, what will you do now?" he asks, watching as I head back down the hall.

"I'll be back. She'll change her mind," I call over my shoulder, passing through the curtain and finding a furious looking Rian standing there waiting for me.

"Do not *ever* do that again," he growls, jaw clenched.

"Let's go," I say, walking straight for the door.

He catches up and stops me with a hand on my shoulder. "Go where, exactly?"

"We're going to get Eve back. I'm not going to just sit around and wait anymore. While we're all finding excuses to do nothing, my *sister* is probably being tortured right now, or worse." I don't care who agrees anymore. I won't let Eve rot in some cell while pretending everything is perfectly fine. I can't.

"I understand how you're feeling, but this isn't the time to rush into something. We need a clear plan and as much as you would like to think otherwise, you need help. You can't do this alone."

"Maybe not, but I haven't been given much of a choice," I say, jerking out of his grip and pushing the door open. I have no idea where I am going, but as I walk through the village I realize it looks somewhat familiar. I turn a corner on instinct and a few houses down is a bakery, exactly like I thought there would be.

I don't take much time to consider it before I turn back and find Rian. He is talking to one of the other guards, probably telling him to prepare us for a trip back home. He'll be quite upset when he realizes I have zero intention of returning home without my sister.

"Rian, we're leaving."

"Mar," he sighs, "I told you we can't-"

"We're going to visit my brothers. Their village isn't far from here and I want to see them." My heart swells as I fight to contain a smile.

"What? Your brothers?" Rian asks, completely lost. For someone so smart, he seems awfully slow to follow.

"Yes. I have three of them and I want to see them, so let's go," I say, gesturing back towards the direction of the rest of our travel party.

"I don't understand. You're giving up?" he asks, his hand half suspended between us, like he wanted to reach out, but thought better of it.

"Of course not." I just need a reminder of why I *can't* give up.

~~~

As we land outside of my brothers' home, a sense of rightness washes over me. Their comfortable three-room house sits in the middle of a large stretch of field. Their father's horses roam, grazing on the grass and enjoying the cooler weather. The front door is thrown open and two small boys come racing across the land, screaming unintelligibly.

I crouch down, resting one knee in the damp grass and bracing myself as the twins tackle me to the ground, forcing me beneath them both. Their arms are wrapped around me in a vice grip as they burrow their heads into my neck.

"Hey guys, I missed you too," I laugh, pressing a hand into their matching sets of blonde waves.

Flint sits back first, staring down at me with his vibrant blue eyes. "You're here!" he bellows.

Hagan crawls off of me, dragging his twin with him. "Get off! You're going to crush her!"

"You crushed her first," Flint replies, sticking his tongue out.

Hagan launches himself at his twin and the two roll around on the ground, trying to get the upper hand.

"Hey, you two, knock it off. Where's Kee?" I ask. The twins are only six, but our other brother, Keegan, is 16. Which means he is old enough to be helpful, but young enough to still be a massive pain in my ass.

"He was in the back playing with his fire," Flint explains, bouncing up and down excitedly.

"What about you boys? Have you been practicing?" I ask, holding out a hand and letting a small flame dance in my palm.

They shake their heads and then their eyes go wide on something behind me.

Looking over my shoulder I watch as Rian walks up slowly, his entire body stiff and awkward. "Boys, this is Rian, he's a guard in the Tower."

Rian crouches down beside me and opens his own palm, a column of flame shoots up into the air and explodes in the sky. The sound of the explosion makes the twins burst into tears and run screaming back towards the house.

I raise my brows at Rian who has gone ghostly pale, his face is a mixture of horror and shame. "Are you alright?"

"I-I didn't mean to make them cry," he stutters.

"Guess you fucked up then," I say with a shrug, heading towards the back of the house. Honestly, I hadn't expected Rian to be good with children. I mean… he doesn't exactly scream *fun* and *loving*. Still, making the twins cry within 20 seconds of laying eyes on each other? That's a new record.

As I come around the corner I spy Keegan trying to summon a wall of fire. He holds his palms facing the ground and brings them up slowly, a line of flames slowly rising. The flames are nothing but a light red as they flicker before going out. Keegan curses and wipes a hand across his forehead before starting the process over again.

Wordlessly I come up behind him, careful not to make a sound. As he goes through the motion again, I mimic him, replacing his weak flame with one of my own and creating a wall twice as tall as him.

"What the-" he exclaims, falling backwards onto his elbows. He stares at the flames with wide eyes as they don't go out. Realizing that something is different about the flames, he tilts his head back and locks eyes with me. "Mar?"

"Thought you needed a little help," I say with a shrug as he scrambles to his feet and throws his arms around me.

It's been a few months now since the last time I saw my brothers, I've been too focused on Eve to visit, but this time feels different, more important. The people in our lives who mean the most to us are often the ones we take for granted the most. It's not until they're gone that we realize how much we need them.

I've never thought about a life without Eve in it because it felt so impossible, but now that I'm living through it, I wish I had held on a little tighter the last time I hugged her.

Keegan moves to pull back, but I clutch him to me a little tighter, resting my chin on his shoulder and breathing him in. "Not yet," I mumble.

Instead of questioning me, Keegan pulls me closer, wrapping his arms around me fully and letting me have this moment with him. Keegan and I have a special relationship, he was only 10 when our mother died and I was the same age he is now. I watched him go from an innocent kid to this almost adult that he is now. It still amazes me how much he has grown, physically and emotionally.

This time when Keegan pulls away, I let him go. "You're late," he whispers, his voice slightly deeper than I remember.

"I'm sorry, I got caught up in some things at the castle. I couldn't get away," I explain, the lies burning my throat. I wish I could tell him the truth, even knowing it would hurt him. He loves Eve and Elani as much as I do. Despite how complicated other people might think our family is, we love each other the same as any other family would.

"Is everything alright?" he asks, his eyes flicking to where I know Rian is standing off to the side.

"Yeah, don't worry. I'm just happy I get to see you and the twins." I pull him back to me, unable to help it. I only let go when I feel another presence join us.

Rian steps up to my brother, reaching out a hand and giving him a tight smile, "nice to meet you, I'm Rian. I'm one of the-"

"Why is *he* here?" Keegan seethes, unusually brash.

"Keegan," I bark, "don't be rude."

"I'm here to guard your sister, to keep her safe," Rian answers, puffing out his chest.

"Sure," Keegan says with a derisive snort.

"What is the matter with you? Why are you acting like this?" I ask, astonished by these outbursts. Keegan has always been polite... at least to strangers. This new attitude is one that I am completely unfamiliar with and certainly not a fan of. Though it does have a bit of an appeal when directed at Rian.

"It's fine, Mar, don't worry about him," Rian says with a tight smile.

"Princess," Keegan says, crossing his arms across his chest and pinning Rian with a harsh glare.

"I'm sorry?" Rian looks between us, confused.

"If you're a guard then you should be addressing my sister appropriately. After all, she is our princess." Keegan raises his brows expectantly.

"Keegan you know that I-"

"No, that's alright. Your brother has a point. My apologies," Rian says with a bow of his head. "If you'll excuse me, I am going to circle the perimeter and make sure everything is secure."

"You do that," Keegan says with a mocking smile.

The moment Rian is out of earshot I whirl on my brother. "What was that?"

"What do you mean?"

"That behavior that's what. I've never heard you be so rude before."

"Well, why is he here?" my brother glowers.

"You heard him, he is here to do his job. To keep me safe."

He rolls his eyes. "You've never needed a guard to keep you safe before. So why now? What's going on that you're not telling me?"

I heave a sigh. "Nothing is going on, I swear."

"Liar." Keegan stares me down.

"Keegan-"

"No. You're just going to tell more lies. I'm going to hang out with my friends," he says, stomping off into the woods without another word.

I groan, looking back towards the house and already regretting my decision to stay the night. Taking a few deep breaths I try to focus on the reason we're here. I need to spend time with my brothers before rushing off to save my sister and possibly getting myself killed.

This could very easily be the last time they see me and I intend to make it a happy memory. For all of us.

Chapter 28

Rian

O f all the enemies I have made in life, the most surprising are the two children sitting in front of me. Mar's younger brothers haven't stopped glaring at me since we sat down for dinner. I tried to explain to them that I would just eat with the other guards in the village, but the boys' father insisted.

I set down my knife and fork, placing my napkin atop my empty plate and clearing my throat. "Thank you for the meal, it was delicious."

The boys' father, Theo, throws his head back with a laugh, smiling behind his thick beard. "No need for all that. It's nothing fancy."

Theo is a large man with an even bigger personality. He is well above six feet tall and absolutely covered in muscles from working in the fields. He has the same blue eyes as all three of his sons, but where they all share blonde waves, his head is left bald. It's as though all of the hair on the top of his head migrated down to his chin.

Despite his generally intimidating appearance, he seems genuinely kind and welcoming...unlike his children. Flint and Hagan, the twins, look a mixture of horrified and disgusted by my presence. Meanwhile their older brother, Keegan, barely contains his hatred behind a scowl. I'm not sure what I did to earn this distrust, but Mar seems perfectly content to let me suffer under their harsh stares.

Once we all finish eating, I help Theo clear and wash the plates so that Mar can spend time with her siblings. When she told me this is where she wanted to go, I thought for sure it was some kind of trick. It is clear in the way she looks at her brothers that she is here for nothing more than to be with them.

The night is cut short when Theo herds the twins up to bed, leaving Keegan and Mar alone to talk. I listen from the other side of the wall as they whisper back and forth. Despite their age gap, the two of them seem close. Something that I envy. Growing up an only child is not so uncommon, though families like Mar's are becoming normal with each new generation, still, a part of me will always be envious of those with siblings. There is no bond quite like it.

When I first met Cryus he wouldn't shut up about his *adorable little sister*. Then there is Mar and Eve who, if not for their devotion to one another, might have been enough to shatter that fantasy. But this, looking at Mar with her brothers, this is what I envy. I peek around the corner and watch as they hug each other goodnight and Keegan heads up the stairs.

"Vana, I am exhausted," Mar sighs as she enters the kitchen. She walks straight to the wall of cabinets and pulls the highest one open, rummaging around before pulling out a glass bottle.

Dark liquid sloshes around inside, piquing my interest. "What's in the bottle?"

Mar pops open the top, swirling the liquid inside so that the heady aroma wafts through the room. "Theo's secret stash." She brings the bottle to her lips, tossing her head back and taking a large gulp. Her eyes squeeze tightly together as she extends the bottle towards me.

I bring the bottle to my lips, taking a large swig of it myself and immediately regretting that decision. I shove the bottle back into Mar's hands as I clamp my lips closed.

"Theo will murder you if you spit that out," Mar says through gritted teeth.

I force the liquid down, the alcohol burning my throat while my taste buds threaten to shrivel up and die on my tongue. I rush to the sink, bending forward and sticking my head under the faucet. Swallowing mouthful after mouthful of water does nothing to get rid of the repulsive taste.

"Someone's dramatic," Mar snorts, taking yet another drink as I watch on in horror. She sets the bottle down on the counter, hopping up so she is seated next to it.

Standing, I turn the water off and wipe a hand against my dripping lips. "What the fuck is that?"

"It's mead made by one of the locals."

Shaking my head I fight back the urge to gag. "How can you drink that stuff?"

She shrugs, "You get used to it I guess."

"Get used to it? By what, burning all your taste buds off?"

"It's really not that bad," she rolls her eyes.

I look her over, taking in how comfortable she looks here. I glance towards the doorway and let my eye trail over the small notches dug into the wood. I found them earlier while Mar was busy with her siblings and Theo was off looking for some kind of sword he wanted to show me.

"You seem different here."

She smiles, looking down the hall where her siblings sleep soundly. "It's my home."

"Here? Not the Tower or Izal?"

"I may live in the Tower now, but this is the home that I grew up in, where I spent the first 16 years of my life. It's where I was born," she says with a sigh.

"What made you leave?" I ask, leaning back against the counter beside her.

"My mother died."

My chest constricts painfully. "I'm sorry. How did she pass?"

She is silent for a while and I'm about to apologize again for overstepping, but she surprises me. She leans back, resting her head against a cabinet and looking at me out of the corner of her eyes. "She died giving birth to the twins."

I can't help but glance down the hall to where I know the boys are hidden away. Mar looks at the two of them with such love and adoration, even though they're the reason she no longer has a mother.

"I know what you're thinking," she says, drawing my eyes back to her, "I don't blame them." She stares at her palms, closing and opening them as I wait for her to continue. "It was no one's fault. My mother was perfectly healthy, but something went wrong during the birth and there was just too much blood. No matter how hard we tried, Theo and I couldn't do anything to help her."

"You were there."

She nods. "But no matter how painful that was, I would never blame my brothers for losing her. She loved them so much, even before they were born. If anything, I feel bad that they never got to know her the way Keegan and I did."

The buzz of insects outside the window mixed with the soft glow of the moonlight create this sort of loud silence. The air feels too thick to breathe. Words too jarring for this temporary world within this room. After what feels like an eternity, Mar hops down from the counter. She stops in the doorway and looks down at the carved divots.

"We should head back to Nat's village in the morning," she says without looking back at me or waiting for my answer. I watch as she makes her way back to the seating area.

I turn around and look out the window at the large open field, far off in the distance is the treeline. A blur of movement catches my eyes, a blip of color among the dark shadows where the trees end. Silently, I open the window and creep through, trying not to draw any attention. I make it across the field in a matter of seconds and in time to see a tall, blonde boy walking into the woods. As he cautiously looks over his shoulder, I am surprised to see it is Mar's brother, Keegan.

I consider going back to the house and telling Mar or maybe even Theo, but as the sound of other voices echoes through the woods, I know I can't do that. Muttering under my breath, I use a concealment spell to hide my presence and keep my steps silent as I follow Keegan through the woods. The voices grow louder the deeper we go until I stop, watching as Keegan approaches a circle of other kids, two at the center with fists raised.

The two boys summon their fire, their fists becoming engulfed in wild, uncontrolled flames. Those around them cheer and cry out words of encouragement, pushing them to use more magic, to make the flames bigger. Sparks fly out around them, catching the dry leaves on the forest floor and creating a bright orange glow.

I watch as the two start to throw punches. Their form is awful and, as one swings a punch towards the other's face, the other fails to block the hit, hissing out in pain. The injured boy clutches his face while another performs some subpar healing magic. I march forward just as Keegan steps into the circle, holding his hands out like he was when Mar found him practicing earlier.

"Enough," I command, walking straight over to the injured boy and quickly healing his face before it can scar.

"Who are you?" a boy says, puffing out his chest as his hands ball into fists.

"What are you doing here?" Keegan hisses.

"You know this guy?" another asks.

"Sort of," Keegan answers, glaring at me.

"Let's go. We're leaving," I say, grabbing Keegan's arm and dragging him behind me.

"No," he says, yanking his arm from my grip.

I whirl on him, "Do you have any idea how dangerous this is?"

"We're being safe," he yells.

"Tell that to your friend's face," I point at the kid who was a minute away from being permanently scarred.

"He was fine, we were healing him. What are you even doing out here anyways? Did you follow me?" he asks incredulously. "That doesn't matter. We're going back to the house, now," I reach for him again, but he jumps backwards out of my reach.

"Why the fuck should I listen to you? I don't even know you. You're just some guy who thinks he's something special because he was sent to watch my sister. Well guess what, she doesn't need your protection. If anyone should leave, it should be you."

"Keegan," I growl.

"What's his deal?" one of the boys asks.

"I don't know, but let's just go," the one I healed answers, pushing his buddies towards the forest edge.

The lot of them take off running, leaving me alone with Mar's brother. Keegan doesn't even give his friends a second glance as they run from us. I stare down at him, waiting for him to say something, but I'm unsurprised when he marches through the woods without muttering a word. He is, after all, so much like his sister.

We make it back to the house quickly, the door slamming shut between us.

Mar rises from her seat on the couch, looking between us in confusion. "What's going on? Where were you two?"

"I was hanging out with my friends when this oaf followed me and dragged me back here," Keegan seethes, conveniently leaving out the part about their little fight practice.

"What?" Mar says whirling on me, "You followed him? Keegan, go to your room."

"Yes, but-"

"Why in Vana's name are you following my brother?" she demands, as her brother makes his way back to his bedroom.

"I was just making sure he was safe."

"From what? He's 16! He might be a pain, but he's a good kid. He doesn't get into trouble. You had no right to follow him," she says, jabbing a finger into my chest.

"I understand but-"

"No. There are no excuses. If I ever find out you did something like this again, I'll have you removed from this mission," she promises, turning to follow her brother.

I suppose that could have gone better. Though I'm not sure it truly matters what happens between us. I can take her being mad at me. I can take her hatred.

What I can't take is her crying over her brother's body.

I can't take her being in more pain.

Not when I'm responsible for the pain she is already suffering.

I already failed one of her siblings, I have to protect the others no matter what. I can't make that same mistake again.

Chapter 29

Eve

"**W**hat're you thinking about?" Nat whispers, moving the tip of her finger around my navel.

I brush back her wild curls, tucking them behind her ears so I can see her clearly. She is so beautiful. Her blue eyes and splatter of freckles. Her skin is like silk beneath my hands and I can't seem to stop touching her. I cup her cheek, bending down to place a soft kiss against her full lips. "You."

She blushes, the tips of her cheeks staining a faint pink. She crawls up the length of my body, pressing her forehead against mine. "You're so different from what I expected," she breathes, her lips brushing against mine.

I pull back a bit, smiling up at her. "Oh? What does that mean?" I chuckle.

She shakes her head, falling to the side and pulling me with her so we are laying face to face, our legs tangled together. "I just... I thought you would be this spoiled princess, I never really thought you would look twice at someone like me."

I raise my brows. "Oh really? And what do you mean 'someone like you'?"

Nat sighs, her eyes dropping to my chest as she places a hand over my heart, "My family isn't exactly royalty. We own a very small herbal shop and my mother acts as a healer and apothecary."

"And your father is a retired guard," I add.

Her eyes jump to mine in surprise. "What?"

"You told me before," I smile at her as her eyes widen.

"You remember that?"

I place my hand over hers, "Of course I do."

Her smile falters. "He travels a lot now."

"Oh?" I trail my hands over the curve of her hips then up her back, following the path of her spine. "Is he a merchant?"

"Something like that." Her breath hitches as my hand moves over her shoulder and then dips to circle her hard nipple.

I pinch the pink bud between two fingers and she lets out a gasp before rolling back on top of me and pinning my hands over my head. I moisten my lips and she leans forward, capturing them between her teeth in a quick nip. "Enough about my family, I don't want to waste another second together."

"Tonight is just the beginning, Nat," I vow against her lips.

Blinking my eyes open, I find myself in another unfamiliar place, although this one is at least warm and dry. I look down and find soft blankets covering me where I rest in a comfortable bed, a stack of pillows keeps me propped up. I'm disoriented, part of me still mentally in that bed with Nat. The dream felt so real, and now, it's like my senses are all out of whack.

A dry, sandy feeling invades my mouth and coats my tongue, my throat burns. I look around the sparse room, searching for anything that will get rid of this awful *dead* feeling. Beside the bed is a wooden chair and a small bucket filled with what looks to be water, though the color is dark and uninviting. Across the room is a table with a tray set on top, a black pitcher next to a wooden box. I throw the covers back and find that I'm completely naked.

I take a moment to acknowledge the fact before the burning in my throat becomes a demand I can't ignore. My head swims as I stand, my legs nearly giving out on me the moment I attempt to put any weight on them. Stumbling to the table, I pick up the pitcher and find it filled with a dark swirling liquid, likely a potion of some kind. Tears sting the back of my eyes as disappointment sets in and I fight to ignore the pain as I swallow my nonexistent saliva.

Determined to find something helpful, I reach for the wooden box, it's old and has an iron lock on it that keeps me from opening the lid. I fight with the lock for a minute before exhaustion forces me to put it back down. Sighing, I walk back to the bed and have barely pulled the covers back over myself when a male appears at the foot of the bed.

"Oh, good, you're awake. I told him that I wouldn't let you die," the male smiles beneath his thin mustache. The scar carving its way down the center of his face seems even more jagged close up.

"Um… who are you?" I ask, pulling the covers up tighter around my chest.

"My name is Chien," he answers, walking over to the chair and taking a seat. He leans back and sets an ankle against his opposite knee, making himself comfortable.

"Right. Where am I?"

Chien crosses his arms over his broad chest, his biceps tensing as he looks me over.

Something about his gaze forces me to swallow, the sensation like trying to shove a wad of paper down my throat. I grimace at the pain and touch a hand to the side of my throat.

"Where does it hurt?" Chien asks, sitting forward as he watches my hand slowly lower back to my side.

"I'm fine, just a sore throat," I try to say it firmly, but it ends up coming out more of a cough.

"One second," he says, rising to his feet. Chien is tall even without any hair to add a few inches. Between his height and the well defined muscles poking out beneath his dark tunic, he has this intimidating aura around him, yet at the same time he has seemed pleasant enough in the few moments that we have interacted before this.

He carries the pitcher back to the bedside, with a snap of his fingers a glass appears in his empty hand. Without missing a beat, he pours the dark liquid and hands me the glass, nodding encouragingly. "Well go on, drink it."

I stare down at the glass, then back at him, then the glass again. *Does this guy seriously think I'm about to drink whatever mystery liquid this is?* I open my mouth to ask him exactly that precisely at the moment my throat feels like it has caught on fire. Without thinking I throw back the liquid and down it in one go, not even pausing to take a breath. Gasping, I throw the glass against the wall, staring at Chien in horror.

"Was throwing the glass really necessary? Honestly, what a waste," he tsks, sitting back down and shaking his head at me.

"What the fuck was that? What did you just give me?" I demand, swiping my forearm over my mouth like that might change something.

"Does it matter? You already drank it and it's not like that would be the first time." He shrugs, like it's the most casual thing in the world.

"Yes, it matters!" I exclaim.

"Well then, excuse me, I had no idea," Chien says, tilting his head down in a half bow. When our eyes meet I can do nothing to avoid his penetrating gaze. His lips curl into a half smile.

"Can you just tell me what the fuck that was? What if-what if I have an allergy or something?"

He stares at me with eyes that say *'really'* and even I have to acknowledge how slim of a chance that had of working.

Sighing, I sit up, fighting past the black dots that appear in my vision. "Look, I don't know what's going on, where I am, who you are, I'm just really confused here. Help a girl out?"

"You see, I'm already doing that. I've been helping you this whole time," he says conspiratorially.

I narrow my eyes at him. "What do you mean, *helping me*?"

Tension is thick in the air as he scooches the chair closer to me, leaning in and gesturing for me to do the same. Holding my breath, I lean close as he looks me in the eyes and laughs in my face. "Don't go getting flattered, I'm only doing it because it's my job. Though I have to admit, I am a big fan of your jokes. We'll have to compare sometime," he says with a wink.

My mouth drops open and as I'm about to reply another male appears at the foot of the bed.

Yuta.

"Well, good to see you awake, *Eve*. Nice of you to join us," Yuta says, bowing slightly at the waist. He's dressed in a pair of fitted gray pants and a deep plum shirt with long sleeves. The fabric looks soft and light, the way it shifts with the slightest movement makes me wonder if the dress I was sent before was made from something similar. He watches me with interest and a sly smile.

"Oh, fuck this. Where am I, *Your Majesty*?" I say, voice dripping with contempt. He doesn't get to just stand there and leave me in the dark.

"Chien, how is she doing?" He smiles at me, his honey eyes glowing.

Chien looks at me proudly before turning to his so-called *King*. "She's doing great. Though she does seem to still be in some discomfort."

Yuta takes a few steps towards me, he strides slow and deliberate as he leers over me. "Is that true? Are you in pain?" he asks, eyes sweeping over me from head to toe.

"Like you care?" I challenge. My throat decides that's the *perfect* moment to start lighting itself on fire again and I have to fist the sheets to keep from crying out in pain.

Of course, Yuta notices and quickly throws the blanket off of my very naked body, exposing me to him and Chien who curses and slaps his hands over his eyes. They're both silent for what feels like an eternity while my skin burns beneath Yuta's unwavering stare. His eyes are locked on my body, unblinking. Fuck, he might not even be breathing.

I've lost a lot of weight since being here. My ribcage is clearly visible, my hip bones are sticking out awkwardly, and my skin has taken on an odd sort of sheen to it. I look every bit the mess that I feel. My hair is matted at the nape of my neck and as I inhale, I can smell myself, which makes me sincerely wish I couldn't. It's really not my finest moment. Though I've done more with less.

"Are you done staring at me now?" I ask, trying to rip the blanket back from him.

"Leave," he growls at Chien who disappears in a cloud of smoke. Yuta slowly pulls the blanket back over me, letting his eyes trail over every inch as he works his way up my body.

"See something you like?" I spit. Though if he did that would work in my favor. Stark realization sets in as my plan reveals itself. This is the first moment, and I have to do whatever it takes to make sure things go right from here on out.

"He said you were in pain, where?" he asks, voice gruff.

I shake my head with a mirthless laugh. "Would you like a list?"

Yuta's jaw ticks, his eyes swirling as power swells in the room. He reaches for the hem of the blanket again, giving me a pointed stare. "Shall I find out for myself?"

Taking a deep breath, I do what I do best. "If you're waiting for a written invitation you'll be disappointed." Heat rises in my cheeks as I force my hands to relax, to sink back into the pillows and appear unbothered. The faintest taste of interest coats my tongue and I have to fight the urge to squeal.

He cocks his head at me and tugs the blanket back down barely an inch. When I don't respond he removes his hands, leaving the blanket in place. Yuta pulls the chair up closer to the bed, taking a seat and crossing his long legs at the ankles. "You know, I'm not the bad guy here."

I lick my lips before smiling slowly. "That's what the bad guy always says," I tease. I pull my arms from beneath the blankets, the movement

191

making them fall a little lower, exposing more of my cleavage and the deep divots of my collarbones.

"Ah, but the idea of the bad guy is completely subjective. Who's really to say who is right or wrong in any given situation?" Yuta shrugs.

"Right and wrong might not be black and white, but it's not entirely gray either." I sit up more, the blanket slipping further as I begin playing with my hair and trying to ignore how greasy and disgusting it feels between my fingers.

Yuta rises, standing above me so I have to tilt my head back to look at him. "Even the best of us are forced to make difficult choices. I would imagine you've had your fair share in life."

"Of course," I agree, licking my lips slowly.

His eyes watch me as he swallows hard. "And mistakes? Have you ever made a mistake?"

A thousand mistakes throughout my entire life fly by like I'm living them all over again. Things that I said. Things that I did. Things that I didn't do. Each moment is painted on the backs of my lids, ready and waiting to remind me of all the reasons why I am in this exact position right now. "More than I could count."

"Then we have that in common," Yuta says with a dark chuckle.

"We have nothing in common," I snap, unable to hold back.

"Only that's the thing, little minx, we have more in common than you are ready to know."

"Like?"

"You'll learn in time. But before you can hear you have to learn to listen."

"That made no sense," I say, staring at him with wide eyes.

"Didn't it, though?"

"No. No it didn't."

He laughs deeply, the sound vibrating through his chest. "It will in time, you just have to be patient."

"I'm afraid patience is not one of my skills," I sigh dramatically.

He smiles to himself. "I have to admit, this is one of the most pleasant conversations I have had since…"

"Since you last kidnapped a completely innocent girl?" I finish for him.

He raises his eyebrows at me, leaning down to whisper in my ear, "There is nothing innocent about you, little minx." He pulls away as my skin burns and my chest heaves. He stares down at me with the delicious taste of amusement on my tongue and I bite my lip. He grabs one of my hands, pulling it into one of his own and kissing the back of my palm. Without another word he vanishes and my hand falls to my side.

As confused as that whole exchange left me, I did manage to get one thing out of it.

A little bit of pleasure, and pleasure means *magic*.

Chapter 30

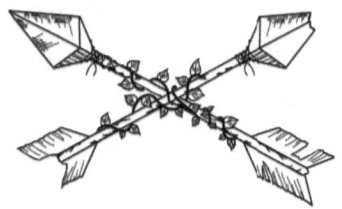

Oak

Burning, aching muscles scream at me as I heft myself further up the wall. My fingertips are bruised and bloody, the skin torn from the rough stones. Sweat drips down between my shoulder blades as I fight to hold myself up. I've come this far, I can't give up now. I'm almost at the top.

I just need to make it to the top and then this will all be over, I tell myself again.

Gritting my teeth, I use my arms to pull myself up and my feet push off of the narrow ledge beneath them. Adjusting my grip, I rest my forehead against the stone, taking wheezing breaths as I try to control my racing heart. This is so much taller than I thought it was. I open my eyes and regret the decision instantly. The ground is at least 30 feet below me.

Dark spots cloud my vision and I clutch onto the wall harder, flattening my body against the stone. *Why the fuck am I doing this? This was such a stupid idea.* I force my eyes up, staring at the purple-pink sky as the sun dips on the horizon. Breakfast churns in my stomach and my throat squeezes against the urge to throw up. That would be *really* bad, in more ways than one.

"Come on, Oak! You can do it!" Lina calls up at me, standing in the splash zone.

"Come on, Oak!" Hala and Symone echo.

When Aine told me that today I would be trying the training wall, I had no idea she meant *this*. A towering stone wall at the very edge of the compound, one used solely for training. It seemed easy enough from the ground.

Now? Not so much.

The edges of the rocks are barely a fingertip deep which makes it nearly impossible to keep a solid grip on anything, not to mention that my toes hang off no matter what I do. Honestly, it's a miracle I haven't fallen to my death yet.

"Don't give up, you're almost there!" Lina calls again. At first her cheering was appreciated, but that was before she became little more than a blob on the ground below.

I force myself up another few inches, staring at the platform at the top where Aine waits for me. She's close enough now that I can see the tension lining her face, inspiring the opposite of confidence. As I get closer to her, I swear I can feel the air growing thinner.

"Don't," Aine says, stopping me from looking down again, "keep looking up. Watch where you're going and stop being so focused on where you've been. It's in the past now."

"*Reallly* inspiring, Aine," I pant.

The top is only a few feet away, the wide ledge beckons to me and my aching fingers. I push up again, but when I reach out with my left hand, the wall crumbles away and I nearly go tumbling towards the ground.

"Ignore it!" Surprisingly this encouragement comes from Farai.

I take a few steadying breaths before crawling my way up the rest of the wall, my teammates cheering me as I do. The moment my hands grip the edge of the platform, Aine reaches for me, pulling me up and over the lip. I collapse onto my back, my chest rising and falling unevenly.

"You did it," Aine states, sounding just a little too surprised.

"I think I might throw up," I groan.

"That's fairly normal." Aine leans over and gives the other girls a thumbs up. Their voices fade into the distance as Aine takes a seat beside me. "You've shown great improvement."

I bite my cheek against my smile. I may not agree with how I came to be here... but I can't pretend that I haven't learned a lot. My form is sturdier, my punches and kicks more powerful, it feels like every part of me has grown stronger. I even took down Hala and Symone this week. It's a weird thing to feel pride in any of this. Like somehow being a Ghost means something.

Not that I *am* a Ghost. Obviously.

I'm a prisoner. Nothing more.

"I was impressed by your work this week," Aine continues, filling the silence.

"Thank you," I say genuinely. Compliments from Aine are rare, she reserves her recognition for those she deems truly deserving which today means me apparently.

"I was thinking..." she starts.

I sit up on my elbows, letting my head fall back as far as it will go. "Oh?" is the only answer I seem to conjure up. I have a bad feeling about this. Something feels off, wrong, too different from this new normal.

"There's a mission. Just a small one. But I think it might be good for you to get some hands-on experience, to see how we do things out in the real world," she says almost hesitantly.

Sitting up fully I fix her with a stare, my eyes wide. "What?"

"I said, you should join us on the next mission."

My brain momentarily ceases to function and all I can think is a garbled mess of noises.

Aine stares at me, waiting for some sort of response.

196

"Seriously?" I ask, finally pulling myself together.

"Seriously."

Without thinking, I throw my arms around her neck. "Thank you," I breathe.

Her body is stiff and non-reciprocating, which is when I realize this is extremely awkward. I start to pull away, but she gives me a light sort of squeeze.

"Don't make me regret this choice," she whispers beside my ear.

She clears her throat and we pull apart, both of us avoiding each other's eyes.

Did I really just hug Aine? This will surely haunt my dreams later.

Aine uses her magic to bring us back down and the first thing I do is tell the others… who apparently were already in on it. They all congratulate me as we dig into our meal, the entire time talking about the next steps and how soon we'll be leaving.

They notably leave details out and ignore some of my questions, but I don't even care. This is it. I'm leaving the compound. Something tightens in my chest and I ignore it, choosing instead to live in this moment and enjoy this feeling while it lasts.

~~~

Two days go by like normal. We train during the day, do our chores, and during meals we talk about the mission. Apparently it's got something to do with a rogue wolf pack who have been attacking travelers as they pass through their section of the forest. Beyond that, I don't know much. No one has said it, but I know this is a test. A show of my loyalty-if I can be trusted.

The thought had crossed my mind that this could be my chance to escape, but I shut it down quickly when I remembered that I still don't have access to my magic. No, I'll need to wait it out a bit longer. If I can get them to trust me enough to give me back access to my power, then I can stand a real chance of making it out of here. The one challenge that I still have yet to figure out… where will I go?

It's not exactly like I can just waltz back into the castle and return to my life as usual. My aunt would never allow it. I'd be back here so fast it would be like I never left. Before Rayan fell, that would have been a good temporary solution, somewhere nearby where I could hide out until things calmed down a bit. Now, my best option is likely Vulca. Which, given its distance, is not much of a solution at all.

No, there are still too many things to consider. So for now I will just play along, earn their trust, and bide my time.

"Are you nervous?" Hala asks from across the table.

"Is it wrong of me to say yes?" I answer, running a hand through my hair.

Hala laughs, "No one would judge you if you are. It's not like we haven't all been there before."

Her sister, Symone, nods. "Our first mission was a mess. We were in way over our heads."

"That doesn't exactly inspire confidence," I grimace.

"Good. Being overly confident will get you killed," Farai says, staring down at her plate beside me. The discolored scars near the corner of her eye seem to glare at me.

The table falls silent, that is until Lina comes bounding over, plopping down between Farai and I.

"Why's everyone so quiet?" she asks, looking around the table.

Hala and Symone share a look before stuffing their faces with food. Lina turns to me and I give a hesitant smile.

"Okayyy then. Is everyone ready for tonight?" she asks, practically vibrating with excitement.

"Oak is nervous," Hala answers for me.

I give her a *what the fuck* look because honestly, *what the fuck!* Lina is the nicest out of my entire squad, but she has a tendency to over dramatize things. A small cut becomes a gaping wound, a stumble over your own feet is likened to falling over the side of a cliff, it's all *greatly* exaggerated.

"Oh? Is that so?" Lina says, raising her brows at me.

"I'm fine. Just… ready to go," I mutter.

"Don't worry, Oak. Someone will be by your side the entire time," she reassures, "we always pair up when we go on a mission."

"How do you decide who goes with who? Is it by rank?" I ask, this being the first time I've heard of such a thing.

"No, we usually determine it by the mission itself and whatever makes the most sense. This time around I'll be with Hala," Lina says, reaching over the table and giving Hala a high five.

"Aine and I will partner up this time," Symone says, mid-bite.

"So I'm assuming that leaves me with Farai?" I glance at her out of the corner of my eye, watching for her reaction.

Farai continues eating as if I said nothing.

"Yup, lucky you," Lina sighs dramatically.

"Seriously, just wait," Hala says excitedly, her eyes cutting back and forth between Farai and I.

"What are you all doing?" Aine snaps, walking up to our table. Most of the other squads have already moved on to training.

The five of us scramble to our feet, quickly depositing our dirty dishes in the bin and rushing to the courtyard.

~~~

Later that night, we gather in the courtyard, dressed in matching brown leather pants and black tunics. Energy hums around our group and the looks of excitement on the others' faces have me feeling it too. It's been weeks, and I'm finally going to be outside these walls. I'm finally going to have a semblance of freedom again.

"Everyone ready?" Aine asks, looking between all of us.

We all nod and then Lina approaches me with a sheepish smile. Before I can process the bag in her hand, it's thrown over my head. The ground seems to shift beneath my feet and I nearly fall over. Two sets of hands grasp me by my arms and hold me steady. When the ground stops shaking, the bag is ripped off my head.

Chapter 31

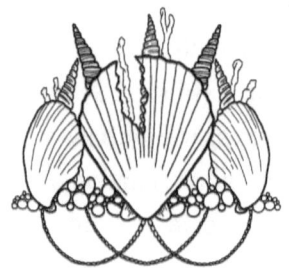

Cay

The courtyard is empty as the morning sun rises, casting a warm glow over us. Terran and I work in tandem preparing the portal. He meticulously places the stones, exactly as instructed while I pour the sand stiffly, the same process as the last time I went home.

Home.

It doesn't feel real yet, knowing that I am going home. Somehow I never thought we would get to this point, yet as I finish the final touch, it is time.

Terran stands off to the side, waiting for further directions. He doesn't rush me. He doesn't ask how I'm feeling or if I'm okay. He just knows. He knows what I need without me ever having to tell him, and for that I am grateful. Terran's presence is a comfort that I need, but can't ask for.

The last time I did this, I was surrounded by my best friends and I felt safe. Like nothing bad could happen to us. My throat tightens as I stare at the place where the portal will appear. The shining image of my city appears like a phantom in my mind. Only the image quickly morphs, becoming twisted and distorted, overlaid with the horrors that awaited me the last time I attempted this spell.

Fear for what I will see this time immobilizes me. My hands begin to shake as magic stirs inside me, awakened by a need to protect myself, even when there is no real threat.

"Steady," a deep voice whispers in my ear.

I take a deep breath, squeezing my eyes shut and slowly letting it go. Opening my eyes, I turn to thank Terran only to find him bent over a pack, searching through the contents. Looking over my shoulder, I find Oliver standing and gazing down at me. His chest is pressed against my back, his hand resting over my hip, the heat from his palm sears my skin.

"Thank you," I croak.

He lingers there for a moment more before peeling away from me and approaching his brother. The two of them squat side by side and go over the supplies we have prepared while I do my best to not pass out.

Swallowing hard, I ball my hands into fists, the sharp bite of my nails into my palm grounds me. "Okay, it's time," I announce, walking towards the inner circle. The moment I step inside, I feel the rush of magic beneath my skin as it awakens.

Terran slings the bag over his shoulder, securing it there as he takes his place to my right. Oliver stares at us, jaw working, before coming to stand beside us.

"What's next?" Terran asks, smiling at me encouragingly.

"Next we hold hands," I say, extending my arms out in either direction. Terran's calloused fingers intertwine with my own, his large hand dwarfing mine. I look to Oliver next, reaching out and watching as he slides his palm against mine, a spark of power transferring between us. I flinch, but before I can yank my hand away, he has my hand in a firm grip.

"What's next, princess?" Oliver asks, staring down at me.

Clearing my throat I nod to their free hands. "You have to complete the circle."

The two brothers stare at each other. Terran is the first to extend his arm, reaching to take Oliver's. Oliver rolls his eyes and takes his brother's hand, the two of them sharing a look that I can't quite understand before turning to me. Their matching hazel gazes bore into me and heat my skin.

"Alright, it's time," I say more to myself than anyone else. I close my eyes and conjure the image of Atran, the docks appearing in my mind, pristine and waiting. I focus on that, ignoring the flashes of destruction that threaten to take over.

Magic passes between us, the flow powerful and sure, unwavering. I watch as the portal begins to open, water cascades down as the image is reflected in it. My palms grow sweaty as my heart begins to race. I feel a rush of power from my left and have to fight the urge to look at Oliver. Instead, I keep my eyes trained on my destination and, with a few muttered words under my breath, we are being sucked in.

Both males keep a firm grip on my hands as the vortex carries us through. Blurry images of the forest and mountains, a flash of bright light, and a wall of darkness all pass us by. I ignore them, looking only to the pristine beach that will deliver me home. Water closes in around us and I feel a rush of cold before we are deposited on the wet sand. I stumble, almost falling to my knees, but Terran and Oliver each take me by the elbow, holding me upright.

"Are you okay?" Terran asks, concern written across his face.

My chest is heaving, as I struggle to take in oxygen. There, straight ahead of me, lies what remains of the tunnel which used to take me to my home, Tepis. The entrance is still standing, though it is nothing more than a flickering dome of magic.

My heart beats erratically, its pounding echoes inside my ears, drowning everything else out. My body grows cold as my skin becomes clammy, my stomach churning. Bile burns the back of my throat as I fight to suck down air, my breaths nothing more than shallow gasps that leave my lungs unsatisfied.

"Breathe, Cay," Terran says slowly, taking in a deep breath and letting it out himself.

I try to mimic him, but find it only makes things worse. Panic overwhelms me as I start to see black spots. *I can't breathe. Can't breathe. No air. I-* The burning slice of a blade against my palm brings me back to the moment.

I look down and find a thin line of red appearing in the center of my hand. Oliver has my wrist in a vice grip, his rough fingers biting into the skin hard enough that it might bruise. I stare up at him as Terran shoves him away. Oliver stumbles back, his eyes never leaving my own. Terran picks up my hand and quickly heals it before whirling on his brother again.

"What the fuck is your problem?" he bellows, marching forward.

Oliver doesn't react as his brother continues to tear into him. He just takes it, listening, but not hearing. He watches me with rapt attention. When I look down at my hand again he follows my eyes. Staring at the place where his blade cut into me.

"Are you crazy? What in the Vana's name would give you the idea to do something like that, honestly, Oliver, do you even thi-"

"She's fine," he says, brushing past Terran and looming over me. "You healed the cut and now she is breathing. Everything worked out perfectly fine."

"That doesn't matter! You should never-"

"It's fine. Let's just... drop it," I cut in. Looking between the two males as my heart continues to race.

Terran appears at my side, taking my hand in his gently, another wave of healing magic passing between us. "Are you sure?"

I smile up at him, a weak smile that I hope doesn't look nearly as fake as it feels. "I'm fine."

He searches my face, sighing when he seems content with what he finds. Without warning, I am crushed against his chest, my cheek pressed against him as heat radiates from beneath his tunic. "You scared me."

"Sorry," I mumble. I pull back, stepping out of his arms as my cheeks flame. My eyes flick to Oliver who looks devoid of all emotion, his face blank.

Laughing nervously, I sweep my dark waves away from my face, "Come on, let's not waste any more time."

We walk along the pier, Terran right by my side while Oliver stays a few paces behind us. As we approach the entrance to the tunnel, a weird sort of feeling creeps in over me. I brush it aside, forcing myself to continue forward, no matter how difficult it is. The city is completely deserted. Homes with doors standing open, stalls left abandoned, clothes and tools thrown about haphazardly. Yet the hum of magic still buzzes through the air as though it was just used minutes ago rather than months.

A familiar tingle creeps down my spine and I immediately throw Terran and Oliver back with a wave of power. I summon a wall of water between us, watching as the ocean ripples and a small horde of figures appear. My magic surges as they walk closer, gliding along the water's surface until they step easily onto the dock.

One steps forward, flicking her dark locs over her shoulder as a sadistic smile spreads across her full lips. "Welcome home, princess," she hums.

"Nalei."

Chapter 32

Rose

Vines shoot from the earth, whipping through the air and snapping at our enemies, forcing them back. My magic swells, thickening the vines and pushing the wolves further back as they cocoon around me. One dares to leap forward and I curl my fingers in, wrapping a thick vine around its hind leg and yanking. I drag the wolf into the air as it snarls and snaps, twisting its body left and right in an attempt to bite through the vine holding it captive.

Meanwhile, more wolves appear on either side of me, creeping closer even as my vines lash out. My attention is split between the wolf I am holding and two others. A hole appears in the vines as one manages to bite through my cocoon and I pull my arm back, flinging the suspended wolf through the air and knocking it into the other one. It's a miracle I don't drop my hold.

"Mateo!"

Reed's terrified yell draws my attention away as he creates a wall of stone around himself and Mateo, another five wolves clawing at the barrier. The sharp scrape of their claws against the stone sends sparks shooting into the air. The bursts of light are enough to distract me, giving the wolf in my hold an opportunity to tear through the vine. He falls to the ground, landing on all fours, and rushes towards me.

Dropping to my knees I dig my fingers into the loose dirt and take a deep breath. Focusing all of my energy, I pour magic into the earth, the ground rumbling beneath our feet as a large creature claws its way out. A moss covered hand appears, then an arm, a head, a neck. Sweat beads down the side of my face as I continue to pour magic from me into this beast until it finally bursts free. It is made entirely of earth, wooden bones, muddy insides, and a thick layer of moss to hold it all together. It's not the strongest defense, but it will have to do.

The wolf launches forward again and I fall backwards, my wooden knight appearing between us and holding the wolf's jaw open. The wolf growls, yanking its head back and forth trying to dislodge the knight. I take the opportunity to crawl backwards, my magic pulsing below the surface, adrenaline fueling me as I stand.

Gael is using his own magic to hold off two wolves, alternating between earth and spells that I have never seen before, light bursting from his fists. The wall is down around Mateo and Reed, the pair back to back as they alternate between attacking and defending in perfect synchronicity.

The ash wolf throws its head back, howling long and loud up at the sky. A thunderous roar swells from deeper in the forest. At least 20 more wolves appear along the edge of the circle, throwing their heads back and returning their alphas call.

Fuck. This does not look good.

"Rose," Reed pants. His shirt is torn, three sharp slashes running diagonally across his chest. The edges are tinted red as if they were soaked in blood. Everything shifts as I see that color.

I release my hold on my knight, returning him to the earth as I summon all of my power. I once again fall to my knees, burying my hands in the earth until the dirt reaches my elbows. Forcing everything else out, I concentrate on building up the magic, of releasing my control bit by bit until it's right on the edge of exploding. Then, I force that power into the ground and watch as it cracks into two.

It starts deep below the surface of the grass. A boom, so quiet you might miss it. But then, the ground rumbles and the crack quickly follows. I stand as it fans out, the small split in the earth quickly becoming a small crater. Growls grow as the wolves are forced further back but it won't be enough, I just don't have enough power, not yet. I pour everything I have into that crack, willing the earth to crumble and give us enough time to get out of here.

Mateo appears at my side. He extends his hand and I stare at him hesitantly.

"Trust me, little Ro," he nods his head encouragingly.

Setting aside my fears, I take his hand. Power feeds into my own and I welcome it, open myself up to it. It feels amazing. Then, I feel a subtle pull on my own magic and fear rises. My panicked eyes meet Mateo's, but he seems sure, he seems...determined.

I watch, mesmerized, as small rocks begin to pull together, one by one. They join into large boulders and then, stacking against each other, a monster is born, not unlike my own wooden knight.

"Vana," Reed whispers from behind me.

Mateo keeps a firm grip on my hand as he mutters under his breath, "Don't move. Wait for my signal."

The wolves begin to pace back and forth on the other side of the crater which continues to slowly grow wider, putting more distance between us. Still, it's not enough to keep them from jumping over and continuing to pursue us.

"Mateo," I caution.

"Trust. Me."

There is a moment of silence and then the creature roars again and I can't help but take a step back.

"Okay, now!"

I'm yanked backwards so hard that I swear my soul is ripped from my body.

Oh. My. Vana!

There, standing in the exact spot I was before, is *my fucking body*! *What the fuck is going on?*

Before I even have time to process this literal out of body experience, I am being dragged away, staring back at…myself. Only, my body is not alone, Mateo stands beside me, but…how is that possible? *He* is the one dragging me away.

"Now would be a great time for you to move," Mateo bites, voice low.

"But-how-I"

"No time to explain, just move."

Gael grabs hold of Reed and drags him away too, the four of us taking off and leaving behind Mateo's wolves and the stone creature. Seeing as I can't ask questions, I am going to have to assume I also left my body back there.

We run for what feels like hours until I force Mateo to stop, collapsing to the ground and heaving up the limited contents of my stomach.

"Are we alive?" The question comes from Reed, whose usually tanned face is currently leached of all color.

"Damn right we are," Mateo answers with a laugh. He shakes his head back and forth, his wild curls flying everywhere.

Gael stalks away from the group and I watch as he disappears behind a tree. "Is he okay?" I ask Mateo.

"Gael? Yeah, he'll be fine," he says easily.

"What just happened?" I finally ask, incapable of holding it back any longer.

"What happened is I just saved all of us, but no worries, I'm male enough to not need your thanks." Mateo beams, his eyes flicking back and forth between the sky and Reed.

I roll my eyes. "Okay well *how* did you save us. Are we- I don't even know what to ask," I mutter the last part to myself.

He rolls his eyes. "What you saw were my illusions. Couldn't have those other wolves chasing after us so I needed to make it look like we were exactly where they wanted us to be."

"What about that stone creature?" Reed asks, his eyes shining in awe.

"Also an illusion." Mateo shrugs.

"But what about your wolves, won't they be in danger?" I ask, suddenly anxious to go

back to the fight.

"Nope, they were illusions too. I sent them away at the same moment we ran. Everything those other wolves are fighting, is one of my illusions," Mateo explains, plopping down onto the grass beside me.

"Won't the illusion just fall away now that we're not there?" Reed presses.

Mateo laughs.

"Seriously? But, we're so far away? How can you possibly keep up that magic from such a distance?" I ask, skepticism creeping in. Maybe it is better we go back.

"You're just going to have to trust me. Right now, I have illusions as far away as the castle. The three of us are laughing in the courtyard as I speak." Mateo winks over at me.

"Wait, so this entire time you've been maintaining the illusions at the castle?" I ask.

"Yup."

"And now you're maintaining the illusions back there in the forest?"

"That would be correct."

"Vana-" Reed breaks off, covering his mouth with the palm of his hand.

"That would take an absurd amount of power," I say, narrowing my eyes.

"Lucky for us, I have just the thing."

Gael makes his way back to the group. "We need to get moving."

Mateo groans, flopping down onto his back. He drags a hand down his face before rolling back onto his shoulders and thrusting himself up into the air, landing on his feet with ease.

He extends a hand to me and I take it, letting him drag me to my feet. "I thought the illusions were working?"

"They are. Buuuut only for so long. These illusions aren't like the ones back at the castle, the wolves here are actually engaging with them, fighting them. It's only a matter of time before they realize what they really are," he says, rolling out his neck and shoulders.

"Okay so how much time do we have?" The question comes from Reed.

A piercing howl comes from the distance and all of us freeze.

"Not enough," Gael groans. He cracks his neck before his wolf form comes bursting through his skin. Gael is huge. His fur is a silvery gray that somehow suits him perfectly. Padding over to Mateo, he shoves his snout into his back, making his alpha throw his hands up.

"Right, well, let's move." Mateo says, pouncing back and forth on his feet.

"What do you mean?" Reed asks hesitantly.

Before the words have fully left my cousin's mouth, Mateo has already shifted, turning into the biggest wolf I have ever seen. *Damn, and I thought Gael was big.*

Mateo shakes out his long black fur and licks a path straight up the side of Reed's face as he stares at me with a mixture of horror and embarrassment staining his cheeks.

"Okay then...what now?" I ask as another howl penetrates the air.

Mateo shoves into Reed repeatedly.

"What, Mateo?" Reed asks, already growing annoyed. This is exactly why they didn't shift sooner, it's way too hard to communicate when half the group can't talk.

"I think he wants us to climb on," I say, watching as Mateo's large head nods enthusiastically. The wolves are more than big enough for someone to ride on their backs, but there is still something about it that makes us hesitate. Yet in the end, Reed climbs onto Mateo's back and I climb onto Gael's.

I've barely gotten settled before Gael takes off. I am forced to lean forward, wrapping my arms around his furry neck and hanging on while also trying not to strangle him in the process. Mateo and Reed pass by us, taking the lead and charging through the forest. We ride like this for hours, until mountains grow before us and we stare up at their peaks as the sun dips behind them.

We're here. We made it to the border. This is Eteri.

Chapter 33

Mar

"I'm sorry, I promise I'll be back soon," I assure the twins as they cling to my legs, begging me to stay. Prying them off of me, I find their eyes glistening. I wipe away their tears and have to fight the urge to go back in for one more hug. The two of them run back into the house hand-in-hand, leaving me alone with our other brother.

Keegan hangs back, staring off into the distance like he expects something to appear out of thin air.

There's something different about him this time, and whatever it is, it worries me. "Keegan," I call out to him. He either ignores me or doesn't hear me, which is extremely unlikely. I walk over to him instead, bumping my shoulder into his. "What's going on with you?"

"Where's that guard?" he asks with a scowl.

Rian has been notably absent this morning, though I know he can't be too far. "Somewhere else. But I don't want to talk about him, I want to talk about you."

"Why? I'm fine."

I grab him by the shoulders, turning him until we are face to face. "No, you're not. I just can't figure out why. So please, just tell me, Keegan. Whatever it is, we'll fix it."

His gaze softens, his voice dropping to barely above a whisper, "You can't fix everything." Keegan pulls away, my arms falling to my side in the process as I watch his back, stunned.

"Are you ready to go?" Rian asks, appearing out of nowhere and making me nearly jump out of my skin.

"Vana, don't do that."

Rian looks away, back to the field where the others are waiting for us. "We should get back."

My eyes narrow, "Back where? Because I told you, Rian, I'm not going home there is still too-"

"Back to Nat's village," he says, cutting me off, "Isn't that where you want to go?""Yes," I answer hesitantly.

"Great, 'cause that's where we're going." He marches back to the dragon waiting for us and climbs on without waiting for me.

Great, he's in a bad mood too.

~~~

The first thing I do when we touch down is head to Nat's family's shop. The door slams shut behind me, but I pull up short when I find the wrong redhead behind the counter.

"Good to see you again," Cyrus, Nat's brother, says with a wide smile.

"Oh, sorry, I didn't mean to interrupt. I was just-"

"Looking for my sister. I know." He walks around the counter, brushing his hands against a worn out apron wrapped around his waist. "Anything I can do for you?"

"Um…"

He laughs, a deep and full sound that eases some of the tension that built up at seeing him. "How about I show you around?"

It takes me a second to process what he said. "What?"

"Let me take you out."

My breath catches in my throat as the back of my neck grows warm. "I'm not so sure that's a good idea. I've got a lot going on."

He nods, his dark copper waves swishing with the motion. "Of course. But the thing is, Nat's not here. She's out flying and probably won't be back for hours. You see, she does that a lot lately. She's awfully predictable. I, on the other hand, am right here and would love nothing more than to show you around," he punctuates his words with a wink.

I can't help but smile. "That's very polite of you, but I actually know my way around here pretty well. I used to come here quite often as a kid."

Cyrus scoffs, sounding offended. "Well then you don't really know anything at all. Lots of things have changed around here, especially over the last couple years. Let me take you out and I'll show you everything." He smiles at me, and damn him and those green eyes.

"Fine," I concede. Maybe he will actually know something valuable.

"Really?" he asks, sounding shocked.

I laugh, "Yes, really. So are we leaving or are we just going to stand around because honestly I'm a very bu-"

"Yes! Just give me two seconds." He rips his apron off, slinging it over his shoulder and letting it fall on top of the counter haphazardly. He appears at my side, grabbing my hand and taking me by surprise. "Let's go."

He flips the sign on the shop to 'closed' before dragging me after him.

~~~

Cyrus spends hours showing me all of the various shops and stalls around the village, introducing me to everyone as we go. There are so many names it is impossible to remember them all, but Cyrus assures me I can do it anyways. Then he takes me to the training square where a small collection of kids are currently using the space to play some sort of game.

The moment the kids see him, they come rushing over, a chorus of his name filling the air.

"Woah, woah, slow down!" Cyrus says, grabbing the smallest girl and positioning her on his hip. The group immediately launches into 20 different stories, all of which he listens to with rapt attention.

When the little girl in his arms reaches for me, I take her from him. "Hello," I say to her, adjusting so that I can see her better.

"Pretty," she says in awe.

"Isn't she?" Cyrus says, leaning over and whispering it between us. His hot breath fans over my cheeks and my neck heats once again. He chuckles and returns to the other kids with excitement.

We pause what we are doing so that he can spend the next hour playing with the kids, all while I braid the little girl's hair and listen to her sing to herself. By the time Cyrus makes it back to me, the little girl has fallen asleep in my arms.

"Here, I can take her," he says, reaching out for her.

I hand her to him gently, careful not to wake her. "Where are we taking her?"

"Follow me." He leads us back through the village, shushing people as they call out to him excitedly and pointing at the sleeping child in his arms. He is positively beaming.

"You're great with them."

"With who?" he whispers.

"Everyone. The kids and the adults seem to love you."

Cyrus laughs, "I guess. I grew up here so I've known most of these people my entire life or, in the kids' case, their entire lives."

"It's nice."

He looks over at me, "What is?"

"Having this... community."

He stops and turns to me, looking me over from head to toe. "What is it about you?"

"What do you mean?"

"You just seem...sad. It makes me want to do everything I can to make you laugh."

I stare up at him.

"There you are!" A woman comes rushing over, placing a gentle hand on the little girl's back and breathing a sigh of relief. "Thank you so much,

Cyrus, she keeps wandering off after the other kids, I just can't keep up." The woman steps back revealing a very large, rounded belly, "I keep telling my mate, this is the last one. No more."

Cyrus hands the little girl to the woman, being careful not to jostle her too much. "I'm always here to help. Just say the word. And if any of the others give you trouble, I'll talk to them."

"Thank you. I swear they listen to you more than they listen to their father or me," the little girl squirms in her arms, "I should get her to bed. You two enjoy your evening now." She smiles at me before doing a double take. She looks up at Cyrus with a mystified look on her face.

"I know," he says with a wink.

The woman hurries off and I am left alone with Cyrus. The sky has darkened, leaving only the faint glow of the moon to light our faces.

"What?" Cyrus asks, tilting his head.

"Nothing, I just-thank you for today. I needed it."

He steps forward, his chest brushing my own. "Tomorrow then?"

"What do you mean?"

"Let me take you out again. Tomorrow."

I chew the inside of my cheek. I've already wasted so much time, I can't keep getting sidetracked.

"Oh no, where did you go?" Cyrus asks, gripping my chin lightly and tilting my head left and right.

I smile, rolling my eyes a little and taking a step back, out of his grip.

"If you let me take you out tomorrow I'll talk to my sister, get her to listen to whatever it is you have to say."

"Cyrus…"

"No, promise me. I'll meet you at the shop at dawn. Don't be late!" he runs off into the night, leaving me standing here with a dumbstruck look on my face.

I walk back to our temporary lodging with a smile spreading my lips, and a lightness in my chest that I haven't felt in a while. Today was amazing. I felt normal again, like I could just live my life here and everything would be okay. There were no meetings to attend or advisors to talk to. I was just me again.

"What's that look about?" a voice says from behind me.

I spin, fists raised as my heart hammers inside my chest.

Rian is leaning against a building, his jaw set and eyes burning.

"What the fuck, Rian? Have you been stalking me?"

He shrugs, "Define stalking."

"Did you follow me around the entire day?" I bite.

"I was guarding you."

"I don't *need* guarding." And just like that, my perfect, normal day, gone.

"You might not think you do, but whether you like it or not, you're a princess. And right now, you're our only Princess," he says, coming off the wall and stalking towards me.

I meet him halfway, shoving him back. "You fucking asshole."

His eyes darken, "Why'd you do it?"

"What?" I say through my teeth.

"Why'd you spend the day with him?"

"Why do you care?" I narrow my eyes at him, watching as his jaw tenses. Blinking my eyes, I take a step back. I look him over and see it written all across his body. "Are you jealous?"

Rian closes the distance between us, his chest pressed up against mine as he practically snarls in my face.

"You are, aren't you." It's not a question. Not when I can see the ways his eyes darken. The way they keep flicking to my lips. There is certainly no question as Rian's lips slam down on mine. I shove his chest, pushing him back as we both fight to catch our breath, only to collide against each other again a second later.

Rian's arms come around me, his fists bury in my hair as he clutches me to him. The sharp tip of his fangs graze my bottom lip and I gasp. He takes advantage of the opportunity and plunges his tongue into my mouth, caressing and playing with my own.

A breathy moan escapes me and he squeezes me tighter in response before spinning us completely and pinning me against the wall. His hands trail down my side, one stopping at my hips, the other continues to move around until Rian has a handful of my ass. His hands tighten, pulling me closer, demanding more. His mouth moves to the edge of my lips, then my jaw, and further and further until he is pressing hot kisses against my collarbone.

"Rian," I breathe.

He growls, the hand on my ass shifting forward to caress my pussy. The heat from his palm nearly burns through the thin fabric of my pants. Actually, my entire body is nearly on fire from his touch. I push against him and he chuckles, leaning back enough that his lust clouded eyes can see my face. "You need something?"

"Ass," I groan, my head tilting back and falling against the brick.

"Careful, little one, someone might think you're offering yourself up," he stares at my neck, at the spot where my steady pulse beats just below the surface.

"Who says I'm not?" I watch him, my heart speeding up just thinking about it.

He bends down, his fangs scraping against my delicate skin. "Yeah?" he asks against my skin.

"Yes." I barely get the word out before his fangs pierce me with a flash of pain that quickly turns into intense pleasure.

He sucks hard, drawing my blood and magic into him as our bodies grind against each other. His hand begins to move, but it's not enough. Rian must know it because without even a word from me, his hand slips beneath my waistband and dives lower and lower until he finds a pool of wetness between my thighs. His rough fingers circle my lips, my clit, and then without warning, plunge deep inside me.

I cry out, the sound silenced as Rian clamps a hand over my mouth with a chuckle.

He pulls back. "Wouldn't want anyone else to hear you, those sounds are only for me." He picks up speed, a singular digit pumping in and out of me with a steady rhythm, as he dives back in and continues to drain me.

My head begins to swim and my eyes fall closed. The hand over my mouth shifts to grip my chin, shaking my head slightly until I open my eyes.

"Your turn," he says, tilting his head to the side and offering me himself as I had done.

My hands plunge into his hair, pulling him towards me. I don't bother teasing, the moment he is close enough I attack, my fangs bite into the soft skin of his neck and he groans deeply. The instant his blood splashes against my tongue I let go of everything, I fall into this and just forget everything else that is wrong.

Rian adds a second finger, then a third, rapidly stretching me. He keeps the same steady rhythm, in and out, in and out. Pushing me closer and closer to that edge without really taking me there. Between the feel of his hard length pressing against my thigh, the pumping of his fingers, and his intoxicating blood, I'm on edge and growing more and more frustrated.

"Please," I gasp, my hips jerk violently against his hand, trying to relieve the growing pressure.

"Please what, little one? Use your words."

Fuck. He wants me to beg for it and he thinks I'm weak enough to-that I'll let him have that kind of power over me now. But the thing is, no matter what I'm feeling, he hasn't earned it. So instead of begging, I bite down again, harder, taking more of his magic for my own.

He hisses. His fingers plunge deeper inside of me, curling and hitting a spot that has me crying out. "Your pussy is clamping down on my fingers so well. You're so tight I can hardly move," he purrs.

Vana, everything is so hot, too hot. It's like I'm burning up from the inside out. I force myself away from his neck, panting as the rush of his magic and my own burns through me. It's all too much, too intense. His words are driving me closer and closer, pleasure builds inside me, wicked and wild, my insides are molten with it. A moan tumbles from my lips as he continues to drive into me, deeper and deeper. Fucking me with his fingers. I buck against him, unable to control myself.

"Fuck, you're drenched for me." He pulls his hand back leaving my pussy aching at the emptiness. It clamps down onto nothing, desperate to be filled again. Slowly, Rian lifts his fingers to his mouth and sucks them in, drinking my juices and making my clit throb at the mere sight.

"You taste so sweet." He leans over me, his glistening lips hovering just above my own. His hand is poised between my thighs, his fingers barely brushing against my swollen clit. "Come on, you know what you want. All you have to do is say the words. *Beg*."

A whimper escapes me and I want to throttle him for drawing such a sound from my lips. Yet my body refuses. His touch and words have created this perfect prison of my own pleasure. The only way to get release is to give in, something that I really, really, do not want to do.

Rian wants me to surrender what little power I have left and accept what he is offering like it's just that easy. But it's not just an intense orgasm he is offering, and we both know it. We've been fighting it this whole time and now, this is going to change everything.

What little control I have over my body cracks and before I can choke them down, the words are spilling into the space between our lips. "Please, fuck me," I beg.

Rian's lips crash into mine. The taste of me mixed with him driving me wild. His tongue traces the seam of my lips and I open for him. He dives right in, stealing my breath and consuming every part of me, claiming me in a way no one else has before. He pulls apart leaving a trail of nips and kisses from the corner of my mouth down my neck.

His fangs tease the spot where he fed from me and my back arches, pushing my chest into him. "Rian," I whimper.

"I could listen to that sound all night. Say it again." His tongue traces the two puncture holes, teasing me even more.

"Rian," I moan, digging my nails into his back and pulling him closer to me. I lift a leg up, wrapping it around his waist and pulling him towards me. He grasps the other and pulls it up so I am wrapped around his waist and rubbing against his length.

Rian slips his hand back under my pants and immediately dips inside me only this time, he picks up speed. His fingers are moving so fast, the sensation is overwhelming. His thumb finds my clit and pushes down on it, making me cry out. Faster, harder, it's everything I need yet it's still not what I want.

I want him inside me. I want to feel his cock driving into me as his hips slam against my thighs. I close my eyes, picturing exactly that and I can feel my climax building. "Rian," I moan. I'm so close I just need-

"I think you can take it from here."

Everything falls away as Rian pulls his fingers out, shoves my shaking legs down, and steps back from me. I nearly collapse under my own weight as he turns and walks away without another word.

What. The. Fuck.

Chapter 34

Eve

Sharp, biting pain radiates from my wrists where they are tied tightly at the base of my spine. Sweat drips down the center of my chest, the thin blouse they gave me clings to my damp skin, the fabric becoming nearly transparent. The cold, hard ground is unforgiving beneath me. My knees ache from the small rocks biting into my skin as I am forced to kneel before him. I shift, trying to relieve a bit of pressure, making my hair fall forward on either side of my face and stick to my neck and forehead.

I watch him as he circles me, stalking, analyzing. Waiting. His eyes never leave me, his gaze locked on the trap he has my body in with an odd sort of appreciation. A shiver rolls down my spine as I pant, fighting to catch my breath. "Please," I beg, my voice hoarse, barely more than a whisper.

Yuta glides towards me, the faint wisps of smoke trailing behind him casting a dark, ominous shadow. He looks down at me, a cruel smile spreading across his full lips as he reaches out, stroking my cheek tenderly. I have to fight every instinct to lean into that warm, comforting touch. The softness of his skin against my tear stricken cheek. In a blur of movement his hand has wrapped around my hair, tugging on it tightly near the base of my scalp and drawing a pained cry.

"You look so beautiful when you beg," his voice is haunting, it fills the space between us and sucks away all the oxygen.

His grip tightens and I have to bite down on my lip to keep from crying out again, my eyes squeeze tightly shut. Worse still, I have to fight to keep my thighs from clenching, from showing even the smallest hint that I-

"Oh for Vana's sake, she did it again," Teru groans, disgusted.

Their voice is so close that I am ripped from this moment and forced back into reality, my eyes flying open. The room around me is far nicer than the one in the visions Teru gifts me. High ceilings, lots of natural lights, the floor is a smooth stone, though I swear my knees still ache. I'm sitting on the floor with my hands unbound and placed delicately in the center of my lap, my knees tucked under me. It's actually pretty comfortable.

Teru is positioned on a short stool directly in front of me, their eyes filled with clear abhorrence. "Brother, care to step in so that I do not have to suffer any further depravity?" They gag dramatically, turning their gaze to the corner of the room.

I follow their eyeline and find Taka lounging by the wall, refusing to acknowledge his twin. It's just the three of us in the room, no Yuta. Something about this makes my skin crawl. The visions have become so real, it's nearly impossible for me to distinguish one from reality and when everything fades away, I am left more than a little disoriented. This time included. "What's happening?"

Teru lets out a long, frustrated exhale. "What's happening is that you are impossible and positively revolting."

"Excuse me?"

"You heard me. Those little visions of yours are utterly vile. As if the king would ever-"

"Teru. Shut. Up," Taka barks, "get out of here. I'll take over."

Teru jumps to their feet. "Finally. Took you long enough," they say, making their way to the door and casting one last look over their shoulder, giving me a subtle wink before they close the door behind them.

I jump to my feet, ready to follow after them, but my head immediately begins to spin, my vision going black in an instant as my body turns cold. Fuck. Not enough then. The visions can only get me so far and it takes a considerable amount of energy to manipulate them in the first place. Even if I have been feeling better over the last week, it still isn't enough.

"Don't." Taka stalks towards me from his spot in the corner, replacing his twin on the stool in front of me.

"So, what's next?" I ask, fighting to stay on my feet.

"We know that you're hiding something. You should just tell us what we want and save yourself the pain. No one is coming for you," he mutters the last part under his breath so I choose to ignore it.

"I have no secrets, I'm an open book."

"*Really*?" Taka drawls, head tilting to one side, "is that so?"

"Of course, I have nothing to hide." I swallow past the rising lump in my throat.

"My twin seems to believe otherwise. My king agrees, and while Teru might be wrong about most things, I am inclined to believe them this time."

"Well you must not be a very good sibling if you speak so poorly about your twin," I deflect.

"On the contrary, we are quite close. Close enough that I know everything about them. They have no secrets from me or anyone else that they love. But even if they did, I would find them out, do you know how?" Taka scoots the stool closer, close enough that waves of his power begin to call to mine where it slumbers deep within me.

I stifle my groan, my heart making a little excited jump inside my chest. It's working. It's really working. This is it, I just have to bide my time now. Play their game while they all unknowingly play mine. I must take too long to answer because Taka seems utterly done with talking as his magic rips into me, far more painful and invasive than any before. There's no manipulating this magic so instead, I endure.

When it finally ends, hours later if the sun is to be trusted, it's Chien who lifts my limp body from the ground, cradling me in his huge arms and taking me back to my room. Cell? I'm not really sure anymore. He deposits me on my bed with surprising care and just like every night for the past week he pulls out a small vial and passes it towards me, waiting until I down the contents before he leaves.

No matter how many times I ask, no one will tell me what it is. All I know is that after I drink it, I don't feel quite so close to death anymore. Something that I refuse to take for granted. This small bit of strength is enough to keep me alive, to keep me fighting, so I'll take it and I won't ask questions anymore. The liquid is smooth as I swallow it all down, the warm feeling of it in my chest makes me hum.

Chien leaves after that, disappearing in a cloud of smoke and leaving faint vapors behind. Almost involuntarily I reach out to them, twirling my fingers around and watching as the smoke dances between them. I bring my hand left and right, mesmerized by the way it curls around me, wrapping me tight, almost like a caress.

"What are you doing?" The sound of Yuta's voice in the room has me nearly leaping out of my skin.

"Vana," I say, clutching my chest. The vapors disappear and an odd sense of longing takes root inside me. "Why are you here?"

"Why wouldn't I be here?"

"You never come after," I answer hesitantly, scooching back on the bed until I'm squeezed into the corner of the walls.

Yuta smiles, crossing the room and smoothing a hand over the bed. "You sound almost disappointed."

I laugh, a short humorless laugh that sounds nothing like any of my laughs from *before*. "As if."

"You might like it here you know, if you would open your mind," Yuta says almost absently, looking at me through thick lashes.

"Never."

"You know nothing about my home, about this kingdom."

"I know everything I need to know," I state firmly.

"Do you?"

"Yes."

"You don't know why we took you. Why you're here. Why the shadows call to you," he says, watching my face.

"I have no idea what you're talking about," I say, my heart hammering.

"No? Well then, I guess there is quite a bit to talk about then," he sits on the edge of the bed, pushing a hand through his dark hair and staring at me with those unusual, amber eyes. "I think it's time you learned the truth. Let's start at the beginning, shall we?"

"Actually, I think it's time you left. You see, I've just been tortured, I'd like some time alone, if you don't mind."

Yuta shakes his head. "You want answers, but you refuse to listen." He stands, looking

down at me with an unreadable expression. "I'll see you tonight." He vanishes.

"I hope not," I mutter to myself.

Chapter 35

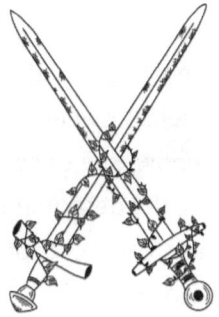

Oliver

Magic crashes into me, the force of it sends me flying backwards. I land on my back, Terran beside me, sopping wet from head to toe. I barely register the pain as I jump back to my feet, rushing forward and slamming against a barrier. On one side, my brother and I, on the other, Cay.

Panic floods my system as our fists begin to pound, desperate for a way in. The barrier is mostly transparent aside from the warping of the spell that distorts the images on the other side. Still, even with the haze and the ripples, it is clear that Cay is not alone. Five dark shadows circle her. Two of them have the audacity to turn their backs to us like we're not a threat. Because *she* forced us away.

A look over at my brother has my blood turning to ice, his own face a reflection of the terror that ravages me from the inside. I fight harder, digging deep into that well and clawing at the barrier with every bit of magic I can muster. There is a steady buzz inside my head as it grows, and grows. Faster than it has since the last time I was locked in a battle. Here, in Rayan. Flashes of that day echo in my mind as a reminder that I have failed before.

Cay is dodging one attack after the other, her magic grows as she calls on the power her home gives her. This land is built on her family's magic, power and energy flows in a direct line from the land into the blood that runs through Cay's veins. Raw energy fills the air from the sheer abundance of magic she is using. She's casting spells while using a myriad of water attacks to defend herself. Between that and the barrier, the magic is draining fast. Though somehow, she doesn't slow, doesn't falter. I can feel the force of her conviction, the determination to win. It's incredible.

"Brother..." Terran's panicked voice cuts through my awe as two of the figures get close enough to grab her.

They're bigger than her, at least a foot taller as they go for her arms, trying to lock her down and stop her attacks. Their hands never even brush her skin before her magic arcs out, hitting them in their chests and sends them hurtling through the air. Two dull thuds sound even from this side of the barrier as they hit the ground. After only a mere moment it is clear they're not getting back up.

My mouth is halfway open on an encouraging cheer when a third figure appears behind her. My words become a warning at the same time that my brother yells out for her. Without even glancing back, large tentacles made entirely of water shoot out all around Cay. They strike at once, knocking her attackers back and turning the tide yet again. One tentacle wraps around the third figure's ankle, hoisting them into the air and throwing them into the barrier.

"Nice," I mutter under my breath, unable to hold the compliment in. My magic is writhing inside me, pulsing and growing unstable with each passing second. An odd sort of ache fills my chest as I try and lock it down. It needs a channel, an outlet, somewhere for all of this magic to go. I close my eyes and press my palms against the barrier, concentrating on funneling every bit of power I can into bringing this barrier down. Part of it is to dispel the power, but the other reason…has everything to do with the girl locked on the other side.

"Cay!" Terran screams and my eyes fly open, my concentration broken.

Cay is down on her knees, her arms hanging at her sides as she struggles to catch her breath. Her long waves have come loose, cascading down her back and brushing the swell of her ass that I'm definitely not looking at. I drag my eyes away from her as a figure stalks forward, looming over her as Cay looks up. Her defiant chin points proudly in the air as her mouth begins to move, though I can't make out what she is saying over the roaring in my ears. Whatever this conversation is about, I don't like it.

"Oliver, we have to get in there!" Terran says, continuing to pound against the barrier. He's pulling and pulling on his magic, fighting to get something strong enough to tear this thing down. He might be the heir to our realm, but his magic is no stronger than mine, especially not here.

"I'm fucking trying," I say between gritted teeth. I push everything I have outwards, pulling more and more magic from my seemingly endless well, but it's not enough. Not to break the barrier. I'm left with only one choice. *Shit.*

I take a step back, kneeling down and placing my palms flat against the sand and taking deep breaths. In, out. In, out. I keep up this rhythm, steadying my breath as I begin to unravel the dampers I have on *that* magic. I picture chains falling away, one by one. Then, an old, rusted lock. I picture myself inserting a key and turning it slowly, fighting even now to retain some semblance of control. The moment the lock clicks, magic swells inside of me.

"What the-"

Power rushes to my fingertips and it takes what little control I have left to launch myself forward, slamming my palms against the barrier again just as power tears itself from me. It's like a piece of me is being ripped away, torn and shredded as it feeds into the barrier. The entire time, my eyes stay locked on Cay.

The barrier begins to ripple and crack as Terran stumbles back, his eyes flicking between me and the girl we are both desperate to get to. Then, with a final crack, the entire thing shatters. We waste no time rushing through, the both of us immediately rushing to Cay's aid. Without the haze of the barrier the figures become clear and the one standing over Cay nearly stops me in my tracks.

Nalei.

Shit. This is very, very bad.

I head straight for the siren while mentally replacing each lock and chain on that wild magic that lives inside me. This might be the worst possible scenario, but it's not enough for me to risk Cay's safety by leaving that magic unchecked. No, it has to be tucked away before it can hurt anyone else.

I rush straight past Cay and slam into Nalei, taking her to the ground. She is pinned beneath me, my body weight holding her down as she grins up at me.

"Oliver, how nice to see you again," she says with her familiar lilt.

"Yeah, Nal, I wish I could say the same." I capture both of her wrists, holding them above her head as she bucks against me.

"Just like old times," she laughs. Her dark eyes begin to swirl and I quickly clamp a hand over her mouth.

"Not quite." Looking over my shoulder I see that Terran has already taken down the one remaining siren and is currently helping Cay to her feet. My heart thumps erratically as I watch them together, his hand on her arm, the hesitant smile she gives him.

"Are you okay?" I hear him whisper to her.

"Fine," she answers, her voice a bit shaky.

Cay's eyes meet my own and I can't help but look her over from head to toe, searching for any sign that she isn't as *fine* as she claims. Thankfully, I find nothing visible to be concerned about. I shift so that I am no longer on top of Nalei, twisting her around so that she is on her knees with her hands behind her back, one of my own hands still clamped tightly over her mouth.

"It's fine, Oliver, let her go," Cay says reluctantly.

"Absolutely not," I snort.

"We've come to an agreement," Cay explains, staring down at Nalei who rolls her eyes.

"Cay, are you sure?" Terran asks, placing a hand on her shoulder.

I stare at that hand, unable to dampen the rage that starts to build inside me.

"Yes, she's not going to do anything," Cay says pointedly. She turns her sea-green eyes on me and raises her brows expectantly.

"For the record, this is a horrible idea," I say, slowly prying my hand away one finger at a time.

"Now, now, Oliver, that's no way to speak of an old friend," Nalei tsks.

Cay's brows pull together, but she says nothing.

I release Nalei's hands and she immediately begins rubbing at her wrists as she stands.

"Remember our deal," Cay says, stepping into the siren's personal space.

"The same to you," Nalei says, voice dripping with loathing.

The other sirens begin to stir and Nalei goes to them, helping them up. Meanwhile I whirl on Cay, grabbing her by her arm and tugging her close so she has to crane her neck up at me. "Never. Do. That. Again."

Cay's eyes burn with defiance.

"What deal did you make? And who is that?" Terran asks, grabbing my wrist and pulling my hand away. He tucks Cay against his side, not even noticing the way she stiffens in his arms.

"It's a lot to explain, it's easier to just tell you as we go along," Cay says with a resigned sigh.

"Okay, but that doesn't answer my question, who is that?" Terran presses.

"*That* is Nalei, daughter of Kareen. Her mother is the leader of the sirens."

Chapter 36

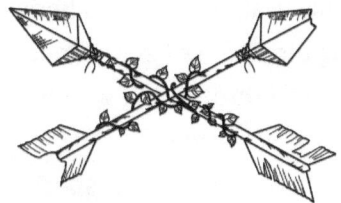

Oak

My eyes struggle to adjust as the bag is ripped off my head. When they finally do, I nearly stop breathing. Trees. There are trees everywhere. New trees. Trees that go on and on, deep into the woods. I spin, looking between every branch and every trunk searching for walls, but there are none.

I'm out.

"Don't go getting any ideas. We're here for a mission, that is all," Aine says. It's only at the sound of her voice that I notice the others. Each member of my squad is staring at me, watching for my reaction with various expressions written across their faces.

Hala is biting her lip against a smile. Symone's mouth is drawn in a tight line, but her eyes betray her, a new light shines within them. Lina is bouncing on her feet, a wide smile splitting her face. Farai looks just as serious as I expect, though if anything she seems *more* tense. But Aine... Aine looks downright murderous.

She stalks towards me, pressing her chest against my own and staring down her nose at me. "From this moment on, your first mission has begun. Don't make me regret this." And just like that, it begins.

Lina takes a few measured steps away from the group before flashing a wink and shifting. Her small frame bends and grows into a ginormous snow white wolf. She tilts her head back and lets loose a piercing howl that haunts the night sky. Hala steps up to her side, she doesn't bother shifting before climbing atop Lina's back. "Good luck!" she says, patting Lina's neck. The two take off through the woods in a blur.

"Wow, I had no idea Lina was a wolf."

"Don't tell her that, she takes pride in her species more than anyone else I've ever met. She would be devastated if she found out her 'wolfishness' wasn't the first thing people noticed about her," Symone says with a snort.

"Symone, let's go." Aine steps forward and I do a double take. She is suddenly double my height... and has four legs. Aine looks the same from her head to her waist and then it's clear what species she is. A long, horse-like body emerges from beneath her tunic, the fur a soft caramel brown that shines under the moonlight. Somehow, her being a centaur makes perfect sense.

"Be safe," Symone says before climbing upon her back. And just like before, the pair take off, leaving only Farai and I behind.

"Okay, what next?" I ask, turning to Farai.

"You said you're good in the trees, right?"

"Yeah," I shrug. Though I have now come to learn that my superior balance had a lot more to do with my magic than I previously thought.

"Good. Lina and Hala will take point, tracking down the pack. Aine and Symone will provide support and circle the exterior circle, making sure no one escapes."

"And us?"

"We will be providing our own support from above." Farai starts walking towards the base of a tall tree, staring up at the foliage and squinting her eyes.

"How are we going to get up there without magic?" The familiar pang rings through my chest as I remember just how long it's been since I had access to my magic. The fact that I know it is there yet I can't reach it makes my skin itch.

"Let me worry about that." Farai goes deathly still in an instant. Every small movement ceases, even her breathing.

Fear forces me to take a step closer. "Farai?"

No response. Another full minute passes and my worry only begins to grow. *What if something happened? What if this is some spell, or poison? What if something is wrong?* I take another step closer just as Farai's eyes fling open. I nearly fall flat on my ass as her completely black eyes stare back at me. But that's not all. Farai's entire body has taken on a dark grayish tinge.

Stone. She's turned to stone.

Farai is a gargoyle.

Holy. Shit.

Before I can really process this new, highly interesting discovery, I am swept up into her arms and we are soaring through the air. A scream gets lodged in my throat as we burst through the tops of the trees. Only as I look down, expecting to feel some minor sign of fear, I am left with my mouth hanging agape. It's positively beautiful.

"Wow," I breathe.

"I know," Farai says and this time I do scream. Her smooth, stone hand slaps down over my mouth as her eyes begin to dance around, watching for any sign of trouble. "Are you trying to get us killed? What the fuck was that about?"

"You can talk."

"Obviously. Why wouldn't I be able to talk?"

I shrug. "I just didn't realize that gargoyles could talk while shifted. I just assumed..." I stop talking.

"Why would you assume that? Haven't you ever met a gargoyle before?"

"Yes, but not while they were shifted." My cheeks begin to flame as I realize how stupid this all sounds. Of fucking course she can talk.

Farai flies us over the treetops, staring down at the ground below with her all black eyes. Her stone brows pull together as she seems to see something, and then I hear it, another piercing howl cutting through the silence. We dive. Farai's arms squeeze me tightly to her chest as we plummet towards the earth. Just before we're about to crash into the branches, the trees wrench apart, a perfect opening for us to dive through.

We land on a thick branch, perched high above the ground where a fight has broken out. Lina is still shifted, biting and snapping at other wolves as they try to trap her. Hala is off to the side, her legs now mirror those of a goat, a thick dark brown fur covering them. She's a faun, so I am willing to bet her sister is as well.

While fauns might not have a lot of power, they're exceptional at spells and magic, which is why it comes as no surprise that Hala is easily fending off half a dozen wolves with attack after attack. I'm watching, mesmerized, as she easily summons the earth and uses it in combination with various spells, bright bursts of magic lighting up the space around her.

"What do we do? How do we help?" I watch as Lina manages to knock two wolves unconscious when two more appear out of nowhere and jump straight into the fray. Some of them are in their mortal forms, fighting with fists and using magic. Yet nothing stirs inside me. Nothing rises to the surface or even begins to call to me. It's extremely unsettling.

"Nothing, we watch. If something happens and we need to step in, then we will. Until then, this is where we are most useful."

More and more wolves continue to pour into the clearing, the majority of them rushing straight for Lina. She quickly becomes overwhelmed by them and I nearly lose sight of her white fur completely.

"Farai..."

"No. She's fine. Lina can take care of it. Do not react."

My hands begin to shake as more and more time passes without even a small hint that Lina is buried beneath all those wolves. The sound of snarls and gnashing teeth echo through the forest as my ears and heart begin to pound. This is not good. This can't be good. There's no way.

"Oakley. Don't." Farai grabs my arm.

A pained whimper breaks through the silence between the fighting and I'm already flying towards the ground. It doesn't matter that I only learned today that Lina is a wolf, there is something about that sound and I just *know* that it's her.

She's hurt, and she needs help.

The tree is a lot higher up than I expect and it feels like I'm falling forever. It's only as the ground grows closer and closer that I realize I have absolutely no magic to catch me and without shifting it is highly unlikely I'll be able to just land on my feet.

Fuck.

I close my eyes, ready for the impact that never comes. Cold, firm arms wrap around my middle and grab me, stopping me just before I collide with the ground. Instead, I am set gently on my feet and spun around so fast my vision goes blurry.

"*Never*, do that again," Farai bites. Her eyes flick to the spot just over my shoulder and then I'm being shoved out of the way as Farai uses her stone arm to block the sharp edge of a blade that was aimed straight for the spot where my head had been. The blade bounces off her arm and shatters. The male immediately shifts to fighting with magic as I crawl out of the way, barely avoiding a stray spell.

I head straight for the spot where I last saw Lina and start going after the people who aren't shifted. My heart is racing as I meet their punches and kicks blow for blow, dodging and blocking just as much as I am attacking. A fist swings for my face and I duck down, sweeping my leg out and catching him in the back of his ankle. He hits the floor with a thud and I pop back up, ready to jump back in. I give myself a second to admire my form and how much better I've gotten.

The ground begins to rumble and I am forced to grab onto the closest tree to keep from falling over. Then, the ground explodes before me, a figure draped in white flies into the air as dirt and mud pour out behind. There, in the center of it all, is Lina. She's shifted back and her clothing is in tattered shreds covered in a large amount of blood. Her white hair is coated with it on the ends, the color staining it a dark crimson red.

"Lina!" my voice is drowned out by the sounds of screaming. All at once, great, thick roots spring up from the ground and wrap around the people, dragging them down and pinning them against the loose earth.

Lina walks over to me, looking me up and down. "Are you okay?"

"Yes, I'm fine but you–"

"It's not my blood." Her eyes are devoid of their usual light. She's turned cold, distant, her gaze appearing far off as she reaches out, grabbing me by my forearm. "Come on, let's go find the others."

Hala is wiping her hands against her tunic, still in her shifted form. She grimaces at the mud and general grossness covering her body. "Well that was a lot messier than I was hoping."

"True, there were a lot more than we were expecting," Lina agrees with a sigh. She blinks her eyes a few times and seems to come back to herself, though the way her lips are turned down is still so unlike her.

Farai marches over, standing over me with a furious gleam in her eyes. "You could have gotten yourself killed."

"I was–""No. I don't want to hear it. You could have jeopardized everything," Farai growls. She's back in her mortal form yet everything about her is still preternaturally still.

"But Lina–"

"Don't go dragging me into this. I was perfectly fine where I was. Whatever you did, that's on you." Lina bends in half, gathering up her blood soaked hair and tying it up.

I don't bother arguing. Whatever I say won't matter. Clearly, I made a mistake. Even if it doesn't feel like that. If that was Rose, or Mar, or Cay, or Eve, I would have done the same thing because it doesn't matter that she was fine. When someone you care about is in trouble you take care of them. They shouldn't need to ask.

"Come on, let's go find Aine and Symone." Hala says, running a hand through her short hair.

"Wait, but what about them?" I say gesturing to the dozen unconscious people littering the ground.

"Leave them, they're not who we came for," Farai says, stalking off into the dense part of the forest.

"Wait then why were we fighting them?"

"Easy," Hala says, "they got in the way."

Lina and Hala both follow after Farai. I look around, studying the faces of the people they are just leaving behind and wondering what the point of all this is. If I thought I didn't understand the Ghosts before, this certainly didn't help the issue. Still, I follow after the others in time to see Aine and Symone approaching, both in mortal form.

"Did you get what we needed?" Farai asks Aine who nods in confirmation.

"How did it go over here," Aine asks, her eyes flicking towards me. When she looks back to her second, they share a knowing look and Aine sighs. The sound has barely passed through her lips when another bag is thrown over my head.

Great.

Chapter 37

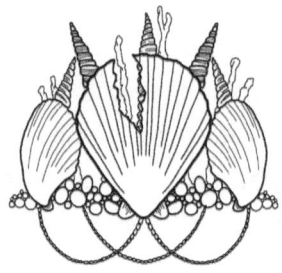

Cay

"What do you want?" Oliver bites. He's standing close enough that his body heat radiates against my side, at the same time, Terran wraps a loose arm around my shoulders, tugging me closer to him.

I sway on my feet, my power growing unsteady as many thoughts war with each other in my mind. Fear turns my blood thick, slowing everything down to a crawl as I fight to breathe. Nalei is standing before me like a dark omen, a representation of just how far I have fallen. How far this kingdom has fallen.

"Why don't you ask *her*," Nalei says, her voice is rich and deep, intoxicating even without the use of her magic. Her mere presence is like a beacon, calling everyone to her like mindless puppets.

"Cay?" Terran whispers against my ear.

He's so close, he's practically wrapped around me and yet somehow I feel cold and detached, like somehow my body is far away from here. I want to lean into him, to accept the support he is offering, but I can't. Because all I want to do is run.

"Back off, brother," Terran is ripped from my side with a snarl. Oliver's large hands grip my shoulders and he starts to shake me.

I stare up at him without really seeing him, caught in an endless loop of pain. I curl my hands into fists, my nails biting into my palm, yet I don't feel it. I don't feel anything. I thought that I could do this. That I could face this. But I was wrong. *I'm not ready. It's too much. I can't do this. I can't do this. I can't-*

"Focus." Oliver bends forward so we're eye to eye. The green flecks of his iris are particularly bright right now, swirling with mixtures of golden browns. His dark lashes fan his cheeks as he blinks. "You with me?"

"I can't," the words are barely more than a whisper, nothing more than a breath of fear and confusion and pain.

"Yes you can, princess. You've got to pull yourself together. Tell us what's going on, beautiful," Oliver says just to me. His thumbs are moving in soft circles against my shoulders, the rough pad scraping ever so slightly.

I focus on that. The sensation of skin against skin. The heat working its way back into my body. Slowly, I knit myself back together again so I can keep going. I ignore all of the little cracks and holes and glue back the pieces so I can do what needs to be done. There's always time to be broken later. Taking a deep breath. I feel the fear settle. It's not as strong, but still there, sitting in the pit of my stomach like a stone might in a lake. "I'm good."

"What's going on?" Oliver says, not pushing for anything more than what I have offered him.

"They have a way back into the city." I look over to the small group of sirens standing off to the side, their lips are curled into matching sneers as they stare me down.

"Yes we certainly do. You see, while you've been off prancing around in the earth realm, we sirens have been getting to work rebuilding the kingdom that *someone* destroyed," Nalei taunts.

"Watch your mouth, Nalei, I'm this close to saying screw it and ending all of you," Oliver growls.

Nalei laughs, the sound full and hearty. "Try that and you'll never get back into the city. Last I checked you have two earth elementals and a half-broken princess, you'll need better to get in and well, I'm better," she flicks her long locs over her shoulder, a familiar clear quartz necklace dangles from a leather band wrapped around her neck. She sees me looking at it and smooths a thumb over the stone reverently.

"She's right," I swallow down the lump in my throat, "I don't have enough magic. We need their help."

"Absolutely not, we'll find another way," this comes from Terran who has been standing off to the side watching, waiting, analyzing. I can see the plan already formulating in his mind, the problem is, it won't work.

"We don't have a choice," I say with a sigh.

"Why not?" Terran says, stepping forward like he means to get between the sirens and me.

"Because, the entire tunnel is destroyed, exactly as I thought it would be. Which wouldn't have been a problem except, unfortunately, Nalei is right, I don't have enough magic." The moment we touched the beach I knew that our plan wouldn't work. There was no way that I could bring Terran and Oliver into the city safely and there is even less of a chance they let me go in alone.

"See, at least the little princess is honest with herself about her inadequacy." The sirens snicker at Nalei's continued remarks.

I knock Oliver's hands aside, barely having realized he was still holding onto me, and brush past Terran, walking straight up to Nalei. "I don't like you. You don't like me. I don't trust you. You don't trust me. All of this is abundantly clear, but the fact remains, we need each other."

Nalei smirks and stretches her arms out wide, spinning in a slow circle, "Well it seems we have an understanding then." She turns back to face me, reaching out a hand.

I stare at it, fighting the urge to turn around and run.

"Cay, you don't have to do this. We can figure this out," Terran reassures from behind me.

242

"He's right, there are other options," Oliver echoes, for once agreeing with his brother.

"Maybe, but this is the fastest." We all know that my mother doesn't have much time, it doesn't need to be said, yet even in the silence I feel the weight of those words pressing down on me.

"Ah yes, tell me, how is auntie Mira?" Nalei tilts her head at me.

Oliver moves faster than my eyes can track. One second he is standing just behind me, the next he is behind Nalei, a blade digging into her throat. "Say that name again and lose the right to speak. A siren with no voice, how does that sound? I don't know about you, but I kind of like it."

"Oliver," Terran warns.

"Settle down, I was only checking in on family." Nalei leans back into Oliver, a hand landing on her thigh and skating up.

I grab her wrist, pulling it away and twisting it back until a hiss escapes her. "Enough, we're wasting time."

Nalei sighs, "Just as boring as ever. Fine, let's go."

Oliver hesitates for only a moment, but as our eyes meet he seems to see my plea and releases her. "If any of those buddies of yours so much as think about laying a hand on any of us, they'll wish they were dead."

"Those guys?" Nalei says, glancing over her shoulder at the small collection of males waiting for her command. "They're harmless. But if you would like to gut them, be my guest. I've grown tired of this group anyways."

Terran shakes his head as Nalei walks back to her small group, greeting them and telling them the plan, if it can even be called that. "What did she mean about *'family'*?" he asks.

Every family has its secrets, mine is no exception. Ours just happens to be as deep as our blood. "Nalei is my cousin. My mother and her mother are half-sisters, the same way as Mar and Eve. They share a father, but that is about where the similarities stop." I don't tell anyone this. No one. Not even the girls. For a while, I refused to acknowledge it myself.

"I'm very sorry, Cay. I know that you have a complicated-"

"It's fine. I don't want to talk about it. Can we just go?"

Terran gives me a small smile, reaching out to caress my face. "I'm sorry for bringing it up, lead the way."

I'm so shocked that I stand there frozen as the others make their way forward. I don't even flinch as Nalei sets her chin on my shoulder. "Looks like you got yourself a brother of your own, pity it's the boring one," she sighs next to my ear and then bounds off after the others, leaving me alone on the edge of the boundary.

Composing myself, I join the rest of the group. The moment I walk up, I am instantly sandwiched between Terran and Oliver. Terran reaches down and takes my hand in his and I'm pretty sure my eyes are about to pop right out of my head. He smiles down at me as I struggle to find something to say.

What the fuck is happening?

Oliver snorts on the other side of me, but otherwise says nothing, he just stands there like a silent sentry.

"Stand back, it's going to take us a minute to get things started," Nalei calls out to the group as she and two others walk forward, hands outstretched in front of them.

"So, what is this plan?" Terran asks, bending down so he is speaking directly in my ear.

"Um-so the sirens are using spells to slowly rebuild the tunnel, but they've been working from inside the city out, this section is still too damaged for you to cross through so they're going to temporarily rebuild it as we walk through," I explain.

The entire time during our fight, Nalei was bragging about all the work she had done, how she was going to be the kingdom's savior, not me. It wasn't until I admitted that I wasn't here to save the kingdom that she was even willing to hear me out. But as much as it destroys me to admit, the only person I care about saving right now is my mom.

"If they're going to fix it, why wouldn't they leave it? Why destroy it after?"

I stare at the back of Nalei's head. She lowers her arms, having completed the spell, and looks at me over her shoulder. Her eyes flick down to where Terran is grabbing my hand and she winks, laughing openly and making the sound echo down the newly formed tunnel.

"Because, not only is she a siren who thrives on chaos, she also doesn't have the power needed to sustain it right now. At least not permanently. That would require power like what my father yielded."

The power that failed to pass to me.

Chapter 38

Rose

The mountain stretches high into the clouds, the peak lost in the fog. When we first decided to come to Eteri, we knew there would be challenges. Namely getting *inside* the city. The people of Eteri are notoriously reclusive, and rarely allow outsiders in. Still, we aren't left with much of a choice if we want any sort of answers.

"Alright, let's move." I start towards the narrow path carved into the mountainside.

Reed reaches out, grabbing my wrist and pulling me back, "What are you doing? You can't just walk up the mountain."

"Then how exactly do you think we're getting into the city?" I ask, staring at him expectantly. This is a familiar argument, one that I have long since given up trying to win. According to my cousin, we have to be invited into the realm. If we aren't, then we'll be seen as trespassing and could possibly get ourselves killed. Not the best idea, but we don't have time for court pleasantries.

"I told you before, we need to be invited. If we aren't, then we might as well have stayed in Sena, because we are not getting in." Reed throws his hands up, clearly frustrated by my disregard for the *rules*.

"Reed, I appreciate your insight and respect your opinion. But," I take a step towards the mountain, "we don't have time. So come with me or don't, but either way, I'm walking up this mountain." I take another step onto the path, reaching a hand out.

He stares at it like it holds the key to his demise. Then, with a resigned sigh, he takes my hand. His entire body seems to cringe the moment our hands touch, and I feel just the slightest twinge of guilt at forcing him to do something he so clearly does not want to do. "If we get killed, then who helps Oak?" he asks under his breath.

"We're not going to get killed, okay? All we have to do is make it to the top and explain why we're here. You and I have royal blood, that has to count for something. Our ancestors knew each other, maybe they were friends even." The stare I receive in response has me laughing out loud, the sound echoing around us like a great roar.

"Shhhh," Reed says, his panicked eyes flicking all around us.

A branch snaps behind us and we both whirl, staring at the edge of the forest with our hands firmly intertwined. Two figures appear at the edge and I breathe a sigh of relief. Mateo and Gael are back.

"Took you long enough," I grumble.

"Aw, little Ro, did you miss me?" Mateo says, clutching a hand over his heart.

"Did you find anything?" Reed says, dropping my hand and rushing up to the wolf shifter.

Mateo's easy smile widens as he looks my cousin over. He reaches out a tanned hand and cups Reed's cheek, leaning forward and whispering in his ear.

Reed stumbles back and Mateo laughs, Gael just shakes his head as he makes his way closer to me.

"Everything okay?" I ask him, hardly expecting a response. In the short time I have known Gael I have learned one thing to be certain, he only speaks when absolutely necessary. A pleasant change from Mateo's constant chatter. Somehow I just know that Eve and Mateo will be fast friends.

Gael simply nods as the others join us. Mateo slings an arm around his second's shoulder and beams at him. "Did Gael give you the rundown?"

"Um…"

"Of course he did, good work." Mateo claps a hand on Gael's shoulder and starts up the path, meanwhile Reed is still staring after him, dumbfounded. Mateo looks back over his shoulder and gestures for us to follow him, "what are you waiting for? We've got a long way to go."

Gael follows after him without question. Reed slowly makes his way up the mountain, stopping when he gets to my side. His cheeks are a vibrant red, the tips of his pointed ears stained the same color.

"What did he say to you?" I ask, whispering in his ear.

"You don't want to know."

~~~

We're about halfway up the mountain when we pause to take a break. It's been hours and we're all exhausted, but for the most part, we've had no issues aside from Mateo's constant need to ask questions and tell stories. It has been entirely uneventful. Which is exactly why I don't trust it.

Mateo is sprawled out on the dirt, an arm slung over his eyes as he lays there. Reed is just a little further up the path, using his magic to sense any disturbances or gaps in the path. Gael disappeared back down the path so he could relieve himself, which leaves me here alone in my worries. Something just doesn't feel right.

Getting to my feet, I walk off after Reed, my heart racing for no reason. *It's fine. He's just around the corner. There is nothing to be worried about.* A loud grunt comes from up ahead and I am sprinting. I round another curve in the path and run straight into a body. We both go down in a tumble of limbs, dirt clouds the air as we hit the ground.

"Vana, Rose, what are you trying to do, tackle me?" Reed groans from beneath me.

I stumble off of him, staring down at him as he clutches his gut. "What happened?"

"What do you mean? *You* tackled *me*."

"No, before that. I heard a grunt." I spin in place, searching the area around us for any sign of trouble.

"I just tripped. Are you going to help me up?" He reaches a hand out for me.

I pull him to his feet, using my magic to get all the dust and dirt off of him. "Sorry, I guess I'm just a little on edge."

"I understand, I feel it too. Let's just get back to the others and keep moving. The path was clear up ahead, no sign of anyone else on the trail or any issues with the path itself."

"Good." We walk back to the others, side by side. As we round that final curve we freeze. Gael and Mateo are both lying face first on the ground, their hands bound at the base of their spine.

Reed takes a step forward, but I stop him, every fiber of my being telling me that this is a trap.

"Rose…"

"I know. Just… give me a second to think." I slowly look up, searching for any sign of an attacker hiding out overhead. There is nothing there. Craning my head back, I stare up into the clouds. A dark shadow appears at the center of one and I squint my eyes up just as the cloud vanishes and a swarm of people dive down towards us.

They land as one in a perfect 'v'. At the point is a tall, lithe woman. Her head is completely shaved, lines of golden paint have been drawn across her dark, brown skin. The lines start at her sharp jaw, arching up and cutting through the center of her eyes, splitting her defined brows and then curving over her head. They continue down her neck, branching off and disappearing beneath a woven tunic. The combination is absolutely stunning, but more breathtaking are her large wings, the feathers are pure white, the edges dipped in gold.

The woman takes a step forward, her wings tucking in closely behind her. "Who are you?"

I swallow hard, stepping in front of Reed ever so slightly. "My name is Rose, I am third in line for the Sena throne."

"We have extended no invitation to you or your realm." Her voice is deep, commanding, with the slightest hint of an accent.

"I know, I apologize. But you see, there was no time to-"

"You acknowledge that you are here without invitation."

Reed squeezes my arm, drawing my attention. He shakes his head and I know that this is bad, but I don't have a choice. We came here for answers, I'm not leaving without them. "Yes."

"Then you are trespassing." The others behind her move forward as one, there is a popping sound and then they're pointing long staffs directly at us.

"Please, if you would just let me explain. We are here because-"

"Enough. All will be revealed upon your judgment." She nods her head and the others move, two grab Gael, dragging him to his knees. As they pull him upright I see the bruises on his face, the dried blood on his lip. Two others do the same to Mateo, his head falls forward, his face curtained by his dark curls so I cannot see the extent of the damage they did to him.

This is bad. This is very, very bad. I don't know what this *judgment* is, but it doesn't sound good at all.

Four more march towards Reed and I, and he immediately goes on the defensive. I grab him, forcing him to look at me. "Don't fight. Trust me." His eyes are wide with panic, but he nods nevertheless, stepping back and allowing them to grab him. I raise my hands up, offering them to the woman.

Hands grab me on either side and then suddenly, there is no ground beneath my feet. A scream dies in my throat as I am lifted into the air, the clouds parting as we fly higher and higher. Looking around, I find the others in similar positions. Mateo and Gael hang limply between their two guards. Reed is staring at the ground in horror as he remains perfectly still. We fly in a straight line, Reed on my right, the others to my left. In front of us, the woman from before.

The sky is full of clouds that seem to part the moment we're about to go through them, reforming behind us. I can hardly make out anything as we get higher and higher. The air grows cold and damp, tiny bumps break out across my body and my neck begins to tingle. It has gradually become harder to breathe and now I have to fight the urge to gasp for breath. The air is so thin, my vision begins to grow black, but then another set of clouds vanish and a city appears before us.

Chapter 39

Mar

"Here you go," the older woman says, handing me a freshly baked pastry.

"Mar!" a voice calls from the other end of the alley.

I use my vampire sight to see past the crowds, focusing on the head of red hair as Cyrus jogs towards me. My smile takes me by surprise, almost as much as my racing heart. Nat's brother stops just short of running into me, beaming down at me with that breathtaking smile of his. "Hi."

His smile turns into more of a smirk as he jolts forward, taking me into his arms and lifting me off my feet as he spins me around. A panicked squeal escapes me as he spins and spins. My pastry falls to the ground and I nearly shed a tear. A travesty. Cyrus doesn't stop spinning and the world blurs as he picks up speed.

"Cyrus!" I cry with a laugh.

He sets me down on my feet, steadying me as I sway, laughter spilling from my lips. "That's better."

"What was that about?" I say, finally getting my laughter under control.

Cyrus shrugs, "I wanted to make you laugh, you looked way too serious."

My heart jumps and I have to bite my lip against what will surely be an embarrassing smile. *What is happening? Less than 24 hours ago I was doing…things with Rian. Now I'm over here smiling at Cyrus?*

"What do you say?"

I mean really, what if someone saw? What if Nat saw and now she hates me? Would she hate me? I would hate her if she played with Eve. But am I playing with Cyrus? No, right? Of course not. What happened with Rian was a one time thing, a lapse in judgment. Though there was that time in Rayan when-

"Mar."

Blinking away my thoughts I watch as Cyrus searches my face, amusement shining in his eyes. "What?"

"What were you just thinking about?"

"Huh," my heart kicks into overdrive.

"Your cheeks got all pink and your hands," he reaches out and pries my fingers apart from their tight fist. He rests his palm against mine and then slowly slips his fingers through mine. "Let me take you on a flight."

"What, why?" I ask, voice shaking.

Cyrus laughs, squeezing my hand and pulling me forward so we are chest to chest. "Because, it will be fun."

I shake my head, sighing. "I don't have time for fun right now, Cyrus. I still need to convince Nat to-""No you don't. Let me take care of my sister. You," he leans forward so our noses almost touch, "just worry about holding on tight."

His green eyes sparkle with a promise that I am so tempted to take. I swallow hard before telling him I can't. "Okay." *Wait, what?*

"Really?"

No. "Yes."

His smile splits his face as he wraps his arms around my waist, crushing me to him. The feeling of him wrapped around me has my body relaxing. I just met Cyrus and somehow I already feel safe with him. I feel at ease, like he will take care of me no matter what. *What is happening in this village?*

Cyrus practically drags me through the village, his eagerness to get to the field nearly overflowing into me. The clearing is wide and open, plenty of space to shift without causing any damage to surrounding buildings. He turns to me, grabbing me by the shoulders and moving me over a few steps. "Stay here. Don't move."

I nod as he turns, jogging out to the center of the field and giving me a wink before he pulls his shirt off over his head and tosses it my way. I roll my eyes and catch it out of the air. There is no reason to remove his clothing, all of them are enchanted to survive a full shift. No, Cyrus just wants to show off. Though the defined cut of his stomach and the deep v that dips below his waistband is not something I am willing to complain about.

My eyes are glued to him as he shifts, his tall frame changes and grows into a huge, vibrant red dragon. His scales are a dark, matte crimson. The soft portion of his underbelly is a pale yellow that bleeds into the creases of his wings. Everything about his creature is magnificent, the sheer size, the coloring, the long horns that sprout from just behind his eyes. I suck in a breath, his eyes. They are the same mesmerizing shade of green.

"Wow," I breathe.

Cyrus chuffs a dragon's laugh and smoke billows out from his mouth. He stalks forward, standing more than three times my size. I think he might be the biggest dragon I have ever seen. *No wonder he is such a coveted guard.* He leans forward, staring into my eyes with a request or demand and I walk forward slowly. He lowers a wing to the ground and I eye it suspiciously.

He makes that chuffing sound again, and I swear I can hear his voice telling me to trust him. I do. I jump up onto his back with ease, positioning myself in the spot between his shoulders where his wings start to sprout from his back. He shakes and I am forced to lean forward, grabbing onto whatever my hands can. The moment I am settled, he takes off.

I scream as Cyrus leaps into the air, his powerful wings beating fast, driving us higher and higher into the air until we're flying just below the clouds. He curves to the left, the right, weaving between the clouds. His spiked tail directs us as he soars.

An unsteady laugh breaks free as I sit up a little higher, only to be rewarded by Cyrus putting on a burst of speed. My hair is ripped free of its ponytail and flows freely behind me, the blonde strands whipping around. My heart pounds as we fly faster and faster, suddenly we're flying straight up and I start to lift off his back. At the last moment, I grab hold of a set of raised scales, holding myself to him as he pushes harder and harder.

Then, he stops. His wings stop beating, curling in tight to him as he tips his head back and I scream as we go fully upside down. It takes everything in me to hold on as we freefall back towards the earth. My hair is flying everywhere now, covering my face and making it nearly impossible to distinguish what is going on around us aside from the feeling of weightlessness.

I take the chance to shove my hair out of my face and find the ground far closer than it was a mere minute ago. Another scream breaks free from me as the ground grows closer and closer. "Cyrus!" I can barely hear my own voice over the whoosh of the wind. I squeeze my eyes shut just as I am sure we're going to crash.

His wings burst open, catching the air and sending us soaring back into the sky just before we would have hit the ground. His wings flap furiously as he brings us back up, my heart pounding and ears ringing the entire time. Once we're a decent way into the air he evens out, slowing down.

The sun is still rising, the sky a beautiful shade of gold as we glide easily through the air. I fight to calm down, focusing instead on the beautiful mix of colors and the subtle scent of rain in the air. Eventually, I relax, leaning back so I am laying down, staring up at the sky. I close my eyes and just breathe.

After what feels like hours, we make our way back to the ground. Slowly this time. Once Cyrus touches down, I slide off his back. I immediately go to work trying to tame my hair. The ribbon I used to tie it back is long gone so I do my best to get it to lay flat. I hear the flutter of clothes as Cyrus shifts.

"So?"

"That was amazing," I say honestly, abandoning my hair as my fingers get snagged on another knot.

"Yeah? You look a little windswept," he says with a laugh, coming up to me and smoothing his hands down on the top of my head.

I laugh, rolling my eyes, "Yeah, well whose fault was that? You know, you almost killed me a few times."

He threads his fingers in the hair at the base of my neck and a shudder rolls through me. "Yeah? You look alive to me, more alive than any other time I've seen you."

I raise my brows, "Is that so?"

"Yeah," he says, stepping closer, moving one hand down the center of my back and letting it rest in the dip at the base of my spine.

"So, what's next?" I ask, breathlessly.

"I don't know, I think I want to stay here for a bit longer." He steps closer, our chests brushing against each other.

"Oh?"

"Oh." He pulls me closer and tugs on my hair, tilting my head up towards him. His eyes heat, flicking to my lips as they part involuntarily.

My eyes flutter closed and I suck in a breath as I wait for his lips to brush mine. Instead, they brush my cheek. I open my eyes as he places his forehead against mine. "What's wrong?"

"I can smell him on you."

I freeze. My heart stalls in my chest and I stop breathing. Shit.

"Shhh, it's okay," Cyrus says, pulling back so he can look down at me, "I understand."

"Cyrus-"

"I don't share. You should know that." He slowly untangles his hand from my hair, removes his hand from my back, and takes a step back.

"I-"

"You don't owe me anything, Mar. I just thought you should know that. You know, in case you were curious."

I stand there, dumbfounded and completely at a loss for words. This male...

"I should go find Nat. I'm late for my shift and she'll probably be pissed. But don't worry, I'll still convince her. Just give me the day." Without waiting for my reply, Cyrus takes off, jogging back through the village and leaving me alone in the clearing.

And not for the first time today I wonder, what is happening?

~~~

"Thank you," I say, smiling at the shop owner. Everyone here has been so welcoming, so willing to give whatever we might need. I walk back to our temporary accommodations with a bag of dried fruit, picking at it as I go. It's nearly halfway gone by the time I make it back.

There, leaning against the door, is Nat.

"Hi," I say, surprised.

"Heard you've been spending time with my brother," she says, continuing to stare straight ahead.

"Um, yeah I guess." I swallow down the lump in my throat.

"He seems to think your plan is foolproof." Her eyes flick to mine.

I have told Cyrus exactly two percent of my plan because that is exactly how much of a plan I have, but if this is what is going to convince Nat...

"It is."

"Do you really think we can get her back?" She turns to face me fully, her eyes are puffy, her cheeks a blotchy red.

"There is no alternative. We're getting my sister back, with or without your help." Though having her help will certainly make things considerably easier.

"Okay."

"Okay?" I echo, staring at her.

"I'm in. Let's go get Eve."

I stumble a step forward, "Wait, really?"

Nat takes a deep breath, her hands drive into her curly red roots and she tugs on her hair. "Fuck it," she laughs, "that's what Eve would say, right? Fuck it?"

"Yeah, that's what Eve would say." I can't fight back the smile.

She shakes her head like she can't really believe she is doing this. "Alright then, let's go."

"Now?"

"We've already wasted enough time." She sighs, looking up at me with a sad smile, "*I've* already wasted enough time."

My heart constricts, the same words I've said to myself at least a thousand times, finally being shared. I'm not alone. Not anymore. But I know it's not enough.

"We have to go back to Izal."

Nat whips around, her hair fanning out around her like a flash of fire. "What?" She seems to panic. "That is in the complete opposite direction as-"

"I can convince my father. I know I can. He wants to help, he just feels trapped. Let me have one more chance to convince him that this is the right thing to do."

Nat stares up at the stars, her eyes squeezed tightly shut. "It's your mission, your plan. Tell me what you need me to do and I'll do it."

"Okay, then let's go."

Chapter 40

Eve

Bruises cover my knees, a mask of dark purples and blues from the hours spent kneeling on the stone floor. I twist, looking over every inch of my body in the mirror. It doesn't matter that I eat every last scrap of food they give me, I keep losing weight. Now, my ribcage is clearly visible beneath the skin, my collarbones stand out harshly and my cheeks are already looking more sunken in.

I run my fingers through my damp hair, trying to free some of the knots that have built up. Clumps of hair fall out, landing on the floor like a dark oil spill. My eyes are ringed with dark circles, the discoloration making my normally dark gray eyes appear dull and lifeless. Maybe they are lifeless. I have no idea how long I've been here, each day that passes feels like one long blink, one insufferable minute.

Pulling on a thin slip, I hobble over to the bed, laying down and staring up at the bare ceiling. Closing my eyes, I start my search for the threads. I look deep into the dark corners of my mind, feeling around for any sign of familiarity, of something there. Something I can grab onto. But just like every other time I've tried since that first, they're gone.

Whatever connection I found to my girls, it's as inaccessible to me as my magic. As if on cue, a sharp, stabbing pain starts up in my stomach. I curl into the fetal position, trying my best to breathe through the pain. The empty well of magic continues to throb. It's becoming more frequent, only a few hours between episodes now. Maybe less. It can't possibly be a good sign.

"Get up," a light, feminine voice says from somewhere in the room.

"Go away, whatever or whoever you are, let me suffer alone," I groan, clutching my stomach.

"Get. Up." The voice sounds closer now.

I can't bring myself to open my eyes to see if someone is really there. Fear that someone is…and fear that someone isn't keeps me stuck just as I am. Hands grab me, rolling me onto my back and prying my hands away from my stomach. Huh, guess there really is someone.

"Fuck. Off," I bite, still squeezing my eyes shut against the sharp stabbing pains.

"The king would like you to join him for dinner," she says again. I have to assume it's Eri. She's the only person I can think of that would fit the voice.

This guy really can't take no for an answer. "I'm not really in the mood for small talk at the moment, just send a plate to my room as usual." Another shooting pain ricochets through me and I arch off the bed with a gasp.

"It wasn't a request." A small hand wraps around my jaw, pinching my cheeks so I am forced to open my lips. Hot liquid sloshes into my mouth and down my throat, making me gag. It's not an unpleasant taste, but the fact that I'm lying on my back and had no warning doesn't make it easy to swallow.

Coughing and sputtering I sit up, my eyes flying open. "You're a real bitch you know that."

Eri stares back at me. Tonight, she is dressed in a sleek black, silk chiffon dress that hugs her slim frame. The collar is stiff but rounded, the sleeves are cropped short and hang loosely. The entire thing is held together by golden buttons that start at the collar and run diagonally to the shoulder before following the seam all the way to the floor. The hem is embroidered with golden swirls. It's exceptionally beautiful and fits her perfectly.

"This is for you," she says, holding out another beautiful gown.

"What is it with that male and his desire to dress me up?" I mutter to myself. *Must be easier to stare into the eyes of the person you're slowly killing when they're dressed in finery.*

"Get dressed." Eri helps me into the dress, holding it open as I step into it.

I use her shoulders to steady myself until I have to slip my arms in. The dress is made of emerald green velvet. The collar is a thick band that wraps around my throat like a choker, intricate bronze beading sewn in. Two strips of fabric connect to the halter's edge, hanging loosely around my upper arms like sleeves that had fallen down, leaving my shoulders bare. A sheer panel carves a deep v down the center of the dress, stopping at the cinched waistline.

Eri kneels down, helping me to slip my feet into a pair of matching flats.

"What, not taking me barefoot today?" I taunt.

"The king wouldn't like it," she says matter of factly. She takes my elbow, guiding me from the room and following the vaguely familiar path to the dining room. When the doors open, I am surprised to find that *the king* is not alone.

Yuta sits at the head of the table, Teru and Taka both on his left. The seat to his immediate right is left open. I eye it suspiciously as Eri leads me over. Yuta jumps up, pulling the seat out as Eri practically shoves me down into it, taking the empty seat on my right. Chien appears beside her, sitting down and placing a hand on her knee that I can't help but notice she smacks away.

"Eve, thank you for joining us for dinner," Yuta says with an easy smile.

"I wasn't aware I had a choice," I sneer, "you know when I said I wanted to be alone earlier I meant for longer than a few hours."

"Ungrateful little twat," Taka bites from directly across from me.

"Oh I'm sorry, Taka, what exactly is it you would like me to say? Thank you?"

"Enough," Yuta sighs, placing his hands down on either side of his empty plate. He looks up at me, those amber eyes flashing in the low light. "I invited you here tonight as a sign of good faith."

"Says the male who continues to have me tortured," I snort.

"You ignorant-" Taka starts, Yuta's glare silences him.

"That is all over now. I'm done with the torture. From this point on, consider yourself our guest." Yuta claps, summoning the servants who begin piling food upon our plates.

I've heard that before. "Why?"

"Because it has proven to be… ineffective," Yuta explains.

Teru and Taka tense in unison, their bodies becoming rigid in their seats. Chien laughs out loud, earning himself a glare from everyone else at the table.

"True, though it's not exactly like you have the best people for the job." I smirk across the table.

Taka bites his cheek as his twin rises to their feet. "I am great at my job, what would you even know about it, you depraved whore."

I snap my fingers. "That's *right*," I say, tapping a finger against my temple, "you did do that *one* thing. You remember, right? That time that you invaded Rayan and killed their king? No? Just me?"

Teru sighs, their chin dropping against their chest. "How many times must I explain. I had nothing to do with that pathetic excuse for a king's death."

"Calm yourself, Teru. We know," Yuta says.

The table falls silent as I process what they just said. "I'm sorry, what?"

"Do you have a question, Eve?" Yuta says, turning to me with a smile.

"A few actually. What the fuck do you mean you had 'nothing to do' with King Callan's death?" I curl my hands into fists to stop them from shaking.

"Must I explain *again*," Teru says, exasperated.

"Yes," I say at the same time Yuta says no. I stand, slamming my hands down on the table. "Tell me what you meant, right now."

Teru looks to their king, I do the same.

"All will be explained in time, for now, let's just focus on getting to know one another." Yuta says, raising his brows. He reaches out to me, placing his hand atop my clenched fist.

The moment our hands touch I get an overwhelming need to listen to him, to tell him everything. To just let it all go and stop holding back. I swallow hard, staring down at our overlapping hands. Narrowing my eyes, I rip my hand away, curling it against my chest.

Yuta sighs, "We wish you no harm, Eve."

"Kind of hard to believe after the whole torture thing, remember?"

Taka laughs. "This is a waste of time. We don't need her to talk or trust us, because I broke through the barriers and I know *everything*," Taka smirks at me. "I know all about who you are. I know about your friends, your little garden, I know all about that dragon-"I bolt. I'm not even really sure when I made the decision to do it, but suddenly my chair is flying backwards and I am running back towards the door Eri brought me through. I barely make it five steps when Teru's magic rips into me. They leave my eyesight, choosing instead to just hold me there, completely immobile.

"Honestly, why do we even try?" they sigh.

Yuta appears above me, staring down. "If you would like to leave, I will have Eri escort you back to your rooms. Otherwise, please sit. Enjoy the meal."

Grinding my teeth I know that I'm not going to make it out of here. Not with Teru and Taka around. Their magic is too strong. I'm completely helpless without my own magic and I'm already so weak. My heart begins to crack as I realize I am well and truly trapped here. I force back the tears even as my heart silently pleads for someone, anyone, to save me. Yet another reminder that I am alone, no one came for me.

263

"Fine," I whisper. After a moment the magic releases me and Yuta extends a hand. I take it, allowing him to pull me to my feet. He guides me back to the table, picks up my chair, and pushes it in for me once I am seated.

Clearing my throat I look at Yuta, "If I am to sit here, you will answer my questions. All of them."

"I cannot make such a promise, but I will answer all that I can," he says with a nod of his head.

"No. Clearly you know *everything* about me," I glare at Taka, "it's only right I get to know more about you."

"As I said, I will do my best."

That's probably the best I'll get for now so it will have to be enough. "What did you do with all those people?" I demand across the table.

Teru rolls their eyes. "Relax, I simply *encouraged* their attention elsewhere."

"What the fuck does that mean?" I growl.

Teru leans forward, "It means that I have a *special little gift* that makes things go a bit smoother when it comes to the things that I want."

"Teru," Taka bites at his twin, a sneer curling his lips.

"No, tell me. What is this gift?" I implore Teru, refusing to meet Yuta's stare to my left.

"Leave us," the king commands, his deep voice filling the room and sending shivers skirting down my back.

Chairs are pushed back as everyone begins to rise, along with my panic. "No, wait, you said I could ask questions! You said I would get answers!"

Teru and Taka leave without a moment of hesitation. Chien and Eri follow closely behind. The door falls shut behind them and I feel my heart crack a little more.

"The gift that Teru is referring to is what we know as the call to the soul. It allows us to make our will, the will of others. In doing so, they become more compliant," Yuta explains.

"So, you just force people to do whatever you want? Just like that."

"In a way. We simply call to their souls with our own desires and share them. In this case, the people of Rayan simply left their kingdom because that is what Teru wanted."

I temper my growing rage, choosing instead to focus on getting more answers. "Why? Why not attack, take the city by force?"

Yuta turns his chair towards me, leaning forward so we are practically in the same breathing space, despite the bit of table still between us. "Because, that is not our way, we do not take what is not ours."

"You took me."

"Precisely."

"I am not yours," I growl, staring into those amber eyes with a burning intensity. *Ohhhh if I had my magic right now...*

He smiles, looking me over from head to toe as if he finds me amusing. "Not yet, but you will be."

"Screw you," I say, spitting in his face.

Yuta chuckles, licking his lips as he leans in even closer, his warm eyes swirling with gold and shadows. "Your words do not hurt me. You'll realize soon enough that you belong here just as much as any of us do."

Sighing, he moves his chair back to normal, gesturing to our full plates. "Eat, you need to build your strength."

"I have more questions."

"We have time."

With that, I silently eat, my shoulders slumping as I start to go over everything on repeat. One thing sticking out more and more each time. This *gift*. This power, it's familiar. The ability to control someone's actions with your will alone... it reminds me of Oak's persuasion.

Chapter 41

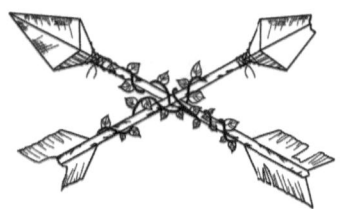

Oak

"This feels amazing," Lina groans, sinking into the hot water.

"Agreed, we should have done this sooner," Hala sighs.

It's been days since my first mission, but despite our work we were given no break. If anything, training has only become *more* intense. Especially mine. Aine has me working with Lina every day running stealth simulations. Which is more or less me trying my best to hide from Lina while she hunts me down. I've yet to succeed in staying hidden.

"Oak, what's on your mind?" Symone says, tilting her head back so her short hair can get wet.

"Nothing," I say, watching the ripples in the water and avoiding eye contact.

"Sure, we've heard that one before," Lina snorts.

"Come on, just tell us what's on your mind," Hala pushes, swimming over to sit beside her sister. Three sets of eyes watch me, and I can only be glad Aine and Farai were on kitchen duty this evening.

"I'm just frustrated. I've been training for what, almost three months now? It feels like I've barely made any progress." I sink lower into the water.

"That's not true, you have made a lot of progress," Hala says adamantly.

"Yeah, don't go insulting all our hard work," Lina says, splashing me.

"But on that mission…"

"Enough, everyone messes up their first mission. Don't even think about it. Besides, if you really were as bad as you think you were, you wouldn't be here. You'd be stuck training until who knows how late. Give yourself some credit," Symone says, reaching out to squeeze my hand.

I'm not sure when or how, but these girls have become more than just my captors. More than just the people who ripped me away from my life and family. Guilt builds as I am once again reminded that in the months I have been here, I still have no idea what is happening outside these walls.

Surely the others have found Eve by now. That much I can be assured of. But what about everything else? Did Cay's mother wake up? What happened with Rayan or all those people? Is Rose alright? Reed? There are still so many things I don't have answers to, and the longer it takes me to get out of here, the more questions I have.

I just need to get good enough to be invited on more missions. Maybe if I don't mess the next one up I'll get access to my magic and to shift. If I could *just* access my magic then I could escape…

"Hey, you're doing that thing again," Lina says, drifting to my side. Hala and Symone are further into the springs now, swimming around in the deep waters. The sisters stay close to each other, one seemingly always watching over the other's shoulder.

"What thing?" I ask, looking at Lina out of the corner of my eye.

She sighs, "Sometimes you just disappear."

My brows pull together, "I'm right here…""Not like that. You just get really quiet, your eyes sort of stare off into space and it's like none of us even exist to you." She doesn't sound mad, just resigned.

"I'm sorry?" I'm not really sure what to say in this situation. With Eve, I never had to worry about this. She just knew. We could both be together, doing our own thing, without really ever interacting with one another. It was easy.

"Why are you sorry?" Lina laughs.

"Um…"

"Look, I'm not sure what it was like for you outside the Crypt, but… in here you can talk to us. You can talk to me." She swims around so she is treading water in front of me.

"Oh."

"Oh?" Lina laughs again, "is that all, just 'oh'?"

"I- I'm not really sure what you want me to say here."

"I don't *want* you to say anything," I open my mouth, but she rushes on, "and before you stop talking entirely that is not what I meant. I just want you to feel comfortable here with us." Lina looks over her shoulder to where Hala and Symone are laughing together. She sighs, reaching forward and grabbing both of my hands. "I know that you aren't here because you want to be, but neither are we. We're just as much prisoners of our circumstances as you are, even if it doesn't seem that way."

"Is it true? That everyone here is an orphan?" The question slips out before I can stop it.

Lina looks away. "Yeah," she whispers.

"How did you all end up here?"

Lina smiles a little, returning to sit by my side. "It's different for everyone. We each have our own story, but only mine is one I'll tell."

I nod, waiting for her to continue.

"When I was a little girl, my pack worked for the high lord and lady. Our pack was pretty small, just a handful of families and there was only one other kid. We lived closer to the mortal lands, on the edge of Sena territory. My father and mother would be gone a lot, they were escorts for some tradesmen who went back and forth to the castle." Lina leans back, resting the back of her head against the edge of the pool and floating to the surface.

"One day, all of the adults went out on some big mission escorting someone important. They left me and the other kid alone back in the village. They were supposed to be right back. Days went by and no one came back for us. Eventually the other kid got worried, he wanted his mom and he wouldn't listen to me," she pauses, squeezing her eyes shut. "I begged him not to leave. To just wait for them to come home, like they always did. But he didn't, he went running off into the woods, and a few days later some guard showed up.

"Apparently the pack never made it to the castle. The high lady sent a guard to check on us. He was expecting to find an entire village, but instead he just found me. I didn't understand what happened at first. When he told me he was taking me to the castle, I thought he was taking me to my family. But then the high lady sat me down and explained that my family was gone and I was going to live somewhere else now."

I nod, knowing exactly where this is going. "They brought you here."

"They brought me here," Lina confirms.

"So, you were raised here?"

"You could say that," Lina says with a chortle.

My brows pull together, "There are no kids here."

"You're just noticing that?" Lina sideyes me.

"No, I mean. If this is where orphans are brought, why aren't there any kids here now?"

"You know some people might think you were upset about the decline in *orphaned children*," she says with a dry laugh.

"But, that's what I mean. Everyone here is relatively around the same age, right?"

"I guess..."

"So what happened that so many children were being orphaned all around the same time? Our lands have been at peace for a millennia. Yet somewhere around 20 years ago a bunch of people just started dying?"

Lina laughs openly now. "At peace? Is that truly what you believe?"

"It's true, up until the attack on-"

"Peace is a fantasy. Peace is a dream. We have never been at peace. Not in this realm or any other. *War* is not the opposite of peace, it's conflict. Just because the fight is not where you can see it, doesn't mean the fight isn't happening somewhere. It could be halfway across the world, or it could be right next door. To think that we have ever been at peace is ignorant and naïve."

"But-"

"I admire your optimism, Oak. I do. I wish it were true, that peace was something we could truly achieve. But as long as there are people, there will be conflict. It's just the way things are."

I stare at Lina, seeing the truth in her eyes. As much as I want to deny it, she's right. What happened in Rayan should be evidence enough, there is no such thing as peace. We're all just ignoring the conflict until it becomes our own. Just like Sena choosing not to help Rayan.

"I'm an orphan, did you know that?"

Lina nods, "Yes, I did."

"So then why wasn't I brought here? Why didn't I grow up here?"

"Oak, you have something that everyone else here doesn't have. Family. You may not have a mother or a father anymore, but your aunt is the high lady. You have a brother, right? And cousins? You have people who care about you. Of course you weren't dropped here."

"But what if I don't? What if no one really cares about me?" I whisper.

"What? That doesn't even make-"

"My entire life I have always been the one who is just there. An extra seat at the table. The friend that no one notices is gone. The one that no one cares as much about." *The one that no one comes to save.*

"Oak, come on. Even I know that's not-""I have always had to earn the love I am given. I'm used to it. I learned to be what other people wanted me to be and I made myself useful. Because if I'm *not* useful, if I'm not everything that they expect me to be, then they won't care anymore. They'll toss me away and forget all about me, like I was never even there."

It's the first time I've ever spoken those thoughts aloud but as I hear them, I know that they're true. I might have doubted before, but if my time here has proven anything, it's that I am exactly the person I always thought I am.

Lina sighs. "Listen, I don't know everything. I don't know your friends or your family, but I know you. You aren't disposable."

"Then why was I sent here? Hmm?"

"I don't know what you-"

"She sent me away!" I scream, my words breaking off into a sob, "I went against her *once* and she sent me away like I'm some *stranger*. She kept me around until I was no longer of use to her and then she sent me here." I wipe at the wetness on my cheeks that has nothing to do with the hot springs we're wading in.

"I'm sure that's not-"

"Oak," Aine's voice calls from the cave entrance.

"I need to go," I grab onto the edge of the pool, lifting myself out of the warm water and making my way over to Aine.

"Everything alright?" she asks, looking over my shoulder at Lina. I follow her gaze and find Hala and Symone on either side of her.

"I'm fine," I say, turning away from them, "What do you need?"

Chapter 42

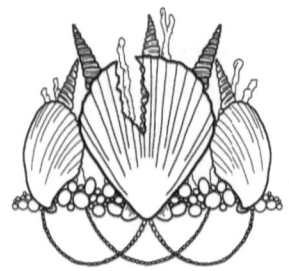

Cay

"**T**ime to stop," Nalei calls out. The sirens form a line spanning the width of the tunnel, raising their arms and making the same movements.

I watch the back of Nalei's head as she performs the spell that will fix the next section of the tunnel. I know she can feel me staring, yet she never glances back, as if I am so inconsequential.

"You okay?" Terran says, wrapping his arm around my waist.

I tense at first, the shock of the contact freezing me, then he squeezes my hip and I relax against him. I don't know what has him so touchy, but ever since that moment in his room…

"Cay?"

"Yes, sorry, I'm fine." I smile up at him. His curls are a bit unruly, the humidity making them far looser than usual. His olive skin seems even darker in the low lighting, making the green of his eyes stand out more. I reach up, hesitating before cupping his cheek. "Thank you for checking on me."

"Of course," he says, turning his face to kiss the palm of my hand. He removes his arm, walking off after his brother as I am left standing there. Terran greets his brother and the two step off to the side, talking in hushed voices.

Oliver is even more tense than usual, his eyes continually finding Nalei like he trusts her even less than I do. Though her earlier words suggest they have a history. I bite the inside of my cheek, studying him. Terran only knows Nalei because of the incident with Rose, and even still, he had no idea who her mother is or our... relation. Oliver on the other hand seems to have some sort of connection to her. One that I can't exactly trust.

"Well, well, looks like someone is all alone."

I jump, so distracted that I didn't notice the male siren approaching me. "What are you doing? Shouldn't you be helping?" I glance over his shoulder, watching as the other sirens continue to form the spell. Terran and Oliver are off to the side in what looks like an argument.

"They've got it covered. I'd much prefer to be right here." He stalks forward. For each step I take back he seems to take two steps forward until I am crowded against the tunnel wall and he is blocking any escape. His arms come up on either side of me, bracketing me in as he leans forward. "You smell divine," he says, dragging his nose up the column of my throat.

"Don't touch me," I bite, magic already beginning to rise inside of me.

"Oh, but how could I not, you're so soft, and this hair," he reaches out, picking up a loose strand that has fallen into my face. His cold fingers wrap around it, he gives it a slight tug before leaning in again, his baritone voice right against my ear. "I'd love to see it wrapped around my fist with you down on your knees. You'd like that too, right?"

I blink slowly, my legs suddenly feeling very weak. He grows taller as I begin to sink down to my knees. His hand reaches back, pulling on the tie holding my hair back and letting the strands fall loose.

"That's right, you love it. Don't you?" he lilts.

I feel myself nod, staring up at him as I move slowly. My muscles are tense, something screams inside me. I can hear a voice crying out and I try to listen closely, to hear what it has to say. My knees just barely brush the cool ground when hands appear under my arms and I am dragged to my feet. My face is crushed against a broad chest as I hear a growl from behind me.

"Touch her again and lose that hand," Oliver seethes, magic rolling off him. His entire body is tense as he holds the siren against the wall by his neck.

"Settle down, I was only playing," the siren chokes, pushing up on his tiptoes to relieve the pressure on his throat.

"No," Oliver says, pushing harder against him so that the only sound escaping his lips is a croak.

I try to tell him to stop, but Terran tugs me tighter against him, grabbing my chin and forcing me to look up. I start to argue with him to let me go, but from this angle it is clear, both males look positively feral. Looking between them you can see it in their eyes, the quiet calm that sends a chill skating down my spine, a trail of heat following in its wake.

"Now, isn't this a bit dramatic, Oliver?" Nalei asks with a sigh, sauntering towards us.

"Control your people, Nalei, and I won't have to," Oliver says through his teeth.

"Please, Javan didn't mean any harm, isn't that right?" she says with a pout.

"Of course not," Javan gasps. He's smiling despite the way his eyes are starting to bulge.

Oliver grinds his teeth. Power pulses through the air and then Javan is sliding down the wall as Oliver wipes his hand against his pants. He quickly walks over to his brother and I, grabbing my chin and tilting my head left and right.

"Oliver, stop, let go," I groan shaking off his grip.

"Are you hurt?" he mumbles.

"No," I huff.

"Good. From now on you're not leaving our side. Where you go, we go. You don't go anywhere without one of us by your side, got it?" he says, raising his brows expectantly.

"No, actually, I can take care of myself. I don't need you to-"

"No, you can't, so until you can, you're going to do exactly as we say, got it?" Oliver says cutting me off.

I look up at his brother, "Are you going to say anything?"

"He's right. We can't trust them. For now, we play by Oliver's rules," Terran says, with a sympathetic smile.

Chewing on the inside of my cheek, I look past them both to where Nalei and the other sirens snicker. "Fine," I groan. Oliver nods at my agreement and marches off, leaving me alone with Terran.

Terran's hands move to my shoulders as he tries to get me to look at him. "Cay, please, you have to understand that this is for your safety."

"I am so tired of everyone treating me like I'm some fragile doll. I can take care of myself." I stare up at him, watching as his hazel eyes soften.

"I know that. You're so strong, Cay, no one doubts that. But... you're also highly susceptible to siren magic and until we can change that, you can't be left alone with them," Terran says, his thumb rubbing slow circles against me.

I step back, out of his reach. "Got it." I turn, walking back towards the others.

Oliver is standing with his arms crossed over his chest, watching as I approach, his brother trailing after me.

"Let's go," I say, stopping beside Nalei.

She leans over, speaking directly to me, "You know, you'd be able to fight the magic if you'd just admit-"

"I said let's go," I snap.

She hums, shrugging her shoulders. "Lead the way, *cousin*."

I start forward, watching as the magic ripples, but doesn't give. The amount of power that the sirens are using is still far exceeding what I could do on my own. No matter how much I wish we could just leave them behind, we still need them.

Hours pass in silence until the main entrance comes into view. The moment it does, I freeze. The others continue forward, only Oliver and Terran stopping at my side.

"You ready for this?" Terran asks.

"We can take whatever time you need," Oliver adds in a surprising show of empathy.

"No, we've waited long enough. My mother has waited long enough. Let's just get what we came here for and get back to her," I say, my mother's face clear in my mind.

It hasn't even been that long since we left, but I can't help the fear that we're too late. Anything could have happened in the time that we've been gone and this could all be for nothing.

"Hey, she's going to be fine," Terran says, placing a hand on the small of my back.

I close my eyes, taking a few deep breaths.

"Are you three just going to stand there or are you going to come inside?" Nalei calls from the other side of the doorway. Her hands are propped on her hips, a cruel smile splitting her lips.

I smile back at her which makes her grimace and turn away. "Let's go."

Chapter 43

Mar

"Let me be sure I understand you, you want to go back to Izal?" Rian asks.

"Yup," I grunt, hauling a bag onto my shoulder.

He grabs it from me, shouldering it as I shake my head. "Why exactly are we going back to Izal when you've been hounding me for *weeks* to go *south*? Do you need a reminder that Izal is *north* of us?"

I whirl on him, reaching my hand out for the bag. "Thanks for the geography lesson," I say, yanking it off his shoulder.

Cyrus appears beside me, grabbing the bag before I can shoulder it again and pulling it onto his back. "I'm down for wherever, just tell me where to fly and I'll go."

Looking him over from head to toe, I have to suppress a laugh. Cyrus is no small male. He is at least a head taller than me and has biceps thicker than my thighs. He's broad shouldered, huge, yet somehow he has shoved his arms through the small straps of my bag and is currently bouncing on his feet like a kid about to eat cake.

"See?" I say, turning to Rian, "Cyrus understands."

Nat comes running over, a bag of her own strapped across her back. She takes one look at her brother and sighs, "You look ridiculous."

"Really?" he says, twisting back and forth, his hands propped on his hips, "I think I look hot. Don't you agree, Mar?"

I laugh, smacking his shoulder. "Yes, very hot. Now go help the others get ready. I'll be over in a minute."

"Your wish is my command, Your Majesty," Cyrus says with a dramatic bow.

I roll my eyes as he runs away. Rian stares after him with a look of utter revulsion. "What?" I bite.

"Nothing. It's just a shame," he says with a shrug.

"What is?"

"That someone like Cyrus would get wrapped up in all this."

I narrow my eyes on him, "It was your suggestion to bring him along in the first place."

"Oh, I know. I wasn't talking about the mission." Rian marches over to the others, barking orders as they rush to get things ready to go.

"Jeez," Nat whistles, "what's wrong with him? He's even grumpier than usual."

"Who knows, it's Rian," I sigh. I look around to examine the pack on her back, notably small, "is that all you'll need?"

"Yeah," she says with a nervous laugh, "I left most of my stuff back in the barracks so I thought this might be a good chance to grab the rest of it."

Nodding, I grab her hand. "You know, you're welcome to come back. Once we get Eve back, I'm sure she'll want you around."

Nah flinches, "I'm not so sure about that. I'm the reason she was captured in the first place. If I had just-"

"Hey, enough of that. We've been through this too many times, it was no one's fault. Besides, the important thing is that we are going to bring her home. You can even be the one to swoop in and rescue her," I say with a waggle of my brows.

She shakes her head, "okay, I like the sound of that."

I smile at her. "Come on, we should join the others, I want to be in the air in the next few minutes."

~~~

The flight back to Izal is entirely uneventful. No weird shadowy figures, no flashes of light. Just a perfectly normal flight. As we make the final descent onto the platform, my heart begins to race.

What if he says no? What if even now, my father decides that it's too risky?

"He'll say yes," Rian says, appearing beside me.

"What are you talking about?" I ask, my words shakier than I would like.

"I know you're scared that the king won't approve. But I know you. You can be very convincing, so just do what you do best and *convince* him." He gives me a small smile and takes off, helping the others unload.

I take a deep breath before heading straight for my father's chambers. The halls fall away, the familiar faces pass by in a blur, and then I'm standing in front of his door. I raise my hand. I knock. It all feels unreal, like someone else's body doing it. It's not until the door is pulled open and I see his familiar auburn hair that it really sinks in. This is happening.

"Mar?" he says, rubbing at his scruff-covered jaw.

"Hi." I swallow hard.

"Where have you been?" he asks, a surprising amount of anger lacing his words.

"I found more people willing to help rescue Eve," the words rush out of me.

His eyes grow wide as he looks back and forth before pulling me into his room. "Mind your words, there are ears everywhere."

"I know, I'm sorry, but... dad, please, it's already been over two months," my eyes begin to burn and the tears I have refused to let free force their way out.

His eyes soften, he reaches out, pulling me into a hug. "I know. I miss her too. I will always miss her, but it's time to think of the future, *your* future." He pushes back, squeezing my arms and staring into my eyes expectantly.

I shake my head, my tears already drying up, "I don't understand. What do you mean? I came here to ask for your help, to give me the resources I need to save her. We have a good group, but there's not many of us and I think if you-"

"I know, and I think it is incredible, how far you are willing to go for Eve," he says, with a broken smile.

"I would do *anything* for her," a dark, inky feeling begins creeping in.

"That's admirable. It is," he says with a nod, "but it's time that you start thinking about your own future and the future of this kingdom."

"What does that have to do with Eve? We can't just leave her, that's your daughter," I snarl.

"She's not."

My body becomes cold. Everything around me slows and a ringing fills my ears. I stumble, knocking against a table.

He reaches out for me, helping me sit down in a nearby chair. "Mar, are you okay?"

"What-what do you mean?" I gasp. *Holy shit. Fuck. I can't breathe.*

"Eve is not my daughter," he says plainly, standing upright.

I stare up at him, my mouth hanging open, dry. My chest is beating erratically. "I don't understand."

"Of course not, why would you? I know this must be a lot for you to take in right now. We never thought that either of you would ever need to know, but given the circumstances-"

"The circumstances? What are you talking about? Eve is your daughter. She is my sister. She is the heir to the throne." *Eve is the heir. Eve is the heir. It's her.*

"No, she is not. Not anymore," he says with a sigh.

I stand, throwing my hand out. "Why not? Why are we even having this conversation? I don't understand!" I yell.

"Mar, please. Eve is *gone*. I know that this is difficult... maybe if it was someone else who took her *somewhere* else, things would be different, but it's not. We have to accept that and move on."

"Fuck that! What does any of that have to do with rescuing her? Eve needs us, she needs our help! You're her father! Why won't you save her?" my voice cracks and the tears are back with a vengeance, pouring freely, choking my words and cutting off the air to my lungs. There is an erratic spark of magic in the palms of my hands.

"Mar..."

"So, what then? What exactly are you saying?"

"Mar, I love your sister, I do. So much. More than you'll ever understand. She is my daughter in all of the ways that matter, but-""There are no buts!" I cry, "I can't believe that you could even begin to suggest that-"

"We have to be honest with ourselves, realistic. We have to think about what is best for this kingdom," he says, practically pleading with me. "Eve is not the heir to this kingdom, not anymore. The fact that she is too far out of reach-"

"Don't say that," I croak, "You're not even trying!"

"Please understand. This is not easy for me. We never thought that this would happen. I am doing the best that I can given the situation. We are under attack here. You might not see it, but we are," he reaches for me, but I rush away from him, standing next to the door. "The queen is not getting better. Eve is gone. We need to take care of our kingdom, *you* need to take your rightful place as-"

"No. Absolutely not. Don't you dare finish that sentence."

"-as heir. This is *your* birthright. You have always been the heir. I'm sorry that I have kept this from you and for all of the secrets, but it was for your protection. Both of you. Eve-"

"Enough lies! I don't believe you," I shake my head, "I'm done."

"Mar."

"No! I. Am. Done. If you won't find Eve and you won't help me, then I'm going to do it myself. I'm not going to just sit around anymore."

"No, you won't. I forbid you to leave the kingdom," he says, his voice hard, eyes devoid of all emotion.

"What?" I say, taking a step closer to him.

"I forbid you from leaving this kingdom. You have wasted enough time already. You are to remain here and fulfill your duties as expected. I will make the preparations and we will inform the kingdom of your status in due time. We cannot afford to look *weak* right now."

I laugh, a gross wet sort of laugh that doesn't quite sound right. "Weak? Duty? Do those words have no meaning to you?" I pause, waiting for him to say something. When he doesn't I laugh again, stepping back towards the door. "I *will* be leaving, and I will find Eve, and when I bring her home she will be our queen as is *her* birthright. Same as it always has been."

"How do you plan on finding her?" he snaps. "She is *already* lost to us, do not make this more difficult than it already is!" His face contorts and the smallest crack in his facade slips through.

I almost fall for it. I almost see the pain he is going through. But then I see Eve in my mind and none of that matters. I won't let him lie to me anymore. "Don't pretend this is difficult for you. You've clearly had your mind made up for some time. Tell me, did you ever intend on searching for her?"

"You don't understand, there is still so much that you don't know-"

"The truth is, father, I no longer care. You can strip me of my power, resources, whatever you want. You can try and lock me away, but I will fight you every step, and I will win. You can count on that. Because when it comes to things that I will do for my *sisters*, you have no idea."

I'm out the door before he can utter another word. The door slams shut behind me as I race towards the landing pad, sending a prayer to the goddess that Nat and the others are still there. Because as of right now, we have to run.

Chapter 44

Rian

"Hey! Be careful where you throw things!" I yell at the two guards haphazardly tossing bags off the landing platform. A strong hand claps me on the back and I grunt under the force of it.

"Hey… there's nothing going on between you and the princess, right?" Cyrus asks, appearing beside me

"What are you talking about?" I grit.

"You and Mar, together? Anything? Listen, I just want to be sure because I really like her, but if you and her… just give it to me straight, are you two a thing?"

I would love nothing more than to punch this male right in his face. Words of denial burn on the tip of my tongue, yet somehow I can't seem to say them.

"Got it… there is a you and her," Cyrus says with a knowing nod.

"What? No-"

"That hesitation says otherwise, come on, I'm your best friend, I know you" he says, bumping his shoulder against mine.

"You are absolutely *not* my best friend."

"You're right, I'm your only friend. It's that whole asshole thing you've got going on, not very friendly," he looks me up and down with a grimace.

"I don't even know what to say to that," I mutter.

"How about you just tell me what's going on between you and the princess. If there is something going on between you two, then I don't want to be in the middle of that."

"There's not," I bite.

Cyrus narrows his eyes at me, leaning in close enough that our noses nearly touch.

"Do you mind? Personal space," I hiss.

"Hey, you two, knock it off and come help," Nat calls from the bottom of the landing platform.

Her brother winks and jumps off the edge, partially transforming so that he can ease his descent. It's something that I have only ever seen the two of them do. No other dragons have ever had the control necessary to only *partially* transform like that. It's insane.

"Jackass," I mutter, racing after him.

When we get to the bottom, Nat puts us to work hauling supplies.

"Is this really necessary? Shouldn't we just leave everything ready? It's not like we're going to be here that long," Cyrus says with a grunt, catching a large satchel I toss at him.

"You don't know that. The king could be hard to persuade, it's better that we take the rest while we can get it. Next time we ship out, we won't have the luxury of taking naps." I catch a bag Nat tosses me, throwing it along to her brother.

"Less talking, more working. I still have to run to the barracks to grab my things," Nat says.

"No worries, I'll grab them for you!" Cyrus says, rushing off towards the barracks.

"Cyrus, wait! I don't want you going through my stuff!" Nat cries after her brother.

"I forgot how insufferable he is," I say, watching him run.

"I didn't," Nat sighs.

We work together to get the last of the things unloaded. Once it's complete, she wipes a hand across her brow and nods in the direction of the barracks, "I'm going to go see what's taking him so long."

I snort, "You're going to make sure he doesn't go looking through your stuff."

"Both," Nat says before jogging off after her brother.

Looking around, everyone else has left, so I take the opportunity to rest. My ass barely hits the floor before I hear a familiar voice screaming my name.

"Rian!" Mar cries out, racing towards me.

I'm on my feet in half a second, catching her as she practically barrels into me. "Mar? What happened? Have you been crying?"

"No time," she gasps, "we need to go. *Now!*"

"Okay, yeah, let's go." I start racing around the room collecting as many supply bags as I can and dropping them at her feet as she struggles to catch her breath. Pausing I push back her hair, damp from sweat and the tears that stain her cheeks. "Are you okay?"

She shakes her head, "No. Where are the others? We need to go, we're wasting too much time."

"They'll be back soon. What's going on, tell me and I'll fix it."

"I-I can't tell you," she croaks, a single tear slipping free.

"Okay. That's fine. Do we need to leave now?" I ask, brushing away the tear.

A choked sob breaks free from her and my blood begins to boil. "He- I don't know, I don't know how much time we have, but not a lot."

"Alright, then we should go. The others will figure it out and find us eventually." I say, pulling on a pack and shouldering another two.

"But what if they don't, we need them. Besides, we'll never make it out of here on our own."

I grab her, forcing her to look me in the eyes, "Mar, why are we running?"

"I-"

"Stop where you are! Unhand the Princess!" a guard cries out from the top of the landing platform. A dozen more appear behind him and I know it, our time is up.

"It doesn't matter. Let's go. We'll leave everything behind, we'll be faster that way." I start dropping bags.

"Are you sure? But what about Nat and Cyrus?"

"They're coming. If we need to leave, then let's leave. The choice is yours." My heart is already racing, uncertainty clouding every racing thought that passes through my mind.

She looks up at them and more tears slip free. "Let's go."

I slip my hand into hers, pulling her along beside me as we race through the tunnel entrance, shouts ringing out behind us. The sound grows louder until I'm sure that at least two dozen guards are hot on our trail.

What is going on? Clearly her talk with her father didn't go well, but Vana, this? This is just absurd.

"Rian!" Mar cries out, yanking me to a stop as a large black dragon drops down in front of us.

Cyrus hops down off of it and jogs over to us, looking Mar over from head to toe. "Vana, Rian, I left you two alone for five minutes and you already made her cry. I guess you're right, it won't be much of a competition after all."

"What is he-"

"It doesn't matter," I say, cutting Mar off, "let's just go."

Mar and I leap up onto Nat's back and Cyrus follows.

"You're not going to fly?" I question.

"Nope, Nat's got the first shift. I have no idea what's going on, but given all those guards we passed on the way to get you guys, we figured it might be best to conserve energy. We grabbed those by the way," he says, nodding towards the bags I had collected before.

"Good thinking," I say, my heart finally calming down, "how'd you two find us?"

"Easy, we heard shouting and followed the pounding footsteps," he answers with a shrug.

"Thank you," Mar whispers. She's practically a gargoyle with how still she is standing. Even as Nat tilts with the curves, she doesn't budge.

"Of course," Cyrus says, looking her over again, "why don't you sit down?"

"No. I'm good."

"Okay… so, where're we heading?" Cyrus says, running a hand through his hair.

"To Eve, we're going to bring my sister home."

I watch her as she falls silent, her eyes growing glassy and distant.

"Still holding onto that 'there's nothing going on' thing?" Cyrus whispers to me.

Chapter 45

Rose

Bright, golden rays of sunshine cast a glow across the city as we grow closer. A mixture of sparkling white marble pillars and ancient stone create an arch, a gateway into Eteri. A collection of towers are clustered together, perched atop the mountain's highest peak, all around are crystal blue waterfalls. Water crashes against rock and stone, creating a mist that mimics the clouds as we fly in.

As we begin our descent, the castle grows larger until we touch down and it towers so high that it could be mistaken for another peak. A long, stone archway is lined with guards, their dark skin in contrast to the vibrant golds and yellows of their attire. Some males wear nothing over their chest aside from a series of swooping metal chains also coated with gold.

"Follow me," the female who seems to be in charge says. Rather than heading into the castle, she turns off to the side, taking a set of spiral steps down into a wide valley. As we descend deeper, we also grow closer to one of the waterfalls, the roar almost deafening.

We walk alongside a small river, following in a single file line, a guard between each one of us. I go first, Reed is behind me, followed by Mateo, and Gael is at the very end. The males have been completely silent since we've touched the ground. Meanwhile, I'm just trying to fight the urge to gasp in awe at every little thing we see.

Everything from the tiled ground to the marble statues scattered around us is ornate. I've never seen anything quite like it. Each realm has its own unique beauty. Sena is known for its many native flowers and trees, like the wisteria. Vulca is known for the bioluminescent glow that lights up the inside of the volcano, and the *literal* river of lava. Rayan has always been known for the stain glass most of Tepis is-*was*- made of. No one knew that Cansu even still *existed*, though I remember something about hot springs in one of the few history books that actually mentions the realm. Meanwhile, Eteri is rumored to be the most beautiful of all the realms. I can see why.

"Where are we going?" I ask, unable to hold it back any longer.

"You will be taken to the ceremony space where you will be judged. If you are found unworthy, as I suspect you will be, you will be cast out of the city," she answers dryly.

A throat clears behind me. "What does that mean exactly? To be cast out of the city?" Reed asks.

"It means that you will be thrown off the side of the mountain," the guard between Reed and I says.

"Seriously?" Reed whispers.

"Seriously."

"Enough questions, we're almost there," the female says ahead of me.

"Wait, I just have one more," I say walking a little faster so I'm only a few steps behind her. Vana, she moves fast. I have to pay attention to every little step I take so I won't fall flat on my face, meanwhile she simply glides across the ground.

She stops, looking over her shoulder at me. Her eyes roam from head to toe, distaste clear in her glare. Still, she nods which I take as permission to ask ahead.

"What is your name?"

Her eyes narrow before flicking down the line. She turns back around silently, completely ignoring me.

Well, that's awfully rude. I really hope that Oliver doesn't act like this when he is acting as emissary. Though I suppose I don't actually know anything about this female, perhaps she is just another guard? Her position and general command seems to suggest more, but I could be wrong. We still know so little about how Eteri structures their realm, maybe it's nothing like the others at all. They are, of course, the only realm with a Chief and Chieftess.

"Asha," she says after a few minutes. Her words are so low that I barely catch them.

"Nice to meet you, Asha," I reply, smiling to myself.

A small circular set of pillars appears before us, the towers standing at least three times my height. There is no ceiling, just an opening that reveals the clear sky, a myriad of golds and pinks mingle together as the sun begins to dip on the other side of the mountain's peak.

Asha walks to the center, nodding to her guards who grab hold of our arms, fanning us out across the room. From this position, I can finally see the others' faces. Gael's jaw is set, his gaze locked on his alpha, waiting for any sign of trouble. Reed is looking all around the room, his mouth slightly agape, his eyes filled with wonder. Then there is Mateo... who yawns directly in his guard's face, stretching his arms out over his head and rightfully getting a smack to the back of it.

"You have been brought here to face judgment," Asha announces, looking over all of us.

"Yeah, you still haven't really explained what that means, do you mind filling us in?" Mateo says, scratching his head. It is a miracle that Mateo doesn't drop dead from Asha's scathing look alone.

"Here, your intentions will be revealed, your soul laid bare," Asha continues, locking eyes with each of us. Her gaze lingers when it reaches me. "One at a time, you will be called upon by the One Who Is Pure of Heart." Asha turns and it is then that I notice the small group of people approaching from behind.

All but one are clearly guards, then, at the center, is an absolute goddess. Tight black curls fall down to her waist, held back by a golden crown, long spikes fan out, arcing over her head like a halo. Her skin is similar to Asha's, a dark brown, but with a much cooler undertone. She is draped in a white, nearly sheer gown that clings to her chest, waist, and hips.

I can't seem to tear my eyes away from her. She is beautiful, ethereal even. Her face is a soft oval, her nose flat and wide with the most adorable rounded tip. Her cupid's bow is deep, her lips full and the most mesmerizing shade of pink. But it's her eyes that are the most breathtaking. A bright, honey brown, hooded yet so striking as she stares into my own.

Stares.

Staring.

I'm staring. She's staring back. *Fuck.*

Her lips spread into a wide smile, a single, deep dimple appearing in her dark, smooth cheek. Those honey eyes sweep over the rest of my group, softening. She steps forward, away from the guards. Asha bows and then quickly trades places with the girl, leaving her front and center and giving me the perfect excuse to continue my staring.

"Hello," her voice is light, crisp, exactly as I imagined it to be. She extends her hands out wide, palms up as she twists to look at each of us in turn, her gaze snagging on me once again. "Welcome to Eteri, welcome to our home."

"About time someone said it," Mateo says loud enough I can hear it from across the room.

My own glare rivals that of Asha's from before, still not quite able to kill from a distance, but if the look of fear in Mateo's is any sign, it got the job done.

"My name is Azariah. I understand that this is all confusing, that you are likely experiencing some fear. But please understand that this entire process will be completely painless," Azariah says, continuing to sweep her eyes between the four of us.

"Um… that guy said we would be thrown off the side of the mountain," Reed laughs nervously.

Azariah nods her head, "He is right."

"Wait what?" Mateo exclaims, "how is that painless?"

"You are all here with good intentions, are you not?" Azariah asks.

"Of course," I answer, drawing her attention back to me.

Her smile wavers and her eyes flick to Asha, so quick I might have missed it had she not stolen every ounce of my attention the moment she walked into this circle. "Well then, let's not waste any more time. Let's start with you, shall we?" She smiles at Gael whose guard grabs him, dragging him forward.

Azariah guides Gael to his knees, "Your hands please."

He looks up at her with no hesitation, reaching his hands out like he's done it a million times. Her palms hover over his own. We all wait for something to happen, none of us daring to move. Then, a blinding light flashes from between their palms. It's gone in half a second and then Gael walks back to his spot, looking entirely unfazed.

No words are said as they bring Mateo forward. He puts on a brave face in front of his second, but it is clear in his eyes that he isn't the most excited about this next part. Same as Gael, he falls to his knees, reaching out his palms. Only, instead of staring at the beautiful creature before him, his eyes remain locked on my cousin. They don't waver until that same bright light flashes and he is back in his position.

Reed stumbles forward, looking back at me over his shoulder. I give him an encouraging smile as he is the next to fall to his knees. It takes longer than the others, but just as before a bright light shines between their palms and Reed lets out a sigh of relief as he walks back to his spot.

I make my way forward confidently, chin held high as I lower to my knees, staring up at her. She's even more exquisite up close. I smile up at her, but quickly lose all confidence as her honey eyes turn to me. The moment out palms meet I gasp as the magic takes over. Everyone else has vanished and instead of a valley around us, the pavilion floats in the air, clouds on every side.

"Hello."

"Where are we?" I ask breathlessly.

Azariah laughs, "The same place we've always been."

"How is this happening?"

"It is a gift from the goddess herself. To see into one's soul, to know their intentions perhaps even better than they know them themselves."

My head whips back to Azariah. "You're Goddess Blessed."

"So it would seem," she shrugs.

"What happens now? Do I... do something?"

She shakes her head. "I simply need to be here with you, in this space, to truly understand your soul. Though..."

"What?"

"Your soul is... difficult."

Fear seizes me and I quickly wish I could still see the others. "Wh-why?"

"It's your blood. The other one had it too, but... it was not the same."

"Reed. He's my cousin."

Azariah nods in understanding. "The part that you share is not tainted, not in a way that stains one's soul."

"I don't understand, my soul is stained? It's... tainted?" *Fuck. Fuck. Am I about to be thrown off a mountain?*

"That's the thing, your soul seems to be... undecided. There is a part of you that has a great capacity for hate, yet there is still so much room for love," Azariah breathes.

I get to my feet, reaching out and grabbing her hands in my own. "I promise, I am here with no intention to harm any of you. I am only here to get answers, to *save* someone I love," I say, squeezing her hands.

She bites the inside of her cheek, "I see."

"Please, we just want to save her. Once we know how, we'll leave. I swear."

Azariah seems to ponder it. She slowly removes her hands, placing them on my shoulders and easing me back to my knees. "I want to help you save her, whoever she is, but I cannot risk my people. I cannot risk repeating the mistakes of our ancestors."

"Wait, please. Just give me a chance. A chance to do the right thing, to make the right choices. Or… if I can't stay, let the others. They're innocent, right? Send me away if you must, but don't condemn them to that fate, not because of me."

She considers me, a hand coming up to rest on my cheek and damn my heart actually skips a beat. "Rose, third in line to the Sena throne, I will allow you one chance. One chance to right the wrongs our ancestors have made, to get the answers that you seek, and then to *go*," she says, putting extra emphasis on the last bit.

"Thank you," I breathe. The word has barely left my lips when a bright light bursts from in between us and I am forced to shut my eyes against it. When I open them it takes a second for everything to come back into focus, but when it does, we're in the valley again, the others spread out around us, an anxious looking Reed half a step towards us.

Azariah helps me to my feet, pulling me in close to say just to me, "Do not make me regret this decision." She steps back, dropping my hands and turning without another word. Then, she becomes nothing more than a wisp, a breeze, a phantom wind. Somehow, she still has form, a vague sort of outline where her body used to be.

She's a sylph.

Then she is gone.

The others come rushing over to me, their guards gathering around Asha, likely for their next steps.

"Vana, Rose, what happened?" Reed says, looking me over from head to toe.

"Nothing? The same thing as you guys, right?" I ask, looking between them.

Gael shakes his head, "You two were frozen like that for nearly an hour."

"What? An hour? No, it was barely a few minutes," I say, shaking my head.

"Rose, he's telling the truth. It was... terrifying," Reed says with a shudder.

"Yup, super creepy," Mateo says.

"Oh."

"'*Oh?*' That's it? Just oh? What happened?" Reed whispers anxiously.

"I-"

"Come with me, you will now be taken into the city," Asha says, appearing beside our group.

"Finally," Mateo groans, stepping forward.

Asha holds up a hand, stopping him. "Throughout your time in the city, you will always be escorted by one of our guards. Also, before you can enter you must surrender all weapons, including magic."

Cries of outrage burst from my group's lips, but I silence them, smiling at Asha. "That will be fine."

Mateo grabs me, yanking me towards him. "This is a terrible idea," he hisses in my ear.

"Trust me, this is the only way we can gain their trust and get the answers we came all the way here for," I say back, pleading with my eyes.

His eyes narrow on me, his gaze unyielding until finally, "Ugh, okay. Let's just give up our weapons *and* magic to enter this foreign realm with *zero* protection, sounds great."

I smile at him, turning back to Asha as she produces four golden cuffs, locking one around each of our wrists. We follow as she starts back up the path we came, Mateo and Gael whispering behind us.

Reed laces his fingers with mine and cuts me a nervous look, "I hope you know what you're doing."

Me too.

Chapter 46

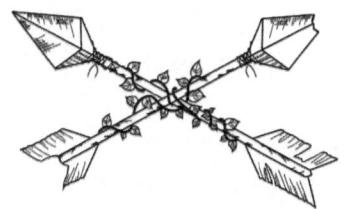

Oak

"Where are we going?" I ask, following Aine as she leads me to an unfamiliar part of the compound.

"You'll see."

Two girls nod at us as we pass through a cave-like opening, descending down into a dark tunnel. The walls are damp, the pungent scent of rust fills the air. Small torches line the walkway, leading deeper under the compound, the path remarkably steep. Our steps echo in the silence, filling me with dread.

"Aine?" I ask hesitantly.

She turns to me, eyes distant, mouth drawn in a tight line. "I need to ask you something and I need you to be honest with me, can you do that?"

"I-" I hesitate, wondering to myself if they know.

"Yes or no."

Biting the inside of my cheek I nod my head, earning myself a scowl. "Yes, sorry. I can do that."

She nods to herself, looking over her shoulder for a brief second. "Is it true that you have a gift? A power unlike anything anyone else has?"

Fuck. How does she know about that? My persuasion... it's so rare, I've always been exceptionally careful with who I tell. This shouldn't be possible. Clearing my throat I meet her stare, "Yes. I do." No harm in that, no harm in just answering her question. I can just leave it there, no need to explain any further.

"And is it true that this power allows you to force your will upon others?" Aine asks, brows raised.

Well shit. *There goes keeping that to myself.* I almost lie, the words are right there, but somehow, I can't seem to speak them. Actually, it feels as though I'm being... choked? My lungs start to burn as I struggle to suck in air, each passing second my throat grows tighter and tighter.

Aine sighs, "I asked you not to lie."

I cough and sputter, clutching my throat while my panicked eyes meet Aine's resigned stare. Shaking my head I realize what this is, how screwed I am. It's an enchantment, a powerful one at that. Whatever magic is at play here is keeping me from lying... by making me choke on my own words.

My panic grows in an instant. I waste no time rushing back through the tunnel, stumbling through the opening and falling to the ground under the disgusted stares of the two girls standing guard. I've barely caught my breath when Aine appears at the opening, she says something to the guards and they both disappear, leaving the two of us alone.

"How're you feeling?" she asks, squatting down beside me.

"I almost died," I croak, voice hoarse already.

"I know. I tried to warn you."

"Yeah, well you didn't try hard enough."

"I did all I could. Now, get up, we need to go back down. And remember, *the truth* this time, unless of course you want to be choking on your own words again."

I laugh, pushing to my feet and wiping my damp hands against my leather pants. "No thanks, I'm good where I am."

"Oak-"

"No. I mean it, why in Vana's name would I even consider going down there when I just almost *died*?"

"Because," Aine says, stepping forward so I am forced to look in her eyes, "I need your help."

Hold on, what? Aine, needs my help? Mine? In what reality does that make any sense? "Huh?"

"I need your help, Oak."

"Why me?" It comes out a whisper.

"You're the only one who can help us."

"Us?"

~~~

"What. The. Fuck. Aine? Why is there a male tied up down here?"

The male in question is lying face first in the dirt, hands tied at the base of his spine, legs chained together at the ankles.

"I had to," Aine says, standing over him. She stares down at the back of his head as he remains completely unconscious.

"Why? What reason would you possibly have for *tying a male up*?" Other than some unique circumstances I once heard Eve boasting about.

"We need answers, he has them."

"Okay, but why do you need me? We are literally in a cave where he can't tell lies."

She sighs, finally looking at me. "Because, it only works if he actually talks."

Oh.

"Look, I don't know a lot about your gift, but if it works the way I think it works..."

"You think I can force him to talk."

"Can you?" she asks, her eyes wide and pleading. I've never seen her like this, so unsure, so... vulnerable. It's unnerving.

I squat, pushing his head to the side so I can get a better look at him. There is nothing overly familiar about him. Though the myriad of bruises marring his face doesn't exactly help things. I look up at Aine, an odd sense of deja vu moving through me. Not so long ago she had me tied up in a way. I was the captive. Still am. "What did he do?"

"Does it matter?"

Closing my eyes I have to speak through my teeth, "Yes. It matters. What did he do to deserve this and why are *we* the ones doing it?"

Aine looks between the male and I, clearly contemplating whether or not to tell me. With one last look at me, she nods. The movement is so small I nearly miss it. "This male is responsible for those attacks, the wolves in the woods. He has been terrorizing travelers."

My eyes narrow. "I thought we took care of that? Have there been more attacks?"

"No, there couldn't have been."

Realization sparks in me as I laugh in disbelief. "Please do not tell me that this male has been *kept down here* since that mission."

"I cannot."

"Vana, Aine. What were you thinking? Does anyone else know about this?" *If they do, would they care?*

"No. I have told no one. It was… forbidden." Aine folds her hands over stomach, chin raised high in the air.

"Forbidden by who," I ask. Aine had said 'we' and 'us' earlier, like she wasn't alone in this…

"The high lady herself asked-"

"No. I'm done, I'm leaving." I start back up the path, my heart already racing at the mere mention of my aunt. Adrenaline is pumping through me steadily as Aine grabs my wrist, yanking me to a stop.

"Don't leave."

"Why?" I say without looking back, "why would you tell me if she forbade it?"

"It was her who told me to seek your help in the first place."

A heavy weight drops in my stomach. *She knows. She knows about my gift. About what I can do.* "She told you to ask me?"

"She told me to use your gift." The message was clear. This wasn't a request. It never is with my aunt. No. She just expects everyone around her to fall into line, do as they're told, regardless of what toll that might take on them. But this time, there is nothing she can do to force my hand. It's my choice.

"No."

Aine stands so still I think for a moment she must be paralyzed. Then, she blinks. Once. Twice. Oh so slowly until her eyes close and when they open again I can see the regret written in them. She doesn't want to do this any more than I do. But that doesn't matter. I won't be *her* puppet any longer.

I've barely made it a few steps up the path when Aine grabs me again, her grip far looser, her touch gentle. As I face her, her eyes speak to something that I know all too well and I can hardly resist it. "Please," she whispers, and my resolve cracks.

"I don't even have access to my magic."

"I will grant you limited power," her eyes narrow, "if you try anything, you'll never make it out."

Rolling my eyes, I pull my arm free and cross the room again, slapping a hand across the male's face and startling him awake. "What the- where am I?" he groans.

"Answer any question she asks," I speak directly to him, lacing my words in a way that he can't refuse.

His eyes take on a sort of glassy sheen that quickly vanishes as the persuasion sets in. It's so quick, I'm sure he isn't even aware of what has happened. A string of curses follow me as I walk back to Aine, stopping only for a moment at her side.

"I hope this is what you wanted." I leave, the echo of my footsteps on the damp ground drowning out the vibrant vocabulary display coming from the male. Yet for some reason, as soon as I am out of sight, I hesitate. Staying just close enough to hear Aine's first question.

"I'll ask you again, have you seen these people?"

Closing my eyes I bite back the bitter taste on my tongue. Had I really expected anything different? *Of course* she would lie about her intent, about what she *needs to know*. Still, I can't help but wonder, *who is important enough that my aunt is using the Ghosts to look for them? And why is Aine lying about it?*

Chapter 47

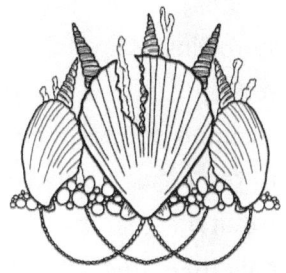

Cay

Somehow, the closer we get to the heart of the city, the more I realize it's not as bad as I was expecting. The castle walls, for the most part, are still standing. It was like I expected it to look as bad as it felt. When my father died and the barrier fell, it felt like the world was crumbling to pieces and all that would be left behind is dust. But here it is, still standing.

Despite the chaos and destruction, there is still beauty here, and life. The stained glass may be cracked and broken, but it's still there. The spires may not stand as tall, but they *are* still standing. The archways and statues lining the outermost circle of the city reminds me that it's not over. There is a chance, I just have to be willing to fight for it. No matter how painful it is.

These walls represent hope as much as they represent despair. It might hurt to walk the halls and see the shadow of my father around every corner, but there is also a promise that one day those shadows might bring me joy rather than sorrow. I swear for a second I can even hear his laugh, just as the grand entrance appears.

I stop right as we pass through the doorway.

"Surprised?" Nalei taunts from beside me.

"Yes, actually. I thought there would be nothing left. It's... it's better than I expected."

Nalei rolls her eyes, "Obviously. We haven't *just* been working on the tunnel."

"Why?" I ask, my eyes narrowing as I watch her wrap a long loc around her finger.

"It's my kingdom too," she mutters, looking away from me.

I let her words hang in the air as I play them over again. An idea popping into my head, one that I hesitate to voice. The image of our people marching to Sena is the only thing that pushes the words out. "If I sent people back, to help, would you harm them?"

"What are you talking about?"

"Guards, staff, whoever might be helpful or willing. If I sent them here, would you help them or harm them?"

"What is this?" she says, waving a hand in the air around me.

"Just answer the question, Nalei. If we're going to rebuild this kingdom, you can't do it alone. You'll need help."

She barks a laugh, "We're sirens. No one is going to want to work with us. Your father made sure of that."

"That's not true."

"Really? Because the first thing you did when you saw us was attack. Or am I remembering incorrectly?"

I pause. When I saw her appear in that water the only thing I could think of was how scared I was. But now that I'm thinking about it... I did attack first. "You're right. But maybe I was wrong. Prove it to me."

"I don't have to prove anything to you. I don't owe you shit," she says, sauntering up to me and looking down her nose, nostrils flared.

"True. Do it anyway. *You* used to love beating me when we were kids. Why not now? Or have things changed? You could be the savior of our kingdom."

304

Vana knows it won't be me.

Her head tilts, her eyes glinting as her skin shifts to reveal dark teal scales. They're only there for a moment before Nalei smiles a cruel, inky smile that sends a shiver down my back. "Fine. Send them here and I will put them to use." She turns on her heels and stalks off down the hall, disappearing around the corner with the other sirens following closely behind.

A rush of relief cools my blood as I let out a rough exhale. This could work. This could be the solution I've been looking for. I'll talk to Regan and she'll coordinate the ones who will return while those who can't stay safe in Sena. My only concern is exactly what Nalei brought up, *what if people aren't willing to work with the sirens?*

"You okay?" Terran asks, his warm hand landing on my shoulder.

"I will be."

He smiles down at me and then leans forward, pressing his lips against my forehead. He pulls back, staring into my eyes as his hand lands on my cheek. My heart stalls as he leans forward again, this time brushing his lips over mine in a featherlight kiss, his curling into a smile.

I suck in a breath and he chuckles deeply, taking a step back and reaching for the hand dangling limp at my side. He brings my hand up to his lips and kisses the back of it before threading his fingers through mine. A throat clears behind us and his eyes flick over my shoulder, never losing his easy smile.

I peek over my shoulder and find Oliver watching us, jaw tight and eyebrows drawn together. Terran nudges me forward and heat rushes to my cheeks as I find him watching me. Laughing nervously, I pull my hand from his, giving him a sheepish smile as I start down the familiar halls of my home to the cavern.

Oliver and Terran follow behind, talking in low whispers that I pointedly ignore. *As if I don't have enough to worry about... Terran is acting* odd. I bring my hand up to the cheek he caressed, the lingering heat still burning my skin pleasantly. As we make our way through the castle, I keep an eye on what remains of the barrier. Bigger sections seem to pulse as the smaller ones slowly knit themselves back together. As they meet, an arc of energy cascades throughout the entire thing.

The sight of it stops me in my tracks, I spend minutes just watching it as it slowly pieces together, bit by bit. So much of the dome is still missing, the gaping holes creating cascading waterfalls yet, it's *healing*. I look across the courtyard, watching as Nalei swims beside the other sirens, palms outstretched before them as they slowly pour magic into the barrier. Once a section is complete again, they move on to the next.

"They're really doing it. They're healing the city," I say under my breath.

Leaving them to their work, we continue on our way. The entrance to the cavern looks exactly as it always has. The roar of the waterfall down the spiral staircase echoes up to us. I step forward, two large males matching the step. I spin, planting a hand in the center of their chests, staring up at matching hazel eyes.

"This area is sacred, you can't enter."

Terran nods, taking a step back, "Of course."

I turn my gaze on Oliver, raising my brows expectantly.

He smirks, taking a step forward.

"I'm serious, Oliver. You can't follow me." I push him back as Terran grabs hold of his arm, nodding towards the stairs. Spinning I race down the steps, nearly tripping over my own feet. As I rush through the water, it parts, closing behind me like a curtain pulled shut. The cavern opens up before me and I feel a rush of relief as it looks exactly the same as before. Slipping off my shoes, I pad barefoot to the water's edge, bending down to trace a fingertip along the surface.

"I know you're there." My voice reverberates off the cavern walls, the sound light despite my irritation.

"Remember the last time we were here?" Oliver says from the bottom of the stairs.

Sighing, I plop down onto the wet stone, the water soaking through the fabric and clinging to my thighs and butt. "I do. In fact, I distinctly remember you peeping on me while I was naked."

"Peeping implies that I was trying to hide."

"Hmm, interesting perspective. Tell me, Oliver, how is it that you were able to enter the cave? Now and before." I poke the surface of the water, watching the ripples as they spread throughout the entirety of the pool, moving on in a seemingly infinite wave.

"I can't."

"Can't or won't?"

"Won't."

I look back at him where he leans against the wall, his head is tilted back, his eyes squeezed shut. Just like before, not a drop of water clings to his curls or wets his cheek. So many mysteries. So many secrets. So many lies. Shaking my head I turn back to the water, pulling a small vial out from my cleavage.

"Did you just pull that from between your-"

"Not the time, Oliver," I say between clenched teeth. Bending over, I dip the vial beneath the surface, letting it fill to the brim and then freezing it so not even a drop can be lost. It hardly weighs anything yet the feel of it in my hand is like a boulder being set upon my shoulders. I expected to feel excited and relieved once I had it. Instead, all I feel is the fear of what happens if this doesn't work.

I grip the vial tightly, and move to stand, a bronzed hand appearing in front of my face. Oliver stares down, his eyes locking on the exposed portion of my breast from his vantage point and I roll my eyes. Taking his hand, I allow him to pull me to my feet, a powerful spark of energy passing between our joint palms. My eyes widen as I gasp, but Oliver seems entirely unaffected.

Biting my lip, I ignore the weird energy, making my way back to the staircase only to realize Oliver is standing at the pool's edge, watching the water with intense focus. "What're you doing?"

"Go on, I'm right behind you," he says without looking at me.

I make it one step up the stairs before turning back, "You can't enter the water, Oliver. I'm serious. This place is sacred and you even being here is disrespectful enough. Don't. Touch. The. Water."

Chapter 48

Eve

"Thank you," I mutter as my plates are cleared from the table, the servants disappearing almost as quickly as they appeared.

"Was the meal to your liking?" Yuta asks, sipping his glass of wine.

"It wasn't the worst," I say with a shrug. It was mouthwatering, genuinely the best food I have ever tasted. There is at least one benefit to this new arrangement. At least when I am forced to eat with him I can enjoy the food.

The corner of Yuta's lips tug into a small smile, and his amber eyes shine. "I am glad to hear it."

Silence hangs in the air, only the faint sound of a clock ticking nearby. I shift in my seat, glancing around the room. There is this odd feeling in the air, like taking a deep breath before releasing an arrow. We're both waiting for the *snap*. Thunder claps outside and I jump out of my seat, my hands clamping down over my ears.

"Are you scared of thunder?" he asks gently.

"No," I snarl, forcing my hands to my side.

He nods, lips drawn thin. "Well, I suppose we should get back to those questions."

I swallow hard, sitting up straighter in my chair, "Yes, we should."

I hardly got anything out of him the first few times, but not this time. Now is the time to get serious. Channel my inner Rose. I can do this. Ask the right questions. Get answers. Escape. That's the plan. *I can do this.*

"What would you like to know first?" he asks, catching me off guard.

"Umm…" my mind empties and I mentally curse myself. *Of all the times-*

"Why don't I first explain who I am. It seems only fair now that I know the truth about you," Yuta says, setting his wine aside and leaning back in his chair.

"Sure," I mutter.

"As I'm sure you realize by now, I am the king of Cansu. Though, I have many names. I prefer Yuta."

"Okay… and the other names?"

Yuta smiles to himself, "Most know me as the 'Second King of the People'."

"Who was the first?"

His smile falters. "My father."

My chest constricts at the memory of my father's smile. "Where is he?"

"Dead."

"I'm so-""I don't want sympathy, especially not from you," he spits.

Fighting back the urge to throw my water in his face, I focus on my next question. "Alright, well what about your mother?"

"Dead."

Vana, this is not going well. "Right, well can you explain to me the meaning behind your title? What does it mean to be 'King of the People'?"

Yuta reaches forward, grabbing his glass off the table and downing what remains in a single gulp. He taps the rim and a servant appears, filling the glass before disappearing in a cloud of smoke. "The people chose me."

"What? What does that mean they 'chose you'?"

His arms extend out on either side of him, a tick of irritation in his jaw, Exactly what it sounds like. Once, the people chose my father as their king. Then, upon his death, they chose me."

"But how can they *choose* a king? A title like that is from blood." Though I suppose once his father was king it didn't matter much.

"You're right, but when that line dies, a new one must be chosen."

"But what about-""Enough, new question," Yuta says, waving a hand between us.

"Fine. What are you?"

Yuta laughs, the sound bursting from him and from the expression on his face, catching him by surprise. "Oh little minx, that mouth."

"How about you focus on answering the question and leave my mouth to me." My hands ball into fists at my side. *What is this, some sort of joke to him? He tells me I can ask questions, learn the so-called truth, yet every time I do, he treats it like some game to be played.*

"Alright. But you're not going to like the answer," he says, a hint of amusement lacing his words. When I don't respond he sighs, sitting back in his chair and fiddling with the ring on his middle finger. "I am a species called grim."

"Grim?"

"Grim."

"That's not- there's no such thing," I exclaim, throwing my hands up. *What's the point of asking questions if he's just going to lie about it? I should have stayed in bed.*

"I told you, you wouldn't like the answer."

"Yeah because it's a lie, and if there is one thing I hate more than everything else, it's being lied to," I snap.

"Well then you're really going to hate what I have to say next," he sighs, "the grim are very much real. They make up nearly the entire population of this kingdom."

"If the grim are real, why haven't I heard of them before?" I challenge.

"Because, *everything* you know is a lie." His words turn my blood to ice, but I don't get the chance to argue before he continues, "When Vana created the creatures of Estarynn, she realized that something was missing. So, she created the grim to fix it, to act as the balance." He picks up a small dinner knife, balancing it on the tip of his finger.

"Balance? How so?"

"Stop interrupting me and I'll explain," Yuta says, raising his brows expectantly.

Rolling my eyes I sit back, gesturing for him to continue.

He sets the knife aside, staring at me from across the table. "As Vana breathed life into the world, she also gave people their souls. The part of them that grants them free will and makes them who they are. But somehow, that wasn't enough. When she realized this she created the grim and, in addition to their own souls, she added pieces of *her* soul. In doing so, she could remain connected to her creations, to look over them, walk among them."

A million questions race through my mind now, but I force them all down, waiting for Yuta to continue. Patience really isn't one of my many virtues.

"For millennia all creatures lived in peace. They took care of each other, but then… realms were created, people divided. Over the years, people *forgot* about what Vana did, they saw our gifts and… things changed. We were no longer perceived as saviors or protectors. We came to represent death, not life. That wherever the grim went, death would surely follow. Like a plague," Yuta's voice deepened, his words spoken like a curse.

"Centuries went by and eventually the grim were cast out of the other realms entirely, banished to a small corner of the world draped in shadows. *That* was how Cansu was created. Out of necessity, because we were not welcome anywhere else. Only it backfired, without the grim in the realms, there was no balance. Over time, people began to get cut off from the land entirely, their magic drained until it was nothing more than a drop of what it once was."

"But-we have magic?" I butt in, unable to stop myself.

Yuta laughs mirthlessly, "You have *some* magic. The magic that remains in the lands is not a gift from Vana at all. No, rather than fixing their wrongs, they found a *loophole*. If the leaders of the realms added but a drop of their power- their blood- back into the land, it would replace what was taken."

"Taken?"

He flashes a cruel smile at me, "Did you think that Vana would simply *allow* the grim to be cast aside? That she would allow them to be treated as parasites?"

I gasp, "She took the magic back." "She took it back," he says with a real laugh this time.

Fuck. This is... if this is real, if what he is saying is true then...

"But this story isn't over," Yuta says, pulling me from my internal spiral, "their little loophole wasn't enough. The magic of the four realms wasn't strong enough to truly sustain the level of magic the land needs."

"I don't understand. How did they-"He gives me a pointed stare and I clamp my mouth shut. "They stole it," he growls, "they knew that they needed a piece of Vana for their plan to work so they *took* it."

"How?" I ask hesitantly.

Yuta stares at me, rage and disgust contorting his expression. "It doesn't matter," he dismisses, looking past me like I'm not even there.

Pushing my chair back I stand, slamming my hands down on the table, "If this is true. If what you say *really* happened, then why does nobody know about it? Hm? It sounds to me like the grim are Vana's favorites or something. So why does no one even know they exist?"

His chair is thrown backwards as he stands. "Because a millenia ago, *someone* rewrote history and just like that," he snaps his fingers, "it's like the grim never existed."

The weight of his words crash down on me and I collapse back in my chair, my head swimming and stomach churning. It's too much. This-this isn't what I was expecting *at all*. I thought I could learn more about *him*, about how to escape. *Something*. Never could I have imagined *this*.

313

"I want to go back to my room," I whisper.

He appears above me, grabbing my arm and pulling me gently to my feet. In the blink of an eye, I am back inside my chamber. Yuta steps back, dropping my arm and clearing his throat. "I understand that this is overwhelming. Take some time to rest. I have decided that from this point forward you will be granted more… freedom," the last word seems to pain him to say. He crosses the room to the door as I stand there frozen. With his hand on the knob, he doesn't bother looking back as he warns me, "try to escape and you'll be right back in that cell. Goodnight."

The finality of the door closing nearly has me collapsing again, but then I realize, he didn't lock it. There was no turn of a key, no click of the lock, nothing. I wait a few minutes and then rush to the door, slowly turning the handle and pulling it open.

"Nope," a deep voice says from outside and I nearly scream. Pulling the door open all the way, I peek out and find Chien leaning against the wall, eyes closed and arms folded across his chest.

Without a word, I slam the door closed, march over to my bed, and lay there awake thinking of all of the questions I never got to ask, and all the answers I never wanted.

Chapter 49

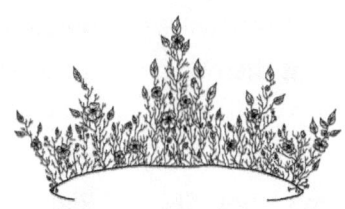

Rose

Everything moves quickly once the ceremony is over. The world seems to blur as we are led through the city to our chambers. Asha explains that there is a small section of the castle dedicated to visitors and that we will be staying there, though she sounds less than thrilled about it. Still, I hardly hear her, my mind is still stuck on someone else.

Azariah.

I don't know what it is about her, but I can't get her face out of my head. We knew coming to Eteri that things would be different, so little is actually known about their customs, but still, the ceremony overall was far outside what we could have imagined. In all of my research I've never heard or seen anything like it. And there she is, at the center of it all.

Why?

What power does she have to allow her to judge a person's intentions like that? To understand their desires before they do?

There is still so much to learn, but all of it will have to wait. We're on borrowed time and we have to use every second searching for an answer on where to find Oak. We can't lose sight of that. No matter what.

"Well that was fun," Mateo says, pulling me from my thoughts.

I have to blink my eyes a few times to truly take in my surroundings, we're already in a room. A *big* room.

"*Fun*? Seriously, Mateo?" Reed asks, exasperated.

Gael silently slinks off as the two other males launch into their usual banter.

"Alright, stop. We need to focus," I announce.

Reed turns to me, brows raised. "Focus? Right, so, where were you the entire walk over here?"

"What do you mean I was right beside you?"

"Physically, sure. But up here?" he taps a hand against his forehead, "you were a world away. Did you hear a word of what Asha said?"

Guilt claws its way up my throat as I realize he's right. I let myself be distracted by questions that don't matter. "I'm sorry. What did she say?"

Mateo chokes on a laugh as Reed sighs, sitting down beside him on the small couch. I take a single seat opposite them. We're in what seems to be a large seating area, various chairs, couches, and cushions are spread throughout the space. There are halls that seem to branch off the main entryway that I can't see, but given Gael still hasn't returned, I am assuming there are other rooms somewhere.

"The most important thing Asha said is that we are not to go anywhere without a guard. They have two outside right now and someone will take us to breakfast in the morning," Reed explains.

"Wait!" Mateo exclaims, bolting upright, "Does that mean we aren't getting dinner?"

Reed pulls him back down beside him, "Relax. She said they're going to send someone with food."

"Why does someone have to bring the food?" I ask, looking over my shoulder to the door.

"She didn't feel the need to explain," Reed mutters and it's hard to tell if he is more annoyed with the wolf at his side or the 'she' in question.

"Okay, what else?" I coax.

Gael appears over Mateo's shoulder and whispers in his ear. Before Reed can answer, Mateo clamps a hand down over his mouth. "You know what, I think I'd rather get some sleep," he says loudly, his eyes flicking around the room.

Reed mumbles against his hand so Mateo leans forward, whispering to him as well. My cousin goes still and Mateo slowly removes his hand. "Me too," Reed agrees, looking at me.

"Okay. Yeah…." I add.

The three of us follow as Gael leads us down the halls and behind a sliding door. I open my mouth as soon as it slides shut, but Reed shakes his head. Mateo leads us further into the room and then into a small bathing chamber. He looks to Gael for confirmation and then sighs when his second gives a thumbs up.

"We're good," he says with a nod.

"What was all that about?" I ask, looking between the two wolves.

"Gael detected a listening spell, they're in the rooms and central living space so we needed to find somewhere it couldn't reach," Mateo explains.

"Right, good thinking," I breathe, "Reed, what were you trying to say before?"

"The two biggest things I noticed were that we're very isolated. The visitor halls are practically their own building, completely disconnected from everything else."

"Which means it will be a lot more difficult to get around without being noticed," I interpret.

"Exactly. The second thing is that all meals are shared, everyone eats together," Reed continues.

"Isn't that a good thing? Everyone will be in the same place at once, won't that make it easier to sneak around?" Mateo asks excitedly.

"Not exactly, if everyone is supposed to be together, our absence will be noted. We can't just not show up," I explain, pressing two fingers into each temple, massaging away my growing headache as the events of the day begin to catch up with me. I'm exhausted, and if what Reed is saying is true, we still have a long night ahead of us.

~~~

Sometime later food is delivered, but I hardly touch it, my head pounding and my eyes burning as I fight to keep them open.

"Rose, you should get some rest," Reed encourages, placing a hand on my shoulder.

We finalized our plans almost an hour ago, but I haven't been able to convince myself to go to bed yet. I know that we're missing something. "I will, later."

"There's nothing more you can do right now. We should all just take the opportunity to get some sleep so we're ready for tomorrow," Reed presses.

"I know but-""You heard him, little Ro, time for bed." Suddenly I'm being thrown over Mateo's shoulder.

"Mateo! Put me down!"

"I will. In bed," he laughs, marching down the hall, and into one of the four rooms. Once inside, he throws me down onto the bed hard enough that I bounce off of it.

"Mateo!" I huff, pushing my hair out of my face.

"Get some sleep, see you in the morning!" he bellows as he closes the door behind him.

My head aches as I lay back in the bed, staring up at the ceiling. I only close my eyes for a second, but then... it's so hard to open them.

There's a pounding on the door and I sit upright, heart racing. There's a burst of pain in my head at the motion, but I ignore it, stumbling to the door and yanking it open. "What's wrong?" I grumble, my tongue feeling thick in my mouth.

"Well good morning to you too," Reed chuckles, "come on, it's time for breakfast."

"Break-what?"

Reed leaves, the ghost of his laughter lingering as I am left standing in the doorway, completely lost. *Did he say breakfast?*

I look outside the window and sure enough, the first rays of morning light are already peeking over the side of the mountains. *What the? It's morning already?*

"You coming?" Reed asks, appearing back in the doorway and startling me.

"Um, yeah, just a second." I speed through getting ready and meet the three males out in the seating area. Mateo is spread out on a couch upside down, his dark curls brushing the floor. Gael is waiting in a wooden chair, his eyes fixed on the door, hands balled at his side. Reed looks up at me from his spot on the floor and gives me a small smile.

"Sorry for making you wait, I'm ready." No sooner have the words left my mouth does the door open. Gael is on his feet in a split second, Reed and Mateo not far behind.

An unfamiliar woman walks through, she looks between us, a wide smile splitting her full lips. "Good morning, my name is Imani, I'm here to take you to breakfast." She has smooth, umber skin, similar to both Asha and Azariah, but not *quite* the same. Her diamond shaped face is framed by a collection of fluffy curls that are styled into an afro held back with a silk scarf. Like Asha, she has golden lines painted over her skin, only Imani's are more like rings around her neck and arms.

I step forward, extending a hand, "Nice to meet you, I'm Rose."

Imani's smile widens as she takes my hand in her own, clapping the other over top and squeezing tightly. "Lovely to meet you, please, follow me." She leads us back through the castle and this time, I pay attention.

Reed wasn't exaggerating when he said we were isolated. It took nearly five minutes before we saw a single person who wasn't a guard. The beauty of the castle itself is amazing, but the fact that there was no help or other visitors along the way makes the back of my neck tingle.

We're led into a ginormous banquet hall, easily three times that of our own back home. Long tables run the length of the room, benches placed on either side. It's packed, the lively sound of conversation filling the space as people take their places and say their morning greetings. Imani walks us over to a table on the far end and instructs us to wait here.

The four of us take a seat and look around, watching as others begin to grab for the food placed at the center of the table, passing it out to each other and serving those sitting next to them. A woman is holding a babe to her breast while another hands her a plate with a wide smile. It's incredible, there is no tension, no hushed conversations or awkward exchanges to be heard. Everyone here seems genuinely happy to do so.

"This is so…" Reed starts.

"Different?" I finish, thinking about the silent meals held once a week back home. Usually, we all eat on our own time except for our family meals held at the end of every week. Most of the time, my mother uses it as an opportunity to ask us about our accomplishments or news around the realm. It's *nothing* like this.

"Yeah," Reed breathes, watching the others the same way I do.

"Beautiful, isn't it?" Imani says, appearing beside our table. She peers over the tables with a broad smile and admiration in her eyes.

"It is," I agree.

"Well, help yourself to anything on the tables. If you have any specific needs just let someone know and anyone around will be happy to help. I'll be sitting over there," she says gesturing to the front of the room, "someone will come for you at the end of the meal. Enjoy!"

She makes her way across the hall and I can't help but notice the others joining her at the table. To her right is Asha, on her left, Azariah. The three women talk lightly, laughing over their food and engaging with the other strangers at the table.

"Who are they?" I ask the stranger sitting next to me.

The male looks me up and down, taking in the others sitting around me. He seems to consider his answer before turning to the person sitting across from him. The two exchange a look and then the second male answers. "That is our chief and chieftess."

I do my best to contain my shock, nodding as if that makes complete sense. Clearing my throat I direct my attention to the three females again. I can almost understand Azariah's presence at the table, given that she was the deciding factor to letting us in. But Asha is just a soldier, and Imani was the one sent to get us, what reason do they have for being seated at the table? "And the others?"

The male's eyes narrow, suspicion building yet, to my surprise, he does answer. "That is Imani, the eldest daughter. Asha, the second daughter. Then Azariah, the third daughter, she will be our next chieftess."

"But she's third in line?" I ask, staring at the trio with outward confusion this time.

This time, the two males ignore me, returning to their meal as if I hadn't spoken.

A warm hand touches mine and I meet Reed's eyes, and I can tell by his expression that he heard what they said. We both turn to the table and find three sets of eyes already on us. Imani looks at us with a warm smile, she even raises her glass to us before taking a sip. Asha's eyes are filled with distrust while Azariah... looks almost *scared*.

Slowly I turn back to the table, pasting on a smile. Mateo and Gael look at me with concern in their eyes, Reed's more filled with panic. I lean forward, whispering as low as I can, "Things just got a lot more complicated."

Chapter 50

Mar

We land in a small clearing, Rian and I jump down first, then Cyrus.

Once we're all off, Nat shifts. "Cyrus you've got next shift," she says, stretching her arms above her head and twisting at the waist.

"Works for me," he agrees easily, walking to Nat's side and helping her stretch out her arms.

Rian turns to me, "What's the plan?"

In the hours since we fled Vulca, I have thought about what to do, where to go. The only thing we know about who took Eve is that they're from Cansu. It's not much to go off of, but there is one thing that seems obvious. "We continue south, we should move further east and try our best to avoid any villages or military outposts."

Nat nods, "That should be easy enough. Cyrus and I know the area well, we've grown up flying here, and he has a good understanding of where the outposts would be."

"There are a few areas that might be a little tricky, but if we're careful and try to use concealment spells as often as possible, we shouldn't have any issues," Cyrus says, echoing his sister.

"We should try and travel by foot as much as possible," Rian urges.

"That will take too long, Nat and Cyrus won't be able to keep up on foot. We should just alternate who flies to conserve energy. We'll only stop when absolutely necessary. I don't want to stay anywhere too long," I counter. My father will have likely already sent dragons after us. Our head start is limited at best, we can't risk being caught.

Nat raises her hand above her head which makes Cyrus smile and Rian snicker. "Two questions," she says, lowering her hand, "first... where exactly are we going? I know you said south and that's great, but... eventually we're not gonna have anywhere else to go so, is there a final destination in mind?"

"I'm done waiting for backup, we're going straight to Cansu and bringing Eve home." I look between the three of them, waiting for any sign of protest. Cyrus and Nat exchange a look, but don't say anything immediately. This time, if they don't want to go, I won't make them. I won't fight them on it at all. It was dangerous enough without my father involved, now... now they could lose everything, and if they did it would be my fault.

"Okay, second question. Why exactly did we just run from Izal? Wasn't the whole point in flying all the way back to get an army? Now we're running from said army?" Nat questions.

Rian steps forward, sparing me from answering. "The king disagrees with our plan. So much so that he wasn't a fan of Mar leaving, which is why we needed to before he could stop her." His answer is as close to the truth as any of them can know.

What my father told me about Eve, about *me*, it's too much and I can't think about it right now, not when my only priority should be Eve.

"So, no army?" Cyrus confirms.

"No army," I echo.

"What about your other friends? You all rushed in to save Rayan, to help Cay, why not go to them?" Nat asks and I can tell that Rian is wondering the same thing, especially after the fight we had to get *him* to help before.

"They are helping, in their own ways. I'm not sure the full extent of everything, but I trust them." Even if I haven't heard from any of them in weeks.

"Good enough for me," Cyrus announces with a shrug.

Rian shakes his head at him as Nat just sighs.

"Thank you." Magic swirls inside me as my emotions begin to spill over. I've fought to keep them under control, but right now it's like every moment is colliding at once. "I want you all to know how much I appreciate you. But I also want you to know that I know it's a lot. There's a lot at risk… I won't blame you if you want to leave."

Nat steps forward, grabbing my hand. "I've wasted enough time. Let's go get our girl."

Cyrus stands at his sister's side, "Where she goes, I go. I'm here to help, however I can."

The siblings step to the side and Rian moves forward. Instead of stopping, he pulls me a few feet away. "I know there is more going on than what you've said. I'm not asking *now*, but I do expect answers eventually."

"I-"

He shakes his head. "Come on, let's get moving." Rian grabs my hand in his, leading me back to the others.

Cyrus's eyes land on our joined hands almost instantly. His eyes flash to Rian before landing on my own, the intensity of his gaze stopping me in my tracks. Cyrus bounds over to us, grabbing me by my hips and yanking me against his chest, effectively removing my hand from Rian's. "Trying to make me jealous?" he chuckles against my ear.

"What? No, I-"

"Relax," Cyrus says, nipping at my earlobe and drawing a gasp from me. "I like that sound, can't wait to hear it again later tonight." He winks at me, stepping back. The heat from his hands linger on my hips.

"Let's go," Rian practically growls, shoving past Cyrus.

"Do I want to know what is going on between you and my brother?" Nat says with a shudder.

"You know, I'm not really sure of that myself," I groan.

"Well you might want to figure that out because those two," she nods towards Rian and Cyrus, "have a history."

"I don't understand, Rian is the one who told me about Cyrus in the first place. I thought they were friends?"

Nat nods, "They are. Were? I don't really know. What I do know is that I'm not really sure it matters when it comes to you." Nat walks over to her brother, smacking him on the back of his head. The two exchange a few words before Cyrus walks off, giving himself enough space to shift.

The shift takes over, his hulking red form and powerful wings as captivating as the first time I saw them. We all quickly climb on his back, Nat and I easily, meanwhile Rian consistently seems to *fall* off. The chuffing noises coming from Cyrus are *totally* not suspicious at all.

We take to the air quickly, soaring through the clouds until we're high enough above them that we won't need to use a concealment spell. Nat and Rian are bent over a small map, marking off areas to avoid as I keep an eye on the horizon.

An hour goes by before we approach our first village. Cyrus follows Nat's instructions and curves further to the east, doing our best to stay out of sight. When we make it through without any warning bells going off, I feel good. More hours pass and we fly easily, rarely needing to adjust our path or stop for breaks. Then, I feel an odd tug on my own magic.

I collapse to my knees, clutching my stomach. Nat and Rian appear above me, talking over each other as questions spew from their mouths. I can hardly hear anything other than Rian's shout to descend. My head is pounding worse than ever before, a sharp stabbing pain is in my chest stealing away my breath.

The moment we touch the ground I am lifted into Rian's arms and carried to the ground. Cyrus shifts and rushes over, staring down at me as

325

Nat explains. Rian's hands cradle my cheeks, his eyes searching mine as I struggle against the urge to scream.

What the fuck is happening to me?

There is a bright, blinding light, and then the pain is gone and I'm slipping into the darkness.

Chapter 51

Oak

Sweat pours down my back, the hair at the nape of my neck sticking to the damp skin. The loose sleeves of my training tunic flutter as I dive forward, rolling through the movement at the last second. "Nice, Oak!" Hala calls from somewhere in the distance.

I don't dare look anywhere else but ahead. This is it. The training course that will determine whether or not I can get my magic back on the next mission. A large log swings overhead, just barely missing me. It's not my first close call, but it doesn't matter. I'm halfway through, and this time, I'm going all the way.

There are a series of platforms suspended in the air at different heights. The size of the platforms themselves vary and some even collapse. There's a challenge to it all. Agility, balance, and most importantly, *speed*.

I take off, rushing towards the end of the runway and launching myself at the first platform. It's a big leap, and I have to put enough power behind it to remotely make it. A chorus of cheers surround me as I safely make it to the first platform. Thankfully, this one doesn't seem too unstable. I look at my options, the platform to my right is smaller, more narrow, but it's not as big of a jump as the left. The left is higher and if I don't jump far enough, that's it.

"Trust your instincts!" Lina calls out to me.

I wipe the sweat dripping down the side of my face. Trusting my instincts is not something I have ever done. My entire life I have constantly doubted myself, doubted others and their intentions. That internal voice screams at me that nothing is as it seems and for so long I fought to ignore it.

But that was then, this is now. If training with the Ghosts has taught me anything so far, it's that we are the only thing that binds us. Our willingness to believe that we are capable of doing more than we ever imagined before is the very thing that makes it true. So fuck it, I might not have wings, but I'm going to fly.

Pushing all of my strength into my legs I leap for the higher platform. The flat surface is level with my thighs as I start to fall with a muttered curse. I reach out, leaning forward so that my torso comes down on top, catching most of my weight before I can be dragged down. My lungs burn, my arms shake with the effort to pull myself up, my legs kick at nothing as they dangle in the air.

Finally, I get a good grip on the other side and manage to pull myself up the rest of the way. I crawl to my knees, my hands planted against the platform as I take harsh, heaving breaths. Two down, four to go. The next two are one after another in a line, nearly identical. Seemingly easy enough, but something about it makes me pause.

"Two more minutes!" Aine calls out, reminding me that it's not just about getting to the other side.

The third and fourth platforms are too far to really get a good look at, but if I can just make it past these two, I can reevaluate. Rising on shaking legs I wipe my palms against my thin pants, hoping to dry them in case I need to catch myself again. I take three deep breaths.

"Here we go," I mutter to myself, leaping to the next platform.

As soon as my weight is fully on the platform it starts to crumble and without taking a second to think I leap to the next. Only my balance is thrown off as the wood beneath my left foot falls away. There is a collective gasp as I stretch my body as far as it can go, barely catching the next platform with the tips of my fingers.

Burning pain sears down my back, it radiates through my shoulder and up my arms. I let out a scream as I fight to pull myself up, my arms shaking with the effort as I slowly inch higher.

"One minute!" Aine calls out again.

"Pull, Oak!" Symone cries.

"You've got this!" Hala bellows.

"Just a little more!" Lina encourages.

But it's Farai's voice that breaks through, one word that has me pulling myself the rest of the way up. "Fight!"

My feet touch the platform and more cheers erupt. Aine's warning of thirty seconds barely breaks through them. I push through the haze of exhaustion and pain, leaping to the third and forth platforms so fast I barely register ever stopping. I collapse onto the final platform, staring up at my squad as Aine clicks the stopwatch, her face expressionless.

"Did I make it?" I wheeze.

Five sets of eyes watch Aine as her lips slowly spread, she turns the stopwatch. Two seconds. I finished with two seconds to spare. Hala, Symone, and Lina fall on me, creating one big pile of limbs as they scream excitedly. Farai and Aine share a proud look with each other before congratulating me.

"We knew you could do it," Lina whispers against my ear, squeezing me to her before disentangling herself.

The sisters are close to follow, both offering a hand and pulling me to my feet. Everyone but Aine heads back to the dining hall for their dinner shift.

"There were some close calls," Aine remarks.

"I know," I agree, still fighting to catch my breath.

"You made a lot of mistakes," she continues.

"I know," I sigh. Shit, maybe it's not enough to make it through. I hadn't even considered how I performed on the course, I was only worried about finishing.

"You can't go back to relying on your magic from here on out, you need to keep working on those skills without it."

"I kno-wait." I stare at her, unsure if I really heard her correctly.

"Why do you look so surprised?"

"Well you said- and I thought- but-""You did good, Oak. You can be proud of yourself. You've come a long way, let yourself have this." She follows after the others and I am left staring at the empty course that just changed everything.

Finally, I am making progress, it's time I got my magic back. I make my way to the dining hall and take my seat at our usual table. The others join me shortly after and launch into all of the *best moments* from the challenge. There are many versions of the challenge so everyone experiences something slightly different.

Instead of platforms, Hala had to swing from her hands to cross, while Symone was forced to crawl with barely half an inch of space to move; she nearly didn't make it in time. Lina was forced to cross a rolling log, and Farai had a slightly different version to my own. When we turned to Aine expectantly, she excused herself.

Rather than get caught up in Aine's early departure, we begin talking about all the ways they almost failed at their challenge. Their stories grow wilder and wilder until Lina spits water across the table, soaking Hala and earning a spoon full of rice to the face. As I laugh alongside them, I begin to feel this odd sense of longing take root in my chest.

"Everything okay?" Lina asks quietly.

The others stop what they're doing and listen in.

"Um... yeah. I guess I just wish my friends were here to see that," I say with a shrug. The table remains silent for so long that I look up, watching the others as they do their best to look anywhere but at me.

330

Hala and Symone excuse themselves first, followed by Lina whose eyes look surprisingly glassy. Farai is the only one who stays.

"Did I say something wrong?" I ask, looking over my shoulder as the three of them disappear down a hall.

"No. They're just... they're hurt is all," Farai explains.

"What? I don't understand what did I-"

"It's not your fault. It's just... you're different from us. Everyone else that you see here, they have no one outside of these walls. When they were brought here, it was because there was nowhere else for them to go."

"So...""When they hear you talking about friends on the outside, it hurts. We are the closest thing that each other has to a family. But you, *you* have an actual family. I think it just reminded them of what they've lost," Farai whispers.

"I never meant to hurt them," I assure.

"They know that, but it doesn't make it hurt any less. Pain has a way of sneaking up on us. One moment everything is fine and then poof, the ache is just as bad as it was in the beginning. It's better to acknowledge it than run from it," she shrugs.

"I shouldn't talk about my friends then." Already the small bit of joy that winning the challenge brought is replaced with the familiar sense of loneliness.

"No. Don't do that. You are allowed to be happy, just because those around you are hurting doesn't mean you aren't allowed to feel joy. If thinking of your friends makes you happy, do that. Never let someone else take that from you." Farai stands, giving me one last reassuring nod before walking off in the direction Aine headed earlier.

It's not that I don't understand, I get it. But I can't just accept that this is my life now. I have people waiting for me, looking for me. At least... I hope they are.

331

Chapter 52

Terran

A steady beat pounds inside my skull as I blink my eyes open. I'm slumped against the wall, the hallway completely empty. I turn my head to look around and wince. I bring my hand up to my left temple and hiss as my fingers find a lump already forming beneath the skin.

"Asshole," I mutter, remembering my brother's fist the second before he slammed it into my face and disappeared to who knows where. Stumbling to my feet, I hear a faint humming growing louder, a silhouette appears at the end of the hallway.

"Well well, what's this? The little lord left all alone?" Nalei taunts, jutting her lip out in a mock pout. She gathers her thick head of locs and runs her hands over them, water pooling on the floor as she gets to the ends. "Do you want to know what I think they're up to down there? Cay and your brother," she drawls, circling me as her eyes flick to the entrance to the cavern.

I step in front of it, pasting on a polite smile. "I know what *Princess* Cay is doing," I say pointedly, all while ignoring the comment about Oliver's whereabouts.

"Rigggght, and what about that beautiful brother of yours? Any ideas? I've got a few in mind." Her head tilts, her eyes flashing as scales ripple over her skin before disappearing.

Oliver warned me about her, how dangerous she is. If there is one thing my brother and I agree on, it's that Cay's protection is the most important thing, even if that means getting between her and her cousin.

"What my brother does is not my concern, he is more than capable of making his own decisions." Even when I don't agree with them.

"Is that so? And what if what he does includes a certain cousin of mine?" she whispers against my ear.

"Mind your tongue," I rebuke.

"Ooo, a bit touchy, aren't you?" she laughs.

"Mind. Your. Tongue."

Nalei spins away from me, dancing to nonexistent music. "I have a better idea, how about we play a game. I ask a question, you answer."

"I don't like games."

She turns to me, looking me over from head to toe, a devious grin tugging at the corners of her lips. "No, I imagine you don't. You're the serious brother, the one who has *everything figured out*. Oliver told me all about *you*."

I clamp my mouth shut, ignoring her and focusing on a spot on the wall where the stone cracked to form a perfect heart shape.

"You know what else your brother told me? He told me a story, one that I think my cousin could find very interesting. Any ideas what it could be about?" She continues to dance around me, her voice lilting as her words stoke the rage inside me.

Still, I stare at that heart and do everything I can to prevent myself from rising to her bait, or worse, going down into that cavern after Cay.

"This story was a bit of a shock even for me. I never thought that… well… you know. And now, there they are, down there in that cavern, all alone…"

My hands ball into fists.

"You and your brother are so alike. Not just in looks, though I must say you certainly share those exceptional genes." Her hand trails across my chest and to my bicep, curling around it. She laughs as I yank it from her grip. "Same temper too. I wonder what else is the same," her eyes flick down and it takes every ounce of self control I have not to react.

Nalei lets her gaze linger, then, as if bored, she sighs and rolls her eyes. Without another word she turns and saunters away, casting me one final look over her shoulder before starting to hum. The sound disappears around the corner just as Cay emerges behind me.

"How'd it go? Got what you needed?" I ask, forcing a smile.

She holds her hand out between us, palm up as she unfurls her fingers to reveal a frozen bottle. "Yep, all set. We just need to get this- Terran! What happened?" Her free hand reaches out, touching delicate fingers against my throbbing eye.

I grimace as she pokes at it, gently reaching up to remove her hand. "Nothing, a parting gift from my brother before he vanished."

Cay sighs, nodding her head back down the staircase as she heals my throbbing eye, "He followed me. He should be right behind me."

My teeth grind together as I nod, "Of course he did."

"Actually I should probably go check-"

Oliver appears around the curve of the stairs, hands folded behind his head. "Brother," he says with a nod.

I grab him by his collar, pulling him close, "You *punched* me."

"Did I? I don't know, that doesn't really sound like me," he says with a shrug.

A light hand lands on my back and I release him, turning to Cay who looks between us with clear concern. We shouldn't be doing this. *I should be in better control.* She has enough to worry about already, let

334

alone adding whatever this is between Oliver and I. Dark circles ring her sea-green eyes, and they lack their usual brightness.

"I'm sorry. We've been traveling a lot and I think we all could use some rest," I say with an apologetic smile.

"Not me, I'm fine," Oliver announces proudly. He's staring out the window searching for something.

"Great well then if you'll excuse-"

"Where's Nalei?" Oliver asks, cutting me off.

"Why?" Cay asks, her eyes widening with growing concern.

"I don't know, Oliver, why does it matter? Go find someone else to expend all that extra *energy* you seem to have," I groan, unable to hold back my annoyance at him upsetting Cay further.

Oliver's eyes burn even as he smirks. "Maybe I will," he says, taking off down the hall.

I tug on the end of Cay's hair as she watches him walk away, stealing her attention. "Why don't we go get some sleep?"

"I don't know...is it safe?"

"It's as safe as anywhere else right now. Come on, you can sleep in your old room. I'm sure you miss your bed, right?" I wrap my arms around her, drawing her into a hug and resting my chin atop her head. After a few moments, her arms wrap around me loosely, her face burying against my chest. I feel her nod slightly and we head towards her room.

~~~

We make it back to her rooms without incident, but before entering I send out a burst of power, searching for anyone who might be inside. Feeling nothing out of the ordinary, we enter and I start laying out protective charms, ones that only I can remove. Once I'm sure the room is secure, I follow Cay into the bathroom where she sits at her vanity, staring at her reflection.

"Everything okay?"

She smiles sadly, opening the drawer and pulling out a small seashell necklace. She offers it to me, "It was a gift from my father to my mother from when they were first married, before he was king. A mating gift. My mother gave it to me on my 18th birthday. I wore it every day for years."

"It's beautiful," I admire, handing the necklace back to her gently.

"It is." She reaches up, pulling her dark waves over one shoulder and bringing the chain up around her neck.

"Let me," I say, stepping forward and taking one end in each hand. I gently clasp the chains together and set it against the back of her neck with care, brushing her hair back. She tilts her head up at me and my eyes fall to her heart-shaped lips.

Slowly, she stands, turning to face me and looking up through thick lashes. Her arms wind around my waist and she presses against me, clinging to me as her cheek presses against my chest, barely an inch away from my erratic heart.

As she pulls away I take her hands, leading her back to the bedroom. I excuse myself as she pulls a silk sleeping gown out from the closet, giving her privacy to change. It takes everything I have in me not to turn around and watch as she reveals every inch of her smooth skin. I feel a tap at the center of my back and nearly stop breathing when I turn, finding her there in nothing but a sheer bit of fabric.

She's a goddess. One I am ready to worship.

She's all curves and smooth skin, the color dusted a light pink from her flush. I try to keep my eyes on her face, but I can't help but look down to those rosy peaks barely hidden from me. "May I?" There is a breath of hesitation from both of us, an acknowledgement of what this means.

Cay nods slowly, taking her lower lip between her teeth.

I reach out, gently tugging on the neckline until it dips low enough to reveal her pert nipples. "Beautiful," I breathe and she shudders.

My hands roam up and down her arms as my eyes trail back to her lips. Intense heat burns between us and I can't fight it anymore. I grab her hips, pulling her against me and bringing our lips together. Our lips move in tandem, light kisses that grow deeper until neither of us can breathe.

Vana, I want to take this slow, to take my time. But the feeling of her pressed against me is everything I have wanted for a long time. I trail my tongue across the seam of her lips and she opens for me.

Fuck it.

I waste no time diving in, my tongue devouring the taste of her as she gasps, pulling me against her harder. My hands shift, moving down until they rest over the generous swell of her ass. "Is this okay?" I mutter against her.

"More," she gasps.

Needing no further words of encouragement I squeeze her in my palms, loving the way she feels in my hands. I growl, deepening the kiss as I shift a hand to her thigh, pulling her leg up and around me. Taking the hint, she follows my lead and then she's in my arms, legs wrapped around me as I carry her to the bed and set her down gently.

My palms run up and down the expanse of her thighs, feeling the smooth skin there and catching on the divot beneath her hips. "I love these," I groan against her lips, digging my fingers in and pushing against her.

"Terran," my name spills from her lips breathily as her back arches off the bed, pushing her chest into me. Her hands are on my back, pushing into the space between my shoulder blades and forcing us closer together.

I kiss down the column of her throat, feeling the rapid beat of her racing heart, almost as erratic as my own. I follow the curves up the side of her body, mesmerized by the way she reacts to every light touch. Her gasps, her whimpers, the way she bites her lip when she thinks she's being too loud. Leaning back on my elbows, I kiss the tip of her nose and pause.

Vana, she is stunning. Dark hair spills around her head, fanning out against the white bedding. Her eyes are closed, her long lashes fanning her heated cheeks. The softness of her jawline makes her appear angelic in a way I can't truly describe. Just soft, gentle, *good*. Everything about Cay is good, and somehow she is here with me. I am utterly undeserving of her.

Her eyes flutter open. "What-what's wrong?" she asks, her voice shaky, though not from nerves.

"Nothing, I just wanted to look at you."

Cay's entire face turns bright red, even the tips of her ears. I chuckle, leaning forward to plant a soft kiss on her lips, slowing everything down and savoring the moment. Whatever this is, wherever this is going, I don't care. Not now. All I care about in this second is the beautiful woman staring up at me with kindness and admiration.

Pushing off of her, I stand at the foot of the bed. Her legs fall closed without me there, the hem of the nightdress barely brushing her upper thigh. I reach out, gently trailing my hand from her ankle to her knee, then wait. The silence stretches for what feels like an eternity, and then her legs fall open to the side. My other hand joins as I push them the rest of the way up her legs, bunching her dress up at her waist.

Swallowing hard, I move to the thin straps of her undergarment, slowly tugging it down. She lifts her hips, helping me. Once they're off, I set them to the side at the foot of the bed. I drop to my knees, pulling her to the edge and drawing a noise from her that is half laugh, half gasp. It does funny things to my heart.

I pull back, tapping the sides of her knees and making her look at me. Her lids are half closed as her ocean eyes find mine. "Do you trust me?"

"Yes," she nods.

With that singular word, I'm given permission to do something I swore I never would. After the first taste, I'm not sure I will ever be able to stop.

Chapter 53

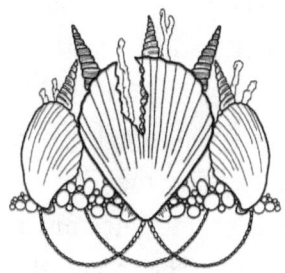

Cay

Terran's hot mouth presses kisses along my inner thigh, carving a path up until he reaches my soft stomach. He kisses me there too, moving across my body and then down the center until he is hovering over my core. He lingers there, staring at the most vulnerable part of me with a look of pure awe in his eyes. His hazel eyes drift up, finding my own. They remain locked on mine as his mouth closes over my clit.

Holy shit!

My back arches off the bed and I slam my hand down over my mouth to muffle my cry. The feeling of his mouth against me sends every nerve ending into overdrive. I'm a mess of sensation. His tongue laps at my folds, drinking in my arousal and humming with approval. The vibration has me crying out again, one hand fisting the sheets. Every inch of my skin is over sensitized. It's like my feelings have been dialed up to 100. My thighs quake with the effort to control myself, to control my… sounds.

He lifts his head, licking the wetness from his lips as he groans, "Let me hear you." He squeezes me and I let out a small whimper.

Terran circles my clit with his tongue before sucking on it gently, toying with it. Every touch is too much, I'm overwhelmed by the slightest brush. I'm burning up from the inside, lava moving through me as tension coils deep inside me, building steadily. My heart is racing, my thoughts running faster than I can keep track of. The only thing I know is the feeling of him between my thighs. The sucking grows stronger, rougher, right on the edge of unbearable as my hips jerk against him.

He backs off, kissing my thigh and trailing his tongue down to my knee before making his way up again, moving back to my heat. "You taste exquisite, angel," he groans against me.

The momentary reprieve lets me catch my breath enough to unclench my fist. But the moment he drives his tongue deep inside my entrance, my hand thrusts into his curls, fisting them and tugging tightly. Terran grunts and I instantly release him, moving my hand back to the bed.

He grabs my hand and laces our fingers together, connecting us. My head is thrown back as he speeds up, spearing me with his tongue over and over again. Devouring me. I'm gasping and whimpering as a tight coiling sensation builds. Tension unlike anything else I have ever experienced before. He wraps an arm around my thigh, pulling it further apart for him while releasing our joined hands. I nearly come off the bed as his tongue is replaced with a long, thick finger.

Fuck. Shit. This is… wow.

All thoughts cease when he adds a second finger and flicks his tongue over my clit all at once. I nearly combust. My magic is writhing almost as much as I am. I can't keep in my moans, I can't stop myself from grinding down onto his face and hand. And when he curls his fingers and they brush against that spot inside me, everything does explodes.

Terran moves quickly, draping himself over me and capturing my lips with his, swallowing my cry as I fall apart in his hands. My inner walls clamp down on him, waves of pleasure rolling over me. His fingers continue to pump and curl until my body finally stops spasming and my breathing begins to even out. When he finally eases from me, I flutter my eyes open, not really aware of when they closed in the first place.

"Are you okay?" he asks, pressing his forehead against my own.

"Ye-yeah, I think so," I gasp.

"Are you sure?"

I wrap my arms around his neck, the movement surprisingly difficult. My limbs feel heavy, weighted to the bed. I'm exhausted and I-I didn't even do anything. I freeze. My heated skin cools in an instant, my throat drying up and every muscle tensing. *I didn't do anything.*

"Cay?" he asks, worry bleeding into his eyes as he sits back enough to stare down at me.

I bury my face in my hands, shaking my head. Slowly he pries them away, smiling down at me as he gently strokes my cheeks. "What's going on?"

"I-I'm not ready to…"

His smile widens. He presses a light kiss to my lips, then my forehead, lingering there. He rolls so he is laying beside me, turning me with him. One hand drapes over my waist, the heat and weight of it soothes something in my chest and it becomes a little easier to breathe.

"Look at me, angel," he places a finger beneath my chin, tilting my face up to his, "this goes as far as you want it to go. If you want to stop here, we stop. If you want to keep going, we can do that too. You change your mind? We stop. It's completely up to you. I will never force you to do anything that you aren't ready for."

The sincerity of his words warms me all over again and I nod my head, my eyes surprisingly misty.

Vana, I cannot cry right now, that would be so embarrassing. I mean honestly, what the fuck? This beautiful, kind, gentle male, just gave me an incredible orgasm and then proceeded to say literally all of the right things. Get it together.

"What about you?" I whisper, looking down to the obvious bulge in his pants.

341

Terran shakes his head, "Nothing for you to worry about." He glances towards the bathing chamber before brushing another kiss against my forehead. He tells me he'll be right back as he jogs into the bathing chamber, returning almost immediately, rag in hand. Holding it up to me he stops at the edge of the bed. "Can I?"

"Um…" he wants to do what exactly?

His eyes soften, "It's to clean you up so you're not uncomfortable later."

"Oh. Um… can I do it myself?"

"Of course," he says, passing me the rag.

"Thanks," my cheeks heat as he turns around, giving his back to me as I slowly wipe at my damp thighs and then… elsewhere. I clear my throat when I'm done and he turns around, reaching for the rag. I swear my face is on fire as I hand it to him and he returns it to the bathroom.

Seriously, what am I so embarrassed about? He literally just had his face buried between my thighs. His tongue touched more than that rag did for Vana's sake.

"Can I lay with you?" he asks upon return.

"I'd like that," I say, crawling up into the bed and turning so I'm laying with my feet facing the foot of the bed instead of hanging over the sides.

Terran climbs in after me, staying atop the covers, but pulling me to him. He tucks me against his side, my cheek resting against his firm chest. His arm is wrapped around me, rubbing smooth circles over my bare shoulder.

My eyes are closed, sleep so close to claiming me.

"I promise to do things right from here on. I won't ever take advantage of you again," he says under his breath, and I'm not sure what he's talking about. I want to tell him that he hasn't taken advantage of me, but before I can get the words out, I'm already asleep.

~~~

Eve is on her knees, crying. Her head is being held back by her dark hair, a thin dagger pressed against her throat. Hot tears pour down my cheeks as the others' cries fill the air, becoming all that I can hear. A dark shadow

342

stands over her, dark mist wrapped around its hands as it clutches the blade.

I'm searching for any hint of magic, but there's nothing, not the smallest ounce of power remaining inside me as I sit here helpless. The figure drags the blade across Eve's throat, dark blood spilling down her pale skin and coating her stark white dress. A scream tears through me as I reach for her, only to be dragged through a dark tunnel and thrown back into darkness.

I'm sitting upright in bed, my screams echoing into this reality. Warm arms wrap around me, holding me against a firm chest. I can't stop the tears from pouring, choked sobs bursting free as I cling to him. *What the fuck was that?*

He rubs his hands up and down my back soothingly. Taking deep breaths I finally calm down enough to stop crying. I feel raw, spent, like every ounce of energy has been used up somehow. I push against Terran's chest. Swallowing against my hoarse throat. But when I open my eyes and peer up at him, it's not Terran, it's Oliver.

"Oliver? What are you doing here?" I look down, clutching the blanket to my chest. I'm still wearing the practically sheer nightgown from before.

"I heard you screaming."

"But what about Terran's enchantments? No one but him was supposed to be able to get in here."

"Like I said, I heard you screaming." He runs a hand over his longer curls, brushing them away from his dark rimmed eyes.

I look around the room, trying to make sense of things. "What time is it?"

"Middle of the night." He yawns.

"Where's Terran?"

"How should I know?" Oliver asks, his eyes narrowing. "Why?"

"Well he was here when I-"

Oliver pushes his palm into my forehead, forcing me to lay back as I fight against him. "Shhh, sleep."

"Oliver, what the fuck? You can't just shove people like that," I grumble, settling back into the bed.

"Seems to work to me."

"You're impossible," I sigh. My eyes flick back to the door and the question nags at me. "Seriously, how did you get past those enchantments?" *Maybe they weren't as strong as Terran thought.*

"Relax, the enchantments are strong," he says, seemingly reading my mind. "I've spent years learning how to get past my brother's enchantments, no one else is getting through there. Not unless we want them to."

His words give me a surprising amount of comfort. I don't doubt for a second that Oliver would dedicate years to messing with his brother, which means he's probably telling the truth about the rest too. At least there's that.

I'm exhausted, my entire body wants to shut down, but as my eyes close even for the smallest of seconds, I swear I can see Eve's throat being slit and hear my friends' screams all over again. I can hear my own screams. I shake my head to clear the images, focusing instead on Oliver who is laying in bed beside me, a small space left between us.

"Oliver, why are you in my bed?"

"This is getting repetitive. I. Heard. You. Screaming."

"And so you had to get into bed with me?"

"Yup."

"Interesting."

"If you say so."

Irritation prickles beneath my skin, but I just don't have the energy to fight with him right now so I opt for the alternative. "Fine, if you're going to stay then at least make yourself useful."

"Who said I wanted to stay?"

"Then leave."

"No."

"Okay, so make yourself useful."

He sighs. "Useful how?"

I bite down on my lip before saying, "Tell me a bedtime story."

"Seriously?"

"Seriously."

He doesn't respond for so long that I think maybe he has fallen asleep. But as I peek up at him I realize he's just staring straight ahead, his jaw tight. He clears his throat and my brows pull together.

"What?"

"Cay, are you wearing undergarments right now?" he asks through clenched teeth.

My mouth drops open at the absurd question, but then my eyes follow his and I see them. There, folded up at the foot of the bed. Exactly where Terran left them. If the rest of this kingdom collapsed around me at this moment, I wouldn't even be mad.

I sink deeper beneath the covers and ignore his question. Maybe if I pretend we aren't looking at what we're both clearly looking at, they'll just evaporate. Maybe the universe will just suck them up into the ether and we can pretend this never happened.

"When I was little," he says, making me jolt, "my father used to train with Terran. Terran was already 15 by the time I was born, but from the moment I could walk, I would chase after them. Follow them around, watch what they do, and one day, they noticed me in the corner of the room, watching as they practiced. My father handed me a sword and told me to give it my best. I was barely four years old and the sword weighed more than I did."

He scoffs, "I couldn't even lift the tip off the ground. But Terran just walked up behind me, got down on his knees, and showed me how to hold the blade. They dropped everything and spent hours working with me on the proper stance, how to block and dodge, everything." He pauses the silence stretching and filling the air with a heaviness that I can feel in my chest. When he continues his voice is gravelly, "I was sick a lot as a kid, but I did everything I could to get strong. On my fifth birthday, my father gave me two blades, twins to each other."

A rare, genuine smile brings out the dimple in his cheek. "They were light enough that I could actually carry them. I swear I didn't leave the training room for weeks after that. I spent night and day practicing with those swords, using them together. Eventually, after years of constantly being knocked on my ass," he snorts, "I actually beat Terran in a duel. My father was standing right there, watching as I held the tip of the sword he gave me against my brother's throat."

Oliver goes on and on about his father and all the things that he did with him before he died. Eventually, I start to drift to sleep just as Oliver begins telling one story that might not be about his brother.

Chapter 54

Rian

The air shifts around us. Mar goes completely limp, her hands falling to the side and the tension releasing from her face. Her entire body is burning up, her skin almost difficult to touch.

"What do we do?" Cyrus asks, looking between his sister and I.

"Aren't you two supposed to be some sort of healing experts? You tell me!" I bark. Brushing Mar's hair away from her face, I see dark lines spreading out beneath her skin. They move slowly, spreading out like spilled ink on parchment. Looking over her body, I find those lines spreading from her fingertips and as I pull back the hem of her pants, at her ankles too. Panic swells as a flash of the queen collapsing infiltrates my mind.

"What is that?" Nat says, dropping down beside me.

"I don't know, but whatever it is, I don't like it. So you two need to figure it out," I growl. Reaching out, I gather Mar back into my arms and carry her further away from the clearing so we are just beyond the treeline. The ground is softer here as I lay her back down, gently resting her head against a log.

She lets out a pained moan and my hands curl into fists. This is yet another example of me failing in my duty to protect her. I bring my hands up, placing them over her stomach and pushing healing magic out. She was clutching her stomach before she passed out, so maybe this is the source of the problem.

Nat appears above us with some small twigs and branches. "Here, we should get a fire going before it gets dark."

I stare at her. "Seriously? Of all the things to prioritize, you choose a fire? We have fire magic!" I snap.

To her credit, Nat doesn't flinch. She simply raises her brows and crosses her arms over her chest. "Are you done?"

"Depends, you have any more idiotic ideas?" I growl.

"Hey, asshole, don't talk to my sister like that," Cyrus chastises as he approaches, setting down a large bundle of flowers.

"What's that?" I ask, eyeing them with suspicion.

"These flowers are known to be good for a multitude of illnesses and even some poisons. Since we don't know what is wrong with her, it's best to remain cautious and choose something more generalized for now," Nat explains. She thanks her brother as he sits down beside her.

"You want me to get the fire going?" he asks.

"Yes, Cyrus, that would be extremely *helpful*," she says, giving me a pointed glare. After a few sparks from Cyrus the fire is burning steadily as Nat meticulously places larger branches to form a kind of teepee over it. She sees me watching and sighs, "These flowers need to be dried out, *slowly*. We can't just blast them with magic, it will make the flower useless."

Nodding, I turn back to Mar, smoothing her hair back from her face again as sweat begins to bead on her brow. Her skin is still so hot, those dark lines seeping throughout her body and turning her skin a dark gray.

"When was the last time she fed?" Cyrus asks, leaning back on his elbows comfortably, as if this wasn't an emergency situation.

"How should I know?" I mutter.

"Aren't you her guard? Shouldn't you be paying attention to these things?" Cyrus scoffs.

"I'm sorry, I was too busy chasing her around and then running from royal guards," I spit.

"Stop… fighting," Mar groans, her eyes slowly blinking open.

"Hey, you scared us, how're you feeling?" Nat asks, reaching forward and placing her hand against her cheeks.

"My stomach…" she grimaces.

Nat reaches into her satchel and pulls out something small and round. "Here, open," she says, placing the items under Mar's tongue. "That should help at least a little."

"What's going on? Where are we?" she mumbles, trying to sit up.

I push her back down by her shoulders. "Stay still, you just need to rest for now."

She rolls her eyes, but remarkably does what I say for once.

"Mar, when was the last time you fed?" Nat asks.

"I've been using blood bottles. There should be a few left in my bag somewhere," she says through gritted teeth as she starts to curl in on herself.

Nat moves her hands over her stomach, pressing down lightly and watching for Mar's reactions. "Pain?"

Mar hisses as she presses down on one spot and nods her head vehemently. "You could say that."

Cyrus appears behind me, tapping me on my shoulder. I glare at him until I see what's in his hands. He's holding two bottles of blood, only the color is far darker than anything I've seen. "Mar, is this what you've been drinking?"

"Yeah," she manages to gasp out.

I twist off the cap, putting it up to my nose and sniffing. It smells completely normal so I bring it to my lips and take a sip. It tastes relatively normal, if not a bit bitter. "Do you know what type this is?"

"Should be O Positive, my favorite."

I don't bother mentioning that my blood type is O Positive, I simply take another sip and try to discern if the blood has already gone bad. "When did you get this?"

"Before we left to get Nat."

"It should still be fine, but who knows, maybe there was something wrong with the donor," I shrug, putting the cap back on the bottle.

"You should feed, it will help your body work through whatever it is that's going on," Nat directs, her eyes flicking between her brother and I. She extends her arm, but I push it out of the way.

"Let me."

"Move, Rian," Cyrus says, shoving me aside. He takes my spot beside Mar, pulling her into his lap so she is leaning back against his chest. "Here, my blood is O Positive, your favorite," he says with a wink.

Mar smiles shakily, slowly bringing his wrist up to her lips. As she bites into his skin, her sharp fangs puncturing and filling the air with the scent of fresh blood, Cyrus *moans*.

"Annnd I'm out. I'm going to go hunt down some real food," Nat announces, jumping to her feet and disappearing into the growing darkness.

Cyrus tugs Mar further back against him, his arm draping over her hips. He continues to let out these low moans practically in her ear, yet entirely too loud for it to truly just be for her.

"Can you stop? That is incredibly unnecessary."

He laughs, his head thrown back and eyes closed. "I don't think I will. This is incredible, I had no idea a vampire's bite could feel so *good*."

Shaking my head, I follow after Nat. Using my vamp speed and enhanced hearing it takes me less than a minute to catch up to her. When

I find her she is picking berries from a bush, not bothering to look up as I lean against the trunk of a nearby tree.

"So, are we going to talk about it?"

"Talk about what?" I sigh, staring up at the sky as it grows darker by the minute.

"Whatever is going on between you and Mar."

"There's nothing to talk about."

"That so?" She walks over to me, shoving a handful of berries into my palms. "Then why are you all the way out here?"

"We shouldn't be wandering off alone," I shrug.

She laughs so loud that a few birds go flying off. "*Sure.*"

"What?" I growl.

"Nothing. I just thought that maybe things had progressed since before." She squats down in front of another bush, pulling off a berry and holding it with one hand while conjuring fire in the other so she has more light to examine it.

"Before? When would that be exactly?"

"Back in Rayan."

"You mean when a city was under attack and all of our lives were at risk?"

"Okay fair, but there was that party in Sena too. You can't deny that."

"What is there to deny? There is absolutely nothing between me and the princess." I walk towards her, wrapping the berries in a small fabric bundle before conjuring two handfuls of fire of my own.

"Thanks," she mutters, squinting her eyes at the berry in her hand.

"If you don't trust it then don't eat it."

"There is certainly something going on between you two," she says, ignoring me.

I grind my teeth. Between her and her brother, I'm not sure who is the more annoying. "Well what about you and her sister, Eve?"

"Don't change the subject, we're talking about you two. Now stop being stubborn and just tell me."

"There's nothing to tell," I groan.

"Bullshit. I saw the way you looked at her, the way you danced with her. You can't deny it."

"Why do you care?"

"Because if you haven't noticed, my brother seems to be growing attached, and I'd like to know who I'm rooting for." She stands, spinning around and thrusting another handful of berries at me while taking the others back. "Come on, let's head back."

"Shouldn't we wait a while longer?" I ask, looking around for more bushes to pick through.

"Why? Scared of what you might see? Or hear?"

"I hate you," I mutter, shoving past her. We make it back to the others quickly and thankfully they are sitting beside each other.

"Hey! What did you guys find?" Cyrus calls out.

Nat walks over and shows her bundle of berries earning praise from her brother. As I show him mine he grimaces, "These are insanely poisonous."

I chuck the berries back into the woods as Nat smirks over her brother's shoulder. I glare at her, but all she does is mouth *I'm on his team*.

Chapter 55

Rose

Two days go by. Each morning we are escorted to breakfast and then taken back to our room after. The guards follow us as we make our way throughout the realm, watching and learning as much as we can. On the third day, we have a plan. The guard escorts us to the dining hall like normal and we enjoy our meal, waiting for the opportunity. Which just so happens to be heading this way.

"Was the meal to your liking?" Imani walks towards us with a smile. It's the same question every day.

"It was excellent, thank you," I answer.

"Good soup," Reed echoes with a slurp.

Mateo and Gael nod appreciatively.

"Good! I will pass along your compliments to our entire kitchen staff. Now, if you wouldn't mind, the chief and chieftess would like to speak with you," she directs at me.

I fight to hide my smile. "Of course, I would be honored."

We all push back from our chairs and Imani holds a hand out, stopping the males. "Forgive me, but the invite extends to Rose only. Her being High Lady Ayana's daughter…" she trails off.

Mateo and Gael share a glance and then the former smiles, shaking his dark curls out of his eyes. "No problem. We were actually wondering if we might get a tour of your training grounds?"

Imani seems to consider the question before looking over her shoulder. I follow her gaze and find Asha watching us intensely. She mutters something under her breath and Imani turns back to us, clapping her hands together. "Of course, my sister, Asha, will escort you."

"Cool," Mateo grins, grabbing Gael and dragging him behind as they make their way across the dining hall.

"Will you not be joining them?" Imani asks Reed politely.

"If it's alright with you, I would like to remain with my cousin. *Aunt* Ayana prefers when we stick together," Reed says, wrapping an arm around my shoulder.

"Oh! Of course, follow me." Imani leads us through the crowds of people, all greeting her with warm welcomes and some even placing light kisses on her cheeks. "You know, I completely understand. My sisters and I are very close, we prefer not to be apart as well." Imani smiles back at Reed.

"I'm close with my sister as well. I miss her every day," Reed breathes. It's not part of the plan, but there is a *chance* that we can gain sympathy from them, they might help us willingly.

"She didn't join you?"

"She's missing," Reed says in a broken voice.

Imani stops dead in her tracks, and I nearly run into Reed's back. She turns slowly, looking between us with sad eyes. "I'm very sorry to hear that," she reaches out, squeezing Reed's hand. Her eyes swim with unshed tears.

"Thank you," Reed replies somewhat awkwardly.

"Forgive me," she swipes at her eyes, "I'm an empath. It can be... overwhelming at times. Though it does give me somewhat of an advantage with the herbs."

"The herbs?" I ask, peeking around Reed's shoulder.

"Yes, I work in the apothecary. Those herbs have a mind of their own at times and I seem to have some way of knowing what they want," she laughs, confirming what we already knew.

"Really! I work in our apothecary too!" Reed beams.

"That's fantastic, I would love to bring you to the workroom and talk remedies." Imani continues walking, continuing to smile at us over her shoulder. There is this calming aura that just radiates from her, something bright and happy and warm. She seems to call people to her without even trying.

"That would be incredible, thank you!" Reed looks back at me and I nod.

This was part of the plan. We're going to need to distract the many eyes watching us if we ever want a chance at getting the information we need. Reed insists we should just *ask* and I can't seem to make him understand that even if they agreed, we can't trust what they have to say. The best way to get what we came for is to do it ourselves. So now we move to step one.

"Here we are," Imani says, stepping to the side. She walks up to a mountain of a male, tapping him on the shoulder lightly.

He turns, smiling openly at her and bringing her into a warm hug. His dark hair is braided down his back, ringed with beads on some strands that clack against each other as he moves. His eyes find me over Imani's shoulder and he takes a small step back before making some sort of gestures with his hands.

Imani responds with her own, and it is then that I realize she is using sign language. I've only seen it a few times and it is fascinating. She gestures us closer and we step to her side, watching as she both signs and speaks. "This is Rose, the girl Asha told you about, and her cousin, Reed."

The chief looks between us and extends his arms wide, gathering us both into a hug. He releases us after a few moments and we watch his hands move.

"I have heard so much about you," Imani interprets, "welcome to our home." She turns to us now, "you can just speak with him as you normally would and I will interpret it."

"Thank you for having us on such short notice," I answer, watching as his eyes flick between my lips and his daughter.

He smiles, laughing to himself. "I heard that you made quite the impression on my second daughter, better hope your friends are tough enough to spend the day with her." My cheeks heat, but he continues signing as Imani interprets, "we are happy to have you here. It has been some time since your brother has visited."

My brows pull together, "My brother?"

"He always brings such joy to the realm, we are sad he did not join you." The chief frowns, placing a hand over his heart.

I glance at Reed, but he only shrugs. "Are you talking about Terran?"

He shakes his head. "Oliver. He has made quite the impression on everyone here."

My mouth falls open and I think Reed chokes beside me. "A good one?"

This time Imani laughs along with her father. "Yes," she interprets. "Oliver is well loved in Eteri," she adds for herself.

"Well it appears I owe my brother an apology. I guess he wasn't lying all those times he bragged about visiting here," I shake my head in disbelief.

"Brag? Are you sure we're talking about the same brother? Oliver is nothing if not humble," Imani says. Her father watches her as she signs for herself and seems to nod in agreement.

This time Reed and I burst into laughter and have to physically hold it in when it gets to be too much. "I'm sorry," I say through a laugh, "it's just… humble is not usually something we would use in the same sentence as Oliver."

The chief seems to consider my words then shrugs, signing back with an easy grin. "I suppose we each view one another through our own eyes. Please excuse me, I am needed elsewhere, but please, enjoy your stay and let anyone know if you need anything."

Imani hugs her father goodbye while Reed and I dip our heads. "So, how would you both like to see the apothecary?"

Reed nods enthusiastically and I know that it's not just for show.

"Actually, would it be alright if I walked around a bit? I'm still getting used to the altitude and think a walk might be just the thing I need." All I need is an hour to check out the layout and commit it to memory, then I can jot it all down and combine it with whatever the others learn on their own.

"Would you like to see a healer? We have plenty of remedies for this sort of thing," Imani offers.

"I would prefer to handle things without them if possible. I have quite the sensitive stomach," I place a hand over my gut.

"She does, I have to brew everything for her separately using very meticulous methods," Reed adds, covering for me, "it can be *very* time consuming."

"Really? Well then please, show me how it is done so that we can be sure to provide them for our guests in the future."

"Of course," Reed nods.

"Well then, sure. Just be careful and stay on the marble paths. A guard will be with you at all times so when you're ready to return to your rooms just let them know." Imani and Reed head off in the opposite direction together and as if summoned, a guard appears behind me.

Smiling at him, I take the first path I find and follow it. Most of the city seems to look the same. White and gray marble. Accents of gold. Stone pillars and archways. It's all very regal, elegant. Something about it tugs at my memory, but I lose the thought as I make my way into the first room.

Tall, glass ceilings let in the morning light, casting an orange-red glow. A sense of longing hits me as I take in the vines clinging to the walls and pillars. The fresh scent of jasmine fills the space, wafting from the delicate white flowers growing throughout the room. On the far wall, large windows peek out over the mountaintops, showing the sea of clouds drifting slowly through the sky.

I move deeper into the room, admiring all of the flora, especially those that do not grow back in Sena. As I round the corner a small pond comes into view. White lotus flowers float atop the water's surface and I can't help but smile as I remember a time in my childhood when I went searching for them and fell into a different pond.

"I knew I would find you here."

My head shoots up from the water. Azariah is just across the pond, sitting along the edge with her knees pulled up, her cheek resting against them. She trails a finger across the top of the water, watching me and waiting for something.

"I'm sorry, I was just walking and I was drawn here."

The corners of her lips tip up ever so slightly. "I know. I was expecting you." She wraps both arms around her knees and waits.

"Um… okay. Should I leave or…"

"Join me." Her eyes flick over my shoulder to the guard and I hear his retreating footsteps.

"Oh, okay." I hesitate, but then she smiles fully and my lungs constrict, my pulse quickening.

"Don't be scared, you are meant to be here."

My brain short circuits, and it takes me a moment to regain thought. Free will. The ability to *move*. I practically trip over myself as I circle the pod. I stand next to her, unsure if I should stand or sit or-

"Have a seat," she turns her head so her chin is resting on the top of her knee, staring at me expectantly.

"Thanks," I mutter, plopping down beside her. We sit in comfortable silence, watching as the sun rises over the mountains. Azariah is staring at the lotus flowers, watching as they drift with the tiny ripples as she brushes the surface of the water. While she watches them, I watch her. Something about her truly captivates me in a way I have never experienced before.

Once, when I was still a child, I became fascinated with a particularly rare flower. I found every book that mentioned it, gathered them up, and read through every single page trying to learn more. I spent hours searching for it all throughout the castle grounds. Everything about the flower drew me in, the color, the shape, the way the scent was described -a light, sweet fragrance like a ripe fruit- everything. I wanted to know that flower at its core, to understand it in its rawest form.

Eventually, my mother had to explain that the flower no longer grew, that it hadn't for some time. I was devastated. How could something so beautiful and rare just disappear without a trace? Certainly there was some magic, some spell that could bring it back. But there wasn't. I had to accept that sometimes we had to let go of what was so that something new could be. Now, watching Azariah smiling down at that little lotus, I wonder if she is that something new. And am I willing to take the risk to find out?

"Can I ask you something?" I keep my voice low, letting the soft howl of the wind outside wrap around my words.

She lifts her head, nodding as she wipes her wet fingers against her soft, lace gown.

"Eteri is unlike anywhere else I have ever been before. And not at all what I expected," I look out the window at the sea of clouds. "I've always been told that your people are cold, standoffish. But... that's not what I've seen or experienced at all. Why?"

She smiles to herself, folding her legs so she is sitting criss-cross. "It does not surprise me that you would hear such things. They aren't exactly untrue, though I am glad to know that you have felt welcomed here." She pauses, seeming to consider what to say next. "It is not often that we open our arms so willingly. My people do not trust easily and I fear that, if not for my gift, they would shut out the rest of the realms entirely."

"But why?"

"When history tells a story, but the truth is far from reach, it is easy to get lost in the shadows."

"I don't understand."

She swings her legs over the edge, dipping her bare feet into the water and stretching her legs out with a sigh. "History is nothing but a story told through the eyes of the one who walks away. Very rarely are these stories told as things truly happened. My people have been the victims of such stories, but they have also been the perpetrators."

"The perpetrators?"

"Yes. My father is the chief, my mother his chieftess, but neither of them carry any sort of royal blood, at least not in the way other realms would recognize." She watches me out of the corner of her eyes, gauging my reaction. When I don't give more than a nod of understanding, she continues. "The generation before my father was the last of the royal blood before it died out. Then the people selected my father to lead them and now he has selected me."

"That is quite an honor," I admire. The idea that a system like that is even a possibility is not one that I have ever considered. It is no secret that power is what decides who leads, not blood, but that doesn't mean that people are always so willing to accept that. Especially not when it means challenging the status quo.

"Yes, it is. I am honored to lead my people, to be their chieftess. But I also value the truth. For so long, we allowed history to erase our past because it benefited us, it erased the worst of what we have done. But not now, not anymore. Ignoring history doesn't mean that it didn't happen. It only means that you are doomed to repeat it."

"You lost me," I admit sheepishly.

"Over a millennia ago, the world was very different. People were one, undivided. Then we became jealous, hungry for power, wanting to rule over each other instead of beside. Eventually, it cost us something great, but rather than fixing what we broke, we found ways to cover it up, to ignore it. So the problem got worse, slowly but surely we began to decay until we had no choice but to rely on those that we had forsaken." Her eyes grow haunted.

"What happened?" My heart quickens, my palms growing sweaty.

"We took something that we can never give back. A life. A life that would alter the course of history from that moment forward."

"Why have I never heard any of this before?" Acid churns in my stomach as I wait for her answer, watching as she climbs from the pond. She uses her air magic to dry her legs and I don't have the heart to be impressed by the show, instead I am caught by her words.

"Because, we wrote the history books."

Chapter 56

Eve

A light knock on the door drags me from the depths of sleep. I sit up, pushing my hair out of my face and rubbing at my eyes. My head is pounding already, the empty pit inside me where my magic should reside aches. Somehow, I'm not dead yet. Despite the lack of magic, the minimal food, and constant boredom, I still manage to wake up every day.

For a while I questioned it, but then I heard my mother's nagging voice in my mind reminding me to be grateful for my gifts. At the time, she was referring to the strength of my magic, but I'm sure it applies to this situation as well.

Swinging my legs over the side of the bed, I take a moment to pause, letting my body grow accustomed to the new position. After a few moments of black spotted vision, I stand. I cross the room on shaky legs, then reach for the handle and pause.

Wait. Why the fuck am I answering the door? I drop my hand, staring at the handle and waiting for it to turn. Minutes go by as I watch, my heart pounding in my chest with every passing second. *What are they waiting for?* The door is hardly a barrier against them. Nothing can stop Yuta or any other Grim from entering when they have the power to evanesce.

I shudder, my spine tingling. I'm still not sure how much I believe what Yuta told me, but... there has to be some truth in it. The magic that they hold, the way that history has all but forgotten Cansu, things just don't add up.

I've never been one for history, but I know for certain that I have never heard even a whisper of a species like the grim. I do however distinctly remember being quizzed on the 16 species, where they're from, what elements they hold, and what skill they're known for.

The knock sounds again, louder this time and I nearly jump out of my skin. I take a step back and the knock comes again. Then again. Then again. Until whoever is on the other side is practically pounding on the door. With each rap against the wood a sharp burst of pain nearly splits my skull. I cover my ears with my hands, but it does nothing to lessen the riot happening outside.

My hand snakes out, grabbing the handle and ripping the door open in one fluid move. "What the fuck do you want!" I yell.

Chien is slumped against the wall, dark shadows ringing his nearly black eyes. "Morning to you too," he says through a yawn.

But it's not Chien who was pounding on my door. Oh no. Far worse... *Teru* is standing between the door frame, arm raised in preparation for another round of knocking. "Took you long enough," they mutter, whipping their long hair over their shoulder.

"What do you want, Teru?"

"I have been sent to collect you." Their lips curl into a sneer as they look me over from head to toe, taking in my exposed skin. I hadn't had time to throw some real clothes on, so I'm standing here in nothing more than a thin slip with barely there straps and a hem that brushes the tops of my thighs. "What in Vana's name are you wearing?"

"Someone decided to start banging on my door so I didn't have time to get dressed," I snarl, placing my hands on my hips.

"Well get dressed. You look ridiculous." They roll their eyes, crossing their arms over their chest and moving to lean against the wall beside Chien.

"I don't know, I think she looks hot," Chien says with a shrug, a smile dancing in his eyes.

"Must you?" Teru sighs, "Also, don't let the king hear you say that, or Eri for that matter." This time, Teru smirks, their eyes flashing with amusement as Chien's body turns rigid.

"Shit." Chien stands ramrod straight and marches down the hallway, disappearing with a string of curses slipping past his lips.

Teru's eyes turn back on me, their brows raising, "What are you still doing standing there? Get dressed."

"No."

"No?"

"Nope," I say, popping the 'p'.

"Are you always this difficult?"

"Most days."

"Why am I not surprised?" Teru pushes off the wall and then stalks into the room, closing the door behind them. "Alright, now get moving, we're already late and I despise being late."

I walk back to the bed, plopping down on my back and picking at the dirt beneath my nails.

"What do you think you're doing?"

I turn my head, fluttering my lashes at Teru with innocence. "I don't know what you mean."

"Get. Up."

My mouth opens wide on a grossly exaggerated yawn. I roll over onto my side, tucking my hands beneath my cheek. "I think I'll get some more sleep." My eyes fall closed and I actually might fall asleep with how comfortable this bed is feeling right now. Most nights it is nearly impossible to get any sleep, but right now? This bed feels like a cloud.

"Absolutely not. The king has requested you, now get up."

I roll onto my back, staring up at the blank ceiling and counting the cracks again. "I have no interest in sitting around a table and getting another history lesson."

"Good, because neither does he."

I roll onto my stomach, propping my head up in my hands as my elbows dig into the mattress. "So then what does he have planned?"

"I believe," Teru hesitates, seeming to gather their thoughts, "That he wishes to show you the kingdom. Though I have no idea why when you have been nothing if not stu-"

"I'll get to go outside? Really? I can walk around? You swear it?"

Teru's lips curl in disgust as I sit up eagerly on the bed, practically bouncing on my knees. "I suppose that would be part of your-""Get out."

"What? You have no right to-"

"Get out so I can change."

Teru rolls their eyes, but does as I ask, slipping from the room and closing the door gently. I race to the bathing chamber and quickly freshen up the best I can with limited resources. Once I feel more like myself, I look at my small collection of clothes and frown. The only things I have are the opulent dresses he has propped me up in and the tattered remnants of the other clothing I've managed to salvage.

"Fuck," I mutter to myself.

There is a soft knock on the door and when I turn to look at it I find a hand sticking through holding a bundle of fabric. Teru waves the fabric in the air impatiently. "Here," their voice creeps in through the small crack in the door.

"What's this?" I grab the fabric, unfurling it to reveal two simple garments. I slip on the pants first, pulling on the drawstring to tighten the waistband. The fabric is a thicker cotton, the ankles are fitted, but the rest hangs loosely around my legs. I slip my arms into the top next, wrapping one side around and tying it at my side, then doing the same with the opposite piece as it drapes over the first. The top is the same material, the sleeves falling just past my elbows, the collar becomes a deep v until the place where the fabric overlaps.

It's so unlike everything else they have given me, yet there is a comfort to it. My skin is oversensitized right now, my bones are a bit more prominent beneath my skin from how much weight I've lost. I feel little more than a ghost yet this fabric wraps me in comfort and makes me feel… safe. It's warm and light, soft and sturdy, all at the same time. It reminds me of being wrapped in a warm towel after a long bath.

"Are you ready yet?" Teru calls from the hallway.

Am I? This will be the first time I am really getting out since I was brought here. The realization hits me that this could be a chance for escape, but as I take a step towards the door I am reminded just how weak I am. I bend over, clutching my stomach as a deep rooted pain steals my breath. Forcing myself to breathe I stand upright. As I pull open the door I bite down on the inside of my cheek to keep from crying out.

"What's wrong with you?" Teru asks, eyeing me with scrutiny.

"Nothing." My legs begin to shake with the effort to stay standing. Fuck no, this is not happening right now. No way am I going to let this stupid magic withdrawal keep me from getting out of here. Even for a few minutes. I can't take staring at these blank walls anymore. My brain needs stimulation or I might *genuinely* die of boredom.

"You're lying," Teru's eyes narrow.

"No, I'm not," I try to say, but the words come out more of a gasp as, sure enough, my legs collapse beneath me.

"Vana," Teru shoots forward and catches me.

I stare up at them in surprise, fully expecting to have hit the ground.

"Alright, let's go." Teru yanks me to my feet, wrapping my arm around their shoulder and then pulling us out of this existence and dropping us into the next. We're in some sort of kitchen. A few people meander around, working silently. One greets Teru with a smile and asks what she can do to help. Teru whispers something to her and her eyes flick to me for the briefest moment before she nods, disappearing behind some closed door.

366

She returns moments later and hands Teru a plate of food and a glass with some sort of dark liquid. Teru thanks her and then glides towards me, setting the two down in front of me. "Go on."

The scent of the food wafts towards me and I barely choke down the sob that rises in my throat. That smell, I would know it anywhere. It's the same sandwich that I ate every time I was sick growing up, the one my mom made me. The plate is arranged with various foods piled around it and not stacked between bread, but that heady, spicy smell is *exactly* the same. I reach for a fork and take a greedy bite, not even considering whether or not this is a bad idea.

A moan slips out the moment the food touches my tongue. My entire body seems to relax as I dig in, stuffing my face so fast that it actually becomes hard to breathe. A bit of food gets stuck in my throat so I reach for the liquid, tossing it back in one go and letting the flood slosh down. When I set the cup down Teru reaches out, taking it to that back room and returning with another.

"So, you're serving me now?" I ask with a mouthful of food.

"That's revolting. Please chew first, then talk. Or better yet, don't talk at all."

I swallow hard, being more careful this time not to choke. "Aw, you care about me."

Teru barks a humorless laugh. "I simply care enough about my own life to not let you die. At least not at the hands of some breakfast. Though later, I might not be as concerned."

"Right," I snort. I clean the plate completely, pushing it back as I go for the second glass. The moment my hand touches it I feel Teru's eyes glued to me. At first, I shrug it off but as I bring the edge of the glass to my lips I swear I can feel their eyes following every miniscule movement. Slowly, I set the glass back down, not a single drop passing my lips. "What did you do to this?"

"What?"

"The drink, what did you do to it?"

"Absolutely nothing." Teru shrugs.

"You're staring."

"Am not."

"Are too." I narrow my eyes at them.

"You're being absurd."

"No, I'm really not."

"Yes, you really are."

"You're imagining things."

"Dont," I snap, slamming my hand down. "Just-if you're not going to answer my question then fine, but don't try and tell me that I'm imagining things. I know what I saw."

"You didn't see-"

"I did and I won't let you tell me otherwise so let's just move on." I push the drink away, ignoring the slight burn in my throat as I deny myself.

"Brat," they mutter under their breath as I step up beside them.

"I'll take that as a compliment," I smile.

They snort. "Of course you would." Their long fingers wrap around my bicep and then we're tumbling through the darkness again.

To my surprise, I don't feel the need to hurl my guts up the second the world comes back into view, though there are still black dots clouding my vision. I blink my eyes to dispel them and when they clear, I suck in a breath.

We're in the center of a city square, with long cobblestone roads stretching out in all directions. The roads are lined with brilliant orange and yellow trees. The bell shaped leaves are so unlike anything else I have ever seen before. Small fruits, about the size of tomatoes, hang from the branches. The colors are beautiful against the dark brown wood that makes up the buildings and the dark silhouette of mountains off in the distance.

I spin in place, taking in the beauty of the landscape. The mountain peaks disappear into the misty sky, but the outlines are still there standing tall. There are small buildings running up the streets and seem to continue all the way up the side of the closest mountain, some areas held up by large wooden beams stuck into the ground. Lanterns are hanging everywhere, casting a soft glow along the empty streets.

"Where is everyone?" I ask, eyeing Teru suspiciously.

"It is still early, the king wanted to see you before things got crowded. Now let's go, we're already running late." They practically drag me behind them as they cut through alleyways and between small buildings until we come upon a large gate. The gate is closed, wide beams framing it on either side as some sort of carved sign sits on top, arching over the center.

I try to make out the many intricate carvings, but Teru shoves me inside through a small gap in the gates. The other side is almost indescribable, otherworldly. Natural black stone is built up on the left, forming a barrier to the river. The water is perfectly clear, the riverbed covered with the same, flat stone. Some of the orange leaves have fallen in, resting upon the surface and floating down with the flow of the river.

We follow the river up another cobblestone path. There are small huts with no windows, steam billowing out from vents in the ceiling and under the doors. The deeper we go, the thicker the mist becomes until the water vanishes and the ground is hard to see. I stumble over a loose rock and curse to myself.

I hear Teru snicker ahead of me, but I am too concentrated on not busting my ass to care. That is, until I slam into their back face first. "Fuck." I rub my aching nose. I glare at them as they spin, pointing into a small house on our left.

"Go in there and wash yourself from head to toe," they say with a grimace, looking me over as if I am covered in filth.

"Why would I do that?" I cross my arms over my chest.

"Just do it," they groan, walking over and pushing the door open.

I follow after them and peek inside. The entire room appears to be some sort of shower, the walls are sleek stone, the floors a smooth wood with a drain at the center. There is a line of products sitting on a shelf built into the wall that piques my interest. I have to admit, this is infinitely better than my current bath situation. With narrowed eyes I slip past them, slamming the door closed and testing the water that is hot almost instantly.

Stripping from my clothes, I quickly step under the spray, groaning at the sensation. Teru tells me to hurry up from outside the door and even though I want to savor this moment, I don't want to find out what happens if I'm not quick enough. I use the fragrant soaps to wash my body and my hair and then shut the water off. Looking around there is a small hand towel that I use to dry my skin, ignoring my dripping wet hair.

The fresh floral scent of the soap clings to my skin as I pull the pants and wrap-shirt back on. I yank the door open just as Teru starts to shout at me again. Their eyes seem to search for any lingering sign of dirt and seem to be satisfied as they gesture for me to follow them. We've only walked another few feet up the path from where we stopped before when Teru stops me again.

"Wait here." They leave me standing there, looking at the flow of something on either side, hidden through the fog. They vanish in the mist just as everything else has, but they're only gone for a second.

"That was fast," I call out, watching as they approach.

Except... they seem taller. Broader even. And... their hair isn't long like Teru. This is *not* Teru. It's difficult to see without access to my heightened senses and I can't help but reach out to them, even knowing they won't be there. The faint pull of something deep inside me surprises me and I tug harder, only to be disappointed when it disappears.

I squint my eyes and then the fog is being shoved aside as Yuta comes stalking down the path, chest bare as his tunic falls open, and pants hanging low on his hips. "Welcome, follow me."

Chapter 57

Mar

We spend the night in the woods, Nat taking the first watch. I curl up on my side, hugging my knees to my chest as the lingering aches begin to dull. *Who knew that some bad blood could wreak so much havoc?* Sure, we hear about the dangers as kids, but for a moment there, I really thought I was dying. The pain in my stomach, those dark inky lines that spread out across my body, it was all very real and not at all something I was prepared for.

"Mar," Rian's voice calls from above me.

I force my eyes open, my cheeks burning up from the fever and a whole lot of embarrassment. "What do you want?" I groan.

"I just wanted to check on you. How're you feeling?" he asks, squatting low beside me. His large hands brush back the damp blonde hair clinging to my face. The rough pad of his thumb trails over the sides and down my neck, chasing the lines of blackness.

"I'm fine, I just want to sleep while we can." I squeeze my eyes shut, shoving away the look on Rian's face as he takes in my weakness. *How could I let this happen? How could I be so irresponsible?* My top priority is Eve, but I shouldn't be neglecting myself. I'm no good to anyone dead.

"Alright, well I'll be just over there if you need anything." The crunch of his boots over the dead leaves fades and I finally crack my eyes open again, finding him sitting a few feet away, his back propped against a tree with his arms folded over his chest.

I peek through my eyes, watching him. Rian is complicated. He is rude, aggressive, and for some reason, territorial. The way his eyes flared when he saw me with Cyrus…if I didn't know better, I would think he was just hungry. But no. The heat behind his eyes was not the heat of thirst, it was something else entirely.

My body heats, remembering the feeling of his hands on me, pushing me into the wall and taking ownership. The steady thrum of his fingers against my needy clit. He knew exactly how to wind my body up. Then again… he also left me there, panting and wound up beyond belief. Frustrated.

Yes, frustrating. That is exactly the word I would use to describe Rian. With his stupid white blonde hair, his stupid eyes, and stupid jawline that could cut glass. *I mean really, whose jawline is actually that sharp?* It's infuriating. I never shy away from what I want, I take it. Especially when it comes to lovers.

Then came Rian. He pushes back, he challenges me. And while it can be fun, it is also maddening. Most of the time I just want to bash his head in. Meanwhile my body has other things in mind. Fun, hot, wet things. The space between my thighs dampens as I am flooded with the memory of what happened against that cave wall. A kingdom collapsed around us, but the only thing we cared about then was each other.

Look where that got us? None of this would have ever happened had I just stayed focused. Sighing, I roll over onto my other side, finding Cyrus stretched out on the ground a few feet away. His soft lips are parted, his lashes fan his freckled cheeks as he takes deep, even breaths. How in Vana's name he fell asleep so quickly is the true mystery.

I smile to myself, thinking about the way he spoke to me as I fed. I don't know how he knew, but the entire time he was in my arms he whispered words of encouragement. He reminded me that it wasn't my fault. That I couldn't have known. He even said that it was okay to be embarrassed if I was, but to let it go because there was nothing to be embarrassed about.

At first, I just grew increasingly more mortified by the second, but now, thinking back on it, I needed that. I needed to hear it from someone who is entirely unbiased. Rian is complicated. Cyrus is simple. Straightforward. He has made it perfectly clear that he is interested in something *more* with me. Something I might also be interested in.

Still, whatever it is that I decide, it has to wait until I get my sister back. There is another sharp pain in my stomach and I wince, sucking in a breath. My eyes squeeze shut against the searing pain and I have to force myself to take shallow, gasping breaths. It's not nearly as bad as before, but fuck, if this is what bad blood does to a vampire, I'm sticking to the fresh stuff from now on.

Arms wrap around me, pulling me against the firm chest of someone. A male. Before I open my eyes to get a look, an arm lands over my waist, legs get tangled with my own, and with the hand on the back of my neck holding my against the chest, I am basically trapped. I struggle against his hold, still not entirely sure who *he* is.

"Shhh, go back to sleep," Cyrus mumbles against the top of my head.

"Cyrus…"

"We're just sleeping."

"Yes, but why am I-"

"Shhh, sleep, don't ask questions." His hot palm slips over the exposed skin at my hips and I freeze, waiting for that hand to shift. Except it doesn't. He tugs the fabric down and rests his hand atop it, holding it in place. His hold on me is firm, yet relaxed. Comforting.

I fall asleep in his arms, breathing in the spice and pine scent of him.

~~~

"What. The. Fuck!" Rian roars off in the distance.

I choke on a laugh and look across the fire to Nat. She shakes her head, muffling her snickers with a hand. Her eyes are already watering from how hard she is fighting to hold in her laugh.

"What's the problem, Rian?" Cyrus groans.

"What do you think you're doing?" Rian fumes, bursting through the treeline and pacing in a small circle.

Cyrus follows behind him, running a hand through his fiery curls. "It's not like we haven't done it before. We used to cuddle all the time back in-"

"Stop," Rian rushes Cyrus, grabbing him by his collar and holding him close, fangs bared. "We. Have. Never. Cuddled."

Nat can't hold her laughter in anymore. She bursts into a fit, falling off the log and rolling around on the ground as my own laughter grows.

At some point Nat traded watch with Cyrus and then he eventually came to get me. When that happened I got up and Nat decided she was too awake to fall back asleep so we left the two males alone. A few hours later when we went to wake them, we found them curled against each other, both holding on like they couldn't bear to let the other go. We laughed so hard at the sight that we decided to leave them and have been sitting around the fire talking ever since, just wondering when they would rouse.

"Don't lie, you and I used to cuddle all the time. Admit it. You missed me." Cyrus opens his arms wide and nods his head as if to invite Rian in for a hug.

Rian shoves him away, his hands balling into fists and small sparks flicking out.

"Careful, Rian, better get control of those flames. If you need some help I'm sure my brother would be more than willing to hold your hands," Nat smirks.

"You shut it," Rian growls at her. "You," he turns his stare on Cyrus, "stay the fuck away from me."

"What happened to us? We used to be so close." Cyrus shakes his head dismally.

"What happened is I finally realized you're nothing more than a clingy, overbearing, pain in my ass." Rian points an accusing finger.

As entertaining as it is to watch the two of them bicker, there are more important things that should be addressed. Namely what happened to me.

I clear my throat, "I want to apologize for what happened. I was careless. I should have been paying more attention to things. I caused a needless delay and for that, I'm sorry."

"You couldn't have known," Nat reassures.

"She's right, the blood seemed good enough," Rian echoes.

"You have nothing to apologize for," Cyrus says, marching over to me and wrapping me in a hug before I can stop it.

My immediate instinct is to shove him away, but surprisingly, I lean into him, letting his warmth and spice comfort me just like last night. "Thank you, I appreciate the support, but still, from now on, I should only drink fresh blood."

A chorus of agreement comes from the three of them. I feel Rian's eyes watching me, analyzing me.

"I know that this means things are going to get a bit more complicated. We can't risk depleting anyone's magic too low, and Nat and Cyrus, you both are doing a lot of flying as is-"

"It's easy, you'll drink from me," Rian cuts in.

"Now hold on. Not so fast. If Mar is drinking from fresh blood that means you'll need to too," Nat points out.

"So it's settled them, Mar you drink from me and Rian you can use Nat," Cyrus says with a clap of his hands.

"Thanks for offering me up, brother." Nat punches Cyrus in his sides, but he doesn't even flinch.

"No, that won't work. If we do that then you'll both be weak. Rian and I will take turns feeding from whoever is not flying, that way they have time to replenish their magic and rest. We won't take too much either, only what is absolutely necessary."

"Cool with me, here" Cyrus stretches out his arm towards me, but I shake my head.

"It's not my turn." I can't hide my smile, especially when Nat honks a laugh.

Cyrus turns his arm to Rian who ignores him and turns to Nat. "She fed from him last night, it's your turn."

Nat works her hair into two braids starting at her forehead and pulling back down the curve of her head. "No can do, I'm flying first."

"Fine, then I won't feed."

"Yes, you will. Stop being so stubborn. We all need to be ready for anything to happen and if I'm being honest… I'm still not feeling so great." I exchange a look with Nat, knowing that she'll be interested to know more, but that now is not the time.

"Alright then, we're settled. Let's get things moving." Nat jumps to her feet and finishes tying off the end of her second braid. She takes a moment to stretch, crack her neck, and jog a bit away before shifting into her giant dragon form. Matte black scales cover her, large wings spread out on either side as we climb up onto her back.

I sit down between her shoulder blades, Rian and Cyrus following close behind. The two immediately begin fighting about feeding again, but I tune them out as we take to the skies. I continue to ignore them, watching the horizon shift with the morning sun and the ground grow more barren the further south we go.

We're getting close. The terrain is changing and the familiar heat of my home is quickly fading away, replaced by an odd chill that permeates the air and down to my bones. There is a sort of incessant pull in my chest, a throbbing that grows stronger the further we fly. Part of me is worried that it is a lingering side effect of the blood. The other part of me can't help but hope that it is a sign we're going to find Eve.

Hours pass and Nat continues to fly, keeping high in the sky and far out of view of whoever might be lingering below. A nervous energy builds inside me. Despite the challenges, despite everything working against us, we're doing it. Soon, we're going to storm in there, find Eve, and bust her out. We're bringing her home. And when we do, someone is going to start talking because if there is one thing that we have earned, it's the truth.

Chapter 58

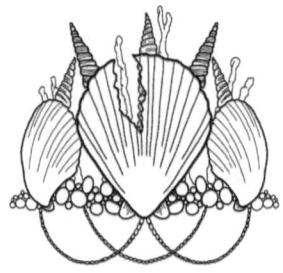

Cay

Light ripples off the barrier as Nalei's sirens continue working to repair the holes. The original plan was to leave as soon as we got the water, but after I saw the work they've been doing, we decided to stay a few extra days. Help where we can. Each morning they swim out and spend hours working on small patches and with each, I feel the magic of the city growing stronger. Nalei swims along the exterior, running a hand over the barrier and looking for any cracks, pushing her magic into them as she goes.

I take a step outside, letting the shift roll over me. It doesn't take me long to catch up to my cousin, swimming beside her and adding my own magic. We work silently, side by side, moving slowly and methodically over the dome that, once repaired, will protect our city again. In the short amount of time they've been back here, the sirens have made incredible progress, and it is feeling more like a reality that we could actually return home.

"What're you doing?" Nalei asks, breaking the silence.

"Helping."

"This little act you're putting on is truly beneath you, cousin." She swims ahead of me. "We don't need your help."

I pause, placing my hand over another crack and letting my magic fuse it back together, imbuing the barrier with the magic that fuels the city. I can't help but wonder if I had actually received my father's magic, *would I be able to do more? Could I fix the barrier alone?* Shoving the thoughts aside, I swim after Nalei.

"I know that, but I'm here all the same."

"For now." She pushes ahead again, and this time I let her go. After all, today is the day we have to leave. We've stayed too long already.

For the next two hours, I swim the length of the barrier, digging deep into my well of power and dragging up every last drop of magic that I have to offer. Draining and replenishing over and over again until I'm too exhausted to continue. My entire body aches as I walk down the halls, my arms feel impossible to lift even to simply reach for my bedroom door. Still, I head inside and go straight to the bath, filling the tub and sinking in deep.

The desire to stay in that tub, soaking my muscles and letting my magic fully replenish is strong, but then I see a letter placed upon my vanity. I slip out of the tub, letting the water drip off of me as I tear the seal open, reading the words over and over again as panic rises in my chest. I don't hesitate as I rush from the room and down the hall to where I know Terran is staying.

I shove the door open without knocking and find both him and Oliver sitting around a table. Their heads whip to me and they're on their feet before a word has passed through my lips.

Terran clears his throat. "Cay, you're naked."

"What's wrong?" Oliver demands. His eyes stay on mine, never straying lower despite, as Terran said, my very exposed body. His hand flicks and a second later I am wearing a silk gown, having used his earth magic to craft the small scrap of clothing.

But none of this matters, not as I thrust the letter into his hands and everything rushes out. "I just found that in my bathing chamber. I swear to Vana, it wasn't there this morning. It just appeared."

"What did it look like? Was there any sign of magic?" Oliver passes the letter to his brother who reads it over quickly.

"No. It was like it just popped into existence exactly where it was," I explain.

"What do you think, brother?" Terran asks, folding the letter and passing it back to me.

I quickly unfold it again, reading the lines over and over and hoping to find something that I missed before.

Cay,
I need your help. Something has gone wrong, I can't say more.
Get to Eteri as soon as possible.
~Rose

"It *is* possible that magic was used to deliver this directly to Cay, though I am more interested in learning why exactly our dear sister would be in Eteri. Care to explain?" Oliver asks calmly.

"Does that really matter right now? She needs help!" I exclaim. *How are they acting so calm right now?* Something is wrong with Rose, she needs our help. We should be on our way there right now, not talking about why. We can't waste time, not again.

"Yes, it does, actually. You know nothing about the customs of Eteri." Oliver takes a step forward and I match him.

"I am not a child, do not presume to know my mind. I have studied Eteri for most of my life, who are you to tell me what I do or do not know?" I challenge.

"Reading a book and living it are two very different things. Eteri is unlike any other realm. They do not take being deceived lightly. She could be killed," Oliver growls.

"Even more reason why we should already be on the way!"

"You say you're not a child, but there you go, just rushing into things. You don't know what you're talking about, so how about you sit back and let us fix whatever mess our sister got herself into?"

"Enough," Terran snaps, "both of you need to calm down. Cay, we need to know everything so that we can figure out our next move. Oliver, Cay is not a child, she is a future queen, you will treat her with respect."

"I'm sure that makes you feel better at night," Oliver mutters under his breath.

"Watch your mouth," Terran snarls, grabbing his brother by his collar. Oliver only smirks as Terran forces him backwards and away from me.

"Can we just focus on figuring out how we're going to save Rose?" I practically beg.

"We will. First we need to know what is happening and why she is there," Terran persists.

"Fine. Rose and Reed went to Eteri to get answers about the Ghosts. She wants to find Oak," I exhale. I'll feel bad about betraying her later, for now, all that matters is making sure she is safe.

"What?" Oliver fumes. He stalks towards me, but Terran steps between us.

"Calm down."

"Calm down? Are you fucking kidding me? Our idiot sister practically signed a death sentence with this fucking plan of hers and you expect me to stay calm?"

"Wait what? What are you talking about?" I interject.

"Yeah, bet you didn't know that, huh, princess? Eteri has rules about who can and cannot enter their city. Those who enter must have pure intentions so tell me, would you say my sister's intentions are pure?" Oliver mocks.

"She is trying to rescue Oak!" I defend.

"That might be true, Cay, but in the eyes of Eteri, that might not be how they see things. Is she being upfront about her intentions? Has she asked for help? If not they could easily see this as an attempt to steal knowledge or infiltrate the city. There is a very delicate balance with these things and... I'm not sure Rose is yet equipped to handle such things," Terran sighs.

"Rose is the smartest person I have ever met. She doesn't have a single malicious bone in her body. What she is doing is right, it is good. Don't try and turn this into something twisted," I choke. My eyes are burning with unshed tears, my throat constricting with the emotion building up steadily.

This is wrong. They're her brothers. They should believe her, support her. How can they say this?

"We aren't trying to say that she is doing anything wrong. I promise you. But it's all about perception, the way things look," Terran reaches for my hands, "Oliver isn't lying that playing with Eteri is a dangerous game. One wrong move and they can have her killed, and we won't be able to do anything about it."

"So what do we do? Is this why she needs help? Is she in danger?" I wail.

"Probably," Oliver mutters, still standing by the wall. His calm exterior has morphed into one of anger and resentment.

"What do we do?" I beg.

"What else do you know?" Terran probes.

"Not much. I know that she had some wolf helping her, though. I can't remember his name, but he has dark curly hair."

"Mateo," Oliver groans.

"Fuck," Terran curses.

"What? Is he going to hurt her?" I shudder. I can't lose Rose too. First my father, then Eve, then Oak too. I can't do this again. I can't lose anyone else. *And my mother, what happens if we don't get the water to her? What if we're already too late? I knew we should have gone back right away, even if it was my choice to stay.*

"No, Mateo is harmless. At least to Rose. But he is also impulsive and dangerously charismatic." Oliver runs a hand down his face.

"I don't understand?"

"Mateo has a tendency to make people trust him. He can get people to believe pretty much whatever he says," Terran elaborates.

"Okay, but isn't that a good thing?"

"Sure, except when those people can see straight through your bullshit. The heir, Azariah, has some sort of power. She knows people's true intentions, and no one can hide from that. If Mateo tries to manipulate her, they could see that as an act of aggression. We could have a whole new war on our hands." Oliver shakes his head to himself.

My heart beats wildly in my chest and my fingertips go numb. This is bad. Oh Vana. *What if something already happened? What if we're too late? What if they figured it all out and Rose is being held prisoner somewhere or worse, what if she is dead?*

"Deep breaths," Terran encourages, squeezing my hands.

"O-okay. So what now? Y-you have a plan, right? You know what to do?" I stammer.

"Breathe, Cay. You need to breathe. Here, sit down," Terran leads me to the chair he was sitting in when we arrived and eases me into it. He kneels in front of me and rubs soothing circles against the backs of my hands.

"You two go back to Sena. I'll go to Eteri and make sure Rose doesn't get her and everyone else killed," Oliver announces.

"I'm going with you," I say, the words slipping out before the decision was even fully made in my mind.

"No way, absolutely not, it is far too dangerous," Terran argues.

"Yes, I am. That letter was sent to me. She asked for *my* help. I won't abandon her."

"Cay..."

"No, Terran. You don't understand, Rose has always been there for me. She never gave up on me. I'm not about to give up on her."

"Terran is right, it is too dangerous and besides, you came here to get the water for your mother. You should be there when she wakes up," Oliver says.

My heart throbs as I imagine my mother waking up, smiling at me. I want to hear her voice again. I want to see her eyes, a mirror of my own. I want to feel her arms wrap around me. But if all of that means leaving Rose to fight whatever this battle is alone, then it's not worth it. If she really is okay, then there will be time for all of that later. "Rose is what is important now. I've done everything I can for my mother, now it's time to help my best friend."

The brothers exchange a look and I can see the moment Terran cracks. His eyes close as he heaves a deep breath. "Okay. I'll return to Sena and deliver the water to your mother. You two go get Rose and bring her home."

"Terran," Oliver warns.

"Let her go with you. I trust you to keep her safe." Terran looks into his brother's eyes and some unspoken conversation passes between them.

Oliver just shakes his head, storming from the room without another word.

"Where is he going? Is he leaving now? Do I need to go after him?" I stand on unsteady legs.

"No, he'll be back. Let's just get you ready to go so that when he does, you can leave immediately." Terran gives me a small smile.

"Thank you."

"For what?"

"For trusting me enough to let me go."

"I think we both know that there is no *letting* you do anything. If you want to do it, you will."

I wind my hands around his waist and bury my face against his chest. He places a tender kiss on the top of my head and I feel myself melt against him. My stomach stirs as fear invades my veins, but I shove it aside, focusing on what I know and what I can control. Whatever happens next, it doesn't matter, so long as Rose is okay and my mother wakes up.

Chapter 59

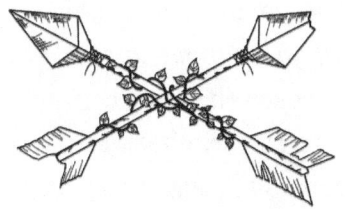

Oak

"Did you hear?" Lina asks, plopping down beside me at the table.

"Hear what?" I mumble around a mouthful of food.

"Aine was called to the castle."

The entire table freezes. The busy sound of the dining hall fades away, replaced with the sound of blood rushing in my ears. My entire body goes numb, the air stalls in my chest. Hala and Symone share a look, their forks left hovering in the air mid bite. My own fork slips from my grip, clattering against the ceramic plate and chipping it.

"*Oak,*" Lina admonishes, her voice sounding far away.

"Lina…" Someone, either Hala or Symone, cautions.

"Aine went to the castle?" The words are barely more than a whisper. *Or maybe I don't even speak them?* It's hard to tell when the world around me is slowly fading to black. One mention of home and I'm crumbling. *And since when is the castle home?*

"Oak? Are you okay?"

It's been months since I walked those familiar halls. Since I heard the sound of my brother's voice. Since Rose and I sat in the garden, reading and just existing in each other's company. Those things feel far away now. Torn from me. Somehow, in such a short time, the Crypt made me forget.

Or was it me? Maybe I haven't been trying hard enough? What if there is something more I could be doing? What if all this time I was the one keeping me here, not Aine, not the Ghosts. It has to be my fault. Right? I did something. I had to. Or I guess in this case, I didn't do something. I didn't save myself. I didn't give anyone a reason to want to save me.

Searing pain bursts across my cheek as my head whips to the side. Lina's hand rears back, ready to slap me again, but this time I catch her wrist. Shoving back from the table I throw her arm away from me, turn on my heels, and walk back to my room. I sense more than hear the others following me. They lurk behind me all the way to my room, and stand outside as I slam the door shut between us.

My vision clears, the room coming into focus as my hearing slowly returns. Farai is sitting on my bed, her arms folded in her lap expectantly. "What are you doing here?" I mutter.

"We've been given another mission."

"I don't care, get out."

She stands, walking to the door. "Be ready to move at nightfall," she says, a sort of resignation in her voice. She yanks open the door and the three loiterers jump to their feet, watching Farai's back as she disappears down the hall, likely to her own room.

Lina walks in without invitation, whispering something to others before closing the door slowly. "You want to talk about what just happened?"

"Nothing to talk about." My voice is hollow, even to my own ears. There is this sort of coldness festering in the center of my chest as I begin to replay the same questions again and again. *Why am I here? What did I do to deserve this? Do they truly care so little that they would leave me here to rot?* Eve wouldn't. She never would. But if Eve isn't here, then I don't want to think of the alternative.

"Bullshit. You completely zoned out back there." Lina makes herself comfortable on my bed, laying out with her ankles crossed, arms folded behind her head. Her white hair spills out around her pale skin giving her an, ironically, ghostly appearance.

"Please leave, Lina." I march into the bathroom, standing at the sink and staring at the faucet as I let it run.

"You'll feel better if you talk about it."

"Not everyone likes to talk about their every thought like you do."

"Yeah, but when you keep all that bottled up inside, it's just going to get worse."

I cup my hands together, letting the water spill over the sides for a few seconds before dousing my face. "I'm fine."

"I don't believe you."

"Please. Just... give me some time." I close my eyes, pressing my forehead against the cool glass of the mirror.

"No."

"Lina-"

"No. You don't get to shut me out. You need to tell me what's got you so upset."

"It's nothing."

"No it's not. Stop lying. To all of us. We care about you, we're your sisters and we-"

"You are not my sisters!" My fist slams into the mirror before I realize what I've done. Thin lines of blood appear over my hand from the glass shattering. For a second I just stand there, staring at the water as it turns red from my blood. Then I crumble, I fall to the floor and tug my knees close to my chest, letting the tears fall silently.

Lina appears above me, passing me a washcloth and sliding down to the floor, leaning against the doorframe. "Did that make you feel better?"

I shake my head. No. It didn't. Not one bit.

"Listen, I know that you have people on the outside, but Oak... this is your life now. You need to start accepting that. Once you're a Ghost, that's it. You're always a Ghost. We didn't say any of this before because we didn't want to scare you, but you need to face the facts. You need to start embracing what it means to be a Ghost. You're never going back to your old life. No one is coming to 'rescue you'. You get that right? I know that you're still… mourning, but you can't keep pushing us away. We're all that you have now and sooner or later you're going to need to rely on us. Hala, Symone, Farai, Aine, *me*. Whether you like it or not, we're your sisters."

I want to argue. I want to scream and shout my refusal into the air. I want to tear this feeling from my chest and beat it with a stick until it is nothing more than a shriveled clump of nothingness. Like how it makes me feel. I want to rage and fight and cry and I just want this to stop. But part of me knows that she's right. They're not coming.

I've known for a while, I could feel it. Even since before I was dragged here, there was a distance. I thought that maybe it was all in my head, that I was just imagining it, but no. Clearly not. Lina just confirmed the thing that has been haunting me for longer than I am willing to admit. I *am* alone. "I have no one."

"That's not true," Lina argues and I realize I said that last part out loud.

"But it is." The tears fall more steadily now. *For what? Why am I crying?* I've always known this. I've always suspected that I was going to be left behind. Like a birthday card; it means something for a moment and then is left sitting in some drawer in your room, forgotten. Until one day you're cleaning out the junk and you find it there and you read it and reminisce for a while only to throw it in the trash in the end. My friends no longer need me cluttering up their lives.

"You have us. Forever. Do you get that? Ghosts aren't just friends, we're sisters, bonded in a way that means more than some frivolous friendship."

Her words cut deep in my heart and I want to defend my friends. I want to say that they're more, that they are my true sisters. But I can't. Any time I try to find the words all I can hear is the endless stream of doubt that loops in my mind. Over, and over, and over again. I can't shut it off.

"I know that this is a lot and you're clearly still working through some things, but I want you to know, whenever you're ready, we're all here," Lina soothes.

I look up and standing in the doorway above her is the entire squad. Hala and Symone have their arms wrapped around each other's waist, their cheeks glistening. Farai is standing just a half step back, a look of sympathy in her eyes. But it's Aine, Aine who went to the castle, my former home, who has my tears drying.

Swiping at my eyes and nose I stand, ignoring the empty feeling inside and focusing on something real, something that I can control. "What's the mission?"

The others step aside, leaving a space straight to Aine who's back goes perfectly straight. "We're being sent to retrieve someone."

"Who is it?"

"Unimportant."

Irritation grates against me, but my head is already pounding from crying and my fist aches from punching the glass. "Okay. Where are they?"

"Eteri."

"Alright then. Let's go to Eteri."

Chapter 60

Eve

Yuta waits for me, his hand extended out towards me. His dark hair is wet, the ends curl and drip against his forehead. His amber eyes are bright as they sweep over me, something dark churns in his gaze. He is holding back the fog, but wisps of that shadow power swirl at his feet, caressing his calves and occasionally whipping up to wrap around his waist.

A rumbling laugh comes from him, and it is at this point that I realize I'm just standing here. Staring. It's not the first time, but I like to think that in the past I wasn't quite so obvious with my... appraisal.

Heat spreads over me and sweat rolls down my spine. I shift on my feet, not saying anything, but not looking away either. If he doesn't want people to stare at his chest then he probably shouldn't be walking around shirtless. It's his fault really.

"Come," Yuta reaches forward, grabbing me by the wrist and half dragging me after him. He leads me through the fog, parting it as he goes. Tendrils of his own power lick at my ankles and I expect it to feel gross and repulsive. Instead, a shudder passes through me and I suck in a sharp breath. The damp air is thick in my throat.

His grip on my wrist is loose, the tips of his fingers brush over the backs of my hands as we move. The point where our skin touches is cool despite the general heat and humidity of our surroundings. It's like sensory overload. The gentle sound of the water, the heat, the cold, his touch, they're both pleasant and overwhelming at the same time. I can't seem to focus, to gather my thoughts enough to question where he leads me.

We walk up a set of stairs that lead into one of those wooden buildings. Instead of a door, there is a curtain that splits into two. Yuta pushes a half to the side and pulls me through after him, being sure to hold the fabric open until we're both through. A wave of wet heat hits my face and it's suffocating. My chest feels heavy as I try to breathe through it.

I expect to see some sort of home or meeting space, instead, I find a wide open pool of water, crystal clear from the surface to the very bottom as steam wafts from the surface. The same black stone as before lines the edges of the pool and then over the floor. There is a small waterfall in the corner of the room, cascading down a sleet of stone that clings to the mountain. And that's what's most surprising. The water looks out over the side of a huge mountain, the peaks so high that they get lost in the clouds. But between them is a cliff that overlooks the crashing waves of the sea.

There is a sort of wooden deck that extends out on either side of the entrance and wraps around three sides of the pool. Yuta drops my hand and walks to the closest edge, dipping his foot into the water. "The water is perfect," he muses to himself.

"What is this place?"

"It's a hot spring. You've never seen one before?"

"No. We don't have anything like this in Vulca."

"Well, you can look at it as a sort of relaxation pool. There are some that are used specifically for bathing, but those are on the other side of the city. Would you like to try it out?"

I look down at my clothes and flick my eyes back to his, brows raised.

He chuckles, pointing to a small table on the far side of the water where towels are rolled up and stacked. "You can use those."

I chew the inside of my lip, staring at the towels and wondering if I'm really going to do this. My entire body hurts and despite having now eaten, I still feel weak. It might be nice to do something relaxing… even if it means getting in the water with the enemy. I've already come this far, might as well see it through. Besides, I have so many more questions and if this is how I'll get answers, then that's fine with me. It's better than sitting across a table again.

I walk across the damp wood, careful not to slip. Once I'm standing in front of the towels I look over my shoulder and find Yuta watching me closely. He's already in the water, having gone in with his pants still on. The water comes up to his hips, splashing against him lightly as he skates his hands across the surface.

I'm about to ask him to turn around when I realize this is the perfect opportunity. I might not have access to my succubus magic, but that doesn't mean I can't be alluring. I turn away from him, pulling on the strings that hold the fabric closed and then letting it slip off my shoulders. I can feel his eyes on my bare back. Then, I slip my hands into the waist of the pants and pull them down slowly, bending over a little so that my ass is sticking out towards him.

It's not my best work, but it will have to do. I step out of the pants, leaving them there with the shirt in a small puddle of dark fabric. I let my hand rest strategically against my upper thigh, reaching for a towel and wrapping it around me. It's small, barely covering the tops of my breasts and the underside of my ass. Perfect. Turning back, I freeze. Yuta is facing the cliff's edge staring out at the horizon… looking *away* from the show that I just gave him.

Hiding my irritation, I sashay to the edge of the water and step onto the first step. The water is insanely hot and I hiss against the pain as it scalds my skin. *What the fuck! Are they trying to boil people alive in here?* I bite my lip, hiding my grimace as I slowly descend into the water.

"Wait."

I freeze, looking up as Yuta wades through the water. He stops in front of me and reaches out. He wraps a finger around a loose strand of hair and tugs on it. "Put your hair up."

I'm ready to argue, but instead, I let go of my grip on the towel and gather up my hair. As I raise my arms over my head, the towel slips and Yuta's hand shoots out to grab my wrist. He slowly lowers my hand back to the folds of the towels and then tells me to turn around. I do as he says, goosebumps rising as his fingertips brush the skin at the back of my neck. His hands move expertly, gathering up my hair and twisting it into a knot atop my head.

Once the hair is secured, he taps my shoulder lightly and I spin again. He takes a few steps backwards and then sinks down onto what appears to be an underwater bench. I follow after him, sitting down beside him. As the water comes up to my shoulders, I sigh. Now that I've gotten used to it, the intense heat is soothing. The lingering aches in my body already start to fade.

"So, why are we here?" I ask, staring at him while he stares off into the distance.

"I thought you might like the chance to relax."

"You feel bad about all the torture?" I snort.

"I just think you should be able to experience the more pleasant parts of this land."

"Mmhm. So, are there a lot of hot springs here?"

"Yes, there are three in the main city and then a few smaller ones towards the far edges of the land."

"So I assume this one is private? Only available for use by you or your court."

He smiles, "No. This is a public space. I just make a point to visit before the rest of the city wakes."

I nod, "Makes sense you'd want this place to yourself. It's admittedly peaceful here."

"I don't come here when I do because I want privacy, I just don't want the citizens to be uncomfortable."

I cock my head, "I thought you were chosen by the people. They don't like you?"

"The opposite. It seems that I can't go anywhere without someone trying to service me in some way." He sighs, sinking lower into the water so that it reaches his biceps now.

"You don't like being serviced?"

He looks at me out of the corner of his eyes, one brow raised. "Is that what you really want to know? Are those the questions you're really interested in asking?"

I shrug, "I'm just being polite."

He laughs, "Oh, little minx, I'm not sure you know the first thing about being polite."

My cheeks heat and I sit up a little straighter. "Says the male who had me kidnapped and tortured."

His jaw locks. He lets the silence hang in the air for what feels like an eternity, but is probably no more than a minute. "What other questions do you have?" he says finally.

"I have a lot."

"Go for it."

"You're gonna regret that."

"Probably."

I sit up straighter, angling myself towards him so I am sitting sideways on the bench. "Alright, question number one. If what you say is true and the Grim are real-"

"They are," he interjects.

"-then can you use other magic? Do you have access to one of the elements? Or is it just that weird shadow stuff?"

"When the Grim were first created we did have access to the elements, but-"

"Which element?"

"Are you going to interrupt every time I talk?"

"You interrupted me," I point out.

"To correct you."

"So?"

"I can't be expected to answer your questions when you continue to ask more *while* I am answering."

"Fine. Save all questions to the end. Got it." I roll my eyes.

He watches me, then continues, "After we were cut off and banished, the Grim lost access to the elements. We could only use the power directly associated with our species, the shadows as you called them."

I pause, waiting for him to continue and when he doesn't I restate my question. "So which element do the Grim have?"

"All of them."

"All of them?"

"Yes."

"Wait wait wait, so one person can use all four elements?"

"Apologies, I should have explained better. No, we do not have access to all elements but we can have any *one* element. Fire, water, earth, air," he shrugs, "It just depends on the person, their soul, what *calls* to them."

"But... I thought the elements were determined by species?"

"They are for most, but Grim are not like other species. We are directly born of Vana. She granted us the ability to wield any of the four elements so that we can maintain the balance."

This is insane. I have never heard of anything like this before. The entire kingdom here could have any of the four elements... that means their army would have all four elements. They would be unstoppable.

"Next question?" Yuta prompts.

"Um, okay. Well, what about mating?"

He raises his brows at me, the ghost of a smile tugging at the corner of my lips and I roll my eyes.

"Not like that. I mean, is it the same as other species?"

"Relatively. At least from what I know. Though to be born a Grim at least one of the parents must be a full blooded descendant."

"What do you mean?"

"Other species can appear seemingly randomly, right? So long as there is some genetic history somewhere in the bloodline, any species could be born despite what their parents are."

"Right, like how a pegasus could be born to two hydra."

"Precisely."

"So for the Grim, it's different?"

"Yes. If a child is born a Grim it means that one of their parents must be full blooded. It is why our species is so rare."

"How many full blooded Grim are left?"

Yuta's face turns haunted, his amber eyes grow dark with shadows. "Not enough."

Chapter 61

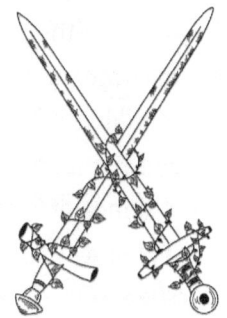

Oliver

I gather the small pack onto my back, walking down the hall to meet Cay where she is preparing the spell that will first drop Terran back in Sena, and then deliver us to the Eteri border. If it were up to me, I would be going alone. But it's not up to me. So now I have to hope that I can not only rescue my reckless sister and cousin, but also keep the princess safe.

Looking out the windows I watch as the sirens continue their work. Admittedly, they've made a significant amount of progress, despite my irritation at their presence. In all of my visits to Rayan, I have rarely found any sirens within the walls of Tepis. I have, however, spent my fair share of time with them on the docks and around Atran.

"Oliver."

Speaking of...

"Nalei." I am not surprised to find her slinking out from some dark hallway. Her locs are pulled up into a thick bun, exposing her long neck and the shimmering of her siren scales. "What do you want?"

She stalks towards me, hips swaying in that familiar way. "You were just going to leave without saying goodbye?"

I don't try to hide the boredom on my face. These games aren't new, in fact, they're a regular occurrence when interacting with the siren heir, as she calls herself. Nalei and I may have a history, but there are some things that I won't just ignore. "Why would I bother?"

"Oh, come on, you know you miss me." She circles me, dragging a finger across my back and around my shoulders, her sharp nail scrapes against any exposed skin. She stares up at me with those warm eyes, eyes that I *used* to stare into with some semblance of fondness.

"I won't ask again. What do you want?"

"What happened? We used to be so close?" she pouts.

"You tried to kill my sister." I growl.

"Oh hush, you know I wouldn't ever *really* kill her. It was all a bit of fun. Besides, the best part was watching that cousin of mine fall apart without ever touching her," she laughs to herself.

I have to fight the urge to snap at her, knowing that it will only give her exactly what she is looking for. Chaos. Strife. Unrest. It's in a siren's nature to desire such things. Something that once brought me at least a hint of amusement. Now, it feels more like a nuisance.

Her hand flattens against my chest. Thick lashes fan her cheeks as her eyes flutter shut, hiding the storm brewing in their depths. "How bad is the pain?" she whispers against my ear. Nalei knows how to put on a show, it is what first drew me to her. But now, I can see right through this facade and I would rather not play along.

I peel her hand off my chest, releasing it without so much as a second thought. I continue walking down the hall, gripping the strap of my bag with one hand while the other remains balled into a fist at my side. The sooner we leave, the better. It seems that no matter how far from home I go, I can never escape the web of lies that have been so expertly woven.

"Does she know?" Nalei asks, skipping up beside me. She cocks her head, watching me as I stop dead in my tracks.

My hand wraps around her throat, squeezing. Not enough to do any real harm, but enough to show that I'm not in the mood for games. "Of course she doesn't. And it's going to stay that way," I growl.

Nalei tsks, "touchy, touchy. Who would have thought the little minnow had it in her, snaring not one but two brothers."

"Watch your mouth." I release her, marching on without looking back. But of course, I've already engaged. I did the very thing I was trying to avoid, *interest* her.

"Now, now, no need to get upset." Her hand wraps around my wrist and I stop. Not because she made me, but because I know it's easier to just get this over with. If I try to avoid it, it will only make it more fun for her.

"Oliver, I'm being serious. You can't keep this a secret forever." Nalei's voice is rougher, the smallest hint of genuine concern hidden somewhere within her words. Confiding in her might have been my first mistake. Though I have to acknowledge that having at least one person who knows allowed some small weight to be lifted. At least temporarily.

"I know."

"You need to tell someone," she encourages, "if not my cousin, then maybe your brother."

"Leave it, Nalei. I don't need nor want your advice."

"Since when? You used to talk to me, you used to come to me with your thoughts. With your anger," she breathes. Whatever exists between us is a mess, but there is no denying the truth of her words. At one time, Nalei was the person who I went to for anything, everything. Those times have come and gone, severed from the moment that she decided my baby sister could be used for one of her many *games*.

"I don't have time for this. Go back to whatever it is you were doing and stop fucking around with Cay." I yank my hand from her grip.

I'm already halfway down the hall when she calls after me, "I bet you're wondering why you're so drawn to her, why you can't seem to get her out of your head."

I resist the urge to turn around. "I don't know what you're talking about." Except I do. I know exactly what she means. I just have zero interest in talking to her about it. Or anyone actually.

"You used to be a better liar," she sighs. "I can help you, you know? I've been doing research. I found the answers that you're looking for, the truth. I can tell you why your magic is the way that it is, what that *power* is. Don't you want to know?"

If she's telling the truth, then that would certainly make things easier. But if there is one thing I know about Nalei, she will say whatever she has to in order to get her way. "Thanks, but no thanks. I'll take my chances."

"You'll regret it," she yells down the hall as the distance between us grows.

"Looking forward to it," I mutter to myself.

Chapter 62

Terran

Cay takes a step back from her work, checking that everything is in place for the third time. Each grain of sand was placed with care, yet she still searches for any speck that might be even slightly off. A small crease forms between her scrunched brows, her hands fidget at her side, desperate for something to do.

I close the distance between us, wrapping my arms around her shoulder and drawing her back against my front. "Everything is perfect, don't worry." I rub my hands over her shoulders slowly.

Her entire body moves as a shiver rolls through her. After a moment of stiffness, she relaxes against me. "Are you sure? What if something goes wrong? What if I can't do it?"

I rest my chin on the top of her head. "You can. You got us here, didn't you?"

She sighs, tilting her head back so she is staring up at me. "That was different. I had time to think, to prepare myself mentally. This just feels so rushed." She shakes her head as I grab her by the shoulders, turning her around so she is facing me.

"Trust yourself, trust in your magic. Your father taught you this spell because he believed that you could do it. And you *have*, twice."

She rolls her eyes. "Yes, but it's not like the first time was that much of a success," she mutters.

I can't help but smile, she looks adorable. "You know why, and this time is different. All you have to do is open a gateway for me to step through, and then one for you and Oliver."

"Speaking of, where is he?" she looks over my shoulder, biting her lip. She gets this look on her face when someone mentions my brother. A look that is *only* reserved for him. It's a look that I both love and loathe to see.

"I'm sure he'll be here." I cup her face, drawing her seagreen eyes back to me. Vana, she is beautiful. I mean truly, she could be a goddess. I let my eyes roam over her.

She is dressed in black cotton leggings that are tight around her every curve. She's paired them with a loose fitted blouse with long sleeves that are tight around her wrists, but billow everywhere else. It's a light shade of turquoise, almost the same color as her eyes. My gaze snags on her mother's necklace clasped around her neck.

Cay follows my eyes and gently brushes her fingers over the pendant. "I can't believe that after all of this, I won't be by her side when she wakes. *If* she wakes," she says the last part more to herself.

"Don't worry about that. Everything is under control. You and Oliver go take care of Rose and I'll take care of your mother. I'll make sure that she gets what she needs and *when* she wakes up, I will be by her side to help her," I reassure.

"I hope you're right," she breathes. The sound of a door creaking open draws her attention away from me and there it is again, that look. I know without turning around that Oliver is here.

"You're late," I scold, not bothering to face him. I focus instead on the stray piece of hair that has fallen loose from Cay's braid, tucking it behind her ear.

"I'm here," Oliver retorts.

"Is everyone ready?" Cay asks, looking between us.

"Yup."

"Whenever you are," I answer with a smile.

She gives me a small smile back and then turns to the circle, concentrating on the spell that will summon the portal. It's unique magic, unlike anything else I have ever seen. Something like this would be invaluable in battle. If we were able to use the spell at will, it could change everything.

Water swirls in the center and then an image appears. We discussed the best place to have Cay drop me and decided on the library, in our spot. It will put me close to her mother and limit the number of people I am forced to interact with. The small table appears and Cay glances back at me over her shoulder.

"Okay, you're good. Just step through like last time and you should be in the library," her voice wavers with uncertainty.

I step up behind her, placing a light kiss on her shoulder. "I trust you," I whisper against her ear.

She shudders and her cheeks turn bright red, yet the image never falters. Her magic stays steady as I approach the portal, looking back one last time to find my brother hovering just behind her. I give him a nod, knowing that he will take care of her, even without my asking.

Somehow, at some point in time, Oliver grew to care about Cay. At this moment, I am grateful. In most other moments, I am cautious. Because whenever something catches Oliver's eye, he rarely lets it go.

"Be safe." I step through the portal, one foot after the other. As soon as both feet are in the library, it closes behind me. I spin slowly, listening for any sign that I am not alone. Using my enhanced hearing, I can hear voices far away, fading by the second. Once there is total silence, I move.

It's early morning and most people are still in bed, but there will likely be guards stationed throughout the halls. I move quickly, using a concealment charm to hide my presence as I head straight for Cay's mother. So long as nothing has changed, she should be with Flora. There is a strong chance she'll beat me for waking her so early, but if this works, it will be worth it.

As I turn down the hall I see the grand doors that lead to the infirmary and quicken my steps. They reverberate off the floor and I slow. *Why can I hear my steps?* An odd sensation moves over me from head to toe and as I search for the concealment charm, I find it missing. I try to conjure another, but the magic just falls away. I raise my hand to try again when two guards materialize in front of the door, their own charms peeling away.

"My lord," the guard on the left says, dipping his head slightly. The other follows suit but remains silent.

I step forward hesitantly, nodding my head in return. I expect them to step to the side as I reach for the door, but instead, they step closer together, effectively blocking me from entering.

"Move aside, I need to enter," I command.

"Are you ill, sir?" the silent guard asks.

"No, simply visiting." Not that it is any of his business. *Who is he to question his future high lord?*

"The high lady is awaiting you in her chambers," the first guard states. Neither guard will meet my eye, they simply stare straight past me like I am not even there.

"Right, well I will join her as soon as I am finished with my visit, it is quite important. Now, step aside." I reach for the handle again and they step forward, barely an inch from touching me.

"The lady insists that you see her immediately."

I look between the two of them. Whatever this is, it's not good. These guards are on my mother's orders and for whatever reason, she does not want me going into the infirmary. *Or is it something else?* "I see. Well, I shouldn't keep her waiting then." I turn to leave.

"Your mother's chambers are in the other direction."

I turn slowly, forcing a smile. "Yes, I am aware. I am simply going this way so I might fetch a glass of water along the way. I am quite parched." I clear my throat, watching for their reactions.

Their eyes flick to each other for no more than a second. They step forward in unison, straightening their backs as their hands subtly drift to the blades hooked into their belts. "I'm sure we can arrange for water to be brought to you. We must insist that you go straight to the high lady's chambers."

"Right. Of course. After you." I gesture for them to lead, but only one steps forward, the other following behind me like I am some prisoner being taken to the cells. Nothing about this is right. A part of me fears that these guards are not guards at all, the other part of me feels that they are exactly who they claim to be and truly are doing my mother's bidding.

It's a short walk to her chambers, a silent walk. I don't miss the way they conceal us, or how any attempt to cast a spell or charm is immediately peeled away. Whatever these two guards are doing, I can't use magic. Two servants walk by and they don't even acknowledge our presence, confirming that we cannot be seen, nor heard.

Fuck.

The moment we arrive, the doors are pulled open and I am ushered in. My mother is sitting at her desk, staring out the window with a glass of wine in her hand. She swirls the liquid absently, taking a small sip as I cross the room. The door clicks shut before I've taken two full steps into the room.

"Mother, I was told you needed to see me." I take a seat across from her. Energy hums inside me, my magic on high alert. We're the only two people in the room, but there is a powerful magic here, a strong presence that can only be felt, not seen. It lurks in the corners and all around me, haunting, waiting. I have to fight the urge to search for it, knowing that there is nothing to find.

She lets the silence hang between us, thickening the air yet seemingly stealing the oxygen as my breaths grow shallow. She doesn't bother looking at me as she says, "So, you're finally here."

"I came as soon as I was made aware that you were searching for me." I lower my head and eyes, showing my *remorse*. I have to curl my hands into fists as my magic bubbles up, pushing closer to the surface with every drawn out breath.

"I see. I am surprised that your brother and that princess are not with you." She sips from her glass.

I plaster on a look of confusion. "Why would they be with me? I suspect that they are both sound asleep, it is quite early."

She finally faces me, her eyes dark and brimming with a sort of uneasiness that I've never seen in them before. "Yet you were in the library?"

"I was doing some late night work, I fell asleep."

The glass shatters against the bookshelf just to the right of my head. "Do not lie to me!" she bellows, her chair is thrown back as she pushes to her feet. She's wearing a wrinkled gown, a dark muted gray that falls to the floor in a shapeless heap.

"Mother, are you well?" I ask cautiously.

"No, I am not well. I thought I got rid of the problem by sending your cousin away but *no*," she spits, "you and those damn siblings of yours had to go and make a mess of everything. Do you have any idea what you've done?" She's shaking with rage, her hands are balled into fists atop the table as her magic rumbles beneath her skin, forcing its way out.

"I understand that you are upset, but I can assure you that everything is fine, we have it under control."

"Everything is not *fine*!" she screeches. "Your sister's mere presence in Eteri is a threat to whatever semblance of peace we have left in the realms. She could ruin everything." Magic bursts from her and whips out. A vine cracks next to my ear and I barely have time to move before it takes the tip off.

Her magic is unstable. I need to calm her down before she does something to hurt herself… or me.

"What do you mean?" I say evenly, resting my hands on the table where she can see them. Her eyes whip back and forth between my face and my hands so I raise them up, holding them on either side of my face so she can see that I am not a threat.

She shakes her head, ignoring me. "It's fine. The Ghosts will fix it. Everything will be fine," she mutters to herself.

I freeze, the air in my lungs gets caught. My heart slows, each beat feels like an eternity, the sound of it banging like a drum inside my head. "Whatever it is you've done, stop it. It's not too late. Just, stop it."

A wild laugh bursts free as she throws her head back. "Your sister should be more careful of the friends she makes. That Princess too."

My blood runs cold. "What have you done?"

"I am protecting this realm, *all* the realms! I refuse to allow these children to ruin everything that I have worked for. That *we* worked for!"

Fear unlike anything I have ever known invades my senses. This is not a person I know. This is not my *mother*. I need to get a handle on this before it's too late, before things spiral too far out of control and I can't fix it. I promised Cay that I could take care of things. She and Rose are counting on me. I can't let them down. I need to wake Cay's mother, *now*.

"I can tell that you are upset. I think maybe you need some time to rest, I'll come back later and we can talk about this, okay? Just-just try to take some deep breaths and then we can fix things, alright?"

Surprisingly she says nothing as I quickly make my way to the door. I'm even more surprised when it opens. What doesn't surprise me are the guards standing on the other side, waiting. Only instead of facing away, watching the hall for any sign of a threat, they're staring directly at me. I keep my eyes on them as I ask my mother, "What is this?"

She takes a sort of gasping breath, her voice already sounding hoarse as she answers, "For now, you are the heir in name only. *You* should take this opportunity to *rest*."

"Mother-"

"Guards, take him to his rooms, make sure he doesn't leave," she commands.

Four sets of arms grab me and I feel the concealment charm wash over me the second they do. I fight against them, knocking two aside completely as the others struggle to force my hands behind my back. My magic is thrashing wildly in my chest, desperate to protect me, but as hard as I try to pull on it, it seems to fall away the second it forms. I manage to get the other two off me and whirl on the group, punching and kicking them away as they continue to attack.

I land a kick to one of them, sending him careening back and into another two. I'm too busy watching those three that I fail to notice the one sneaking up behind me until it's too late. By the time I move to block, he's already hit me on the back of the head. I stumble to the side, bumping into the door frame as my mother watches from inside, filling a new glass with wine.

Black dots appear everywhere until it overwhelms my vision and I collapse, everything going dark as I am dragged under.

Chapter 63

Mar

The sky changes colors as Nat soars through the clouds, her large, matte black wings stretch out on either side of us, beating steadily. We're making good progress, the landscape on the ground is shifting with every passing hour. Thankfully, we've only truly had to stop a few times to switch since we're able to feed while still in the air.

Cyrus is all too willing to offer himself to me, baring his neck or thrusting his wrist in my direction every few hours. Admittedly, the more I drink, the better I feel. Now, it's like that rotten blood is just a bad dream.

Thankfully, it's not awkward. Cyrus spends his time telling stories about Nat and him growing up, what it was like learning from their parents, why he became a guard in the first place, everything. It's easy to listen to him and allow myself to relax, despite the burning stare against my neck.

I swear Rian spent the entire last hour giving Cyrus a death glare. Now, he is staring off into the distance, refusing to meet my eyes or engage in even the slightest hint of conversation. I don't know what his problem is, honestly. He acts like he wants me, goes as far as fingering me against a village wall, and then he just walks away like nothing ever happened. One second he is all about me and the next he wants nothing to do with me. It's infuriating and I'm done. I won't let him play these games, there is far too much at stake for some petty feud he has made up in his mind.

Rian jumps to his feet and walks closer to Nat's head, calling out to her that it is time to switch as she chuffs in acknowledgement. She tips her nose down and dives for the ground, landing softly and shifting as soon as we've jumped down. She stretches out her arms and legs and then takes a bottle of water from her brother, downing it in one go.

"Be ready to get back in the air in the next ten minutes," Rian orders, stalking off into the nearby woods.

"Geez, what's his problem?" Nat asks, staring after him.

"He's just mad because Mar's mouth has been all over me and not him," Cyrus chuckles.

"That is not true," I argue, "Rian is always like this."

Nat shakes her head, laying down in the grass and starfishing. Cyrus sits next to her, leaning back on his elbows. "Nah, this is new. He's always been a grump, but never like this. It's definitely got something to do with you."

I sigh, sitting down on Nat's other side. "I have no idea why, though. We hardly know each other. I've seen him around the Tower plenty of times, but it's not like we ever really interacted before leaving for Sena."

Nat rolls to her side so she's facing me. "Really? That's not the vibe that I got."

I shrug, "He's practically a stranger." As soon as the words leave my mouth I regret them. I might not know much about him, but calling Rian a stranger just feels wrong.

Can you really call anyone a stranger after going through what we went through? Would a stranger run from his kingdom and life all because I told him we needed to?

I stare off into the woods, wondering what it is that he could be doing and if I should go after him.

The sun disappears behind a cloud and our little circle grows dark.

"Shit!" Cyrus hisses, jumping up and dragging Nat up with him.

"What?" I say, scrambling to my feet. I stare up at the sky, but there's not a cloud in sight. Then I see it. "Shit."

Two large dragons fly overhead. The second they're above us, the sun vanishes again as we're stuck in their shadow. The three of us race to the forest, stopping just inside the treeline.

"What the fuck are they doing so far outside their usual zone?" Nat mutters quietly.

"I have no idea, but that can't be a good sign." I watch them as they continue flying above us, making wide circles. They don't seem to be flying any lower which could be a sign that they didn't notice us.

"What's going on?" Rian asks, appearing behind us.

"Look," Cyrus says, pointing towards the sky.

Rian curses and pulls us back a step. The four of us crouch low to the ground. "We can't risk flying with them around."

"Agreed," Nat and Cyrus answer in unison.

I take a hesitant step back out into the clearing and feel Rian right at my shoulder, ready to grab me at a moment's notice. "I don't recognize them, but that doesn't mean that they aren't part of my father's guard. Rian?"

"It's possible that he sent word to the outposts and told them to keep an eye out for us," Rian muses.

"They're way outside of their usual fly zone so I doubt they're on a standard patrol. I wouldn't be surprised if you're right, Rian."

"Alright, so what's our plan? Wait them out?" Nat looks between us, her eyes lingering on Cyrus.

Both males seem to consider the plan. The two share a knowing look that I can only imagine comes from the years of friendship they have. It makes me pause as I realize that maybe there is some truth to what Cyrus said before. After all, he's known Rian for a lot longer, it would make sense if he noticed things that I didn't.

"We should keep moving. They seem to be flying in a pattern and if I had to guess, there are likely others out there doing the same." Rian looks around as if enemies are going to jump out from behind a bush. At this point I wouldn't be surprised if some crawled out from the ground with how unpredictable all this has become.

"Rian's right, we should spend some time on foot, we can use charms to cover our tracks and draw less attention than if we were flying," Cyrus agrees.

"And what if they have people on the ground?" Most of the guards are vampires, dragons, or succubi, which leaves at least two non-flying species hiding out somewhere. At this point, I wouldn't put it past my father to call them in. Especially if what Rian said is true and my father really did send out a call to the outposts.

"It's better to risk it on the ground where we can all fight rather than in the air." Rian looks between the siblings, "Nat, how're you feeling?"

She shrugs, "Good I guess. I'm a bit tired and sore, but my magic is good to go."

Rian looks to Cyrus, who jumps up and down a few times, bringing his knees to his chest. "I'm great. Rested and ready for a fight."

"Let's hope it doesn't come to that," Rian says with a grimace.

"And you?" I ask.

"What?"

"Are you good to go?"

Rian's jaw tenses, his pupils dilating. "I'm fine."

"Here," Cyrus says, extending his arm, "I'm practically overflowing with magic, why don't you feed."

"I said I'm fine," Rian growls stubbornly.

I sigh, knowing that there is no point in arguing. "Okay well then let's go, no point in standing around here any longer. We're just wasting time at this point."

They all nod and then Rian starts forward, leading us through the forest. We use the remaining sunlight to guide us so we don't stray from our path south. We stick close, keeping an ear out for any sign of others on the ground and doing our best to avoid them. After a few hours, we hear no sign of anyone else around us and we stop to take a break.

"Thank Vana." Nat practically collapses to the ground, sprawling out and groaning.

"Seriously," Cyrus grunts as he finds a tree to sit against.

"Don't get too comfortable, we need to make camp and set up concealment charms," Rian orders without even taking a second to sit.

I walk up behind him, grabbing his hand in mine and taking him by surprise. "Take a break, we can figure all of that out in a minute. We've been walking for hours and you need to rest. You also need to feed," I add quietly.

"I'm fi-"

"Do not say that you're fine. You need to feed. We're all going to need our strength and now that we're on foot that means resting when you can and not neglecting to feed."

"My magic is nowhere near empty, I can last until morning."

"You shouldn't be putting it off like this."

"Nat needs time to rest, to replenish her own magic."

"So feed from Cyrus," I hiss.

"No," he growls.

"Are you really so stubborn that you would starve yourself and your magic? Because what? Cyrus flirts a little?"

Rian steps forward, yanking me against his chest. We're so close that the tips of our noses brush against each other. "I won't feed from Cyrus because if there is even a chance that you need blood, I will not be the one to take it away from you."

I push back, unable to go very far as his arm is now banded around my waist, clutching me to him. "That's ridiculous."

He shakes his head. "No, it's not. Nat didn't get enough time to truly replenish her magic so she's out. Cyrus is the only other option and if you-"

"He's not."

"What?"

413

"Cyrus, he's not the only other option. If you're so worried about that, then I can always feed from you."

He tightens his grip on me, leaning forward to speak directly into my ear, "No, you can't. Because, the next time your mouth is on me, your lips will be wrapped around my cock, not my neck. Understand?"

My entire body heats and I suck in an involuntary breath. We stay like that, pressed up against each other, for what feels like an eternity. He stares into my eyes with a mixture of desire and hatred. I can feel the war going on inside him through the harsh rise and fall of his chest. His fingers bite into my hip painfully, but I don't move. I don't pull away.

Someone clears their throat nearby and Rian releases me so fast I nearly crash to the forest floor. "What?" he bites.

"Where do you want us to set up camp?" Cyrus asks gruffly.

"I'll do it," Rian mutters, brushing past him.

Cyrus raises his brows at me, "Everything okay? I hope I wasn't interrupting."

I clear my throat, "You weren't. We're fine. Let's go help." I grab his arm, dragging him after me as I make my way back to the others. Nat is sitting on the ground, palms pressed into the earth as she mutters a concealment charm under her breath. Rian is using his vampire speed to gather wood so we can build a fire and conserve our magic as much as possible.

We all make quick work of building a camp and then we're sitting around the fire, listening to Nat and Cyrus bicker. I close my eyes and let the sound fade away. It's something that I've done for longer than I can remember. I just let the entire world fade away and go somewhere deep inside my mind. I let myself drift away and become nothing for a while.

The silence wraps around me. The darkness too. It's in this space that I allow myself to think of Eve. Not how to rescue her, not imagining all the horrific things that they could be doing to her, I just think about my sister and all of our best moments. Lost inside memories of running through the city, dancing to music, and staying up late reading together, I feel a tug at the center of my chest.

414

It's not intentional. I didn't try to do it. But somehow, I feel her. This tug, strong and insistent, calling me to her. I follow it, letting it pull me through the haze of fear and anger until I can practically hear her voice. I feel a weight pressing back against me and it's like she is reaching out, trying to claw her way to me as desperately as I'm trying to get to her.

A hand lands on my shoulder and my eyes fly open. My heart is racing as I stare into Rian's concerned eyes. Disappointment rushes in at the loss of the connection, but… no. It's there. I gasp, slapping a hand over the center of my chest as three sets of eyes meet mine.

"I can feel her. I can feel Eve."

Chapter 64

Rose

"So, are you saying that history is *wrong*?"

Azariah shakes her head, "It's not that simple. What I am saying is that not everything is as it seems."

"Then what's the truth?" I ask, sitting up straighter.

Azariah looks around the room before standing, she reaches out a hand and I take it, letting her guide me to my feet. "What do you know about the time before peace?"

I shrug, "What everyone knows. There used to be five realms, then Cansu rose up and tried to steal all the power. There was some kind of war and the leaders of the other four realms banded together to stop them."

"And do you believe it?" She looks over at me as we walk leisurely through the greenhouse.

"Why wouldn't I?"

Azariah pauses, squeezing my hand which I hadn't realized she never let go of. "It is our responsibility to question everything. It is not enough to simply agree to the easy reality, to the pretty reality. We must look deeper to find what lurks in the shadows, to find the truth."

"Do you know? The truth?"

She tugs on my hand and I let her guide me deeper into the garden. I'm vaguely aware of the fact that I no longer know where the exit is, but I don't have it in me to care. "Some people are born with gifts, gifts that are sent to them from Vana herself."

"Like you?"

She smiles, "Yes, like me. Vana gave me the ability to see one's true intentions. But at times… it is not enough."

"How so?"

"Take you for instance. If I were to judge you purely based on the intentions I saw, to sneak into our realm and steal our knowledge, you would have been thrown from the mountaintops."

My blood runs cold.

"But, I didn't. I could feel that there was more to your story. This is not the first time that this has happened. Years ago, when I first noticed my gift, I felt a sort of pressure to look deeper into our history. It was like Vana wanted me to learn the truth."

"What did you find?"

"I found evidence that we had been lied to, that our ancestors were not the great people we once thought they were."

I can't help but think of my mother. Of what she did to Oak, sending her away like that. My entire life I have always thought she was on my side, that she would do whatever it takes to protect me. I never thought she could be capable of what she did. Now? I hesitate to think about what she *wouldn't* do.

"I can see in your eyes that you know this feeling."

"A bit," I whisper.

"I am sorry to hear that. But, Rose, there is still so much more to learn. And I believe that we can help each other." She stops next to a small stone archway that seems to lead back to the main building.

"How?"

"You came here seeking answers, correct?"

"Yes. I tried to find them back home, but they were too well hidden. I was told by a friend that he believed your realms might know something." Hopefully she doesn't make the connection that said friend is a certain overzealous wolf.

"I cannot say for certain that we have what you seek, but I am willing to help you if you are willing to help me in return." Her angelic face turns serious.

Is this the right path? Can I really trust her? She is offering me everything that I came here for and possibly more. But what does helping her entail? On the one hand, it feels like too much of a risk. But on the other hand, it's far less of a risk than the alternative. Besides, her earlier statement reminded me of one small detail. At any point in time, we could be thrown off a literal mountain.

"Of course, I'll do whatever I can."

Without warning, she pulls me forward and wraps her arms around me, hugging me tightly. "Thank you," she whispers in my ear. She's a tad shorter than me, maybe an inch or two. Her dark skin is so smooth, so soft, it feels like silk against mine. She releases me slowly but keeps our hands intertwined. "Come, follow me."

She leads me through the stone archway. "For the past few years I have been searching for the truth. My sisters help, but it's like we've hit a dead end. At the least, I know that Cansu never tried to steal power."

I trip over my own feet. "Wh-what?"

"Yes, I was quite surprised myself, but no, the Land of Mist has never sought to steal more power than they have."

This changes everything. *Or does it?* Relief floods my system as I think of Eve. *Maybe they're not as bad as we thought? Maybe she's not in that much danger. But what does that mean for Cay?* Whatever happened in the past doesn't change the fact that they invaded her kingdom, murdered her father, and put her mother in a coma. *We can't just move past that. Right?*

"What I was able to learn is that there was some sort of prophecy. The rulers were summoned to the mortal lands to hear it and whatever was said terrified them." She pauses.

"What? What is it?" I ask anxiously.

"Our histories say that the rulers came together to defeat Cansu before they could destroy all of Estarynn but..."

"You don't think that's true?" I finish for her.

"No. All of the true history that I could find stops with their arrival to the mortal realms. Everything after that has clearly been altered. The question is, why?" She stops outside a grand door and I look around, hardly realizing how far we'd walked.

"So what now?"

She pushes the door open and pulls me in after her. "Now, we find out."

I stop barely two steps into the room. There, sitting on the floor at the center, is my cousin. He raises a hand in a sheepish sort of wave. My eyes cut to the other side of the room where Gael leans against the wall. Everything about his posture tells me that he is on edge, especially the way he stares at the corner of the room. I follow his gaze and find Asha, sitting cross legged on a stool and staring right back at him.

I continue searching the room and sure enough, there's Mateo. Only, unlike the others, he is bound instead of free. His wrists are tied together at his stomach with a golden rope. His mouth is taped over and his eyes are wild, frantic. This is bad. Oh fuck this is really, *really* bad. I whirl on Azariah, ready for a fight.

She must see the panic in my eyes as she holds her hands up placatingly. "I understand what this must look like, but I assure you, they have only been brought here to help, as you have agreed."

"Why is he tied up!" I thrust a finger at Mateo who tries to talk through the tape.

"He was annoying me," Asha answers, sounding bored.

I march over to Reed and kneel down beside him. "Are you okay? What happened?" I whisper.

"Yeah, I'm fine. Imani told me we were going to check out the apothecary, but instead she walked me here and then just left," he shrugs, keeping his voice low so only I can hear. "Mateo and Gael were already here with Asha and when I tried to help she told me to back off." He sighs, peeking over his shoulder at her.

I'm about to confront Azariah when the door opens. Imani enters, holding the elbow of an older woman. The woman's dark skin is covered in those familiar golden swirls, bands wrap around her wrists and up the column of her neck. She's dressed in a plain, floor length dress made of simple fabric which seems out of place against the ornate designs inked onto her skin.

"Sol, thank you for coming," Azariah breathes, greeting the woman. She dips her head, bending low in a bow of respect. Whoever this woman is, she is important.

"Anything for you, child. Now, is everyone here?" the woman, Sol, answers.

"Yes, right this way," Azariah gestures towards the seating area, taking Sol's free arm and helping her sister guide the woman into the closest chair.

"I'm very sorry, but what is happening?" I demand.

"You must be Rose. We've been waiting for you, child." Sol smiles at me.

I turn my gaze on her and suck in a breath as I find her eyes glowing, a bright golden light pulsing from them with no irises. *Is she blind?*

She chuckles, "I know what you're thinking. But believe me, I see plenty."

"I-"

"I'm a seer," Sol explains, raising her palms to the ceiling and tilting her head back, "Vana speaks to me."

"Sol is our realm's greatest seer. She is the one who spoke of the prophecy." Azariah gives me a pleading look, begging me with her eyes to accept this.

My mind is racing with all of the new information. In a matter of hours all of our plans have been thrown out the window, and now I'm left with no choice other than to just go with the flow. I am *not* a go with the flow sort of person. The only thing I can do now is... try.

"You agreed to help me," Azariah reminds me.

Mateo makes a sort of distraught choking sound while Reed starts spewing questions out rapid fire. I spin, looking my small group in the eyes one by one. "I know that this isn't what you signed up for, but this is where we're at. I don't like it any more than you do, but... can you trust me?"

Mateo's eyes narrow before he sighs, nodding slowly. Gael follows as soon as his alpha agrees and Reed is right there with him.

"Great, I'm so glad that we can all work together!" Imani says, sounding relieved.

"I'll be honest, I'm not exactly comfortable with all this right now-"

"The feeling is mutual," Asha interjects.

"But I'm willing to try. I have a lot of questions though." I hold my breath, waiting for their response.

Azariah exchanges a look with her sisters and then nods, "We will do our best to answer then. Sol, can you start by telling Rose about your vision?"

Sol's smile slips. "Yes. It was no more than a flash, but I remember it perfectly. There were seven figures standing in an open field, a dark cloud was moving towards them. A great, powerful magic beat between them, tying their fates together. I heard Vana's voice, *'a bond of blood, a bond of love, a bond of fury, a bond of fate, a bond of truth, a bond of trust, and a bond of life to save us all.'*"

I play the words over in my mind, memorizing them. I pay close attention to the bonds. There are seven figures and seven bonds. Some of the bonds seem more obvious, like blood. But a bond of fury? A bond of life? There are so many different ways you can interpret them that it could be impossible to ever truly know.

"Why do you think that I could help? I'm not saying I can't, but it doesn't really make all that much sense if I'm being honest."

Azariah looks to Sol, nodding at her to continue.

"The vision showed seven figures. They were no more than shapeless shadows... all except one. There was one figure who I could see clearly. You."

"Me?"

"Yes, child."

"But... I don't understand. Why me?"

"Why not you?" Sol counters.

"Because, it doesn't make any sense. What do I have to do with any of this?"

"That's what we want to know. If you help us find these answers, we'll help you find out more about the Ghosts," Azariah answers.

I look back to the others and they're all staring with the same expression. Apprehension. There is a lot that could go wrong. I'm not even sure I know where to begin with something like this. But still, I can't just do nothing. *Even if they would let us leave here, how can I ever return home without Oak? No. There is only one thing to do in this situation.* "Okay."

Chapter 65

Eve

I sink lower into the water, watching as Yuta stares out over the mountains. The water glistens against his sandy skin, the defined muscles of his back showcase his lithe form. He's got this grace to him, even as his body grows tense, he seems fluid. An odd sort of desire to trace the lines of his body has me drifting closer.

"What happened? Why are there '*not enough*' Grim?" I'm not sure why I ask, or why I care, but I can't help the question. This is all so new. Besides, it's obvious that there is something bigger going on here. I might not trust Yuta or any of his people, but I am not going to pretend that what he says doesn't at least make some sense.

He keeps his back to me. "When the magic was cut off, we didn't just lose access to the elements, we also lost the ability to feed the land." Yuta runs a hand through his dark hair, the water curls the ends slightly.

Energy buzzes in the air and the hair on the back of my neck stands on end.

Yuta's body seems to vibrate with building anger, the harsh set of his jaw setting off my warning bells. "The land is alive, you know. It is just as alive as you or I. It needs the connection, the magic. It was never going to accept being cut off like that. No. Instead, it found a way to get what it wanted." The rough timbre of his voice skates over me and I shiver.

"How?" I ask, my own voice surprisingly low. The air seems to shift and I wish I could snatch the question back.

The water ripples as he turns back to me, dark power swirls in his eyes. His face is shadowed, menacing, *terrifying*. "By sucking the life out of us."

He stalks towards me, his eyes unyielding, his lips set in a firm line. I fight the urge to back away as he towers above me, power rippling off of him. He places one hand on the wall behind me on either side of my head, caging me in. "For 1,000 years my people have been slowly dying as the rest of the realms boast about *peace and prosperity*," he spits, "For 1,000 years we have suffered. Do you have any idea whose fault that is?" His nostrils flare.

My mouth has barely parted when his hand closes around my throat, squeezing firmly and cutting off the air to my lungs. It catches me off guard and I can do nothing but stare at him with wide eyes, seeing the depth of his rage clearer than ever before. This isn't about me. This isn't about some magic. This is about revenge.

"Those kings and queens, those so-called rulers, stole something from us. They destroyed our kingdom and stole our power and now, we want it back," he growls.

Rather than fight, rather than struggle against him, I relax. I let go of any tension in my body and even lean into his harsh hold. He's mad? Fine, let him be mad. He doesn't scare me, and I'm not about to let him think he does. His eyes narrow at my relaxation. Yuta might be a king, he might be the one with power right now, but he doesn't want it, not really.

I wait for him to realize this just as I have. Neither one of us moves for minutes. Our eyes bore into each other waiting for the other to give and eventually, I win that fight.

He tears his hand away from me, taking a step back and seeming to get his rage under control. His eyes close momentarily and when they open, they're back to normal. Honey brown. "Apologies."

"And here I thought you wanted to be friends," I scoff. It's barely a half joke, but I can't ignore the subtle truth. They came to me with promises, with offers to learn and the *'truth'*. It doesn't matter that all I actually want is to go home. No, they just want to use me.

His head cocks and brows raise. "Friends? Well then it appears that I have given you the wrong impression. No, I simply seek to solve a mutual problem."

His answer surprises me, I genuinely expect him to continue to lie. "Mutual? How does your problem have anything to do with me?"

Yuta doesn't bother responding, instead just backing away slowly and creating some much needed distance between us.

"Enough bullshitting. This is great and all," I wave my hands around, "but I would really like to get back to my life so how about we skip all this and get to the part where you tell me what you want, yeah?" Not that I have any real intention of actually giving whatever that is to him.

He dips under the water suddenly then pops back up, shaking his head and sending droplets flying.

"I thought we weren't supposed to put our hair in the water?" I scowl.

"I never said that."

"But you-"

"You have a lovely neck, you should show it off more," he shrugs.

"I-what? What does that have to do with anything?"

"It doesn't, but that doesn't make it untrue." Yuta rises above the water, his bare chest gleaming. He has an amazing body. I'm not ashamed to have noticed. I even let my eyes roam over him, tracing the defined lines and secretly wanting to lick it. It doesn't make sense, yes he's attractive, but fuck, he is also the person that just tried to choke me as a means to get answers. Under different circumstances...

"Eve, are you willing to make a deal with me?" His voice snaps me out of my straying thoughts.

"No."

My answer must catch him by surprise because he chokes on air. "What do you mean, 'no'?"

"Simple, no. No, I will not make a deal with you." I begin slowly scooting back to the stairs, keeping close to the edge in case I need to make a quick escape.

"You don't even know the terms yet," he grits out.

"Because I don't need to."

He follows after me, moving almost as slow as I am so that it makes it difficult to really notice that either of us are moving at all. "You do realize that you're my prisoner?"

"I thought I was a guest?" I challenge. Ah yes, keep revealing more of your lies, more of your manipulation, this is going perfectly.

"For now. But to be a guest means that you are willing to learn the truth and help us."

There it is again. This promise. *What does truth even mean?* Truth is a figment of our imagination, it's a fancy word dressed up to mean something special. Truth is relative and easily manipulated. The promise of some magic answer to everything has no power over me anymore. "Guess I'll be a prisoner then."

"You can't seriously mean that?"

"Yes, actually, I can. I would rather suffer and lose every piece of who I am than betray those who love me." Even if they haven't come to my rescue yet.

Yuta seems to consider me, consider whether or not I'm being serious. I can see the moment he decides I am. His honey eyes soften and the power slowly dissipates. "I understand, I might even be able to respect that. But until you've seen what my people are going through, I won't take no for an answer." He drifts to the pool's edge and drags himself out of the water, muscles straining.

426

I watch him as he walks to the other side of the deck, picking up a towel and draping it over his shoulders. He walks towards the door and slips between the curtains leaving me alone. I release a deep breath, forcing out all of the tension that built up in the short amount of time that we've been here. It's like I'm barely holding on, constantly on the verge of breaking in one way or the other.

Physically, I'm drained. It's been too long without magic and despite whatever sort of care they think they're giving me, I'm fading. I can keep trying to deny it, but I've already made it far longer than I ever thought possible. If I could replenish my magic, just a little, I'm sure I would be able to think clearly enough to form a decent plan instead of this shit show I'm currently working with. It's one thing to have magic, but be unable to access it, it's completely different when you have none at all. That empty pit inside you.

Physically, I'm dying. Mentally? I might already be dead. I want to believe that they're coming, that my friends, my sisters, wouldn't just give up on me. But if that were the case then *where the fuck are they?* I can take torture, I can handle being starved, I can even do what I think I might have to do to get out of this… but if it's all to return to a life where no one even cares that I'm gone, what's the point? Better to be dead than unwanted.

A sharp pain flares in my chest and I gasp, clutching at the pool's edge with an iron grip. The pain changes, becoming more of a harsh tug, like someone has tied a string around my heart and is trying to yank it out through my ribs. My head pounds and a bright light blinds me as a scream gets caught in my throat.

The light clears and dark, looming shadows tower above me on every side. No. Not shadows. *Trees.* I'm in some sort of forest? What. The. Actual. Fuck. Hushed voices sound from somewhere nearby and my heart kicks into overdrive. *Where the fuck am I?* I take a hesitant step forward, being careful not to make too much noise in case the voices aren't friendly.

"We should keep moving. They seem to be flying in a pattern and if I had to guess, there are likely others out there doing the same."

Wait. Is that…

"Rian's right, we should spend some time on foot, we can use charms to cover our tracks and draw less attention than if we were flying."

It is him! That asshole guard my father made come with us to Sena. The other voice is completely unfamiliar, but that first one, definitely the ass.

"And what if they have people on the ground?"

I stop breathing. Then I'm running. Pushing through the trees and bushes and bursting into a clearing with hot tears spilling down my cheeks in an endless stream. "Mar!" I scream, rushing towards her. I look around, the clearing empty.

"It's better to risk it on the ground where we can all fight rather than in the air. Nat, how're you feeling?"

Nat. Nat's here? But, where are they? "Nat! Mar!" Hot tears spill down my cheeks endlessly, I ignore them, spinning in place, searching all around me for some sign of them.

"Good, I guess. I'm a bit tired and sore, but my magic is good to go."

I can hear her, I can hear Nat. Her voice is like a phantom in the air, all around me yet she is nowhere to be seen. They're talking about going somewhere, leaving. Panic rises as I search frantically, screaming their names and drawing out their exchange. The only thing around me are these fucking trees! There's no sky, no ground beneath my feet, just this growing, empty darkness.

The trees are fading. The voices are becoming more distant.

"No. No. No. No. No!" I chant. "Mar! Rian! Nat! Anyone! Where are you!"

The trees vanish and bright light begins to grow.

"No! Wait!" I thrust a hand out, hitting something firm and fleshy and grabbing on as tight as I can. The bright light consumes the darkness and blinds me yet again. When the light fades, I sit up gasping, shoving aside the figure crouched over me.

"Eve, are you okay? You passed out in the water, it must have been too hot. You can't stay in there for too long, I'm sorry, I should have said something," Yuta rushes out.

My entire body is shaking and shivering, my teeth chatter together despite the heat. I'm vaguely aware of the towel falling open around me. My wet hair is clinging to the skin at the base of my neck where Yuta's hand is holding me. I try to shake off his hold, but I can hardly breathe, each breath is like swallowing small blades.

He moves quickly, his hand at my neck catches my chin and forces my gaze to his. I blink up at him and he curses. "What did you do?" he says through clenched teeth.

I shove him off of me, falling to my side in the process. "Get. Away," I pant.

"You're messing with things that you know nothing about," he grits.

"Fuck off," I groan.

"You're going to get yourself killed if you keep this up." He stands, leaving me on the deck dripping wet.

I lay back with a groan, ignoring my towel as it falls completely open, baring me to the sky. A deep sense of longing replaces all the fear, anger, and resentment that have been building. I heard her. I heard *them*. They're coming for me. They might not have said as much, but I know it. I have no way of knowing what that was or how I saw them, but I don't doubt that it's real. There's no way it's not real.

My sister is coming.

Mar is coming.

That is the only truth that I care about.

Chapter 66

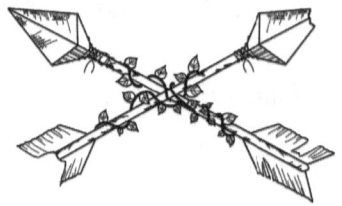

Oak

"**A**re you okay?" Lina asks, hovering nearby.

After our talk, I was finally given some space and time to gather my thoughts. But now it's time to go, we've got a mission and… I'm a Ghost. Lina was right. My life on the outside is over. I need to start focusing on the here and now. I've spent all this time thinking of how to escape, thinking of how to get back to a life that never seemed to want me, but now I'm tired.

As much as I hate to admit it, maybe my aunt had the right idea sending me here. Maybe she could see something in myself that I couldn't. Of course she's still a bitch no matter what. But maybe she's a smart bitch, after all. I mean, I can't deny how much I have improved in the few short months of training with the others. Imagine what else I could do, what I could accomplish.

It's hard to imagine that something I hated so much could actually be something good. Lina is right, I'm still mourning my life, but maybe it's time I start looking at the possibilities. This mission is the start of that. I will give all of myself to this and when we come back, I will leave the outside world where it belongs, on the outside.

I give Lina a nod, "let's do this."

Like always, I know next to nothing about this mission. In fact, the only thing that I know is that we are going to Eteri to get someone. Who that person is, no clue. Does it matter? Not to me. For once I'm going to focus on just doing what has been asked of me. I look around at the others and find five sets of eyes staring at me.

I take a startled step back, "what?"

Aine steps forward, the others following her and forming a ring around me.

"What're you doing?"

Aine reaches out, grabbing my wrist and clasping it between her two hands.

"You're kind of freaking me out," I chuckle nervously.

She mutters something under her breath and then it's like a weight is being lifted off of my chest. I gasp as the full force of my magic comes flooding back into my system, completely free of all binds. Excited energy builds in the air and hums in my ears. It's like I'm waking up. I'm flooded with power, with magic. I can sense the earth again, I can feel the vibrations and the pulsing of the magic all around us.

"Told you she would cry," Symone snickers.

I reach up, touching my cheek and finding it damp. I fall to my knees, digging my hands into the dirt and pushing out as much magic as I can. The ground is torn apart as a giant oak tree bursts from the soil, springing up in the center of the courtyard.

"Really? An oak tree?" Hala sighs.

"I was expecting something bigger," Lina says with a shrug.

"How do you feel?" Aine asks, looking down at me as I sit with my hands buried in the ground, eyes closed as I soak it all in.

"I feel whole again," I breathe. When I look up at them, eyes glassy, they all laugh, smiling with me.

Farai places a hand on my shoulder, "it's time to go."

I stand on shaky legs, feeling almost overwhelmed by the sheer force of the magic swimming in my veins. "Okay, I'm ready." I close my eyes, waiting for the bag to be placed over my head and for that familiar power to drag me under. After a few seconds I peek to see what's taking so long only to see them all staring at me like I'm insane. "What?"

Hala and Symone try to smother their laughter. Aine smiles tightly and Farai and Lina share a look. Lina steps forward, wrapping her hand around mine. "You're gonna love this." She guides me forward and then places my hand next to hers on Farai's arm.

"What are we-"

The world falls away. An all consuming darkness wraps around me and steals my breath. I scream, the sound swallowed by the endless abyss. There is no light, no sound, just the emptiness of space and time. Panic swells inside me and just as I'm about to start blasting out my newly returned magic, the world snaps back into place around me. I fall straight on my ass, rolling over onto my knees and vomiting.

"Okay, who bet that she would throw up?" Lina sighs. I fall to my back, wiping my hand against the back of my mouth and staring up at them as Hala and Symone both raise their hands proudly. A few seconds later Aine raises her hand slowly. Lina just laughs as I groan.

"What about you?" I ask Farai.

She shrugs, "I thought you could take it. Guess I was wrong."

I stumble to my feet, shaking my head. "So what was 'it'?" I look around us, taking in the forest edge in the distance. We're at the base of a mountain. "Wait," I turn back to the group, "is that-"

"Eteri. Yes," Aine confirms, marching up to the mountain like that is not the most insane thing I have ever heard.

"How did that just happen?" I ask, my mouth hanging open.

"Farai's got this special power, it's super cool. She can just think of wherever she wants to go and poof, she's there," Lina says in awe. She flicks her white hair over her shoulder, staring at Farai like she is the most incredible thing she has ever seen.

Farai is staring off into the distance, her shoulders tight and lips drawn thin, clearly uncomfortable. Despite being one of the best fighters I have ever seen, she doesn't seem to want the attention or admiration. Farai is humble, yes, but it's like she will do whatever she can to draw the attention away from herself.

"Let's get moving, we've got a long hike." Aine leads the way up a narrow path carved into the mountainside. It's not steep per se, but it is also nothing like any other hike I've ever been on. The air grows colder almost instantly as it thins, making it more difficult to breathe the higher we ascend.

We don't stop, we don't take breaks, we keep moving one by one in a single file line. Aine is at the head, followed by Farai, then Lina. I'm in the middle with Hala and Symone behind me. There is a comfortable silence, only the sound of small rocks shifting beneath our feet to break it. The wind howls around us, yet it doesn't bother me, somehow, I feel completely at ease. Questions flood my mind, but rather than voicing every thought, I sit with them, trusting that I will know what I need to when I need to.

I fight back a smile, thinking of how different things are in the short time I've been with the Ghosts. That I've *been* a Ghost. Trusting any of these girls seemed insane at the beginning, yet somehow, I know that they've got my back in a way I only ever thought the others would. Still, there is something missing, some piece of the puzzle that hasn't clicked yet. Maybe once it does, I can actually move on with my new life.

There's still pain when I think of Cay, Rose, Mar, and Eve, but not as much as before. I know deep down that Mar would never abandon her sister so I can trust that Eve is safe. Rose and Cay have a bond of their own and so long as they have each other, they'll be fine. So long as they *all* have each other, it doesn't matter that I'll be gone.

Lina stops and I nearly slam into her back. I peek around her to see Aine crouched low to the ground, her palm pressing into the mountainside. Farai drops to one knee, doing the same. We all follow suit and push our magic out. The earth vibrates with energy, but beyond that, nothing. I search deeper, trying to sense whatever it is that caught Aine's attention.

She stands quickly, whirling around to face the rest of us. "Farai, you're going to need to fly, take Oak and Lina. Use concealment charms and *do not get caught*."

Before I can fully process Aine's orders, Lina and I are being scooped up into Farai's stone arms as she leaps off the edge of the path. We're flying through the air in the next second, a concealment charm rippling over us as we do. I keep my eyes on the others as they huddle close, Aine fires off orders rapidly and Hala and Symone go racing back down the mountain edge, leaving Aine alone.

"Wait! She's alone, we can't just leave her," I cry out.

"We have orders," Lina answers back. Her arm is wrapped around Farai's neck, same as mine. We're facing each other, staring past Farai's face as she remains totally expressionless.

I bite my tongue against my argument. Lina's right. For once I am just going to do as I am told. *Trust*, I remind myself. We fly towards the peak of the mountain and remain silent as a horde of harpies come flying from the opposite direction. There are at least a dozen of them, all headed straight for Aine. Still, we don't slow, we don't pause, we just continue flying forward as if we saw nothing.

A beautiful city comes into view as we break through the clouds. Farai lands in a small, isolated corner and what appears to be some sort of temple. She sets Lina and I down and shifts back. Her grayish black skin returns to its deep umber, her curls become loose again, moving as she takes a step away from us. Her dark eyes are downcast, avoiding my penetrating stare.

"What now?" The words come out harsher than I would like, more accusatory than necessary.

Farai flinches. "We need to find the target."

"And who is the target?"

"A girl," she answers vaguely.

"Okay… what does she look like?"

"I don't know."

"You don't *know*?" I bite.

"Oak," Lina warns, bringing a finger up to her lips to shush me.

"How are we supposed to find the target if we don't know who it is?" I whisper harshly.

"The target has a magical tag placed on her," Farai answers quietly.

"How?" I'm asking too many questions. I know it. *Trust.*

"I'm not sure, it could have been something she touched, it could have been placed by one of our people here, it could be a number of things," she shrugs.

I take a moment to breathe, to center myself and ignore the panic rising in me at all the unknowns. *Trust.* "Alright, then I guess we better start looking."

Chapter 67

Rose

Me. Sol saw *me.*

But... why? What do I possibly have to do with all this? What does the prophecy even mean?

Maybe it's just a vision. Maybe it was just the seven of us here, now. Gael, Mateo, Reed, Azariah, Asha, Imani, and me. I look around the room, looking at them one by one. Searching for some meaning of those "bonds".

"Rose, are you okay?" Reed asks, coming up behind me and placing a gentle hand on my shoulder.

"I-"

The door flies open and three armed guards come rushing in. "General, we need you."

Asha follows them out the door without a single question, Azariah and Imani watching her go. Imani turns to Sol and grabs her by the arm, "Come, whatever is happening, we should get you back."

The pair leaves, and then it's just the five of us. Mateo starts yelling beneath his taped mouth and Gael finally takes pity on him, walking over and ripping it off ruthlessly. Mateo screams and then begins yelling at him while he works to untie his hands.

"How could you let this happen to me!" Mateo cries, sounding more hurt than angry.

Gael shrugs.

"Seriously? I thought we were brothers, I thought you had my back. And you!" he yells at me, "what happened to the plan? You just gave up at the first sign of trouble?"

"Mateo-"

"No. I don't want to hear it." He huffs, shuffling to his feet and pushing his hair back.

I'm not sure I've ever seen Mateo like this before. He's usually so carefree, easygoing. It's kind of unsettling to see him so worked up.

"Come on," Reed says, walking over to him and grabbing onto his wrist. He pulls him behind him down the hall. Gael follows behind them, but almost immediately returns, moving to the far window and sitting down, his face sullen.

I walk over to the couch and fall into the deep cushions. Azariah follows, sitting right beside me instead of on one of the free chairs or at the open end of the couch. She's close enough that her shoulder brushes mine when she takes a deep breath.

"So, what now?" I ask, exhaustion starting to sink in.

Azariah hums. "Well, I suppose we can start with what you're thinking. I know that this is a lot."

I laugh, "Yeah, it is." I came here for answers about the Ghosts, to find Oak. I never expected some puzzle that needs to be solved. A part of me yearns to go back to the day before my birthday. When things still made sense.

All of my friends were with me. My family was all together. I knew who I could trust. Except I didn't, I only thought I did. Apparently, you can't hide from the truth once it comes to light, even if staying in the dark is easier. No. I can't run from this. It might not be what I came for, but I won't abandon Azariah to figure this out on her own.

"I'm still processing everything, honestly. What about you?"

"I've found everything that I can on my own, but there's not much. I've tried to find some mention of bonds in any text, but there's nothing, nothing that makes sense at least. Though I have a sort of theory," Azariah adds cautiously.

"Theories are better than nothing, right? What is it?"

"What if this vision has something to do with Cansu?" she whispers, turning to face me. Her legs curl up under her and her knees push into the side of my thigh.

I consider it, thinking back on the bonds. "Maybe it has something to do with the bonds of truth? You said that the history was wrong, right? What if it has something to do with that?"

"It could be. But even if it is, what does that mean? What can we do with it?" she sighs.

"What can we do with any of it," I echo. I stare up at the ceiling, willing my brain to think of something that will help us. Anything, a sign, an idea, a start. One pops into my head, half formed and with all the potential to backfire, but it's something. "Azariah, what does your father know about all this?"

She shakes her head, "Nothing. He does not like to talk about what our ancestors did. He believes that we should be focused on the future, not the past."

"What do you think he would do if you told him?"

She considers it. Really taking the time to mull it over. She closes her head and then nods once. "He might be willing to talk if we bring Sol, if she shares the vision with him."

"Can we trust him?" My mother's face flashes in my mind, and I'm forced to shove it aside.

"I trust my father with my life," Azariah confirms. We make a sort of loose plan to go to her father and ask him if he knows anything. Even if he doesn't, maybe he knows someone who does, or at least where to start looking. It's not the *best* plan, but it's what we've got right now.

"Tell me about yourself," Azariah says seemingly out of nowhere.

"Oh, um, what do you want to know?" I say, staring down at my palms sitting in my lap.

"What do you like to do for fun?" She asks, bumping into my shoulder teasingly.

"I like to read. And I love riding my horse through the woods. It makes me feel more at home than in the castle." I peek out of the corner of my eyes and find Azariah watching me intently.

Her full lips widen into a grin. "I can see what your brother means."

"Wh-what?"

"Oliver, he is your brother, correct?" she asks with a laugh.

"Well, yes, technically, but what did he say to you?" I swear to Vana if he has been traveling the world telling everyone about the time I ran into a window because I wasn't paying attention and I thought it was a doorway...

"He talks very highly of you. Brags, really. He seems very proud."

I stare at her, waiting for her to finish the joke. She stares back, an amused smile curling her lips and making the apples of her cheeks more pronounced. "You're not joking?"

"Why would I lie about such a thing?"

"Oliver talks about me? And he says *nice* things?"

"Is that so hard to believe?" she chuckles.

"Yes, actually."

"Interesting, I thought that the two of you were close," Azariah cocks her head, her hand pressed against her cheek.

I shrug. "Maybe once, but no, not now. Though I'm very close to Terran."

"Terran, that's your eldest brother, correct?"

"Yeah. And I am close with Reed and Oak too."

Azariah nods. "My entire family is quite close. As heir, I spend a great deal of time with my father, but he makes it a point to spend time with my sisters too."

"Are you close with them?"

"My sisters? Yes, they are my most trusted companions."

My mind is instantly flooded with the girls' laughter, those moments in the garden. "Yeah, mine too."

"I didn't realize you have sisters," Azariah asks, sitting up straighter.

I laugh, "I don't. Well, I do, but not in the way you do. They're my friends but..."

"They're your sisters," Azariah finishes.

"Exactly."

"I suppose we all need some of those. Friends can be family as much as family can be friends. Love runs deeper than any blood, and blood does not always mean love." Azariah reaches down, clasping my hand in hers. She flips my palm upright, tracing the lines from my fingertips to my wrist and back.

A shiver goes up my arm as she continues to trail her finger along my skin. "Can I ask you something?"

She pauses, looking up at me and nodding. Her dark eyes are warm, they shine with trust and a sort of nervous excitement that I can't help feeling is reflected in my own eyes.

"Your father... why didn't they heal him? His hearing?" I've been curious since we first met him earlier, but I thought it would be rude to ask. I guess the feeling of her skin against mine made me forget about that.

"My father was born this way. It is a part of who he is. There was never anything that needed healing."

I nod, understanding what she means. I remember at a time thinking that maybe there was something broken about me. That something was missing. Now, I think I know what that thing was. "What about your people? They don't care?"

Azariah shakes her head, smiling down at our palms as she presses hers against mine. "Never. My people have always accepted him for who he is. They trust that he is a good leader. Strong. Compassionate."

"And do they sign the way you do?" I nod to her hands which she raises.

"Not everyone in the realm can sign, though those closest to him have learned," she says, signing along as she does.

"It's incredible," I say in awe. I bite my lip, holding my hands out to her in offering. "Would you teach me?"

Her smile widens. "You want to learn to sign?"

"Well, if I'm going to talk to your father I want to know at least something." I'm not sure why or when I made that decision, but now that the words are out there, I know they're right. Somehow, I know that this is about more than just a conversation that she could easily interpret. It feels bigger than that.

"Okay, I'll start with some basics." Azariah starts with easy stuff. Hello. Goodbye. Thank you. Please. Yes. No. I'm sorry. She's a few letters into the alphabet as Reed and Mateo appear around the corner.

This time, Mateo is the one dragging Reed behind him. Mateo's scowl and pouty eyes have been replaced with an expression that I can only describe as downright gleeful. Meanwhile, Reed is doing absolutely everything he can to avoid my eyes.

I study his face, noting the redness along his jaw, the slight swelling of his lips. He looks up at me and his face turns bright red. I fight to contain my laughter, but fail, earning a quizzical look from Azariah.

Mateo comes bounding over, plopping down on the armrest and staring down at us. "What're you two up to?"

"Working on solving a prophecy, got any ideas?" I sigh. Sure maybe that wasn't what we were actually doing, but he doesn't need to know that. Just like I don't need to know about whatever just happened between him and my cousin. Not that I won't be hounding Reed for answers later.

"I'm great with riddles," Mateo says proudly. He moves to the floor, plopping down at my feet. He holds his hands over a small table and a stack of paper appears. "Let's get to work, this puzzle isn't going to solve itself."

Azariah reaches out a hand and releases the hold on Mateo's magic, when we both give her a surprised look she shrugs, "If we're going to work together it's probably best that we use *every* resource available."

Chapter 68

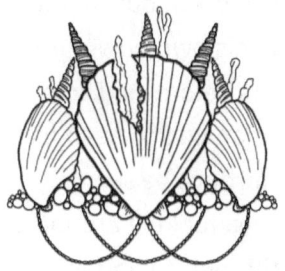

Cay

The portal closes with Terran on the other side and I let out a shaky breath. Oliver's warm hand lands on my shoulder and I look up at him.

"It's going to be fine. Your mother is going to wake up and Terran will be there with her," he says emphatically.

I nod my head. "Right. Okay, let's go." I step forward and start the spell again. Reaching back, I grab Oliver's hand and tug him so he is standing beside me. "I need you to tell the portal where to go."

"How?"

"Just picture the place where you want to go. See it clearly in your head. The spell will do the rest."

He closes his eyes, the heat from his palm burning against mine. The portal begins to open, the cascading water reflecting an image of a mountain. As we step through, the world becomes a swirling vortex of colors and light. A constant stream of power propels us forward, flashes of trees and buildings move past in a blur.

There is a sharp tugging sensation at the center of my chest and I gasp as I feel the portal begin to change. The color fades to darkness then light, then darkness again. There is a sort of haze around us and panic begins to set in as I feel the magic begin to spiral out of control. Oliver squeezes my hand tightly, drawing me back to him.

His eyes are still tightly closed, but he must have sensed my unease because he seems to push his own power into the spell. The haze clears and a sparkling city appears before us. The portal opens up and drops us out. I stumble, but Oliver manages to keep us both upright as we get our bearings. Oliver releases me once he seems sure I won't fall on my face.

"Where are we?" I whisper, looking around at the towering pillars and golden light beaming in through a window. I walk over to it, looking out into a warm sunset hidden behind fluffy clouds. "Wow," I breathe.

"Shit."

I whirl on him. "What?"

He runs a hand across the back of his neck. "I didn't think it would work."

"Didn't think *what* would work, Oliver?" I march over to him, craning my neck back to glare at him.

"I didn't think that the barriers around the city would let us in. I thought we would have to walk in like usual." He shrugs.

"Isn't it better that we don't?"

Oliver snorts a laugh. "Depends on who you ask. Come on," he grabs my wrist, "we're going to be in a shit ton of trouble if we don't go now."

"Go where?" I ask, tripping over myself as I struggle to keep up to his steady pace.

He slows, "We need to check in. If we don't, they'll probably kill us."

I laugh. Then I see the hard set of his jaw and realize he isn't joking. I yank him to a stop, "Kill us? Why would they kill us?"

"They have a certain way of doing things here. If we don't follow those rules, there is a good chance they'll just kill us to save themselves the trouble," he says like it's the most obvious thing in the world.

Shit. They could kill us. What if that's why Rose needed help? What if they have her somewhere, being tortured or worse… what if she's dead?

"Hey, whatever catastrophe you're imagining right now, stop. All we need to do is find Riah and we'll be fine." His thumb makes small, soothing circles against my wrist and I relax a little. Oliver knows what he's doing. He's been here before, he knows how to stay alive. Everything is fine.

"Okay. Let's go find this Riah person then." I swallow hard.

Oliver leads us through the city with ease. He uses shortcuts and ducks around corners before any guards find us. He even smiles at a group of women who wave at him enthusiastically.

"I thought we were hiding?" I mutter, unable to hide my irritation.

He smirks as he rests one forearm on the wall above my head and leans over, his face hovering above me. "Are you jealous?"

My mouth drops open. "What? Why in Vana's name would you think that?"

He shrugs, "I don't know, maybe it's that look you've got on your face. Or the way you scowled at those ladies earlier."

I give a dry laugh. "Very funny. Now answer me, are we hiding or not?"

Oliver steps back, returning the oxygen he stole between us. "Yes and no. We're in a bit of a rush and certain people will be more of a hassle than they're worth." He peeks around the corner and then leads me forward.

We enter a long hallway with a beautiful arched ceiling, there are paintings lining the walls between the full length windows. I can't help but find myself peeking out of every one we pass, staring at the horizon as the sky shifts from golds to pinks and purples. Eteri is a lot like Rayan. Isolated, protected, cautious. But in a lot of other ways, we're the complete opposite.

I thought it would be years before I ever set foot in this city, if ever. I thought I would be queen. Now, it feels tainted, ruined. Like what should have been a happy memory marking a momentous time in my life is now nothing more than a half-assed rescue plan that could very well end in either of our deaths.

Oliver stops outside a door and raises his hand, then lowers it, turning to me with a stern look. "Let me do the talking, alright? They won't be happy that we didn't follow protocol and Asha might actually kick my ass this time."

"Asha? I thought we were going to see someone named Riah?"

"Yeah, well, there is a good chance they're together so..." he knocks lightly on the door, stepping slightly in front of me so I can't see who it is that opens the door.

"Oliver?" an unfamiliar voice questions.

"Hey, Riah," he chuckles. He steps forward to hug the mystery woman, but I ignore them both as I see who is sitting on a couch across from me.

Rose is staring in shock at her brother until her eyes flick to me. A pile of papers go flying as she leaps over a table and comes running up to me. From the second our eyes meet to the moment her arms are thrown around me, I don't move. It's only when I hear her voice in my ear that I breathe. "I missed you," she says against my hair.

I wrap my arms around her waist, crushing her to me. "I missed you too." We stay like that for a full minute, just breathing each other in and hugging each other close.

She pulls back first, staring down at me with wide eyes. "What are you doing here?"

"Yes, what are you doing here, Oliver? Unannounced, in my *room*," the other girl, Riah, says. She has beautiful dark skin and a narrow waist which her hands are set upon. She stares at Oliver with an accusatory glare yet her lips are tilted ever so slightly at the corners, revealing her amusement.

"You know me, Riah, I'm so special I don't need to go through all the theatrics," he chuckles. Oliver walks over to where Reed and two others are still sitting on the couch, watching the exchange. He says something to his cousin who tenses and then turns bright red. He continues walking until he is sitting by a window, staring out.

446

She rolls her eyes, then turns to me. The small hint of a smile vanishes and she sighs. "You know the rules, she can't be here. You *both* can't be here. You have to be judged before you can enter the city."

I turn to Rose, mouthing judged. She mouths back it's a long story and I nod. I turn to Riah, "I'm sorry for the intrusion, my name is Cay, I am the heir to the Rayan throne."

"I know. My name is Azariah, I am to be the next chieftess." Her eyes flick to Rose and back to me.

"Oh, it's nice to meet you then. Again, I am so sorry for just barging in here. We-" I stop myself, looking between Azariah and Rose. *Can I mention the letter? What if she is the reason Rose needs help?*

"What is it you are here for?" Azariah pushes.

My eyes find Oliver across the room and he gives me a reassuring nod. I keep my eyes on his as I explain, "I received a letter from Rose asking for help. She said she needed me, so I'm here."

Azariah's dark eyes move from me to Rose with a flash of pain. "Rose?"

"I swear I have no idea what she is talking about," Rose assures her. She turns to me, grabbing my hands in hers, "I didn't send you any letter."

My eyes grow wide, "What do you mean, you didn't send the letter?"

"No, I didn't send anything."

"But, if you didn't send the letter, who did?"

A siren blares through the air, bright lights flashing in a strobe throughout the room. I slap my hands over my ears as it continues to wail, making long whooping sounds. Azariah takes a step back, staring at Rose with an expression akin to betrayal.

"It's not us, I swear to you," Rose says to her, begging with her eyes. She looks around the room and watches as Oliver marches up beside them.

"Riah, we only came because we thought Rose needed help," Oliver places a hand on his sister's shoulder, stepping between them subtly. Rose's eyes never leave her, her hand hangs half outstretched between them. I watch the conversation happening silently between them and wonder what I might be missing here.

447

"What's going on?" Reed asks, joining us along with the others.

"That siren means there has been a breach, someone is attacking the city," Azariah breathes harshly.

My entire body goes tense. My arms and legs lock up and the air gets caught in my chest. There's an attack. Someone is attacking the city. The city. Attack. City. Attack.

"Breathe, Cay," Oliver says, suddenly in front of me. He blocks the rest of the world out, shielding me from it with his broad chest.

"I-I can't," I gasp.

"Yes you can," he grabs my hand and places it on his chest, above his heart, "come on, breathe with me." He takes a deep inhale and I do the same. He holds it and then slowly exhales. He repeats the steps a few times until my breathing evens out. "Better?"

"Better."

"Alright, we need to go, now," Oliver commands, turning back to Azariah. His eyes flick towards the window and she sucks in a breath.

She rushes over, peeking out and then slapping a hand over her mouth. She races over to a wall and pulls back a curtain, revealing another hallway. "This way," she instructs.

Oliver drags me after him and I drag Rose. A glance over my shoulder shows a long chain. Rose holds onto her cousin's hand, followed by the guy who I believe is called Mateo, and then a stranger. We move single file down the hallway until it splits off.

"Which way?" Rose asks, sounding breathless already.

I know the feeling. It's like my entire body is on edge, waiting for something to happen. I can feel phantom rumbling beneath my feet, even as the walls do not move. I can hear the echo of castle walls coming down and distant screaming. One look around and I know it's all in my head. Though Rose's sweat lined brow and pale cheeks speak to whatever she saw the last time we were in this situation.

Azariah squats down and moves a small rug aside, revealing a wide trap door. There is an odd sort of whistling sound coming through it and an almost blinding white light. Azariah looks between all of us. "I'll go first. Oliver, make sure they all jump through one at a time and then use your earth magic to close the hatch behind you."

Oliver nods and then she is jumping through the hole in the ground. We all stare after her, not a single sound aside from that whistling howl coming from the hole.

Rose steps up next. "Alright, guess we're doing this," she closes her eyes and jumps. I step up next, but then take a step back, shaking my head.

"I'll go," Mateo offers and then he steps through the hole like it was no big deal. The stranger follows and then Reed looks at me with a terrified smile. He nods and then follows after the others.

I'm left staring at the hole with an overwhelming sense of dread filling me. My limbs grow stiff and my heart begins to race again, but before it can get worse, Oliver is there.

"You can do this," he encourages, staring back down the hall towards the curtain we came through.

I shake my hands out and then nod to myself. I step forward and squeeze my eyes shut. I feel my body begin to fall and prepare for the ground. Only there is no ground. My eyes fly open and all that is around me is empty sky as I fall through the world.

Chapter 69

Mar

Eve is close. The longer we follow that power I sensed, the more I know it. That thread that ties us together is growing stronger, pulsing and guiding me towards her. The others can't feel it. Instead, they follow me blindly through the woods. But the trees are growing sparse, the gaps growing larger and making it more difficult to stay hidden. Concealment charms help, but it's a drain on our magic to constantly keep them up.

I look around our newest camp, noting how close we all have to sit, how small the fire has become. We can feed that part of our magic, but it only goes so far in keeping us sustained. Rian and I have it easy drinking blood. Nat and Cyrus are struggling without being able to fly. They can keep their fire magic fed, but their dragon gifts have to be weakening.

That tether to Eve pulses again and I stand, walking in small circles as the restlessness sets in. We're taking too long, we should be there by now. Every moment that we spend sitting around is another moment that my father's men could find us. It's another moment that Eve spends likely being tortured.

"Mar, sit down, you need to rest," Nat calls from beside the fire.

"I'm good."

"Hey," a warm hand wraps around my elbow, "stop for a second."

I refuse to meet Cyrus' eyes. The last thing I want right now is pity. I know that I'm failing, I don't need to be reminded of that every time someone looks at me. "I'm fine."

Cyrus pulls me against his chest, guiding my lips to his throat. "You're hangry," he says with a chuckle.

My teeth ache with the urge to bite him. My throat burns as I remember the feeling of his hot blood slipping past my lips. I imagine trailing my tongue over a vein in his neck, but I hold back. He needs to conserve his magic. We're getting close and we might be in a fight sooner rather than later.

I pull away, placing my hands on his chest and staring into his sage green eyes. I shake my head. "I'm good, seriously. I just need some time."

He pushes back my hair, letting his hands linger at the back of my neck. "Are you sure? Because, you know I'm all about you sucking on me," he wiggles his brows.

My heart squeezes. The gesture is so familiar, it reminds me of the teasing looks I would share with Eve. I force a laugh, taking a step back, "Careful Cyrus, someone might misunderstand you."

Cyrus smiles, "Maybe it's not a misunderstanding."

This time I laugh for real. I press a chaste kiss to his cheek and then dip deeper into the woods. I can feel *him* following me, always a step behind. I duck under a low hanging branch, holding onto it for a second before letting it smack backwards. There is a satisfying curse that brings a smile to my lips.

"Was that really necessary?" Rian grumbles.

I shrug, "No, but it made me smile." I lean against a tree, crossing my hands over my chest and watching him.

He stops in front of me, running his fingers through his hair. It's longer now, the tips keep falling into his eyes. It's created that fun little habit that shows off his biceps and makes my core clench as I'm reminded about his strength. The feeling of his hand between my thighs. His eyes narrow on me, "What are you thinking about?"

"I can't just stand around waiting anymore."

"*That's* what you're thinking of?"

"Rian, I'm serious. I can't do this. It's driving me crazy, all this waiting. I *need* to find her. I need to see her with my own eyes and know that she is okay." I step forward, my arms hanging loosely at my side.

"Okay, then let's do something." He looks around then grabs my wrist and practically drags me back to camp. Nat sits up as we come marching over, looking at Rian's hand around my wrist and then raising her brows at me.

Cyrus keeps his eyes locked on Rian, tense and questioning, "Everything okay?"

Rian drops my wrist, bending down to grab his sword and strap it into place against his hip. He nods his head to me, "We're going to run ahead, scout the area."

"Are you sure that's a good idea?" Nat says, standing. Her brother follows suit and they exchange a worried glance.

I walk over to them grabbing Nat's hand in mine. "I need this. I need to do something."

If any one of them understands, it has to be Nat. Since the moment we ran from Vulca, I've seen the look in her eyes. She's scared for Eve. They might have only had a short time together, but it clearly left an impression. Nat wants to find her just as much as I do.

Nat watches me, studies me. She must see my determination because she squeezes my hand and nods. She sits back down, poking at the fire and ignoring the pointed look her brother is giving her. He sits back down slowly and leans in to whisper something to her that she simply shakes her head at, keeping her eyes on the flames. It seems private so I tune them out, focusing on the task at hand.

I quickly grab my staff, tucking the small cylinder into its case hooked to my thigh. Rian guides my way out and then we are running. Trees pass by in a blur, the sky is already dark, but with our heightened senses we can see easily. We make it to the edge of the forest and emerge into an open plane. The land is almost completely barren, the ground cracked and full of craters.

Still, we keep running. We spread out, covering more ground and occasionally calling out to one another to check in. It's a risk, but worth it to ensure that neither of us gets lost or strays too far. The sky is clear, the bright light of the moon shining above us as we search. There is a strong pulse of magic calling me to the right and I call out to Rian, letting him know.

He follows me as I push harder, run faster. The pulse is growing stronger. The beat seems to kick up, racing and matching the pounding of my heart. I look out of the corner of my eye and find Rian there, determined. We run side by side, moving so fast that I don't notice the shift in the air, the dense fog growing around us.

Rian calls out to me, but I ignore him, focusing on that magic, on Eve. *She's here, she's close. I know it.* I trip over something hard, nearly falling. Rian catches me and keeps me upright, but instead of letting go, he yanks me to a stop. There's too much force and we go tumbling to the ground, curses streaming out from the both of us. The second we stop moving, I'm back on my feet.

I barely make it another hundred yards when Rian appears in front of me, catching me around the middle and forcing me to stop. "What the fuck!" I scream at him, punching and kicking in his hold, fighting to get free.

"Stop. We can't go any further. Look around, you can hardly see," he grunts, struggling to keep me contained.

"Fuck you! We're so close! We have to keep moving!" I bring my knee up. He moves at the last second, barely avoiding a direct hit to his dick. He spins me around so my back is pressed against his chest.

"Enough. This isn't helping," he growls low in his throat. The sound vibrates through his chest, rumbling against my back. He kicks a leg between mine, moving so I'm trapped within his grip, unable to move even the slightest.

A guttural scream tears through me as I throw my head back. I smack against his face, earning myself a curse and the tightening of his grip. I'm thrashing wildly, throwing everything I have at him. I resort to casting spells over my skin, making it searing hot until he is forced to release me. The second his grip loosens I whirl on him.

My leg arcs up, hitting him against his ribs in a perfect roundhouse kick. I follow up with a kick to the center of his chest, sending him flying through the air and landing on the ground with a harsh thud. I spin again, taking off towards the source of the power that almost immediately flutters out. I stop, spinning in place and searching inside me for that tether.

"No, no, no, come on, where are you?" I mutter to myself.

Every breath that comes out is harsh, the air doesn't quite fill my lungs. My head is pounding to the same beat of my heart and the sound of blood rushing fills my ears. *Where is it? What happened to the magic?* I close my eyes, digging deep inside myself and praying to Vana to bring it back. I just need that thread. I'm so close. So so close. Just a little further.

"Mar," Rian growls, grabbing me by my shoulder and shaking me wildly, "what the fuck do you think you're doing?"

"I was so close!" I scream, my eyes flying open. I force Rian off of me, then immediately punch him in his jaw. "How fucking dare you! I could have found her!" I don't recognize my voice, the pure ferocity of my words. I'm practically foaming at the mouth with rage.

"No, you couldn't! It's too dark and the fog is too thick! You could be walking straight into a trap. How do we even know that what you're feeling is even her?" He challenges, screaming back.

"It's her! I know it's her!"

"How? How could you possibly know?"

"I would recognize her magic anywhere," I say through my teeth.

"Would you? Are you absolutely certain? If that's the case then why has it taken you so long," he snorts.

My nostrils flare, my entire body burns as I rush forward, aiming another punch at his face. "Screw you!"

"Actually I think if anyone is screwed it's Eve, seeing as it's been months and we still have no idea where she is."

I slap him.

"Is that it?" He spits out a mouthful of blood and then smiles at me with red stained teeth.

Flames burst from my fists and light up the space between us. I close that distance in half a second. I shove him to the ground, pinning him beneath me as I bare my fangs and dive straight for his jugular. He flips me at the last second, but I manage to keep the momentum going, forcing him to roll again until I'm back on top.

My fangs drive into his neck with a snarl. Flesh tears and the heady taste of blood coats my tongue all in one breath. I moan at the taste, dragging deep, drawing in his power and feasting on it. Every inch of me is on fire, burning with rage and desire. I might actually murder Rian. I could drink him dry and not think anything of it at this moment. Which is why I'm the tiniest bit grateful that he pulls me off of him.

He sits up with me in his lap. His hand is fisted in my hair, the long strands wrapped around his fingers at the root. "I told you the next time your lips are on me what would happen," he snarls.

I tilt my head back, licking my lips slowly, drawing every drop of him in. My chest heaves with my labored breaths, each inhale pushes my chest against his, forcing us closer together. "Yeah? Well then do something about it," I challenge.

Chapter 70

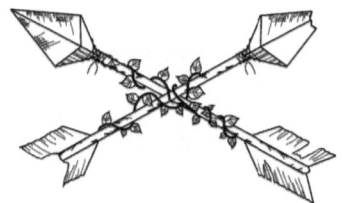

Oak

The city is quiet as we creep in, hiding in dark corners and using concealment charms. Lina leads us in, using her ability of scent to guide us through without running into people. Farai follows a few steps behind while I take the rear. Lina holds her palm out, using the tracking charm Aine taught her. Something that Farai left out.

I want to be mad about being in the dark, *again*. But was I really? Did I just not give them enough time to tell me? Everything still feels so fragile between us, but maybe it's just me. Clearly there was a plan. Aine thought ahead enough to know that Lina would need the tracking charm. Farai knew this, but didn't tell me… because why would she? If I was just trusting her the way I should be, then there wouldn't be this awkward tension.

A small group of guards comes rushing past, a female at the head, barking out orders. "Yes, general!" the guards chant in response. We remain frozen as they pass, keeping pressed up against a wall and hoping that they won't see us.

This is what we've trained for. Every moment in the Crypt was for this exact purpose. We might not know who the target is, but we're ready for it nonetheless. I bounce on my toes, a nervous sort of excitement overwhelming me. Six months ago I could have never anticipated this feeling, this *life*. Everything around me changed in an instant and, for the first time, I think it might be the good kind of change.

The sound of footsteps fade down the hall and Lina leads us onward. We have to cross a large, open walkway and we all pause. Lina rushes across the space first, stopping on the other side and checking the area for any sign of others. Farai and I wait on the other side and then rush across the moment she gives the signal.

Lina runs down a narrow corridor, her palm held outstretched the entire time. She makes it to a fork in the path and takes the right. We follow close behind, staying close enough to not lose track of one another, but far enough to react if something happens. Ghosts have a rule, no one left behind. I always thought it was an admirable rule until I realized the real reason for it.

No one left behind to tell our secrets.

Farai stops in front of me and I peek around to see Lina holding her hand up. We stay put as she moves forward slowly, disappearing around a corner. Farai creeps forward and then spins, shoving me into a small alcove off the main path.

"What's going on?" I whisper.

"Go."

"What? Go where?" I ask, completely lost. This is not protocol. We should be waiting in position for the all clear.

"You need to run, now." Farai turns me around and shoves me forward towards a dead end.

"What are you talking about?" I stumble, turning back around and fighting against her.

"We don't have much time, Oak, you need to go," Farai tries to shove me again, but there is nowhere to go.

"Wait! Okay, just, wait a second. First off, where would you like me to go? If you haven't noticed, this is a dead end." I have to fight to keep my voice down. This wasn't the plan. I know it. They might not have told me everything, but I remember the rules. We can't just leave Lina behind. If we're going to run, we run together.

Farai reaches past me, pushing on a stone lightly. There is a soft click and then the wall is pushing back to reveal another dark tunnel. "This is your chance, if you're going to leave, you need to go *now*." She glances back over her shoulder nervously.

I narrow my eyes. "Is this another test?"

Farai shakes her head, holding out her hand between us and conjuring a large stone. She shoves it into my hands and holds it up between us. "No, there's no test. You need to hit me hard enough to knock me out and then you need to go. Close the door again behind you." She turns around, giving me her back and quickly casting a silencing charm.

"What the fuck are you talking about?" I drop the rock like it burns. Farai dips to the ground to pick it up, quickly shoving it back in my hands. I turn it to dust and remove her silencing charm. "Tell me what is going on," I demand.

She sighs, looking back over her shoulder and then bringing me in close. "Listen to me, we don't have a lot of time. You need to get out of here and you need to run. This is the only chance that you're going to get. Once the Ghosts get you, you never leave. Do you understand that? You will never see your friends or family again."

"I-yes, I understand that. I've accepted it," I say quietly.

Her hands dig into my shoulders. "Don't accept it. You have a life and people that love you, don't confine yourself to a life like this because you're scared of losing the life you already have." Farai's warm eyes are full of a passion I've never seen before. She's serious. She really believes this.

"Farai, what is going on?" I whisper, raising one hand and placing it over hers where it rests on my shoulder.

Farai squeezes her eyes shut. "All of the Ghosts are there because they have nothing, no one. There was no family for them aside from the one they create in the Crypt."

"Yeah, I get that but-"

"We had families, Oak. All of us."

"Okay so…"

"Our families were killed. My parents… they did something that people didn't like and for that, they were killed," Farai breathes.

I take a moment to process. To make sure that I understand what she is saying, but none of it makes sense. "What are you talking about? What does that mean?"

"There are people who disagree with the way that the realms are run. Do you get that?" Her grip tightens.

"I mean, yeah of course, there's always going to be some people who don't agree with everything, but what does that have to do with any of this? What does that have to do with your family?"

"No, Oak, I'm not just talking about small stuff. I mean there are people who go against orders from the rulers. *Rebels.*" Farai raises her brows, looking to me for some sign that I actually understand.

And that's the thing, I understand what she is saying. But that doesn't mean it makes any fucking sense. I get it, I certainly haven't always agreed with the decisions my aunt has made. My parents certainly didn't. My mother spoke about it often, even to her sister. I was too young to really understand it at the time, but I know that it wasn't that serious.

I shake my head, "What is there to rebel against? Truly? What have the rulers done that is truly so bad?"

"They slaughtered an entire race. They *destroyed* an entire kingdom."

Farai's words hang in the air. My heart beats slowly as I unpack them, one syllable at a time. "What are you talking about?" I can barely hear my own question.

"The Land of Mist, The Land of Darkness, Cansu. They erased it."

"Ho-how? What are you talking about?" My hand falls away from hers and I take a half step back, creating some semblance of distance between us. It feels like a rubber band has been wrapped around my chest, no matter how hard I try to take a deep breath, it just gets tighter. Slowly stealing my breath.

"I don't have time to explain it all, but they did something a long time ago, and they were wrong, Oak. Deeply, truly wrong. Those people were innocent, but they killed them anyway. They messed everything up, and now we're all suffering for it."

"Innocent?" I croak. "Those people attacked Rayan. They murdered King Callan. They kidnapped one of my best friends," I seethe. My hands shake with my rising fury. Magic hums to life beneath my skin. My shoulder stings, then burns. Anger unlike anything I have known rises to the surface.

"I don't know anything about that, but Oak. None of that matters. What matters is that you need to go. This isn't the life for you. Can you at least trust me about that?" Farai begs.

I glance back over my shoulder, staring down the dark passageway that might lead to freedom. There is a lot to process. Somehow Farai is connected to these so-called rebels. She wants me to believe that they're fighting for a good cause, but all I know is that it has something to do with Cansu and that... that is something I'm not sure I can get past.

But what if this is it? What if this is my one shot to return back to my old life? I could see Rose again, Reed. I could make sure that Eve is alright and that the others are still together. Mar and I could finally move past all the stupid, petty fighting. I could help Cay get through this, stay by her side the way she did when my parents were killed.

Does leaving mean that I'm a rebel too? What am I signing up for in taking her help? And what if she's lying, this could all just be a test after all. Farai asked me to trust her, but I've barely begun trusting any of the Ghosts. Now this? It's all too much. I can't think past the roaring in my ears.

I look up to Farai, but a flicker of movement has my eyes drifting past her. Lina rushes past the alcove and I quickly slam the door closed behind me. Farai follows my eyeline just as Lina appears at the opening.

"There you are! Vana, I thought something happened to you. Come on, we've gotta keep moving." Lina is rushing back down the hall before her words have fully reached us, becoming nothing more than a distant echo.

I stand there frozen, Farai staring at me expectantly. She conjures another stone into her hand and holds it out to me. My hand shakes, my fingers curling slowly as I raise my hand almost in slow motion. The movement feels disconnected from my body, like my mind is in one place and everything else in another. My fingertips brush the stone and Farai nods encouragingly, turning around and giving me her back yet again.

Raising my fist over my head I take a deep breath and count down from ten. This is it. This is going to change everything. No turning back now. My arm starts to come down as I hit zero and then a long, blaring siren cuts through the air. My eyes fly open and the stone falls from my limp hand, hitting the floor and cracking in two.

"The warning siren," Farai gasps.

Lina appears again and this time she isn't leaving without us. Farai follows after her down the corridor and I'm right behind them both, sparing one last glance at the hidden door before it disappears from view around the corner. My decision once again stolen from me.

Chapter 71

Eve

Yuta returns with a bottle of water and another large towel. He extends them both to me as I remain laid out on the deck. I take the water from him and swallow the entire thing down, ignoring the towel. The wet towel that was wrapped around me has fallen open, exposing me to this male who doesn't let his eyes even flicker down from my face.

I take a gasping breath as I set the empty bottle to the side, reaching up to accept the new towel from him. I push up to my knees, my head swimming and my stomach churning. My hands shake as I slowly wrap the dry towel around myself. Every attempt I make at securing the towel ends with it slipping out of my grip and muttered curses.

He shakes his head, reaching out and taking over the task for me. As soon as I am covered, he grabs my elbows and guides me to my feet. His hands stay there until he seems sure I'm not about to collapse. "Can you walk?" His voice is rough as he asks, his jaw locked.

"I think so, wouldn't hurt to do that whole smoke thing-"

"Evanesce."

"Yeah that. Just take us back to the castle using that stuff and I can curl up into bed." I fight off shivers, focusing instead on getting somewhere relatively safe so I can search for Mar again. I'm not entirely certain I'll be able to access that power again, but if I'm not at risk of drowning I can take my time.

Yuta's honey eyes narrow into thin slits. He lets go hesitantly and I sway. He sighs, reaching forward and placing a hand beneath my knees and at my back before scooping me up into his arms. My protest dies on my lips as his warmth seeps into me. I can't help but curl into his hard chest as he walks back through the curtain, leaving the hot springs behind us.

"Now would be a great time to use that power," I groan. Each step jostles me just enough that my entire body aches. Sharp pain seems to ricochet through my bones, bounding around like a burst of energy that is looking for a way out. It's more than unpleasant, but less than excruciating, just enough to push me to the edge of begging.

"We're not going back yet," Yuta explains, adjusting his grip. I don't move around as much this way, but he doesn't seem to slow down at all, especially as he takes the steps two at a time. He marches back towards the entrance I was brought through before, but instead of exiting through the large gates, he makes a hard left into another small hut.

As we enter, I realize it is more like a small house than anything else. The main room features a short table, surrounded by cushions. There is a bookshelf that is lined with texts I have never seen before. At the back, a small kitchen takes up the majority of the space. There is a small doorway off of it that we go through.

The next room is barely big enough to fit a narrow bed. Yuta walks forward, depositing me on the bed unceremoniously before turning to slide another door open. It's a small closet, filled with all sorts of clothing. He grabs two hangers, passing me one and keeping the other for himself. He nods his head towards what appears to be a tiny bathroom, "Get changed."

Biting my lip against the pain, I push to my feet. I hobble more than walk to the door, squeezing my eyes shut as my head begins to pound. The door slides shut behind me and I have to brace myself against the small counter. The mirror reflects back a face I am unfamiliar with. It's sallow, with lifeless eyes and lips that are cracking.

I blink a few times only to realize, it's me. *What. The. Fuck. Is this what I look like? Seriously? No wonder my master seduction didn't work earlier. I look like a walking corpse! Did I look like this this morning? No...right? I couldn't have.* I pull at my wet hair, looking between the stands in my hand and the dull reflection.

Even dripping wet it's clear that there is something wrong with it. It's like all the life has been sucked out of me. Just a husk of a person left behind. It's like everything clicks into place all at once and my heart begins to beat erratically. I shake my head, denial burning on the tip of my tongue.

No. No way. I need more time. I have to find a way to get more time. Somehow. Mar is coming. She is coming and she is going to take me home. I just have to wait a little longer. Taking a deep breath, I drop the towel, shuddering against the cool air. I slowly pull the dress Yuta gave me over my head.

It's a simple thing. It hangs loosely over my body, the sleeves falling just past my elbows. It's a dusty purple, and made of a very soft, comfortable fabric. I'm grateful for it as my skin feels oversensitized. Every move that has the fabric brushing against my flesh nearly has me crying out in pain, though as I pick up the towel I realize just how much worse it could be.

A short rap at the door has me dropping the towel again. It slides open before I can say anything and Yuta looks me over head to toe. "Follow me."

I force myself to stumble after him. I ignore the pain of every step, the way my head beats in time with my heart, I even ignore the gnawing sensation deep within the pit of my stomach... where my magic should be. Honestly, it's my best performance yet. "So," I say, barely holding back a pained gasp, "where are we off to?"

The city is my best chance of escape. If he won't take me back to the castle or my room then I need to find somewhere to hide. Wait things out until Mar can get here. It's not a foolproof plan, but it will have to do. The alternative...

"I would like to show you around." Yuta leads me back through the house, only looking back once to see that I've fallen behind. He slows his pace, keeping stride with me as I struggle along.

"That's great!"

He stops, looking at me with his head cocked. "It is?"

"Yeah, I-I want to learn more. You told me all this stuff and... I want to see it for myself. To know the truth." I nod as the complete bullshit rolls off my tongue.

Once we get to the gate he pauses, reaching out to steady me as I lean a little too hard to one side. His shadows slip out, slowly moving over my arm and up to my head. I suck in a breath, waiting for him to root around in my brain and see my plan. I prepare myself to run, to fight back with whatever I have left in me.

But the pain never comes-the invasion. Instead, his shadows slip back into him without doing anything. He loops my arm through his, letting me lean on him as we walk slowly back into the city. It's still quiet, most people are clearly either asleep or just waking up. There is a sense of peace in the air that makes the hair on the back of my neck stand up.

"Most of the homes here are families, many generations all living under one roof," he explains, nodding towards a cluster of buildings with small patios facing the street.

"Yeah?" I ask somewhat breathlessly. *Fuck, I need to either keep my mouth shut or figure out some way to breathe through the pain.*

"The stores that you see have likely been run by the same household since we first arrived. Though over the past few centuries more have been forced to close." There is a heavy sort of silence hanging between us. I want to fill it, to take away the uncomfortable moment or change the topic, but I am barely able to suck in enough air to stay standing, let alone talk.

465

Luckily, Yuta does that for me. "Of all the stores, the bakery is one of the most popular. It always has a line wrapped around the corner. People will spend hours waiting to get their hands on one of their pastries." He smiles a bit to himself. "I once waited an entire afternoon for a single slice of cake."

"Was it worth it?" I gasp out.

"It was." He seems lost in the memory, completely ignoring my struggles. I stumble over my own feet, but his grip on me stays firm, keeping me upright. "Down this path is a temple, it's been here longer than we have, possibly since Vana herself walked these lands."

I don't try to hide the awe that fills my eyes, even as the disbelief sits in the background. I get what he's trying to do. Really, I do. But I'm smart enough not to get sucked into this pretty picture he is painting. Even if what he says is true, there has to be more to the story.

"My father used to hold meetings in the town center. He would let the people come and share their concerns. He would work with them to find ways to make their lives easier, better. Even when there was nothing really he could do, he would listen." Yuta turns down a small alleyway, the buildings towering above us on either side.

He pauses, staring up at the sky. "I used to climb these walls and sneak up to the roof so I could watch him work. Once, I fell right before I reached the top. I screamed as I fell. But before I could hit the ground, my father caught me with his magic. His magic set me down on the ground, patted me on the head, and then returned to him as though nothing had happened. He hadn't even paused his speech, he just kept going."

"He sounds incredible." I take the moment to lean against the wall, breathing deeply and trying to muster enough strength to keep going. *This is such a horrible plan. At this rate I'm better off waiting for Mar at the castle. At least there I can sit down, breathe.* Breathing is kind of a necessity despite my lungs' current aversion.

"Are you alright?" He asks, looking down at me, finally noticing just how much I'm struggling.

"Um, actually no. I-I'm feeling a bit sick."

"Sick?"

"Yes, I think I might have gotten overheated at the hot springs," I say sheepishly, waiting for his condescending words and scathing look. Instead, he just grabs my chin and tilts my head up to look at him.

"Right..." he doesn't seem convinced, "let's get you back then."

I'm only half surprised by how easy that was. I thought for sure he would see it as some sort of plan, or at least an excuse to continue hating his people. I barely have the energy to think more of it. I just nod my head and reach out to him, hating that I need his help like this.

I expect him to just whisk us away, but instead he leads me back out onto the main road. I'm about to ask why when a blinding pain shoots out across my entire body and an agonized scream bursts free. I collapse to the ground, my limbs going numb and vision dotted with black. My entire body feels like it's been soaking in an ice bath as shivers begin to take over.

I'm blinking in and out of consciousness, hearing distant shouts and seeing faces appearing above me. I'm lucid enough to recognize Teru, but then the image shifts and I'm not sure if I saw them at all. I try to sit up, to talk, but my body won't respond. I can't move or speak. My tongue is completely numb in my mouth and my eyes roll back in my head.

My head pounds as the voices grow louder. Something is pressed against my lips and then a liquid is sloshing down my throat. A hand holds my mouth shut, tipping my head back as I stare with unseeing eyes. Every sensation feels dulled. I feel my heart slowing, the pounding in my head retreating, but I don't feel better. I don't feel at all.

There is a vague sense of being moved. Odd, shapeless faces flicker in and out of my eyeline as I float in a void of nothingness. Something else is pushed against my lips and this time, I don't need to be forced. I drink greedily, accepting the liquid and hoping that whatever it is, it will make this better. What feels like hours, but could also likely be seconds pass by and nothing happens.

No sensation returns and I am forced to lay there. I can't see anything. I can't hear anything. I can't feel anything. All I have left are my disjointed thoughts. Memories and flashes of things that I don't recognize. Faces and names and a dark, menacing power that seems to want to devour me.

The ground moves beneath me, shaking violently so I am thrown around. No. Not the ground. *Me*. I convulse and shake, my mouth filling with some sort of foam as my heart begins to race again. I want to scream and beg for help. To break every rule I have and to do anything I must to make this stop. I'm here, somehow, in the moment enough to have an idea of what's happening, yet I am helpless to stop it.

This goes on forever until finally there is a warmth somewhere beside me and I seem to slowly stop shaking. The heat grows, washing over me from head to toe. I let it. I give myself over to it fully. That heat becomes *everything* to me. I shove aside all other thoughts and focus on that one thing. It works for a while.

My vision clears a bit and I can see a haze of shapes above me as I start to regain some sort of consciousness. That heat, that lifeline, starts to burn a bit too hot. Too hot. It's too fucking hot! I try to jerk away from the heat searing my side, but then hands appear, holding me down by my ankles and shoulders. I take a small moment to relish the fact I can feel them before I start thrashing.

A face appears above me and I start to panic again. The image shifts and I make out Teru, staring down at me with their long hair hanging on either side of their face. Their eyes are full of a concern I have never seen before and that sends fear skittering through me. I jerk again but Teru shushes me and it's then that I realize I can hear. I force myself to stop, to listen.

"You're okay. You won't feel pain anymore. Everything is going to be alright," they soothe and it's as if those words set me free and I am dragged completely under, untethered. Completely free of everything all at once.

Chapter 72

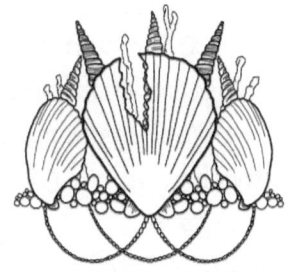

Cay

I remember watching the seagulls dive for fish with my father and mother when I was a child. I thought they looked so graceful swooping through the air like that, splashing into the water and reappearing triumphantly. This is not like that. Not like that at all. Wind whips around me as I fall through the air, arms and legs flailing. I feel myself falling backwards, my head tips towards the ground and a scream builds in my throat.

Just as I'm sure I'm going to dive headfirst into the ground below, my momentum is slowed and a featherlight touch wraps around my arms and legs, then the rest of me. I can't see anything, but I can *feel* it. A blanket of air carries me down to the ground slowly. The second my feet touch solid ground again, I fall to my knees.

I look around to find Mateo patting Reed's back as he wretches into a nearby bush. Rose leaves them, walking over to me and extending a hand which I take. She helps me stand, smoothing down my hair for me with a tight smile. "Are you okay?"

Nodding, I rub at my watery eyes. "Yeah, I just need a second." I close my eyes, breathing in and out slowly, trying to calm my racing heart. That was one of the most terrifying things I have ever experienced. Part of me is glad that I don't remember the flight back to land after Rayan fell, I'm not sure I could have stomached it if I was more aware of how high up we were.

I stare above us watching as Oliver comes flying down. His arms are crossed over his chest as he falls through the air. Azariah throws her hands up, catching him with her invisible air magic and gently carrying him back down. The second his feet touch down, she releases her magic and turns around, checking that we're all good.

A glance over my shoulder reveals the others walking up to us, Reed swiping at his mouth. We've landed on a small ledge of the mountain side, a path, barely two people wide, leads down towards the ground. We watch the city above us, looking for some sign of whatever this attack truly is. Then we hear them.

Screams.

Screams that seem to come from everywhere as they echo their way down to us. There is no sound of fighting, no battle to be heard. Just screams. They grow louder, multiplying until there is nothing but a chorus of terror filling the air. I meet Rose's eyes and I can see the same fear reflected there. Whatever is happening, it's awful. Azariah appears frozen, staring up at the city as her hands tremble and shake at her side.

Oliver pushes past his sister and steps up beside her, whispering in her ear. She looks up at him and gives a small nod. He turns to us and keeps his voice low, "We need to move. No one makes any sound until we're less exposed." He waits for confirmation, moving between each set of eyes and finally landing on me.

We follow after Azariah as she takes off running at full speed. She's running uphill which seems like the opposite of what we should be doing, but I'm not about to argue now. Not when the screams just keep getting louder. Only a short ways up the hill, a small door is carved into the mountainside. Azariah places her palms against it and speaks under her breath.

The door pushes open slowly, and she quickly runs in, stopping just inside until we've all followed after her. I expect her to close the door, but instead she seems to create a solid wall of air in the opening.

"Once the door is closed, it will not reopen again for some time. I am hoping that my family is not far behind me," she explains, her voice sounding small and fragile. She takes one last look through the doorway and leads us deeper in.

"What is this place?" I ask. It appears to be nothing more than an empty cave. The ceilings are low, making my unease rise slightly. The only light comes from the cave entrance and I hate to think of how dark it would be with the door closed.

Mateo and the other male help lower Reed to the ground, the former keeping a hand on the back of his neck as he pushes healing magic into him. Rose and Oliver both linger closer to the entrance, watching Azariah. "It's a safe room," she explains.

Screams fill the entire cave and she closes her eyes as Rose and I both look around frantically. "What is that?" Rose gasps.

"The city."

"How are we hearing it so far away?" I gasp.

"We're under it now. The sounds are carrying through the mountain and... projecting here. It's so that we can know when it is safe to leave again." Azariah sits down, curling her knees into her chest and staring at the cave entrance longingly.

The screams get louder until I am forced to cover my ears. Only that is a bad idea because as soon as I do, they become muffled. Muffled like my screams were in Rayan. My heart begins to race as memories flood me and I'm right back in that room. I try to shove them aside, to ignore the coldness that creeps inside of me. A particularly shrill scream echoes around the cave and I let out an involuntary whimper.

471

I shake my head, trying to force the sounds and images away. Oliver walks over slowly, lifting his hands and draping them over mine to help hold the sound at bay. He stares down at me, telling me with nothing more than his gaze that it's alright. A warm magic pushes into me, driving the chill away, and I finally start to relax. I don't remove my hands, but they at least stop shaking.

Oliver takes an exaggerated breath in then lets it out slowly and I follow suit. This is becoming somewhat of a regular occurrence for us, and it's starting to make me think-*how does Oliver know what to do?* Any time I have ever had one of these moments, when the panic takes over, he brings me right back to reality. Somehow, he is able to calm me down and keep me grounded better than anyone else ever has before.

When it seems like my breathing has returned to normal, he lets go. I drop my own hands and, thankfully, find that the screaming has lessened. Still there, but not as invasive. Rose is crouched next to Azariah, whispering to her. She looks up at me and then her brother and smiles at him sadly. He starts forward, but I make it there first, dropping down beside my best friend and the girl that seems to have all of her attention. Something that we will surely be talking about later.

I take a seat beside Azariah, reaching out and pulling her hand into mine. She doesn't pull it away, but she does look at me in suspicion. I try not to take offense, breathing deeply and letting it out slowly as I force myself to ignore the way I want to fall apart. Today isn't about me. It's about her. "It's okay to be scared for them. It's okay to be scared for *you*."

She looks up at me with wide eyes. Azariah looks back to the cave entrance and sighs. "They should be here by now. We all know the plan. Our realm has prepared for this for years. There are safe rooms all across the city. People should be going towards them as soon as they hear the siren."

I nod. "Then maybe they're in one of the other rooms. That's possible, right?"

"I-yes, I suppose they could be. But that goes against our plan. We're supposed to be here, together. It's safer that way."

"You're not alone. We're here for you and we're going to do everything we can to protect your realm. I swear on my mother's life." I see Rose and Oliver both tense out of the corner of my eye, but I don't have the time to think why. I mean every word. I won't let what happened to my home happen here. Never again.

Azariah nods her thanks and goes back to staring silently. I let her, following suit and waiting for her family to walk through that door. And I know it's never going to happen, I know that this fate is sealed, but I let myself silently wish that my father might walk through as well.

Chapter 73

Mar

Energy pulses around us. The challenge I laid down hanging there, waiting to either be met or ignored. I'm panting, frustration burning through me and making my skin itch. This isn't the first-and likely won't be the last- time that Rian has sparked such rage in me. But it is the first time I have seen that look in his eyes.

The hand curled in my hair tightens and I gasp. I wait for him to pull away, to put distance between us, only of course just when I'm starting to understand this game he plays, Rian goes and switches things up on me. His lips crash against mine with a snarl, his fangs rip into my bottom lip, making me whimper. The sound only seems to spur him on as he deepens the kiss, forcing his way past my lips and devouring me.

Rian's kiss isn't gentle, it isn't sweet or kind, it's every bit the fight that we wage with each other every day, only this time I have no real desire to win. But that doesn't mean I have any intention of making it easy for him. I shove my hands against his chest, breaking our connection and forcing him away. A low growl of warning vibrates in his chest and I feel the sound in my core. I ignore it, swiping a hand across my lips and smearing the lingering blood.

"You never were much good at following through on threats," I taunt, cocking my head.

His pupils dilate until there is only a thin ring of blue around them. His fist tightens to the point of searing pain as he forces my head back. His free hand pushes me off of his lap until my ass hits the ground. His grip never lessens as he stands, he undoes his belt with one hand, ripping it off and dropping it down beside us like it offended him.

He uses my hair to pull me to my knees, forcing me to kneel before him, staring up at him like he is some god. The look in his eyes is predatory. He watches me with rapt attention as he forces his pants open, then shoves them down his thighs along with his briefs.

I don't bother trying to be modest, I stare right back at his cock as it bobs in front of my face. Heat floods me as I take in the size. Not only is it thick, but it's long. Far longer than any I have seen before.

Fuck.

I swallow hard and he tracks the movement, his lips splitting into a cruel grin. "What's the matter? Scared of my big fat cock suffocating you as you choke it down?"

My mouth drops open, ready to argue, only he takes that as an invitation, and before I can mutter a single syllable, his smooth head pushes past my lips. My own eyes widen and almost immediately begin to water. Fucking fuck. I force myself to take a breath through my nose as he shoves deeper, already almost hitting the back of my throat and not even close to his base. He must see the panic in my eyes because he chuckles.

"Relax and take my cock like a good girl," he rumbles, slowly trailing a hand from my jaw down the column of my throat. The touch is surprisingly sweet which catches me off guard, almost as much as his words. He sinks further, and when I feel him at the back of my throat I take another breath and relax my throat, letting him go all the way in.

Not because he told me to. No. Fuck him.

But if I'm going to suck his dick, I'm going to suck it right.

"That's it, swallow my cock all the way," Rian groans, pausing there and wrapping his hand around my throat loosely.

I stare up at him as his eyes stay glued on my mouth. I may be the one on my knees, but if that look in his eyes says anything, I'm the one with all the power. I shift as much as his hands will let me, getting myself into a comfortable position and placing both hands on his hips, waiting for his next move.

Barely a second after I'm settled, he moves. His hips jerk back and then slam forward, making me gag. He does it again and again. Fucking my face with all the rage and desire that has been building for months. I take it all. He uses my hair to guide my movements, dragging me up and down his cock just the way he likes. He's thick and smooth against my tongue. "That's right, choke on it," he growls.

My jaw aches as I am forced to keep it wide open to accommodate his sheer size. Saliva rolls down my chin, stopping when it meets his hand which tightens in response. His fingers flex on the sides of my neck, pushing against my carotid and cutting off blood flow.

My moan vibrates in my throat and he curses, picking up his pace as he thrusts relentlessly. I move my hands around, grabbing his ass roughly and pulling him closer. Rian pulls my hair in response, drawing out another moan. My clit is throbbing from the lack of attention, my nipples chafe against the rough fabric of my shirt. I release his ass, ready to take care of them myself, but the hand at my throat moves before I get the chance.

Rian yanks at my shirt, barely getting it to move. He growls, shoving his hand underneath instead. He pinches my aching nipples between the rough pad of his fingers until the point of pain. I let out a pathetic whimper, my eyes watering between the pain and the force of his cock hitting the back of my throat. Tears run down my cheeks, mixing with the saliva.

The pain finally morphs into the kind that soaks my panties, but of course, it doesn't last.

He lets go and I whine. Rian brings his hands up, smearing my tears with his fingertips and then bringing them up to his mouth, licking them off. "Mmmm, your tears taste almost as good as your blood." I roll my eyes and he quickly drives his free hand into my hair, tightening his grip to the point I fear he might rip my hair out, and picks up the pace. "You want to act like that? Fine, then take my fucking cock and don't you dare gag."

It takes every ounce of self control I have not to. Each thrust moves deeper, cutting off my air supply and forcing its way in. His new grip doesn't allow me to move at all, I am simply held there as he pounds his way in, over and over. Each thrust makes the urge to gag stronger, but I focus on the pain at my scalp instead, even as he gets rougher. His pace slows, but the fierceness only grows. The longer I go without gagging, the wider his smile.

"That's it, take it like a good girl. When I come you better swallow every last drop. You better not spill any of it or I'll spank your ass raw," he says gutturally.

My pussy clenches at his words and I moan again. Only two more rough thrusts and then his hot cum is spurting down my throat. The salty taste of him explodes across my tongue. I swallow it all, guzzling it down like I did his blood. He pulls away from me slowly and I suck harshly as he slips past my lips. I move with him, wrapping my lips around the head again and letting my tongue swirl over it, chasing every last drop of cum just like he wanted.

I release his cock with a pop as he takes a step back, the hands in my hair falling to his sides. "Stand up," he orders roughly. When I make no move to do so, his hand shoots out, wrapping around my throat again and squeezing. I feel the wetness between my thighs grow, the throbbing of my clit almost uncomfortable now.

His hands move to my pants and quickly yank them open, one hand dives beneath my panties almost in one fluid movement. He wastes no time, finding me absolutely soaked just from having him in my mouth. He growls at the wetness, spreading his fingers through my folds and then plunging two deep inside me with ease. "You're fucking dripping for me, little one," he groans.

Normally the nickname would piss me off. For one, I'm almost as tall as him. But beyond that, I'm not some child. I'm not some little girl. Yet somehow this time when he says it, I know that's not what he means. It might piss me off when I'm thinking of it again later, but for now it just feels like his way of calling me his. Not that I *am*.

Rian starts fucking me with his fingers, adding a third almost immediately and filling me up. He curls them perfectly, brushing against a spot that makes me cry out. My legs threaten to give out on me, but his arm wraps around my waist, holding me up and against his side. My head drops against his shoulder as he picks up speed, curling and pumping, building me up. I'm practically shaking from how turned on I am.

The hand at my waist snakes up, moving underneath my shirt and finding my nipple again, pinching it roughly. I moan, grinding down against his hand and pushing my chest into his hand.

"That's it, keep fucking yourself on my fingers, give your greedy pussy what it wants, " he says beside my ear. He palms my breast, alternating between kneading and pinching. His nose brushes against my cheek and my head lolls to the side. He drags his tongue down the side of my neck then sucks on my collarbone.

I'm a writhing mess in his hands. My eyes fall closed as my entire body shakes and I move closer to that peak. His thumb pushes against my clit at the same time as his fangs drive into my shoulder. I scream out my orgasm as it comes crashing over me, wave after wave. My pussy clamps down around him, but he keeps pumping me through it, drawing it out and making it last.

When that final wave slows and I can breathe again, he eases his fingers out of me. His fangs retract and he licks away the small pinpricks of blood. I expect that to be the end of it only of course not, this is Rian, the male who has decided that now is the perfect opportunity to do the exact opposite of what I am expecting.

Rian yanks me so that my chest is pressed against his, capturing my lips in the same move. He wastes no time thrusting his tongue in and sweeping it across my own, they move together in a perfect dance. He moans into me, stealing my breath as he bites down on my lip again, sucking deeply. His hands move to push my pants down and then he drops to his knees, breaking our kiss and pulling them all the way down until I can step out of them.

I'm lost in the moment, so overwhelmed by the fact that this is actually happening that I'm not prepared for his mouth to close over my already over sensitized clit. I barely had any time to recover from my first orgasm, yet he's already pushing me towards a second.

My hands tangle in his hair, holding him against me yet wanting to push him away all the same. Fuck. I'm already moaning again, grinding my hips against his tongue as he laps at my juices, drinking in the taste of me like he did with my blood.

A second orgasm is right on the horizon when he stands again. I whimper at the loss but his hands move to my bare thighs and lift me up so fast that it turns into more of a surprised yelp. My arms wrap around his neck. The head of his cock pushes against my entrance and I stop breathing. He isn't polite as he shoves all the way in, spearing me on him with one brutal thrust. I cry out, clinging onto him for dear life and letting out a stream of curses.

"Fuck, you feel so good. Your pussy is choking my cock so well," he groans, thrusting in again.

My head falls back as I struggle to form words. Rian seems to have enough for the both of us.

"You're so fucking wet, I can feel it dripping all over my thighs," he grabs my chin, forcing me to look deep into his eyes, "you like making a mess all over my cock, little one?"

He drives up into me harder and I let out a garbled yes. Chanting it over and over again. I lock my ankles together. I'm wrapped around him as much as someone can be and he uses this as the perfect opportunity to move his hands, trusting that I can hold myself up. He pulls out and pushes back in over and over, bouncing me on his cock. One hand wraps around my throat and I welcome the sensation, leaning into it and feeling a sense of bliss wash over me.

When his thumb presses against my clit again, I go tumbling right over the edge, leaving all thoughts behind. I'm crying and mumbling and begging all at once. He follows after me, his hot cum mixing with my own and dripping all over us as he pulls out. We take a few moments to catch our breath and then I untangle myself from him, stepping down lightly.

Rian reaches out towards my pussy again and I nearly start begging him to stop. He just shakes his head, reaching into his pocket and pulling out a small rag that he then uses to clean me up. Once I'm good, he wipes at his own thighs, and dick. He stares at the rag for a moment then curses, lighting it on fire until it turns to ash.

Well, that's one way to get rid of it.

We're both working on putting ourselves back together silently. There is this awkward sort of tension in the air and I want to break it. I want to ask so many questions, but it all just feels like too much. I wince as I adjust my shirt, my nipples still sore. The action makes Rian pause for a moment, but he doesn't say anything. As soon as our clothes aren't so disheveled I start trying to smooth my hair back into a ponytail.

I can't help but think of what Nat and Cyrus will say if they see me looking freshly fucked. Of course, Rian looks absolutely the same even after I messed up his hair. All it takes is two seconds for him to put himself back together. Fucking asshole. Cyrus' smiling face flashes in my mind and I feel a wave of guilt. It's not like I owe him anything, but… it's not exactly like there isn't something there. Or at least something worth exploring. Though I have to admit that now probably isn't the best time.

Rian watches me struggle to fix my hair with a scowl.

"What?" I mumble.

He scoffs, "Nothing."

"No. Say it. You were awfully vocal a few minutes ago. Go on, tell me what's on your mind." I'm almost taken aback by my own words and how harshly they come out.

Rian raises his brows at me then crosses his arms over his chest. "Nothing, I've just never seen a woman I've fucked have such a look of instant regret before."

What. The. Actual. Fuck. "I'm sorry? What exactly do you want from me here?"

He turns and immediately stalks back towards camp, muttering under his breath, but I hear him anyway. *I don't know.*

Chapter 74

Rose

I watch Cay as she sits with Azariah, talking softly and watching the entrance to the safe room. Cay's hands are shaking, but if Azariah notices, she doesn't say anything. When I saw Cay standing in front of me I was overwhelmed by a lot of emotions, most notably panic. Because if Cay is here and not with her mom then I can only really imagine two things have happened. One good, the other impossible to speak.

Whatever letter Cay received was never sent from me, something that I am sure would be taking our full attention if the realm wasn't currently under attack. I continue watching over my friend, looking for any sign that she might… shut down again.

The moment the siren wailed, I felt that panic rise straight to the surface. Like I was back in Rayan, watching my friend's home crumble around me, completely unable to help. That sense of helplessness, of panic and fear just came flooding back as if it hasn't been months.

A lot happened in such a short amount of time and now I'm not sure if this feeling will ever truly go away. Maybe it will follow me through life forever until I finally crack. But not right now. Now, I need to be focused and think clearly. There are too many people I care about here to let anything else happen. I pull my brother aside from where he stands watching over Cay's shoulder. Cay looks up at us, but I smile reassuringly, nodding to Azariah and hoping she understands.

Oliver follows me albeit not far from the two girls. The urge to ask him a million questions about why exactly he was with her in the first place is shoved aside as I think of the more pressing questions.

"What in Vana's name is going on? What did you see outside that window?" Even as I ask, I'm not sure I really want to know that answer. The screams continue to filter into the small cavern in waves, constantly reminding us that *something* is lurking beyond these walls.

My brother sighs, sparing one last look at Cay before walking me a little bit further away, out of earshot. "Something is in the city."

I wrap my arms around myself, clutching onto my elbows as a way to keep myself grounded. This conversation feels a little too familiar. I'm already starting to panic before even really hearing what we're facing. It reminds me of waking up from a bad dream, you know you're safe, but your heart still races and you still gasp for breath because your mind remembers what it feels like to *not* feel safe. I take a second to compose myself. "What is it?"

Oliver hesitates. Just the small flick of his eyes away from me and I can already see that he doesn't want to tell me. I smack his arm. Hard. He stares back at me, offended, and maybe slightly pissed off. *Well good. So am I.*

"You better tell me everything that you know, right now. I'm not playing games, Oliver. We need to know what we're up against." I raise my hand, ready to hit him again if need be, but he grabs my wrist, forcing it down to my side.

"It's not a what," Oliver snaps, releasing my wrist. His jaw ticks and my irritation starts to bubble up, but lucky for his arm, he continues. "It's a who."

"A who? I don't understand." My brows stitch together.

He sighs, taking a step closer to me and leaning down so we're practically sharing the same breathing space. I try to step back, but he grabs my arm, stopping me. He jerks his head towards the others and I roll my eyes, but stay put. "There are stories, tales of some warrior that has a power over fear. I always thought that it was just rumors and overactive imagination at play, but…"

"Okay so what does this mean? You think whoever this 'warrior' is, is the one attacking? Just one person causing all that havoc? Do you really believe that?"

Oliver shakes his head, "No, but…. in the stories, the warrior doesn't just invoke fear in people. He uses your greatest, deepest fear against you. One look, and you're stuck facing your worst nightmare. Only it's not even there."

"Isn't that a good thing?"

He shakes his head slowly. I'm faced with a look that I have never seen from my brother before. Dread. Foreboding. *Fear*. Oliver has never *feared* a threat before. It's just who he is. He faces things head on, ready for whatever comes his way. Yet somehow, whoever this warrior is has shaken my brother before even laying eyes on each other.

"Elaborate. Now. Why is it not a good thing?" I rush out. My eyes continue to stray back and forth between Cay and Azariah, Reed, and the doorway.

Oliver closes his eyes, speaking very softly. "The fear can be strong enough that a person just… drops dead. On the spot. It's not real which means you can't fight it, it's not something you can win against. This is not something we can face, Rose. Do you understand? If this is truly that warrior, with that power, we're better off hiding and hoping we never have to face it."

A wave of heat washes over me, my blood becomes thick with adrenaline. My heart kicks into overdrive before I have even fully comprehended what he is saying. *Oliver*, my brother who never hides, wants us to sit here and just… wait it out? This power is unlike anything we've faced before. Unless it isn't. "Is-is-is-" I stutter, clutching onto Oliver's arms.

"Slow down, take a deep breath," Oliver commands, grabbing my shoulders and staring into the eyes that we share. "I know that this is overwhelming, but you can't let the panic take control. Breathe through it. Find your center. Focus on me."

I nod my head, slowly take a breath in and then let it back out. No matter how much air I suck in, my lungs won't cooperate. My hands become numb as a sort of pinprick sensation skirts over my skin, running down the length of my arms and legs. I find myself staring back at Cay as she zeros in on me. The look on her face is enough to bring me back.

I smile at Cay, nodding reassuringly. Her eyes seem to question what is going on, but I do my best to school my expression. I let go of Oliver, wrapping my arms around myself again, nearly shivering from how cold I suddenly am. "Is it Cansu? Are they behind this?" I ask, my voice surprisingly steady. I should have known, in the face of the unknown, my friends will be the ones to guide me through it all.

His expression changes, the fear bleeds away and only anger is left in its place. "No, it's not Cansu."

"You know that for certain?"

He doesn't answer, he looks back at the others, paying close attention to Cay who is now whispering to Azariah, ignoring us.

"What aren't you telling me, Oliver?"

"I think the *warrior* might actually be a Ghost," he practically growls.

That is officially the tipping point of what I can take, what I can process, right now. Later, I will ask him how and why he thinks that, but now? Now I need to tell the others and hope that they don't freak out the same way I do. I don't bother telling Oliver my plan, he would just try to stop me. But even if I allowed him to pull me away to tell me this, I won't keep the others in the dark. Not when it's their lives at stake here.

Oliver curses, almost immediately catching on as I march back to the larger group. Reed, Mateo and Gael notice and move to stand behind the girls. "What's going on?" my cousin asks.

I waste no time in relaying what I have learned. I do leave out the part where someone could just drop dead. I think that might have been the part that set me off. Though the rest of it is equally disquieting. They let me finish before asking any questions and aside from the general look of fear on their faces, they seem to be taking it rather well.

Then Reed turns around and starts throwing up again. Mateo pats his back while Gael starts pacing, clearly anxious to be far away from here. Azariah's eyes grow distant, a sort of absent look on her face as her skin becomes ashen. Cay jerks to a standing position, staring at the door like she expects some monster to come barreling through at any second.

Alright, maybe in hindsight it *wasn't* the best idea to tell them. Oliver moves to Cay's side, bending down to whisper something in her ear. She ignores him, taking a small step forward. She turns to me with a look of determination, not at all the look I am expecting.

"What is it?" I ask, taking a step towards her. We've been here before. Last time, Cay lost more than any one person should ever lose in a lifetime. I know what it's like to lose a parent. But to lose everything she has ever known all at once... I can only be here by her side.

"I've faced my worst fear before," she says, echoing my own thoughts. "I won't cower away this time."

Before any one of us realizes what she is going to do, she races towards the door. Oliver and I are quick to respond, racing after her. We follow her back down the path and I'm ready to do whatever it takes to drag her back inside, until I see Imani coming up the path with a blood soaked shirt. Her arms are wrapped around both her father and Sol.

It's enough to make me pause, staring after Cay's head as she races off back towards the city. Oliver quickly signs something as he passes a shocked looking Imani, but he doesn't slow. He doesn't stop to help. He follows my friend with the sort of fierce determination that I know from

486

him. He might have been scared just telling me about this warrior, but now? All that he seems to care about is following Cay.

They're moving faster than I can keep up with and even as pissed off as I am, I mentally give Cay a high five. Clearly she has been working out or training. I won't be able to catch up now, and... I trust Oliver to keep her safe and bring her back.

I rush over to Imani, grabbing Sol and letting her lean on me instead. The four of us make it back to the cave and Azariah rushes over with tears in her eye, frantically signing away.

Her father is barely conscious, but he brings up a single hand, making a simple sign to her and then collapsing to the ground. Imani and Azariah immediately start fussing over him while I help Sol to the ground. Gael comes over and starts healing her so I leave her, rushing back to the doorway.

I'm about to cross over the threshold when Azariah's panicked cry has me turning back. She stares up at me with tear streaked cheeks and as she whispers my name, I know I can't leave.

Chapter 75

Eve

When I was a child, I used to have nightmares about being stolen away in the night. My mother used it as a way to caution me against sneaking out. My father saw it as an excuse to amp up my training. To hire more specialists and turn any bit of free time into another class. Eventually, those nightmares stopped, the training slowed, and I was granted more freedom.

I was strong. I was powerful. I could take care of myself. I once asked my father if I should undergo some type of torture training, but he insisted that so long as I trained hard enough, I would never be in a position of being tortured. It made sense at the time.

Then, I was taken. I tried to be strong, to withstand anything that they threw at me. I could take being cut off from my magic. I could take the dingy cell and shitty water pressure. I could even take the invasion into my mind. In all the times that they rifled through my memories and picked apart every bit of who I am, I never broke. Not outwardly at least. But *this*, this torture is unlike anything I could have ever prepared for.

Waking up should be a relief, at least I'm not dead. But instead all I can focus on is the pain. Not a single inch of my body is spared from it. I imagine this is what one might feel like if they were eaten by a dragon, spat out, and stomped on by a horde of centaurs, then ripped apart by a hydra. Still, I blink my eyes open, even that small bit of effort is too much and I instantly regret the decision.

Yuta appears above me and places his hand on my forehead, wincing and pulling it away. He disappears and returns a bit later, a dark swirling liquid in his hands. I want to fight him, but there is nothing I can do as he sits me up slowly, wincing every time I groan and whimper. Once I am sat up enough, he holds the vial against my lips and tells me to tilt my head back. There's not really an alternative here so I do it, letting the smooth liquid slosh down my throat.

It's cold and sweet, something that I wasn't expecting. As it settles in my stomach I seem to cool down from the inside, some of the pain fading as well. It reminds me of the numbing paste that Mar favors, except in a liquid form. The pain doesn't quite disappear, but it at least lessens, it dulls enough for me to hold myself upright.

I look around and then down, realizing I am not only in an unfamiliar room, I am also in somebody's bed. Yuta perches on a stool next to me. He watches me, paying close attention to every move I make, seemingly ready for whatever I might do. In any other situation, I would tease him for it, maybe try to get a rise out of him. But now, it's just not worth it. I don't have the energy for that.

He clears his throat, sitting up straighter in his chair. "What do you remember?"

I close my eyes, trying to think of the last thing I do remember, but everything after the hot springs is hidden in a haze. The memories are there, I just can't seem to decipher them. "Nothing really," I shrug, wincing at the movement.

"How are you feeling?" he asks hesitantly, his eyes flicking down to my hands where they strain to support my body weight.

I scoff, raising my brows at him. "Why do you care?"

He tenses, his jaw clamping tight and a small indent appearing in his cheek as he sucks it in. "You've gone too long without magic. Your body was shutting down. You were dying," he says matter-of-factly.

"Well fucking obviously! That's sort of what happens when you cut someone off from their magic for so long. They die," I mock.

"Yes well-" Yuta stands, knocking over his stool as Taka comes strolling into the room, looking between us confused and obviously uncomfortable. Yuta walks over to him, leaving me in the large bed unattended.

I use the opportunity to look around the room while the two of them whisper back and forth to each other. This room is stunning. The walls are painted a soft, almost purplish gray. The bed itself is large and comfortable enough for at least three people, but not overbearing or obscene. The sheets are made of some soft material that matches the color of the walls. The headboard is a dark, woven wicker that compliments the color nicely.

There is a general sense of opulence about the space without looking gaudy. It's...nice. Comfortable. Almost homey. There is a small table only a few inches off the ground, surrounded by cushions. It reminds me of the home we saw when we were leaving the hot springs, the last clear memory I have before I essentially started dying.

It hits me. *I was dying. I was actively on my way to being dead, but now I'm not. Why?* Yuta confirmed my suspicions that my body was finally giving up after so long without magic, but he didn't explain why I'm not currently dead. This train of thought is cut short as Taka stalks across the room, coming to stand beside me and grabbing my wrists roughly. I force myself not to make a sound as he ties my wrists together.

I yank against him, but with how weak I am, it makes no difference. In under 30 seconds, he has my wrists bound together in front of me. The bright side to that is that my legs are still unrestrained. If I could get enough strength back I might actually be able to do some damage. But that's a big *if.*

Taka stays by my side, looking back and forth between his king and I. I don't like how tense he is. How he hovers there, almost appearing reluctant to leave. The choice is taken away from him as Yuta orders him away. He walks slowly to the door, lingering there for a second to share one last look between us. The door closes behind him and I have to fight to stay sitting up.

My back muscles strain with the effort, sweat begins rolling down between my shoulder blades which is extremely disgusting. Waking up sweaty was bad enough, I would rather not add to the grossness.

Yuta walks over slowly, coming around to the side opposite of me and crawling in. *Why the fuck is he crawling in? This is really, really weird. Also, again, gross!* The sheets are practically soaked with my bodily fluids. I shudder.

I open my mouth to make a joke about it, but Yuta cuts me off. He shifts so he is on his knees, staring at the corner of the room. I follow his gaze. I freeze, my heart nearly stops beating. I become acutely aware of myself, of *every* part of myself. I can't seem to force my eyes away from the fire burning not even ten feet away, warming the room and casting a soft glow. I only manage to look away when Yuta clears his throat.

"The fire isn't replenishing your magic fast enough. It's not enough on its own. We've given you potions to try and help with the process, but... this is the longest you have stayed awake in days," he admits.

I nod my head. Understanding exactly what he is *not* saying. "Damn. So, this is it then. I have to admit, I always thought my death would be much cooler than this." I turn back to the fire, staring at it longingly.

He grabs my jaw, forcing my eyes to his. He's a lot closer now, his knees press against the side of my thigh. "No."

"What the fuck do you mean no?" I manage to spit out before my arms give out and I collapse back against the bed. My body begins to shake again. This is probably what he meant by not staying awake long. Though, it does make me wonder if this is the first time we've had this conversation. "Have we-what are you doing?"

Yuta yanks the covers away from me, throwing them towards the end of the bed. As if that wasn't surprising enough, finding myself in nothing but a thin slip does the trick. He moves slowly, cautiously, climbing over me until he has one knee on either side of my hip. I'm slack jawed staring up at him and completely, utterly, confused. *What is happening right now?*

His eyes never leave mine, even as I watch his every movement. My pulse is racing, fear for what's to come flooding my senses. I might have joked about dying, but whatever his new idea is doesn't seem much better. If he strangles me to death I might be even more pissed.

But now, that's not what he does. His hand moves, but not to my throat. To his waistband. Then lower. I watch completely stunned as his hand dips into his pants and grabs his cock. My head completely empties as he begins to drag his hand up and down. *What kind of sadistic fucker jerks off over a dying girl?!*

Yuta's eyes drift closed, his head falls back, a light moan slipping past his lips. The second the sound fills the room, I taste it. *Pleasure*. It's like a piece of me clicks into place as power floods my body. My back bows off the bed, overwhelmed by the sudden onslaught of my magic replenishing.

"We-we've tried everything else, but nothing has been potent enough. This-this is the only thing we haven't tried yet," he says through clenched teeth.

My body hums with energy, that well inside of me slowly filling up. Each stroke of his hand and groan from his lips has more power pulsing beneath my skin. I'm too consumed by the feeling to even notice what he is doing anymore. My own eyes fall shut and I focus on myself and nothing else.

In just a matter of minutes, I already feel stronger now than I have since they first brought me here. I feast on his pleasure. Devouring it and using it to fuel me. I steal that essence from him greedily, letting the taste wash over my tongue as my own body grows heated. Not from arousal, but from magic. I know now why they bound my wrists. Not that it will help anymore.

I break the bindings easily, pulling them apart so that both hands are free. Yuta's eyes snap open and he stops moving, cutting off his own pleasure. I whimper, feeling that connection break instantly. I snarl, moving to sit up and immediately being shoved back down.

"You do not move. Do you hear me? Move and this ends." He waits for a response that he won't get. When I don't answer, he uses his free hand to grab my wrists, pinning them above my head. "Hands up here, little minx."

That intoxicating feeling of magic flowing through me is already gone, nothing but a low hum somewhere deep inside of me. I'm forced to acknowledge that even with the small bit of magic I have now, it's not enough to do any real damage. It might not even be enough to truly keep me alive. So, reluctantly, I agree, nodding my head and opening my palms in concession.

Once he is sure that I'm not planning on moving, he picks up the pace. His breathing becomes rougher the faster his hand moves. I expect him to close his eyes again, but instead, he just stares down at me. It's wildly uncomfortable. Him just pumping himself over my chest, maintaining *direct* eye contact. In another world I would find that incredibly hot... okay, it's still sort of hot, but in a weird way.

I do my best to resist the urge to glance down even though his pants are still fully on and I can't see anything that he is doing. Succubi are drawn to pleasure, we seek it out and try to enhance it. It's part of our nature. It's not *necessary* for us to see what is happening, but it also is an innate part of us to *want* to see. I fight that part of me off.

Shutting my eyes again, I focus on how I'm feeling. Yuta's pleasure comes in waves but I can feel it reaching that precipice. I wonder what he is thinking about. If he really is a sadist and somehow this is just doing it for him. He could also be thinking of something else entirely, imagining that he isn't here, this isn't happening. I know that's what I'm trying to do.

It seems insane to think that just a short time ago I was writhing on the ground in agony, dying. Then waking up and realizing all of this. *Fuck, is Taka just sitting outside? Why did Yuta call him in the first place? Does he know what is happening inside these walls? Maybe he is here in case I actually manage to take on some decent power.*

It makes sense that nothing else has worked since lust and pleasure are the most powerful. The two just go hand in hand. I just happen to be feeding off Yuta's lust at the moment. But it still seems sort of insane that he would go as far as this.

A sharp burst of energy flows into me and I don't have to open my eyes to know he is finished. The magic settles inside me, barely even a quarter of what I usually have, but still, it's enough to take the edge off. Not only do I feel stronger, I feel more clear headed. Like somehow the lack of magic was messing with my mind. I feel Yuta climbing off me and I blink my eyes open.

The door opens and Taka rushes in, confirming my suspicions about him just waiting outside. Yuta walks out of the room in a rush and I sit up, staring at Taka as he glowers in my direction.

"So, does this mean I'm going back to my room now?"

Chapter 76

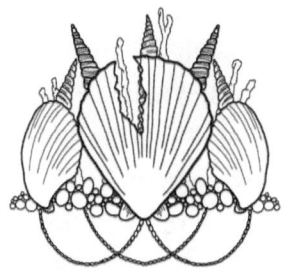

Cay

Usually, when I rush into a situation, I have at least some small part of me that thinks it is the right choice. A good idea. This is absolutely not one of those times. As I leave safety behind me and run head first into what is possibly a horrific death, I can only hope that I don't accidentally drag one of my best friends in with me. I rush past a woman struggling to carry two injured people and I know that Rose would never leave them. Not even to run after me.

What I don't expect is Oliver running straight past them, following without even the slightest hint of hesitation. He calls out my name, but I ignore him, running towards the sounds of screams. I have no idea how to get back up to the main city from here, but maybe I won't have to. Maybe that warrior is closer than we thought and they will save me the trouble. One can dream.

Logically, I know I should be scared. I know that what Rose told us about this person's power should have me cowering into a ball back within the sanctuary I left behind. But that was never a real option. I might have failed to protect my own kingdom, but I won't make the same mistake here. Whatever it takes, I'll make sure that this warrior is taken down. Even if it means using that power again. Yet another reason I can't allow Rose to follow.

A hard weight knocks into me, and before I can protest, I am thrown over Oliver's shoulder like I weigh absolutely nothing. My cheek presses against Oliver's mid back as his arm clamps down over my thighs impressively. He turns quickly and races back towards the cave, running far faster than I would have thought possible with me slung over his shoulder like this.

"Oliver, put me down!" I scream.

"Are you going to run back towards your certain death?" he asks nonchalantly.

"Those people need our help! We have to help them!" I argue. His grip doesn't budge even as I start to thrash in his arms. There is a small shift and then a hand cracks against my ass, stinging lightly. "Did you just slap my ass?!" I exclaim.

"Yes, and if you don't listen I'll do it again."

"You can't do this!"

He slows, then sets me down and blocks my path. "I can and I will. I didn't go through the trouble of saving your life multiple times just to have you throw it away for people you don't even know."

"How can you think like that? Vana, you are such an ass! Those people will die if we don't help them." I shove a finger back in the direction of the screams.

"You're not ready for something like this. You need to turn around and walk your pretty self back into that room. Right now," he demands. He starts marching forward, crowding me so I am forced to take steps back. I bring my knee up, driving it towards his groin, but he dodges it easily, raising his brows at me, "really?"

"You have to let me do this," I practically beg.

"No."

"Oliver-"

"No."

"I am ready for this! If there is any person here who can face this stupid warrior person it's me! I've already faced my worst fear, there is nothing that it can show me that I-"

"Well I haven't! Okay. So turn around and let's go." He grabs my shoulders, attempting to force me to comply.

I scoff, shaking off his grip. "What are you so afraid of?"

He refuses to answer, a storm brewing in his eyes as his mild irritation begins to turn into genuine rage. He grabs me again, but before he can try to move me, a horrified screech reaches us and we both move without a word. We run side by side back towards the sound, knowing we won't have to go far based on how close it sounded.

Sure enough, right around the corner are three young women, maybe a few years younger than me, huddled together under a large tree. Their mouths are all open on another scream as a grotesque monster races towards them. They don't move, absolutely frozen into place as whatever the monster is circles them.

The body is like one long centipede, the top more of a cross between a griffin and a hydra. It has a hulking pincer at the end of its tail that snaps at the girls every few seconds. I watch it move only to find it changing its head, instead a cross between a centaur and a gorgon appears and it is an image that I might never be able to erase.

"What is it?" I breathe to myself, startling when Oliver answers.

"When I was a child, my mother used to tell me bedtime stories about a shapeshifting creature that would consume children and steal their form, adding it to their collection when they misbehaved. I imagine it looked a little something like that," he mumbles beside me.

"Yeah, we had something similar in Rayan. Though the pincer is new," I say with a hollow laugh.

"It's probably something unique to Eteri, the girls all seem to share at least that image, even if the... face keeps changing."

The tail of that thing whips forward, smacking into the tree above the girls heads as they scream. Oliver and I move, him wrapping around to face it on the opposite side as I approach from the front. The beast seems to only be focused on the girls, ignoring the two of us completely as we start throwing every bit of magic we can at it.

Oliver said that there was no way to fight the beast, but maybe if it's not your nightmare you can. Or maybe it just depends on the nightmare itself. A large snake-like head snaps forward and I send a torrent of icicles shooting towards it, stopping it from removing one of the girls heads. If it even can do that. *I mean really, this monster isn't real so how much damage can it really do?*

As if hearing my doubt, the monster latches onto a tree branch, tearing the limb from the trunk and tossing it away like it was nothing more than a twig. The branch crashes to the ground nearby, the monster roars into the air defiantly. I create a wall of ice between it and the girls, Oliver adds his own wall behind it, reinforcing it so nothing is getting past.

Once we've got the monster cut off, we alternate between blasting it with water and earth, driving it further away from the women until one of them seems clear headed enough to drag the others away to safety. It takes some effort, but the three of them manage to make it out of sight before the beast can even crack my ice, let alone get through Oliver's stone. It roars again, the sound shaking the ground and making leaves fall from the tree, raining down over us.

The monster's face morphs into a cyclops, and I shoot a jetstream of water directly at it. Its singular eye blinks and then turns its full attention to me, completely unaffected. Well shit. I didn't expect that. I sort of thought that now that the girls are gone, the whole thing would just disappear. I watch in horror as the face melts and molds until it's half dragon half gargoyle. Its large mouth opens and a stream of fire bursts free.

The soft grass catches on fire instantly, the blaze slowly spreading around me until I am forced to redirect my attention towards stopping the spread. Vines start sprouting from the ground and for a second I think it's

Oliver, then I realize the vines aren't helping, they're trying to grab hold of me. Looking up I see that the dragon side is now fae, the human looking arm outstretched as it controls the earth.

That's *really* not good. It's bad enough that this thing can use the powers of the creatures, let alone the elements. I swear to Vana if this thing turns into a succubus I might vomit. No way do I want *that* power falling over me right now. I reach down, grabbing the small cylinder that contains my trident and I let it pop free, quickly forming the three pointed tips. But that's not what I need.

I mutter the spell as fast as I can, closing my eyes for the briefest second as the trident becomes a sword, the tips fusing together and elongating. I don't have as much practice with this form of the weapon, but that doesn't matter anyways. As my eyes blink open I see a dark skeletal creature taking over and the sword falls from my hands, clattering uselessly against the scorched grass.

"Fuck," I breathe. Oliver's voice screams my name, guttural and full of panic. I watch in slow motion as he comes around the other side of the monster, his head is split open from a gash on his forehead and his eyes filled with tears. He looks devastated as he races towards me, hand outstretched. My own eyes widen as I see a light burst from his palm, shooting through the air and hitting the beast in the dead center.

It seems to freeze, all motion stopping as Oliver's power skates over it and then it *actually* freezes. The monster rumbles and cracks and then shatters into a million tiny shards. In a matter of seconds, those shards turn into dust that floats away on the breeze. I reach my hand out, feeling the icy cold of the dust, almost like the first flurries of winter.

I stare down at my hand, wondering if somehow my own power is coming out. But it's not mine. I spin slowly, watching as Oliver crumples to his knees with tears streaming down his face silently. I walk towards him, stepping over my discarded sword. I drop down in front of him, looking at the burnt skin on the palm of his hand. When I look up, his gaze is far away as I ask, "What did you do?"

Chapter 77

Mar

A thick layer of sweat coats my skin, underneath it, a much thinner layer of shame that I wish I could pretend didn't exist. But I'm not ashamed of what happened. I made a choice and I stand by it. So why do I feel like I did something wrong? Like I *should* be ashamed. I know that I didn't, yet somehow I can't shake the feeling that there's no going back from this.

I take the walk back to camp slowly, gradually stitching myself together with every step. As I approach Nat and Cyrus the two look up at me, looking around and noticing that Rian isn't with me. A part of me knew he wouldn't come straight back to camp, not when he was as mad as he was. Though what he was mad about still makes zero sense no matter how I look at it.

Cyrus stands, walking over to me and letting his eyes roam from my head to my toes suspiciously. "Everything alright?" he asks. He's tense, his eyes keep flicking down to a spot on my neck that seems to burn with every lingering second.

"Yeah, we just… we got separated. I'm sure Rian is fine, we didn't really find anything out there. Nothing worth noting at least. I felt Eve's magic growing stronger so it seems like the right direction. We should get some rest and then keep moving in the morning," I ramble on, unable to stop myself.

His eyes darken. "Of course. Whatever you want to do," he says, lips drawn thin. Shit. He definitely knows. With a shake of his head, he smiles up at me, letting go of what I'm sure he has figured out. "Come on, let's get some rest. We've got another long day of traveling tomorrow, right?"

I follow him, taking a spot to his left while he plops down beside Nat. "I don't know. I think we're close. The ground was all cracked, it was really weird. There was also a lot of fog and that pulse of her power was pretty insistent. I think it knows we're getting close." Nat and Cyrus freeze and I go on high alert, looking around wildly. "What? What is it?"

Cyrus glances at his sister out of the corner of his eye, but Nat just shakes her head. "Nothing," she says, clearing her throat. "Did you say there was fog? Was it like in Rayan?"

Rayan? I try to think back to the fight and what I saw. I don't remember much fog. Though a lot was going on and it's possible I just don't remember, or I might have missed it. "Um, no I don't remember anything like that. It was just this super dense cloud. Ring any bells to you?"

Cyrus places a hand on Nat's back, looking over to me sadly. Nat cuts him off before he can get the chance to explain on her behalf, "The person who took Eve disappeared in a cloud of smoke, or fog, whatever you want to call it."

I sit up straighter. "That's a good sign right? That means this is really it, we're so close. Maybe we should just leave now, I'm sure Rian will catch up with us." I'm on my feet in my next breath.

"No!" Nat exclaims. She shoves past her brother, tripping over her legs as she reaches out to grab my arm. "We should just wait till morning. The fog is dense right? Probably hard to see through? We should wait till we have better light."

"I also think we should wait for Rian to come back," Cyrus tacks on.

The crunching of boots over dead leaves has all three of our heads whipping up. Rian emerges, running a hand through his light hair. When he looks up, his eyes skim right over me, landing on Cyrus instead. "Everything good?"

"Yeah, Mar was just telling us what you found. We decided we should wait until morning to keep going. We should all get plenty of re-" Cyrus' words seem to die in his throat. His eyes are locked on Rian, staring directly at his waist. "I think you lost something."

Rian glances down and slaps a hand over his belt loops. His *empty* belt loops. "Ah, I must have left it back there when I went to take a piss," Rian explains with a shrug. He joins us by the fire, sitting down on the far side of me, next to Nat.

"You make it a habit to take your entire belt off for a piss?" Cyrus says through clenched teeth. If there was any doubt that he knew before, I can toss that aside now.

"Why do you care?" Rian seethes.

"Woah, what is going on right now? It's just a belt, Cy." Nat places a hand on her brother's arm, but he shrugs out of her grip, marching off into the woods.

Rian mumbles something about getting his belt and then follows after him.

"So. We going to talk about how you fucked Rian or..."

My head whips towards Nat and I shove into her shoulder. "Not cool."

I get a hard punch to my arm in return, taking it with no more than a wince and a glare. "That's for my brother," she says with a shrug.

"I didn't hit you when you slept with Eve," I point out.

"And had you slept with Cyrus, I wouldn't have hit you. That's the point," Nat groans. She looks over at me with a serious expression that quickly turns into a roll of her eyes and a sigh. "Alright listen, I don't care who you do. But I don't like seeing my brother upset. We've been through a lot and I just want to protect him the way he has always protected me."

"I get that. If you ever hurt Eve I wouldn't hesitate to take you out," I say pointedly.

Nat takes my hand, squeezing it as she stares into my eyes. "I would never intentionally hurt her. Since the moment I met Eve, all I have wanted was to protect her. She is…"

"Yeah, I know."

"We're going to find her."

I smile, thinking about how her power felt and for once knowing that we absolutely will. Soon.

~~~

My eyes open at the first sign of light. Nat and Cyrus are quick to rise, the two of them disappear for a bit, likely to take care of their bladders before we start this next leg of our journey. Still, as much as I understand basic bodily needs, I can't say I'm excited to be stuck here alone with Rian.

Thankfully, he doesn't say a word. The two of us work silently to ensure that we have all our supplies, and when the siblings return we're ready to go. I'm double checking I have my staff secured when I feel it. Not just a pull, a *yank*. Hard. Right in the center of my chest. It nearly knocks me off my feet with the force of it.

I clutch my hand over it and bend in half, breathing harshly as it grows stronger. Nat is by my side in a second, her hand pressing against my forehead. She pushes healing magic into me, but I shove her aside, forcing myself upright. "I'm fine," I pant, "it's Eve."

"What are you feeling?" Nat asks. Her arm is still outstretched, like she is ready to catch me any second.

"It's weird. It's like before, but stronger? It feels insistent. It's like she is on the other end yanking me towards her this time, not just guiding me."

Nat looks over her shoulder. Cyrus walks forward and dips to whisper in her ear. He steps forward, seemingly ready to scoop me up, but I push him aside too.

"I can walk. Actually, it feels a lot like I should run."

Rian steps forward this time. He ignores the worried looks from the others and speaks directly to me, "Lead the way."

I don't hesitate. I take off running with Rian hot on my tail. I know the other two can't keep up, but I don't have it in me to care. Not when we're so close. Every step closer the power grows, the connection hums happily in my chest. It's warm and buzzing with energy, it's oddly comforting.

We race through the trees, appearing on the other side where the ground begins to crack and decay. We run side by side, jumping over craters and trying our best not to accidentally break an ankle. There is a whooshing sound and a dark shadow looms over us. I don't bother looking up, already knowing it has to be Nat or Cyrus. For being such large dragons, they're remarkably quiet.

We're forced to slow as the fog gets denser, eventually becoming too much. Rian stops by my side and the fog clears momentarily as Cyrus descends, his red wings flapping. Nat jumps off his back and meets us before her brother shifts back. "Did you really have to run?" she snaps.

I ignore how harsh her words are, waiting for Cyrus to join us before pointing in the direction the power is pulling me towards. "We need to go that way."

Cyrus grabs my arm, "No more running. This fog is too thick and we need to stick together."

Nat steps forward, taking a deep breath to calm herself. "He's right. We should buddy up. Mar, you and I can stick together. Cyrus will stay with Rian."

One glance at the males and I already know I got the better partner. Sticking with Rian made sense when we were running, but now? A possibly slow, definitely tortuous walk with almost no visibility? Pass. Even Cyrus seems on edge. His usual easy going demeanor is absent.

"Alright, but hurry up, the power is growing, and last time it got cut off. I don't want that to happen again." They all nod their agreements and then we move through the fog as a unit. Nat stays no more than an arms length away from me, close enough that we can see each other.

504

The fog is almost impossibly thick, the ground uneven enough that we have to shuffle our feet to avoid falling into any holes or cracks. There is a steady pulse to the power drawing me in, almost like a wave, rising and falling with every breath. The closer we get, the more it intensifies.

All light is swallowed up around us and I curse to myself. Even with enhanced eyesight, I can barely move forward, I look back over my shoulder and Nat is still right there, even though I can't see the others. I reach back, pulling her hand in mine. "This might be a good idea."

We walk hand in hand for at least another hour before the visibility finally starts to improve. The fog dissipates slowly and I speed up, Nat's hand slipping through mine as I can't help but run forward. I burst through the last of the fog, the air clearing around me as I look left and right. Rian walks out of the fog a little further down the path, looking at me with a surprised grin. He comes to stand at my side, and together we stare out over a city.

"Fuck. We really did it. We found it," I breathe.

"How's that power feeling?" he asks, nodding towards my chest.

"Like it wants me to get inside right now."

She's in there. Eve is right there.

There is a shuffling of feet behind me and I whirl around excitedly. "I'm sorry for running off again, but Nat, look!" I glance back at the city. When I turn back around, I expect to see Nat and her brother, what I see instead is the inside of a bag as it is pulled over my head.

Chapter 78

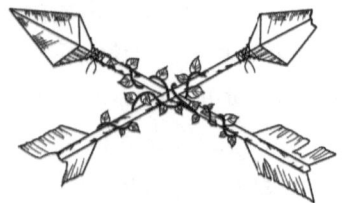

Oak

The siren continues blaring, growing louder the deeper we move into the city. With each wail, a strobing light flashes overhead. Then the screams start. That first shriek stops us dead in our tracks. Lina closes her eyes, cursing under her breath as Farai turns to me with wide eyes.

"We need to keep moving," Lina calls out over the cacophony.

A small group rushes past us, screaming in terror every time they look over their shoulder. I rush forward on instinct, my hands already outstretched and ready for the fight. Lina catches me around my middle, shoving me back and against a wall with a hand clamped firmly over my mouth. I struggle against her, but she shoves me harder.

"Stop, we can't help them. That's not what we're here for, and… they're sort of running from us," she explains with a grimace.

I reach up and remove her hand so I can speak, "What do you mean they're running from us?"

"They're running from Aine, or at least her power."

I turn to Farai, whose eyes flick to Lina and then back to me. I still have so many questions for her. The choice that she tried to give me is playing over and over again in my mind as I think of all the ways it could have gone. *If I were given the chance again, could I run? Would I? Even if I'm not running back to anything?* I shove all the what ifs aside and focus back on Lina. "What do you mean it's her power? What kind of power makes people run screaming like that?"

Lina explains that somehow Aine is able to conjure people's worst nightmares, that she can invoke such terror in them that they just drop dead. It's unlike anything I've ever heard before, an unimaginable power. There are things that I have realized we know little about. Magic being one of them. My power of persuasion, the way Farai can just transport us from one place to another, and now this? "So, what, we're just supposed to let these people die?"

Farai takes a step away, moving slowly around us as Lina shakes her head. "It's not like that, we're not trying to kill anyone."

"But we are. Aine's power could kill someone, or at least hurt them," I counter.

"That's true, but it's just a part of the job. Sometimes fights happen and people get hurt. That's not our fault."

"Lina, how is that not our fault? You said we were sent here to find someone, not to attack. There is no reason why any of this needs to happen. I won't just stand by and do nothing." I shove her off me and start towards the screams that sound the closest. I barely make it ten feet before Lina grabs me again, yanking me back against her chest.

"Oak, you can't. You're a Ghost now. This is what we do. We need to stay on task and find the-" Lina's words cut off abruptly. Her grip on me slackens.

"Let her go. Now," Farai demands, her voice steady and firm.

Lina slowly lets me go and I spin to see what's happening. Farai has a small blade pressed into the side of Lina's neck, right over her carotid. A small trail of blood is already running down over her pale skin. One tiny move and Lina could be dead in seconds, faster than we would be able to heal her.

"What the fuck are you doing?" Lina whispers harshly.

"Oak, you need to go. Right now. Find Rose and disappear. Don't let anyone else see you. Now, go!" Farai jerks her head to the side, one hand still holding the blade against Lina's neck while the other is wrapped around her midsection, immobilizing her.

I stand there, my feet feeling glued to the floor. "Wh-what are you talking about? Rose is here?" Confusion, fear, and excitement war inside me. *Why is Rose in Eteri? Is she hurt? What if Aine's power somehow got to her? Will she be happy to see me?*

"Farai," Lina admonishes, "remember the mission. I don't know what is going on with you, this isn't you. Just take a second and calm down."

"Mission? What are you talking about? I thought the mission was to retrieve someone?" My eyes flicker back and forth between them, waiting for some kind of explanation.

"It is. We were sent to-"

"Farai, no!"

"retrieve Rose. The high lady ordered us to find her and bring her back to Sena using any means necessary," Farai speaks directly to me, ignoring Lina's interruptions.

"I don't understand. Why? What is she doing here in the first place? Why does my aunt care?" I begin pacing, my hands shaking at my sides. This was all just another one of my aunt's games. A way to get us to do what she wants, regardless of how anyone else feels. I learned to expect it, but Rose? She still has blinders on when it comes to her mother, even if she got a small glimpse at what she is really like.

Lina keeps muttering about not saying anything else, but again, Farai ignores her. "She is here because she is looking for you."

"What?" it comes out no more than a whisper, the sound drowned out by the growing screams.

"Rose has been searching for you this whole time. She came all the way to Eteri to find answers about the Ghosts and find you." Farai's words change everything.

For months I thought that she had forgotten me. That they all had forgotten me. I always knew that would happen, that eventually I would just disappear and their lives would go on like nothing ever happened. But... it didn't. Rose is *here*. Here because she is looking for me. Trying to find me. To bring me home.

"She never gave up on me," I breathe. I turn back to them slowly, walking over until I am standing right in front of Lina, making it impossible for her to avoid my gaze unless she is willing to risk bleeding out. "You lied to me. This whole time, you made me think she didn't care."

"Oak, listen to me. You belong with us. You're a Ghost now. This doesn't change anything," she rushes out.

"This changes everything!"

"You're better with us! We're your family. We're your sisters."

"So are they! So. Are. They. Those girls were my sisters first." Nothing else matters now. Rose was looking for me. She didn't give up on me. I won't give up on her. On any of them. I look up to Farai and she gives me a reassuring nod. I take off, back in the direction we came from, hoping to find the secret passageway again.

There is a commotion behind me and I glance back in time to see Lina free herself. She manages to knock Farai back and is racing after me, calling out, "I can't let you do this!" She tackles me to the ground, the air whooshing out of my lungs at the moment of impact.

Lina straddles me, reaching back to grab something and I just know that whatever it is, I can't let her. I buck my hips, throwing her off of me and jumping up to my feet. Farai races towards us with blood dripping down her nose. The two of us square off against Lina as she stands. "It doesn't need to be like this. You can still come home, Oak," Lina pleads, ignoring Farai entirely.

"That's not my home. It never was, you just wanted me to think that my real home didn't want me." I dig deep inside my well and send a burst of power out. Lina jumps, easily avoiding the blast and landing on her feet a little further down the path.

"You always did rely on magic too much," Lina quips.

"And you always talk too much." Farai charges forward. The two meet with flying fists. It looks exactly like one of our training sessions in the sparring ring. The two of them equally matched, moving blow for blow. But this isn't training. There are no rules here.

I join the fight, coming up behind Lina as she grapples with Farai. My hands land on her back as vines begin to shoot out of my palms, wrapping around Lina and binding her arms and legs to her sides. She continues to struggle, managing to break a few vines and wiggle a hand free.

Farai curses, jumping back and yelling at me to do the same. A split second later, Lina shifts, a large pure white wolf bursting from the vines and leaving them scattered across the floor. Lina prowls in a wide circle, her teeth bared as she growls deep in her throat. She watches us with keen eyes, her head whipping around at the slightest movement. It's times like these that I wish my physical shift was more than just some heightened senses.

"What's the plan here?" I call out, hoping that Farai knows what to do in this situation.

"We need to get her under control. No way you can run with her like this. She's too fast and her sense of smell is too good. The only option is to either knock her out and tie her up or tie her up and knock her out."

Lina snaps her muzzle at Farai, barking out angrily. Apparently she doesn't appreciate either of those plans. But I have a better one. One that I know will work.

"Or, I could do this." I walk towards Lina slowly, her eyes instantly following my advance. She leans back on her haunches, clearly ready to pounce the second I'm where she wants me to be.

"Oak, what're you doing?"

"Trust me," I say, looking over Lina and at Farai, giving the wolf exactly what she wants, an opportunity.

Farai curses as Lina jumps forward. But she makes it barely an inch off the ground and then whimpers, sitting down like a good little pup.

I walk forward, stopping right in front of her as I whisper my next command, a little louder this time so Farai can hear me. "*Shift.*"

Lina shifts back, appearing before me dazed and confused. Farai comes to my side and looks her over from head to toe. "What did you do to her?"

"I simply told her to stop. Want to see something cooler?" I take a deep breath, steadying myself as I formulate the perfect command in my mind. "*You will come with us willingly. You will not fight, you will not argue, you will do exactly as I say until I tell you otherwise.*"

Lina blinks slowly, staring at me with glassy eyes. Farai slowly approaches, waving a hand in front of her face. "I don't know how I feel about this," she glances back at me, "you can just make anyone do whatever you tell them?"

"For the most part. I have to be stronger than them though, at least from a magic perspective. If their mind is strong enough, they can fight it off," I explain.

"And you're stronger than Lina?"

"Apparently."

Farai's mouth drops open, "You didn't know for sure?! What would have happened if you weren't?"

I shrug, "Guess she would have captured me. Possibly killed me depending on her orders I suppose."

"She wouldn't kill you," Farai sighs. "No matter what the truth is, why you were brought to us and what this mission is about, Lina *does* care about you. She sees you as a sister."

"I know." And I do. I get it. But that doesn't mean I can just let everything else go. Still, I release some of my control, granting Lina the ability to speak freely while ensuring she doesn't actively try to fight her way out of this one. Lina immediately starts sprouting off expletives while Farai watches with a mild look of annoyance.

"So, what's next?" Farai asks once Lina finally seems to shut up.

"Let's go find Rose."

Chapter 79

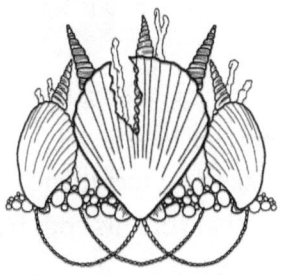

Cay

"Oliver, what did you do?" I ask again.

He stares at me with wide, glassy eyes as tears continue to stream down his bronzed skin. His entire body shakes with this sort of panicked energy. His hands clench and unclench at his sides as he breathing becomes uneven, his breaths coming out faster each time until he's hyperventilating.

"Oliver?"

His mouth drops open and a horrified scream comes out. It's raw, wet, guttural. It's... the stuff of nightmares. I look around, but the beast is gone, scattered in the wind, nothing more than the dust after Oliver's power hit it. *Whatever that power was.*

I reach out to him slowly. He flinches as my hands touch his bare skin. Heat pulses off him in waves as his screams become names. One after another. Rose. Terran. Reed. Oak. *Cay.* He says my name over and over again, chanting it into the air.

"I'm right here," I whisper. My hands tighten around his wrists, squeezing.

He looks up at me looking utterly miserable. His lip quivers as he shakes his head, a steam of *no, no, no,* falling from his lips. He tries to tear his arms out of my grip, but I hold on tighter. He throws his head back with a mournful wail. When he looks back to me, his voice breaks, "I-I couldn't save them."

"Save who? Oliver, what are you talking about?" I beg, willing him to see past whatever horror is clouding his mind.

"I didn't protect them. I can't protect them. I failed. I failed them. I-I-I-" his words break off into another sob. His body heaves with the force of his tears. His magic swirls around the air, powerful and hungry.

I feel it brush against my own and I suck in a breath. Whatever that power is, I don't trust it. "Oliver, you have to focus. You have to get your magic under control," I demand, raising my voice higher than I dared to before. He flinches, but I keep going. I grab his shoulders, shaking him roughly, only managing to succeed in making him cry out again.

Changing gears, I slap him clean across the face. It should be satisfying. It should give me a sense of fulfillment at finally getting back at him for all his comments and taunts. Instead, I feel a piece of me die inside at his pained whimper. I don't know what to do. I shake him again. I scream. I beg. I push healing magic into him. Nothing works.

Pushing to my feet, I look around, trying to find something to fight, something to do to break him free from the torment of his mind. When I look back at him, he is unsheathing a small blade from his hip. I throw myself back towards him, grabbing his wrist as he brings the blade up, hovering over his chest.

"Oliver! No! What are you doing?! Stop!" My cries fall on deaf ears.

His hands shake as he wraps his long fingers around the handle, the tip of the blade poised to drive into his chest. Into his heart. I grab his hands, fighting against him as I try to pry the blade from his grasp. He grits his teeth, breathing harshly as he struggles against me.

My grip slips and his hands recoil, moving towards his chest. I only barely manage to catch him again, the tip ripping a small hole in his shirt. He screams again, his head thrown back in agony.

My throat starts to close up as the panic sets in, sweat coats my body and my heart pounds as I try to think of some way to break him out of this. My strength is already wavering and if I let go, I have no doubt that Oliver will plunge that blade into his heart to escape whatever misery blinds him.

A single thought pops into my mind. I don't even take a second to consider it. I drop his hands, grab his face and yank him towards me, crashing our lips together. He remains frozen at first. The only movement from either of us is his shaking. After a few seconds, that slows, then stops altogether. His hands fall to his sides, the blade slipping free of his grip and landing on the ground innocently beside us.

I stay like that, forcing his mouth against mine and sending a prayer to the goddess that she will save him from himself. His breathing is still uneven, his harsh exhale brushes against our joint lips. Finally, after what feels like forever, he stills beneath my hands. His chest rises and falls in measured breaths. Tension bleeds from him and slowly his body relaxes.

Hesitantly, I pull away, leaving my hands on his cheeks in case I need to do something drastic like kiss him again. His hazel eyes are still glassy, distant, but then his lashes flutter closed, and open again with a newfound sense of clarity. He looks at me, not through me.

"Cay?" he croaks, his voice hoarse from all the screaming.

"Hi," I breathe, smiling at him as relief washes over me.

He collapses in my arms, his arms wrap around my waist as he buries his face in the crook of my neck, breathing in deeply. Oliver clutches me to him like he thought he would never see me again. He holds me like I am something precious that he cannot fathom a life without. He breaks. But he holds me as he does. And somehow, in his arms, I feel like I can breathe again.

I wrap one arm around his shoulders, hugging him back. My free hand tangles in his curls, massaging his scalp as I make soothing noises. The distant screams slowly fade away until the world is silent around us, only the occasional breeze rustling the trees to be heard. I sigh, slowly building up the courage to ask again, "What was that power?"

Oliver pulls back, his eyes puffy and red, his cheeks wet with tears. He wipes at them furiously, clearing his throat a few times as he seems to slowly stitch himself back together. He doesn't say anything about what happened so neither do I. We let that just exist in the moment and move past it. He closes his eyes and when they open, he looks like Oliver again.

"When I was a child, I was often sick. My parents weren't sure how to help me so they took me to Rayan to seek help."

I nod, already having heard this before.

"Your mother and father were the ones who saved my life. They gave me something that ensured I would never be sick again. At least not like I had been. They gave me power and some sort of magic."

My heart skips a beat. "Okay. So, what is it?"

He shakes his head. "I'm not sure. Whatever it is, it's volatile, dangerous. It doesn't belong to me and it knows it. To say we don't exactly get along would be an understatement."

"You talk about it like it's alive. Like it has a mind of its own."

Oliver laughs mirthlessly, "Sometimes it feels like that. I can't always control it. When I try to, it fights back." His face turns haunted.

"Then we need to get it out," I state the obvious.

"I've tried. Time and time again, I've tried. It never works. Nothing ever works."

"We'll just have to figure it out then! We'll figure it out together," I announce.

"How?" he asks. His voice is small, so different from his usual self. This version of him is hurt, broken, scared even. He doesn't want to get his hopes up, but I don't care, we're going to fix this. I will make sure of it.

"We can ask Terran for help."

He shoots the idea down immediately, "Absolutely not. He can't know. He can *never* know, Cay." His eyes beg me silently.

I nod, agreeing even as guilt bubbles up. I don't want to keep this from him and I don't think we should. But... ultimately it's Oliver's decision. He has to be the one to ask for help. This train of thought sends me down a rabbit hole and I start to think about the kiss. *Should I tell Terran? Does Oliver even remember?*

"Cay?" Oliver snaps his fingers in front of my face and I realize he's been talking to me.

"What? Sorry."

"I asked what do you want to do next."

"Oh, um... well I'll be honest, I don't particularly want a repeat experience and it seems like the fighting and screaming has died down some."

"Agreed." He pushes to his feet, offering me a hand and pulling me up after him. The position puts us awfully close, albeit further than we were just a few minutes ago. "By the way, how did you pull me out?"

"Hm?"

"When I was... stuck in the vision."

"Oh, you don't remember?" I ask, looking anywhere but at his face, already feeling the heat rising to my own cheeks. He shakes his head and I consider telling him the truth. But he already looks so upset about everything, and now with this magic stuff going on... better not. "I just called your name," I answer with a shrug.

"Really? It was that easy?"

"Yup."

He seems to accept that answer and then suggests that we meet up with the others. He's worried about the chief and the others who we passed earlier. I feel bad that they hadn't even crossed my mind. Still, I follow him as he leads the way back towards the cave.

We turn a corner and run straight into a small group. I'm already apologizing as I take a step back and then I realize who it is. Oak. She's with two strangers, one looks exceptionally cautious and the other *very* pissed off. Before I can even mutter a hello, the cautious one draws a blade and Oliver shoves me aside.

Chapter 80

Mar

The bag makes it impossible to see anything aside from dark shadows. I can still hear Rian close by, yelling and fighting. There's a loud groan and then silence. I don't bother fighting. They've already got bags over our heads, my connection to my magic feels far away- there, but significantly lessened.

Even if it wasn't, even if we could escape, I somehow think that we wouldn't get that far. No. This is better. We'll let them bring us straight to Eve and then all of us will fight our way out together. That is the only option now.

There is a sound of metal squeaking, possibly a gate or something. I'm shoved forward by a hand at the center of my back and I bite my tongue, refusing to rise to their bait. I'll be silent and compliant until I have the chance to tear their throats out one by one. Let them bring the monster to their front door.

A hand on my elbow yanks me to a stop. Voices murmur around us, but I can't quite make out what they're saying. There is a sound of agreement and then two sets of hands are on me and it feels like the universe collapses around us. I hit the ground on shaky legs that give out on me the second my full weight drops.

I scramble to my knees, not wanting to be on my ass for whatever comes next. The bag is ripped off my head. The lighting here is so dim that I barely have to adjust to make out the stone walls and metal bars. The ground is damp and dirty, a thick layer of dust and debris sitting on the surface. I grimace, looking around for anything to break up the disgustingness and finding nothing.

A low groan has me moving to the bars, looking across as Rian slowly comes to in the cell across from me. His hand moves to his head as he touches his temple lightly, wincing at the contact. He locks eyes with me and stumbles to his feet, rushing forward and banging against the bars.

"How's that working for you?" I ask mockingly.

"Are you okay? Did they hurt you?" he asks, slowly sinking back to the ground as his eyes fall shut.

"No. What about you? You're not exactly looking so hot over there."

"They hit my head with something. Hard."

"That sucks."

His eyes open, meeting mine through the bars of the cell. Slowly he shakes his head. "I really don't have the energy for your childishness right now. We need to figure out our next move."

I shrug, "I already know what it is."

"Oh? And what's that?"

I stand, my own head pounding as my vision swims for a second. "Simple. We find out where they're keeping Eve, bust her out, and then fight our way out of here."

He laughs. Loudly. The sound echoes off the walls and reverberates back at us. "Of course that's your plan."

"It's a good plan," I growl.

"It's bullshit. It's a dream. In case you haven't noticed, we don't even have full access to our magic right now. Or is it just me?" he scowls.

"We don't need magic. We're powerful enough without it," I shrug.

"You're delusional," he mutters under his breath.

"Well what's your genius plan then?!" I screech.

Rian throws his head back, leaning against the stone wall with his eyes closed again. "I'm working on it. Now shut up, my head is pounding and your yelling is only making it worse."

I look around, ignoring him. Our cells are facing each other across a wide walkway that leads to a door. I walk to the far wall of the cell, sinking down so I can watch the door without having to look at Rian. There are two other empty cells down here, positioned slightly closer to the door, but not close enough to really be of any help, not that anyone is in there.

"What do you think happened to Cyrus and Nat?" I ask quietly.

"They probably got grabbed in the fog. Cyrus was muttering to himself almost the whole way and then he just went silent. I assumed that he gave up or got bored with himself, but who knows now," Rian sighs.

"Nat was with me until right before we made it out of the fog. Do you really think that we wouldn't hear if they grabbed them?" I can't help but try and peek inside the cell next to Rian, wondering if there is any sign of them being brought down here.

"It's not like you made very much noise when they grabbed you," Rian scoffs.

I roll my eyes, hugging my knees to the chest and deciding that I would rather sit in silence than listen to his constant complaints. Sure, we're in prison and have limited access to our magic. But that's not the worst thing. All we need to do is figure out how to escape these cells, and then we can make the rest up as we go along.

Still, I can't help but worry about Cyrus and Nat. Hopefully, they somehow managed to avoid getting nabbed. That would be ideal. Though I have a sinking feeling in my chest that that seems a bit too good to be true. Either way, at least they aren't locked up down here with us. If I had to listen to Cyrus and Rian going at it again, I would lose my mind. I swear, one second they're best friends and the next they're on the verge of killing each other. Actually, they're almost always on the verge of killing each other.

The door creaks open and three figures enter in a single file line. The first is a petite female, her hair pulled back into a bun at the back of her neck. Next to her is an insanely tall male with a shaved head, thick mustache, and a gnarly scar. It splits the center of his face and makes me wince at how much pain he must have been in to receive that. The third person has porcelain skin and long black hair that flows down their back, hanging just past their waist.

"Well it's about time the welcome party showed up." I stand, placing my hands on my hips.

The long haired one groans, "Great, another one."

Their words have my heart racing. Eve. They're talking about Eve. She is the only other person I know who can annoy people the way I can. We practically made it an artform. I try to keep my cool, not expose myself.

The girl turns around, watching Rian as the long haired one steps forward. They crack their neck and then reach their hands out, dark mist spilling from their fingertips. "Now, let's just jump right in, shall we?"

I watch as that smoke creeps closer to me. I raise my brow at it, cocking my head to the side. "What's this? A little mist? So what?" I take a step forward and learn very quickly that that was a mistake. The mist surrounds me, invading my mind and picking me apart bit by bit.

Rian calls out to me as I begin to thrash and groan, desperate to fight off the invasion. The mist searches through my mind, sifting through my memories and then suddenly pulling back. The long haired one gasps, turning to look at the others and then rushing from the room at a full sprint.

I'm panting, somehow having ended up on my hands and knees as sweat pours off my face. The sound of retreating footsteps has me looking up, watching their backs as the girl and the bald guy walk back through the door without so much as a word. My arms collapse from beneath me and I land with my cheek pressing into the floor with a grimace.

"Are you alright? What just happened?" Rian demands from his cell.

I roll over onto my back, wiping an arm across my forehead as I realize that this situation is far worse than I thought. "They went through my memories," I admit.

"Shit. Okay, that's definitely not great. What are we most worried about here?" Rian asks, already trying to figure this out when I know that there is no fixing the mess that I just put us all in.

"Well, to start, probably the fact that Eve isn't really my father's daughter," I wince as I say the words aloud.

"What?"

"Yeah… which also means that I am the heir to the Vulca throne."

I roll onto my stomach, propping my head in the filthy palms of my hands. I watch as Rian's face morphs from mild concern to utter horror.

"Surprise?"

Chapter 81

Rose

Kneeling beside Azariah's father, the chief of Eteri, I take stock of his many injuries. Thankfully, it only takes a few minutes to realize that they're all superficial. Reed is working with Imani to treat Sol. Both of them appear to be more exhausted than anything else.

Azariah signs frantically to her father, her tears still streaming down her cheeks even as I reassure her that he is going to be fine. Chief Zion reaches up, taking her hands in his own and squeezing them tight with a smile on his face. He brings her hands up to his lips and presses a gentle kiss on the back of her hand.

"I was so scared," Azariah speaks aloud.

Her father shakes his head, then turns to look for his other daughter. Imani looks over and then leaves Sol in Reed's care, sitting down beside her sister. "How are you?" Imani asks, signing along.

Zion releases his youngest daughter's hands, answering with an easy grin that gives him a sort of youthfulness I've seen reflected in Azariah. I haven't had much time to learn, so I'm not sure what he says, but it makes both his daughters laugh.

Azariah wipes at her cheeks, drying her hands off on her pants before she replies. "You shouldn't joke about stuff like this. What if you were seriously hurt? What if you were killed?" Her hands hang in the air like her words.

"Riah's right. You can't be so reckless," Imani adds.

I watch, completely lost, as he begins signing back. Eventually, I excuse myself from the conversation, joining Reed as he continues to tend to Sol. "How is she?"

My cousin looks up at me with a slight frown. "Physically she seems fine..." he jerks his head towards the back wall and I follow after him. "She seems terrified, even now. She's barely spoken two words to me and hardly responds to anything I say or do."

Glancing back at her, I find her staring off in the distance, her eyes seeming far away. I turn back to him with a sigh. "There's not much I can do. The screams seem to be dying down, maybe once they stop she'll snap out of it?"

Reed leans back against the wall, crossing his hands over his chest. "I hope so. I don't know much about prophecies and all that, but something tells me it would be helpful to have her around while we try to figure all this out."

"Agreed. I still don't fully understand what I have to do with any of this, but... it can't be a coincidence that the attack happened while we were here."

"You think?"

"Oliver said that he believed this power over fear came from one of the Ghosts. Maybe they sent someone after us because we were getting close to finding answers?"

"That's only slightly terrifying."

"Seriously, Reed, think about it. Why would the Ghosts come to Eteri and just attack out of nowhere? It doesn't make sense. Clearly they're here for a reason," I say, keeping my voice low.

It's not that I think they would blame us, but... I couldn't fault them if they did. If we really are the reason why the realm was attacked, then I will never forgive myself. Knowing how much it hurts Cay, her realm being destroyed, I can't imagine Azariah losing hers too. It's too much for any one person to bear.

"So, what's the plan? We just wait it out here?" Reed asks, anxiously looking around the small cave like the walls could close in at any moment.

"For now, yes. Even if she's not injured, it's too big of a risk to move Sol right now. Zion has some minor injuries, but beyond that, the others seem too shaken up to throw into some unknown fight."

Reed nods, looking past my shoulder and then back to me. "Mateo is giving me a look. Can we invite him into this little huddle?"

I can't hide my smirk, "Oh, a look? What kind of look? The kind that says he wishes you were alone right now so he could do all sorts of-"

"Rose!" Reed admonishes, slapping my shoulder as the two wolves make their way to us.

"What?" I ask with a laugh.

"You know exactly what, now cut it out," Reed whispers, smiling as soon as Mateo and Gael join us.

"What're we talking about?" Mateo asks, looking between us.

"Just plans for what to do next," I answer with a shrug, watching Reed from the corner of my eye as he relaxes. *Honestly, what did he expect me to say?*

"That's great because I'm not going to lie, I sort of hate it here," Mateo grumbles.

"He's just mad because he got his ass kicked," Gael says with a small smile.

This of course sets off an argument between the two of them, Gael laughing to himself while Mateo struggles against Reed who is trying desperately to hold him back. I would be worried about them, but something tells me this is just another day in a long lifetime of friendship.

Someone clears their throat behind me and I turn, finding Azariah there waiting for me. I walk over to her with a racing heart. Even after crying, she still looks so beautiful. Her dark skin is glowing even in the dingy light, her hair is still perfectly styled, despite having fallen through the air only maybe an hour ago. She's too beautiful for words.

We stand there, staring at each other with the weight of everything going on around us pushing in. It's like no time has passed at all, yet at the same time, it feels like an eternity. In the silence of our eyes meeting in the darkness, I feel that weight lift off my shoulders. There is something strange and exciting about meeting someone who feels like they've been a part of your life forever.

"I wanted to thank-"

"How's your father do-"

She laughs and gestures for me to continue.

"How is your father doing?"

"He seems to be his usual self, cracking jokes and trying to make us feel better," she says with a roll of her eyes.

"I'm glad. He seems like an excellent father."

She looks over her shoulder, watching as her sister and father sign back and forth to each other with mirrored smiles. "He is. He does everything for us."

I remember what that was like. How my father used to take care of me, spoil me even. Terran did his best to fill in the gap, but it's not the same. Fathers are meant to protect and adore their daughters. They're meant to be there for them whenever something goes wrong, promising to make it right. Nothing can ever really replace the longing of a little girl to hold her dad's hand one more time.

The familiar burn at the back of my throat has me shoving those thoughts aside, focusing on something I can actually control. "What do you want to do? I haven't heard any screams in a long time, maybe it's safe to leave?"

"Honestly? I don't trust it. My sister, Asha, will know to come here as soon as it is safe to do so. Until she does, I think it is best we stay put. I know that your brother said that this is just one person's power, but there is a chance he could be wrong. I won't risk my family's lives needlessly."

"I understand. So we stay here, wait it out a little longer," I reassure her. I expect her to return to her family after that, but she surprises me by taking a seat and patting the spot next to her. I lower myself to the ground, sitting criss-crossed.

"My father is not much of a warrior. He's more like a gentle giant if you ask me. It's my mother who lives for the thrill of the fight. I'm sure that's where Asha gets it from," she muses.

"That sounds a lot like my brothers."

She laughs, "Yes, everyone expected Oliver to be quite fearsome when he first arrived. We had no idea how sensitive he could be. My father respects that about him." My face must show my disbelief because Azariah raises her own brows at me, "You don't agree?"

"No, it's just... most people back home wouldn't describe Oliver as sensitive. He's more like your mother. Hungry for the fight."

"Hmm, well I don't know about anywhere else, but any time he has been here he has shown no desire for anything resembling a fight." She watches me, placing a hand on my knee, "You don't seem happy to hear that."

"It just makes me think that maybe I don't know my brother all that well."

"Maybe, maybe not. I think we often become the person we think others need us to be, even when that means becoming someone different. It's a rare, beautiful thing to be who we truly are with those around us."

I think back to the girls, the roles that we all play with each other. We might love each other equally, but we will always have our own relationships that are different from one another. I smile, realizing that of course that makes sense. "You're right. I just hope that I might get the chance to know who he truly is."

"I'm sure you will, there's plenty of time," she says with a smile.

My heart stutters in my chest. "I hope I get the chance to know you too," I breathe, completely incapable of holding the words back.

"I hope so too."

"Riah!" Imani calls from the other side of the cave.

When we look up, Asha is walking in along with a small horde of guards, looking mostly unscathed other than some mud.

"Is it over?" Azariah asks, climbing to her feet.

Asha nods, looking around the room at all of us, "it's over."

Chapter 82

Eve

Taka wastes no time bringing me back to my room, slamming the door shut, and ensuring it is locked up tight. Normally that would piss me off, or at the very least frustrate me. Now, I'm grateful for the time alone.

My magic swirls deep inside me, humming happily as I reach out and pull on it tentatively. It's slow at first, just waking up, then I feel it move through my veins until it is pumping steadily through my heart.

It's intoxicating. Having this much power again is like drinking the most decadent wine, the taste of it as it coats your tongue and moves down your throat. Thick. Full. I bask in it, letting the feeling wash over me, simmering just beneath the surface of my skin.

I close my eyes, reaching out and feeling those threads again, right within my reach. I wish I could just pull them all and bring my girls to me, but a tiny voice in the back of my head says to wait. Instead, I look for that thread that brought me to Mar. I push my power into it, calling to her and guiding her to me.

Secretly I hope to catch a glimpse of her again, to hear her voice and know that she is closer. It feels easier this time around. Less taxing. But even so, I can feel the drain. Reluctantly, I release my hold on the thread, letting it settle inside me. It takes a solid half hour before I feel my magic steady. It's not as much as when I first arrived back in the room, but still, it's better than before.

Better than feeling like I was one sneeze away from eternal darkness. I run over to the mirror, staring at my reflection and for once not seeing some frail version of myself. My hair is shinier, my skin pinker, my eyes brighter. Actually, my eyes appear more gray than they ever have. Almost the color of a freshly made steel blade.

Despite how much healthier I look, I can feel the layers of grime coating my skin. It's like sweat and dead skin have become a paste over my body. I quickly jump into the shower, washing my body as quickly as possible, but taking a little extra time to run the soap through my hair.

When I jump out, I dry off and then search for something clean to wear. With the towel wrapped around me, I skip back into my room. I pause in front of the mirror again, biting my lip as I let the towel drop and take in my naked reflection.

There is no hiding how much weight I have lost. My ribs still stand out harshly, my collarbones too. My knees look extra odd, like the skin has been pulled too tight around them. I poke at my stomach, wondering how long it will take to finally look like myself again.

A throat clears behind me and I look over my shoulder in the reflection. Yuta is sitting on my bed with his eyes pointed towards the ceiling. "Would you mind covering up?"

I turn slowly, placing my hands on my bare hips as I do. "Why? You're in my room."

His jaw ticks, "And you are still my prisoner. This is not your *room*, this is your cell."

"You know, I'm kind of getting whiplash here. You say you want to be my friend or some kind of an ally, but then you insist on calling me a prisoner.

Which is it?" I lean back against the glass, holding in my yelp at the cold pressed against my back.

"It's complicated. You have so much to learn, so much that you still cannot begin to comprehend."

"You've told me all about the Grim and the *history* that landed you all here. What do I not understand?"

"Do you believe it?" His head drops forward, but his eyes stay firmly fixed on my face, not even daring to sneak a peek.

What is with these people not wanting anything to do with my body? I know it's a bit of a mess right now, but how would he even know if he didn't look? "What does it matter if I believe it or not?"

"It matters."

My first instinct is to snap back, but something in the way he says it makes me pause. For the first time I really consider everything that he's told me. Not just as some ruse or some way to get me to trust them, but as a potential truth. It's hard to believe that my entire life has been a lie and the history books are so absurdly wrong, but what if they are? Eventually, I realize that I can't just decide one way or another without getting the full story. It's just not enough.

"I don't know yet."

Yuta nods, "Well, when you decide then I guess we'll see how that changes things." He stands as the door is flung open, bouncing off the wall as Teru comes rushing in. They run straight to his side and whisper in his ear. Yuta shoots a look my way and then bolts from the room faster than I have ever seen before.

"What's going on?" I ask Teru as they linger just inside the door, catching their breath.

"Nothing for you to worry about. Just-Vana's sake! Where are your clothes?!"

I shrug, looking around the room, "There was nothing clean to wear."

"So put on something dirty then, anything!" Teru chucks my wet towel at me as I roll my eyes.

"No. I want something clean," I demand, even as I wrap the towel around myself.

Teru looks like they're about to argue, and then there is a rushing of feet somewhere outside and they curse under their breath. "Fine, I'll have someone bring you fresh clothing. Behave," they mutter, quickly rushing after Yuta.

I watch as they go, waiting for that familiar sound of the door locking. It never comes. I creep hesitantly towards the door, pressing my ear against the wood and listening for any sign of life outside. Nothing. Not a whisper. Hesitantly, I reach for the handle, surprised when it turns with ease.

The door creaks open slowly, no more than enough space for my head to poke out. Turning to look left and right, there are no signs of any guards in the hall. Just a commotion somewhere deeper in the castle. I pull the door open fully and take a step out.

"Sorry, Teru. Behaving just isn't who I am."

Taking a deep breath, I test my power to see if I can use a concealment charm. To my surprise, it works. Though it feels like an immediate drain and I know I won't be able to keep it up for long. I tiptoe down the hall, listening to each door as I pass by, wondering which will be the door I need.

It would help if I had any idea where I am going. Still, I'm out of my *cell*. Free to roam the castle and do whatever the fuck I want. I make it to a familiar door and realize I'm outside the dining hall. I slip inside, then quickly make my way through a servant's door that leads back inside the kitchens.

I freeze as I find two cooks working on chopping vegetables. I wait for them to sound the alarm, to call out for help, something. I creep by slowly, wondering how strong this charm is and if it will hide my sounds too. When neither of them respond, I take the opportunity to knock over a bowl of chopped onions, spilling them everywhere.

"Really?" one cook groans to the other, dropping down to start cleaning up.

The other cook protests his involvement and starts helping to clean, ducking behind the counter as I cross the kitchen and slip through the door that Teru had led me through. The corridors are long, dark, and confusing. It takes me far longer than I would have liked to finally find a door that didn't just lead into some bedchamber or office space.

The next door I open leads to a sort of balcony. I step out on it and instantly hear voices. I drop to my hands and knees, nearly losing my towel in the process. I crawl closer to the railing, peeking through at the scene below.

Yuta is seated on his throne, one leg crossed over the other. One hand rubs along his jawline, the other taps against the carved armrest. I get a vague sense of deja vu watching him like that, thinking back to the day they brought me here. Taka is standing beside him to the left, leaning over and whispering something to him that only seems to make his body more tense.

Teru runs into the room, straight up the center aisle. They stop at the foot of the throne, announcing something just before the doors are thrown open. Chien and Eri walk in, each escorting a person with a bag over their head. The one with Chien is tall, almost taller than he is. The one with Eri is taller by at least a head.

I sit on my knees, peeking over the railing instead of through it to try and get a better view. Yuta sits upright as Chien and Eri pull the others to a stop a few feet in front of the throne. The hooded pair don't struggle, they don't fight at all. I wonder if they have access to any magic here or if they were like me, drained.

My heart races as Yuta raises his hand and Chien rips the bag off his person's head. A bright red head of hair on an unfamiliar male is revealed. It instantly strikes me as odd as I haven't seen a single person since arriving here who didn't have dark hair. Then, Eri removes the other's bag.

Another head of red hair is revealed, only this one belonging to a female. A *very* familiar female. One whose head has been between my thighs. One who has been the object of my dreams many of my nights spent here alone. One who I am both excited and terrified to see.

Nat was with Mar, I know it. I heard their voices. But that male beside Nat is certainly *not* my sister, nor is it Rian. I reach out for the thread again, but as I do I feel my concealment charm waver and I quickly stop. I can't risk exposing myself here. Not if Nat is captured. If she's captured then that means there is a good chance Mar is too.

No, I can't rush in. I need to listen, and wait, and figure out what the fuck is going on. I take a deep breath in and let it out slowly, calming my racing heart. I settle back on my heels, readying myself for the perfect moment. As soon as I know what's happening, I'll make my move. This is it. The time is finally here. Better hope I don't fuck this up and get us all killed.

Chapter 83

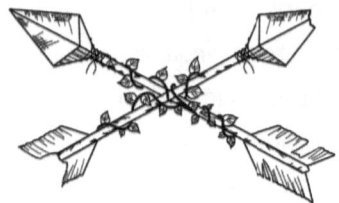

Oak

Cay stares back at me with wide eyes, a mixture of shock and suspicion written across her features. My own shock is not at seeing her here, it's the way Oliver shifts closer to her side, a hand outstretched towards her as if to pull her back. As soon as I realized Rose was here, it became obvious that she wouldn't be alone. Cay was anticipated, at the least, but Oliver?

I guess I should have anticipated this after what happened in Rayan, though there is no part of me that believes he is here for me. No. It is abundantly clear even from this distance that there is only one person Oliver cares about on this mountain.

My body remains frozen. Stuck between the desire to run to her and to stay with Farai. It makes no sense. This is what I've wanted, what I've been fighting for for months. Except my stupid body won't move. I manage to take the slightest step forward and that's all it takes to break the spell.

She runs towards me, her arms winding around my shoulders and crushing me to her chest. My own arms wrap around her waist instinctively. Her chin rests on my shoulder, her voice right in my ear. "I was so worried about you. When Rose told me what happened, I couldn't believe it. I'm so sorry I wasn't there to stop her." She squeezes me tighter.

I return the hug, clutching onto her shirt fiercely. "Stop, there was nothing you could have done." I push away from her so I can look her in her eyes, watching as they fill with tears. "What happened with your mom? Has she woken up?"

She gives a sort of wet laugh. "I'm not really sure. Terran and Oliver took me back to Rayan and we-" her words cut off as she looks over my shoulder where Farai and Lina stay close by.

I take her hand and we walk a few feet away, leaving the others behind. I use a concealment charm to ensure that only we can hear each other. "Go ahead, they can't hear us."

"We went back to Rayan, got water that should wake her up, and then I got a letter from Rose asking for help, so, here I am," she gestures around her.

"Did the water work? Wait, where's Terran?"

"Terran went back to Sena to give my mom the water while Oliver and I came to Eteri."

"So did it work, did she wake up?" I ask nervously.

"I still don't know. And now, it turns out that Rose never even sent the letter," she sighs. She shakes her head sucking her teeth. "Oak, it's a mess. All of it. The sirens are making all sorts of demands and I can't do anything but agree. I want to be here for Rose, and you of course, but I also hate not being with my mother. Not to mention I left Finn behind. I just don't know what to do."

I grab her hand, "Hey, it's okay. We'll figure this out. I know that things with the sirens weren't in the best place to begin with, but you don't have to do any of this alone."

She smiles, nodding her head and then pulling me into another quick hug. She practically shoves me away from her, staring at me with panicked eyes. "Wait, are you free? Did you escape? Vana, I feel awful, I didn't even ask how you were!"

Nodding back to the others I explain what happened with Farai and Lina, leaving out the part about the so-called rebels and focusing on how Farai helped me escape. "Now, I'm looking for Rose."

"Oh, well I can help with that. She's in this cave nearby with the others." She starts walking back towards Oliver and I follow.

"Others?"

"Yeah, there are some people from Eteri, these wolves, and oh! Reed is here too!" she exclaims with a snap of her fingers.

I stop, feeling a thump forming in my throat. "Reed is here?"

"He came with Rose to try and find answers about where they might have taken you," she explains.

"He did that? He came all the way to Eteri just for that?" I think of my shy, timid brother. The brother who would rather spend his days with his nose buried in a book than trek halfway across the world. Let alone up a mountain. He hates heights.

"Of course," Cay says with a furrow in her brow. "You knew we were coming right?"

"I-"

"Oak, we would never just abandon you like that. You're our sister. You're part of us," Cay takes my hand again, intertwining our fingers the way she always does with the others.

I stay quiet as she leads me back to the others and follows a path back towards a cave. Oliver heads straight inside, Cay tugging me in behind him. As soon as we enter, I feel the air shift. Farai and Lina stay at the door, not daring to move any further in as we find it crowded with guards, all eyes on us.

I hear Reed's voice before I see him. His arms are around me almost as soon as my name has left his mouth. I feel Rose come up behind me, forming a sort of sandwich with me in the middle as my cousin and my brother rattle off a hundred questions without taking a breath. Finally they let me go and I look around the room.

There are plenty of unfamiliar faces, but I do recognize the two wolves Cay had mentioned before. They hang back, letting us have this reunion, even as the others start on an inquisition. Rose intervenes, answering all of their questions as I just stare up at my baby brother.

"You came all the way to Eteri," I say in awe.

"We thought they would have answers about the Ghosts. We never imagined we would actually find *you* here."

I laugh, "Yeah well, believe me, I wasn't expecting any of this either."

"Lina?"

We both turn in time to see a dark haired wolf, Mateo if I remember correctly, stumbling forward and then breaking out into a full sprint. He collides with Lina, taking her to the ground as she stares up at him.

"Mateo?" she says in disbelief.

"I can't believe it's you!" he cries, nuzzling into her neck as she laughs wildly.

"I thought you were dead!" She wraps her arms around him, nuzzling him back with her face, something that I know wolves do, but have never seen her act on before.

"I thought *you* were dead!"

Reed leans over, speaking directly into my ear, "What's happening right now? Who is that?"

"I don't know, but that's Lina. She's one of the other Ghosts." Reed's mouth drops open, but I just shake my head, "I'll explain later."

"Actually, you'll explain right now." The demand comes from behind me and as I turn, I see a dark skinned female with beautiful golden wings sprouting from between her shoulder blades.

"Asha, give them a moment," another person pleads from somewhere nearby.

"No, there are a whole lot of people in this room who don't belong here. As far as I'm aware, unless you have been invited into this realm, you are not welcome here," Asha spits.

"Let's all just take a second to calm down and then we can figure this all out. There is a lot going on, and we're all clearly dealing with a lot of emotions, let's just pause," Rose suggests.

Arguments break out throughout the room, voices shouting across each other as they echo throughout the room. I can barely keep anyone's names straight and eventually give up trying, chiming in with an occasional explanation when I can. But it's no use. It's complete chaos.

"The bonds," a frail voice croaks and the arguing stops.

Another person whose name might be Riah or might be something else entirely, I'm not really sure at this point, walks over to a woman propped against the walls. She kneels down beside her and reaches out her hand, "What was that, Sol?"

"The bonds are being woven together, one by one the threads will sew the fate of the realms," she groans.

"What do you mean? Are you talking about the prophecy?"

I look over at Rose who gives me an *I'll explain later* look, and I'm starting to doubt that later is really the best time for that conversation.

"Seven figures- field- darkness," Sol whispers, her voice fading in and out.

"I-I don't understand, I'm sorry. What is it?"

"Blood, love, fury, fate, truth, trust, life, you need them all," Sol says through a wet sounding cough.

Cay steps forward, "is she okay?"

"I checked on her not that long ago, and she seemed fine, nothing was physically wrong with her," Reed answers quickly.

Sol begins to mutter a string of incoherent sentences, something about bonds, and blood, and cloaked figures, all of it makes zero sense. Eventually she passes out and we all stand there in silence, unsure what to do next.

Help, a voice whispers.

I spin in place, looking around the room for the source. It sounds so familiar, but no one else reacts, no one else seems to hear it. My stomach churns, a sinking feeling building. I grab Cay and Rose, pulling them to the side. "This is going to sound weird, but did either of you just hear a voice?"

They both shake their heads. "Are you alright?" Rose asks.

"I don't know, I just got this weird feeling. Like something bad was happening," I say as a shiver runs down my spine.

"It's probably just leftover energy from the-"

Help, the voice whispers again.

"You heard it, didn't you?" I ask, based solely on the looks on their faces. Rose nods her head, "What was that?"

"Did that sound like…" Cay's already pale skin blanches.

It hits me and that sinking feeling might as well be my heart falling out my ass. "Guys, what happened with Eve? You found her right?" They share a look and I nearly throw up. "What happened? What do you know?"

"The last I heard, Mar was on her way to get Nat so they could look for her together," Rose rushes out.

"Same," Cay echoes.

"Alright well, how long ago was that?"

"I-I don't remember," Rose admits sheepishly.

Help. The voice is louder this time, more like a scream. It's also clearer. So clear that none of us can deny it.

That voice calling out to us for help…it's coming from Eve.

Epilogue

Yuta

I watch as Chien and Eri remove their hoods and reveal two heads of red hair. I look between them studying the way their jaws clench and their eyes shift around the room. It's clear that they were raised together. Even their posture holds the same degree of rigidity. I focus on that, ignoring the presence lurking up on the balcony.

She thinks I can't see her, that her silly little concealment charm could ever truly hide her from me. Little does she know that my gifts are many, including the ability to see straight through such charms. I could call her out, drag her down here and make her watch what happens next up close. But it will be better this way.

Still, I send a message straight into Teru's mind, instructing them to make their way to the balcony so she doesn't get any new ideas of escaping. Not that she would get far. She's too weak, her little experiment a bit ago drained her beyond her comprehension. Such magic is not meant to be played with.

In time, she will learn. She'll have to. Just as she will come to learn that reality is a fickle thing. Easily manipulated. Easily distorted. I intend on showing her the truth, the *absolute* truth. Even if it destroys who she is inside. It won't matter in the end, I'll simply build her up into the person she was always meant to be.

Eri and Chien bow at their waists before stepping to the side, leaving the two prisoners at my feet. I cock my head, letting another of my powers wash over them as I search for any hidden tricks up their sleeves. They have none. Nothing beyond the fire in their veins and the dragon souls that slumber within them, cut off by the mountains that encircle this entire land.

My people were exiled here because of such power. The fools of the past believed they could cut us off entirely, underestimating the nature of the grim. They may have stolen our magic, they may have severed our connection with the land, but they will never truly be able to erase the bonds that tie us to this existence.

"What are your names?" I ask, starting things off easy.

Their chins tip up in defiance. Then, the male steps forward, looking me dead in the eyes with a burning intensity. "Cyrus," he answers evenly. He takes a deep breath, "This is my sister, Nat."

I'll give him credit, he maintains his composure even as he betrays his blood. It won't last for long, though I am glad that his little display is helping draw out my show. I fight the urge to look up into the darkness, to see her face as she listens in. "*How did you make it through the mist,*" I demand, voice dripping with the power that will force the truth past their lips.

Their jaws clamp, fighting against their words. The male struggles more than the female so I turn my attention to him fully. He seems to choke on his words, his face turning red as he struggles. He breaks just as his lips are starting to turn blue. "We followed her," he says with a gasping breath, a curse following soon after.

"Who?" It's a needless question. I already know who. She's practically a beacon, calling everyone to her with a power that she can't control and knows nothing about. Still, harnessed in the right way, it is exactly what I need.

The female glares at her brother, barking out a warning. His look is resigned, almost as if he knows his fate is already sealed. "Eve. We followed Eve."

I smile, feeling the waves of emotions pulsating from her. The panic, the fear, the excitement. She held out for so long, holding tight to those dreams of being rescued. Eventually, those faded too. It sends a small thrill through my body as I feel that again. *Delectable*. "Why?"

Even the male, *Cyrus*, holds his tongue. I turn to the girl, expecting to find her equally determined, but instead finding the first signs of cracks. The quiver of her lips, the wetness filling her eyes, the color draining from her face. I walk down the steps, slowly, letting my shadows seep out, trailing behind me.

She keeps her eyes pointed at the ground, even as her body begins to tremble. I stop right in front of her, placing a finger under her chin and lifting her face. She stares up at me with wide, pale blue eyes. Icy. Familiar. I let my shadows wrap around her, noting the way she shivers. Only it's not repulsion that moves her.

"Why have you come here?" I push again, not even needing to use my power.

Her breath hitches in her throat and then to my surprise, she drops down on one knee, then the other. She folds herself in half until her forehead is nearly pressed against the floor. Then, slowly, she peers up at me through thick lashes and breathes two words, "My king."

Disbelief coats my tongue. *Hers*, not mine. I feel my smile spread, savoring the taste as it builds and grows. I watch as the brother drops down next, echoing those same two words with the kind of reverence I am only used to from my people. Taka steps forward, standing at my side as his own power reaches out to them. I hold a hand out, stopping him. "Wait."

Taka takes a step back, following my order without question, trusting me. "Rise," I command, watching as the pair slowly make their way to their feet. They keep their eyes downcast, their hands bound at the wrist in front of them. "Look at me."

Instantly their heads shoot up, the females cheeks flushed. Her eyes are brighter now, enticing. I step forward, caressing the female's cheek with a gentle hand. Fury burns in the back of my throat and I chuckle. Oh, how my show is unraveling beautifully. I rub my thumb across her soft cheek.

"Tell me what brings you here, beautiful," I tack on that last part, excited to see what taste that might draw out. It's unexpectedly bitter.

"We are here to serve you. *I* am here to serve you," she explains.

"Oh? And how exactly do you plan on serving me?" I tease.

"We will do whatever it takes to right the wrongs of the past and return the power that has been stolen," she recites like some sort of mission statement.

I chuckle darkly, letting my hand roam back so my fingers can tangle in her fiery curls. "Well then, let's start here," I tilt my head and brush my lips against hers lightly. Her taste mingles with the sour tastes of jealousy. I groan as I deepen the kiss and let the flavor explode inside my mouth.

A burst of surprise has me pulling away, licking my lips as she stares wide eyed at me. There is the hint of something there, regret? No. Confusion? Maybe. I look up in time to see Teru dragging my little minx from the shadows. They evanesce down to our level, Teru's hand wrapped tightly around her bicep as she struggles to break free. Tears flow freely down her cheeks as she stares at the female, her gray eyes swirl as power builds inside her.

"Eve," she croaks, the sound broken and small. So unlike her declarations to me.

"Well, isn't this a lovely reunion?" I clap my hands together. I turn to the dragon, pulling her against my side and whispering next to her ear, "This should be fun." I reach out and grab hold of my minx, forcing her under my other arm. I evanesce before she can even think of speaking.

We land back in my rooms and Eve slumps to the ground. The other girl crouches down beside her, reaching out as if to hold her. She slaps her hands away, screaming out her defiance, "Stay away from me!"

"I'm sorry, please, you have to understand," the redhead pleads.

Eve turns away from her, letting her tears fall silently as the pleading grows and grows. My little minx is all mixed up inside. A mess of feelings. I let them fuel me. Silently feeding off her the way I have since she first arrived in my kingdom.

What a fun turn of events. I thought I would play nice, make things easier on her, but this? This is so much better. After all, things are just getting started.

To Be Continued in Book Three of the Sovereign Sisters Series:
REALMS OF FATE

Acknowledgements

I can't believe that Realms of Secrets is complete. This book was such an undertaking and I am so grateful for the many people who had a hand in getting it to this point. As an indie author, the support of my readers is so important that I cannot begin to capture it in words. So, to keep things simple, thank you! Thank you for supporting me and this series. Thank you for diving back into this world. Thank you for trusting the process and sticking around as I learn the ins and outs of self-publishing. And thank you for being a part of this journey with me.

Realms of Peace was my debut novel and throughout that process I learned so much. This has been such a rewarding process, getting to see my own growth, and I hope that you can also see it in this book. But it wasn't just about me growing as a writer, it was also about learning what works for me and what my editing process should look like. After months of editing, I am incredibly proud of this book and I truly owe so much of that to my editor **Nora**. Thank you for being so meticulous and ensuring that every tiny detail has been considered. I know that my dyslexia leaves you with some interesting typos, but somehow you always understand just what I am trying to say. I value you so much, not only as an editor, but as a friend. I couldn't have done this without you. Thank you for being here for me, offering me endless encouragement, and for everything else that you do.

Of course, a big addition to Realms of Secrets starts right from the beginning with that STUNNING map designed by **Cody James King.** When I wrote Realms of Peace I knew that one day I wanted to see a map of this world inside my head. Cody, you brought it to life. I am so grateful that I found your TikTok and decided to reach out. I truly could not imagine going through this process with anyone else. Your constant patience, willingness to make changes, and ability to make sense of my vague ramblings is so greatly appreciated. You also found a way to make this process even more fun through your humor and overwhelming kindness. Again, I am so grateful for you and I can't wait to continue to support each other in the future.

Then there is Delilah Cay. Not only are you one of my best friends, an inspiration behind this story, and a sister of my own, you also are the face of this series. The first thing that a person see's when they see my book is the cover that you designed and I am in love with what you have created. Not only the cover but all the gorgeous interior artwork for the characters too. You never cease to amaze me with what your mind comes up with, even when neither one of us can seem to articulate what we see in our heads. Thank you for being patient and kind as I regularly asked for changes… even going as far as asking to start from scratch. I don't deserve you! You are an icon that deserves the world, thank you for being a part of this one with me.

There are so many people who I would like to give thanks to, Sharity, Kaitie, Ali, Beck, Delilah, the list goes on and on. The impact that you have had on me is immeasurable and no matter what role you've played, I am forever grateful to have you in my life.

About the author

Teanna Lynne grew up in Orlando, Florida where she spent her childhood surrounded by stories. She is the youngest of three girls, and an adoring aunt to her nephew. Teanna graduated from Florida Gulf Coast University with a B.A. in Communication and a minor in Creative Writing. She then went on to receive a M.A. in Communication from the University of Central Florida. Teanna is a proud member of the LGBTQ+ and works closely with Diversity, Equity, and Inclusion in her work.